PRAISE FOR

SHADOW OPS: CONTROL POINT

"*Shadow Ops: Control Point* is *Black Hawk Down* meets *The X-Men*. Fast-paced and thrilling from start to finish, *Control Point* is military fantasy like you've never seen it before. Cole's wartime experience really shows in the gritty reality of army life and in the exploration of patriotism as the protagonist wrestles with the line between the law and what he sees as right."

—Peter V. Brett, international bestselling author of
The Desert Spear

"Cross *The Forever War* with *Witch World*, add in the real-world modern military of *Black Hawk Down*, and you get *Shadow Ops: Control Point*, the mile-a-minute story of someone trying to find purpose in a war he never asked for."

—Jack Campbell, *New York Times* bestselling author of
The Lost Fleet series

"Myke Cole takes you downrange where the bullets fly and the magic burns with precision-guided ferocity that'll put you on the edge of your seat before blowing you right out of it."

—Chris Evans, author of the Iron Elves series

"It was very entertaining, and the Magic 8 Ball says 'will enjoy' . . . It's impossible to blow up so much . . . between two covers, in such style, and not have a hit. I would watch it in 3-D." —Mark Lawrence, author of *King of Thorns*

"*Control Point* . . . sees the beginning of something new and awesome: guns 'n' sorcery. Blending military fiction with urban fantasy, this novel was an absolute blast to read— action packed, tightly written and plotted, intense, and utterly gripping." —*Civilian Reader*

continued . . .

"Realism is tightly interwoven throughout Cole's writing, giving the book such power . . . A nonstop thrill ride that's almost impossible to put down."
—*Fantasy Faction*

"An intense masterwork of military fantasy that grips you from start to finish until your eyes practically devour the words as you approach the thrilling ending . . . Whether you're a fan of superhero fiction or military thrillers—heck, even if you like your epic fantasy with elves and goblins—we absolutely recommend you give *Control Point* a read."
—*The Ranting Dragon*

"[Cole has] created a military urban fantasy for the twenty-first century, with all of the complexity and murky gray areas that entails. The action is sharp and vivid."
—Tor.com

"Fast-paced, nonstop action."
—Violette Malan, author of *Shadowlands*

"A thrill ride, from the first page until the very last. *Control Point* had me hooked."
—Shiloh Walker, national bestselling author of *The Reunited*

"A solid and entertaining novel: a really kick-ass premise/milieu and potential for many stories to be told . . . Cole has launched a solid series that I hope to continue reading."
—sffworld.com

"*Shadow Ops: Control Point* is both entertaining and thought provoking; just one of those would make it a good novel, but the combination is what makes it a great one. If you're in the mood for something that's action packed but still delivers depth, this is a great choice. Recommended."
—*Far Beyond Reality*

SHADOW OPS:
FORTRESS FRONTIER

MYKE COLE

ACE BOOKS, NEW YORK

THE BERKLEY PUBLISHING GROUP
Published by the Penguin Group
Penguin Group (USA) Inc.
375 Hudson Street, New York, New York 10014, USA

Penguin Group (Canada), 90 Eglinton Avenue East, Suite 700, Toronto, Ontario M4P 2Y3, Canada
(a division of Pearson Penguin Canada Inc.) • Penguin Books Ltd., 80 Strand, London WC2R 0RL,
England • Penguin Ireland, 25 St. Stephen's Green, Dublin 2, Ireland (a division of Penguin
Books Ltd.) • Penguin Group (Australia), 707 Collins Street, Melbourne, Victoria 3008, Australia
(a division of Pearson Australia Group Pty. Ltd.) • Penguin Books India Pvt. Ltd., 11 Community
Centre, Panchsheel Park, New Delhi—110 017, India • Penguin Group (NZ), 67 Apollo Drive,
Rosedale, Auckland 0632, New Zealand (a division of Pearson New Zealand Ltd.) • Penguin Books
(South Africa), Rosebank Office Park, 181 Jan Smuts Avenue, Parktown North 2193, South Africa •
Penguin China, B7 Jiaming Center, 27 East Third Ring Road North,
Chaoyang District, Beijing 100020, China

Penguin Books Ltd., Registered Offices: 80 Strand, London WC2R 0RL, England

This is a work of fiction. Names, characters, places, and incidents either are the product of the author's
imagination or are used fictitiously, and any resemblance to actual persons, living or dead, business
establishments, events, or locales is entirely coincidental. The publisher does not have any control over
and does not assume any responsibility for author or third-party websites or their content.

SHADOW OPS: FORTRESS FRONTIER

An Ace Book / published by arrangement with the author

PUBLISHING HISTORY
Ace mass-market edition / February 2013

Copyright © 2013 by Myke Cole.
Map by Priscilla Spencer.
Cover art by Michael Komarck.
Cover design by Annette Fiore DeFex.
Interior text design by Laura K. Corless.

ISBN: 978-0-425-25636-7

ACE
Ace Books are published by The Berkley Publishing Group,
a division of Penguin Group (USA) Inc.,
375 Hudson Street, New York, New York 10014.
ACE and the "A" design are trademarks of Penguin Group (USA) Inc.

PRINTED IN THE UNITED STATES OF AMERICA

10 9 8 7 6 5 4 3 2 1

ALWAYS LEARNING   **PEARSON**

For J. R. R. Tolkien, who planted the seed, and Gary Gygax, who watered it until it took root.

ACKNOWLEDGMENTS

Once again, my name is going on a project made possible by a small army of people. They include (but are not limited to) my agent Joshua Bilmes (and Jessie Cammack, Eddie Schneider, and John Berlyne) and the staff at Ace (Anne Sowards, Jess Wade, Danielle Stockley, Kat Sherbo, Rosanne Romanello, Brady McReynolds, Jodi Rosoff, and many more) and at Headline (John Wordsworth et al.). Thanks also to Michael Komarck, Larry Rostant, Nick Stohlman, Paul Jacobsen, Sarah Semark, and Priscilla Spencer, who plied their particular arts to bring this work to life. Thanks also to Joel Beaven, Tamela Viglione, and David Fields for careful test reading, and to Chris Evans, Robin Hobb, Ann Aguirre, John Hemry (Jack Campbell), Mark Lawrence, Shiloh Walker, and Violette Malan for lending their names to the effort to get people to believe that my work was good enough to spend money on. Special thanks to Mihir Wanchoo for consultation on the Hindi/Sanskrit language and Hindu mythology, and to the staff and class of Viable Paradise VI. Thanks also to the Drinklings, the staff of Qathra, and the New York Public Library (where this book was largely written).

Thanks also to my family, in particular Madeline and Jasper, who daily teach me patience, passion, and not to be afraid to get excited about bugs, rocks, and bad British television.

Thanks also to Ted Arthur and Chris Meawad, who have acted as delegates from my old DC haunts and paid careful attention to making sure I never lost touch with my drinking and running (or maybe running and drinking?) roots.

Thanks to United States Coast Guard Station New York and Training Center Cape May (CO – Captain William Kelly, and XO – Commander Owen Gibbons), who continue to hold me to standards

I would never achieve without their incredible example. You lead from the front, and I am all too happy to follow.

With Peter V. Brett again saved for last: brother, friend, mentor, battle-buddy. None of this would exist without you omnipresent on my six, ignoring your own hell to push me through mine. Thanks.

NOTE

A glossary of military terms, acronyms, and slang can be found at the end of this book.

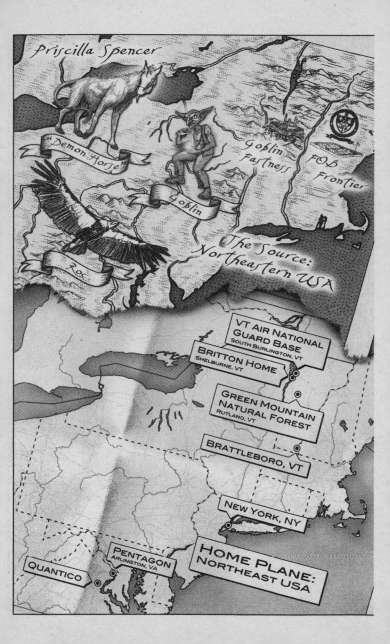

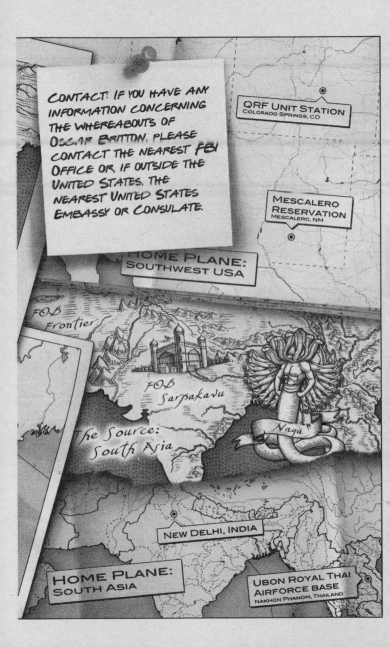

MEASURE OF A MAN

It was kind of a bummer, honestly. No special incantations. No wands or staves. No hat with moons and stars on it. I just get sappy and point and boom. Where's the fun in that?

—Former Ambassador to Finland Katherine Arajarvi
Speaking to reporters on graduation from SAOLCC
and assignment to a SOC Coven

CHAPTER 1
TIDE COMES IN

Oscar Britton is wanted for the murder of several soldiers and civilians, including his own father. He allegedly traffics in prohibited magical schools, most likely Negramantic practice. He has plotted the violent overthrow of the United States government and mishandled classified information. CONTACT: If you have any information concerning this case, please contact the nearest FBI office or, if outside the United States, the nearest United States embassy or consulate.

—FBI Web site: Ten Most Wanted Fugitives

He races into the water, kicking up clods of wet sand, waves sloshing over the glass-polished surface of his shoes.

A little ways out to sea, his people are drowning; those he loves, those in his charge. There is his wife, Julie, his daughters Kelly and Sarah. There is Sergeant Pinchot, who has made him coffee and given him his messages for the last three years. Beyond them are the thousands of men and women whose pay and housing he ensures. They wave their arms, gurgling salt water. The green of kelp mixes with the sodden green of their uniforms.

The ocean reaches his waist. He ignores it. He cannot save them all, but maybe he can reach one of them. Kelly screams, Pinchot's head disappears underwater.

The water is freezing, it reaches his chest, his neck. He paddles furiously, but his charges are no closer. The current resists him; he slogs forward as if he moves through molasses.

Pinchot surfaces briefly, vomiting water. Crabs dance on her head. She vanishes beneath the surface.

Bookbinder pushes forward, chest and arms burning with the effort of paddling. "Julie! Hang on, bunny! Sarah! Daddy's coming!"

But now the water is over his head. The exertion of his rush into the ocean has emptied him of breath, he must draw air.

He draws seawater instead. The light of the surface is gone. He is too far, too deep.

His lungs sag, heavy with brine. He drags to the ocean floor. Drowning, drowning. He has failed them all.

Colonel Alan Bookbinder snapped awake, still freezing. He'd kicked the sheets aside, his body plastered with drying sweat. Beside him, Julie murmured, her slim body gone to the padded comfort of middle age but still beautiful.

"Just a dream," he whispered. It came out as a croak. He couldn't breathe.

Dream or no dream, he was still drowning.

He threw himself out of bed, hands flying to his chest. His veins felt too narrow to contain his roaring blood. He paced a circle at the foot of his bed, panic rising. Was it a heart attack? The doc had given him a clean bill of health just last month. No tingling in his extremities, clear vision. No faintness or weakness.

Just a sensation of being . . . swamped. The panic mounted. *Can't breathe, can't breathe!*

"Stop," he said out loud. "Get ahold of yourself."

He opened his mouth and filled his lungs, felt his head swim with the intake of oxygen. He could breathe just fine.

He looked around his room. His officer's saber, never drawn, hung over the nightstand. The television's screen reflected the moonlight. Julie reached for his side of the bed, snagging a pillow in his absence. Harvey, their fat, ancient beagle, lay beside their bed. He lifted his head drowsily at the sight of his master awake and thumped his tail happily against the floor briefly before putting his head back down.

Everything was as it should be. But the drowning feeling didn't subside.

This is ridiculous, he thought. *You don't need to be awake for another two hours. Normal behavior would be to go back to sleep.*

He would act normal until he felt normal. He took a step toward the bed and banged his shin hard against it. He swore, Harvey chuffed, and Julie came awake with a start.

"Oh, bunny. I'm sorry," he said.

"It's okay," she said, rubbing her eyes, "Are you all right?"

"Yeah, I'm fine. I had a bad dream and . . . I think I might have come down with something. I don't feel right."

"Did you go to the bathroom? You know how sometimes . . ."

"No, bunny, it's not that."

"How bad is it, do you need me to . . ."

"No, no, sweetie. I'll just talk to the doc tomorrow."

Julie flopped back down on the pillows and extended her arms. "Well, come to bed, then. Bunny needs snuggling."

Bookbinder smiled. She had put on a few pounds. She talked incessantly about his bowel movements.

But bunny needed snuggling, and he loved bunny very, very much.

He nuzzled her neck and kissed her earlobes. She grunted affirmatively and drifted back to sleep in his arms.

But the tide stayed with him, and he drowned, wide-awake, until the alarm went off.

Kelly and Sarah squabbled over breakfast like only sisters could. Harvey sat expectantly beside the table, vigilant for dropped crumbs. Kelly's dark ringlets bounced in frustration as she pointed at her younger sister. "Dad! Sarah finished the good cereal!"

Bookbinder stared at the paper, not reading it, consumed by the current roaring through him.

"Don't bother your father, Kel," Julie said, putting another cereal box down in front of her. "He's got a busy day ahead of him."

"I don't want shredded wheat!" Kelly groused.

Bookbinder put down the paper and hugged his daughter, who leaned away, wrinkling her nose. "Shredded wheat loves you, and so do I," he said. "And I promise to pick up more of the cereal you like on the way home."

The drive to work rankled, the drowning feeling making the traffic more unbearable than usual. Even with his privileged spot, it was a long walk across the Pentagon's north parking lot. He fell in with other soldiers making their way toward the entrance. With only generals outranking him, his arm was tired from returning salutes by the time he'd gone twenty feet.

He navigated the maze of hallways, rife with historical displays lauding heroes. The army's sole criteria for heroism was time spent behind a trigger. He couldn't remember the last time he'd shot a gun, and they didn't give Purple Hearts for paper cuts.

He stopped by the building's central gazebo, squatting amid a swath of green in the midst of the concrete maze. The cafeteria inside buzzed with uniformed personnel, sharp-suited civil servants, and contractors. Bookbinder stood on line for his morning coffee, then fought his way out of the crowded entrance.

"By your leave, sir," said a navy lieutenant. He hesitated at that last word, his eyes searching Bookbinder's chest for something he could respect. No combat infantryman's pin. No expeditionary medals. No jump wings. Bookbinder was a high-ranking administrator, and his record screamed it from his uniform. There were soldiers and there were *soldiers*, and it was clear which category this lieutenant felt he fell into. Bookbinder read the lieutenant's record on his ribbon rack—surface warfare qualified, Horn of Africa campaign medal. But he was still just a company-grade officer, and he owed Bookbinder respect. This he rendered as coolly as possible, the salute cracking so sharply that his hand vibrated.

Bookbinder made his way to his office and pushed through the doorway reading ARMY MATERIEL COMMAND on the Pentagon's E ring. Sergeant Pinchot greeted him with a wave from behind her desk just outside his office door. She looked like she'd been stuffed into her immaculate uniform. He paused, seeing her in his dream, drowning in freezing ocean water.

"Oh." She frowned, noting his cup of coffee. "I just made you a pot."

"Well, I appreciate that, sorry. Good morning, by the way."

She shrugged. "Good morning, sir. Everything okay?"

He nodded. "Yeah, I'm just a little off. Can you do me a favor and see what the doc has open today? Put the appointment under your name and rank, I don't want them kicking other people out of a time slot because a colonel called down."

"Will do, sir. Speaking of medical . . ."

"Did you email me the body-weight waiver?"

Sergeant Pinchot nodded. "It's in your inbox."

"I'll sign it, but this is the last time. You've got to start taking physical training seriously." He glanced down at his flat belly, due more to genetics and no great love of food than any commitment to exercise.

"Hooah, sir. I'll take care of it." She wouldn't take care of it, just as she hadn't taken care of it the last two times he'd warned her. He should have given her a command referral to the weight-control program already. He scolded and scolded, but he knew that deep down, Pinchot sensed that he would never do it. He wore a commander's uniform with a commander's silver eagles on his shoulders, but he lacked a commander's heart.

Bookbinder sighed and went into his office, closing the door behind him. The office radiated official dignity from its dark-stained cherrywood furniture to the walls completely covered with the trappings of a long and storied career; plaques, folded flags, challenge coins, trophies. Framed posters depicted dignified scenes. Washington accepted Cornwallis's surrender in one corner. On the opposite wall, the Continental Congress signed the charter creating the army. There were no battle scenes.

He settled into his leather commander's chair and brought his computer out of sleep mode. The huge split-screen monitors were overkill, but they helped with keeping track of the giant spreadsheets that were his stock-in-trade. He'd left at 1900 hours last night. Three hundred emails already awaited him.

He sighed, the current battering him unsparingly.

The phone rang.

He picked it up. "J1. May I help you, sir or ma'am?"

There was a brief pause as the caller took the line off speakerphone. "Colonel Bookbinder, sir? This is HS2 Wainwright in Lieutenant Colonel Thompson's office. We've had a cancellation if you're free to stop by."

The doctor's office had taken exactly three minutes to get him in. There was no cancellation. Pinchot had not used her own name and rank as he'd instructed. Who knew what poor soldier with a more urgent problem had just been bumped so the lofty colonel could be accommodated. But with the drowning sensation dogging him, he was grateful for the chance to get examined.

Bookbinder massaged his temples and stood. He passed through the outer office and tapped Pinchot's shoulder. "They're taking me now," he said, meaning it as a remonstration for her failure to follow instructions.

She tapped away at her keyboard, ignoring him. "That's great, sir. I'll take your calls."

The trip to Lieutenant Colonel Thompson's office took longer than he'd expected. The elevator was being repaired, and there was a snarl of contractors on pedal-driven carts running cable down two of the usual thoroughfares. He passed flat-screen monitors dedicated to the perils of unauthorized magic use. Slick electronic posters featured grizzly digital photos of Selfers gone nova, their burned carcasses scarcely recognizable as human. It was followed by a Ten Most Wanted slide. Oscar Britton continued to hold the top spot.

Bookbinder entered Doc Thompson's and stiffened as half the waiting room got to its feet. "Good morning, sir," they chorused.

"Good morning, everyone. Sit down, please. That's not necessary."

"Good morning, Colonel. Dr. Thompson is waiting for you," said a young orderly in blue scrubs.

Bookbinder glanced an apology at the assembled convalescents. More than a few met his glance, irked at having their wait lengthened by the system's tendency to jump whenever top brass needed something done.

But there was nothing to be done about it now. The tide was insistent, and the doc was waiting.

Bookbinder sat in the exam room for a few minutes before Thompson came in.

"Good morning, sir!" The doctor said, pumping his hand vigorously. Thompson was mustachioed and bull-necked. The silver oak leaf cluster and gold caduceus pinned to his white doctor's coat were the only things that marked him as a soldier. "Your admin seemed worried about you. Everything okay?"

"I feel ridiculous," Bookbinder began, "there's really nothing wrong with me."

"Describe it."

"It feels like I'm drowning. I can't breathe. Well, I can, actually." He demonstrated, spreading his arms and filling his lungs with air. "I just feel like . . . I'm underwater. I can't shake it."

Thompson stroked his moustache with the butt of his pen. "When did this start?"

"Last night. I had a nightmare."

"Does it get worse when you lie down? Are you having trouble climbing stairs?"

Bookbinder shook his head. "It's constant. Always the same."

"You haven't started smoking, have you?"

Bookbinder frowned. "Come on, Doc."

"Okay, well, let's have a look at you."

Having a look at him took all day. After Thompson found nothing abnormal with his blood pressure, he went at him with the stethoscope with similar results. He shined lights in his eyes, looked up his nose and ears, took blood. Bookbinder tried to leave after an hour, worried about the men outside whose days were being wasted waiting, but Thompson wasn't going to let a sick O-6 out of his sight without making damned sure that everything was all right.

The big tests began. Chest X-ray, CT scan, echocardiogram.

By the end of the day, Bookbinder was exhausted, sitting naked in a blue examination gown, his skinny butt freezing against the stainless-steel surface of the examination table. Thompson entered the room, shaking his head.

"Nothing?" Bookbinder asked.

Thompson shrugged. "Nothing. We still have to wait on some lab results, but I don't expect to find anything."

But the current was there. Bookbinder gulped air, feeling the drowning sensation more acutely than ever. "Jesus, Doc. What's going on?"

"If I had to put my finger on it? You're having a panic attack."

Bookbinder cocked an eyebrow. "That's ridiculous. I'm forty-five. I've never had a panic attack in my life."

Thompson shrugged. "Well, there's nothing physically wrong with you, sir. And there's no age limit on anxiety issues. You said it came on right after a nightmare, correct?"

Bookbinder nodded.

"Must have been one hell of a nightmare," Thompson said.

Bookbinder shuddered. "It was."

"Well, look. I'd take the rest of the day off." He handed Bookbinder a small plastic bag full of white pills. "This is a generic zolpidem. It'll help you sleep. Eat something, piss, then pop one. Go directly to bed, do not pass go. Give me a call in the morning and let me know how you feel."

Panic attack. The thought ate at him. He was supposed to be a commander. Panic attacks didn't come with that territory.

"Doc, could we—"

Thompson cut him off, his voice sympathetic. "We'll keep this between us. You're not the first field grade I've had in here with this condition, sir. It's stressful at the top. Sometimes you have to make room for that. You just call me tomorrow."

The doctor paused in the doorway. "There's one thing, sir."

Bookbinder pulled up his pants and buttoned them. "What?"

"It's silly, really."

"What is it?" Bookbinder was tired and hungry and irritated at having wasted an entire working day.

"Well, I have to ask you to call your command's SOC liaison."

Bookbinder's jaw dropped. "You think I'm Latent?"

"It's just that some of your symptoms are consistent with new Manifestation. Protocol is that it gets reported, but there's no reason you can't take care of that yourself. Don't worry, you're not Latent. You're not actually displaying any magical power, which only ever happens with Rump Latents, but they don't have sensations as strong as what you're describing. A lot of them don't even know they're Latent until someone else picks up their current."

"Believe me, this is superstrong," Bookbinder said. "I can barely concentrate on anything else."

"I know," Thompson said, "which is why I'm sure you're not Latent, but you still need to check in with the SOC LNO. Just takes a second for them to send a Seer over. Again, don't worry. Even if you are Latent, you're not Manifesting, which means it's Rump and no real danger to anyone."

Bookbinder pulled his shirt on and nodded. "Okay, Doc. Thanks."

Thompson nodded, waved, and left him alone in the drowning tide, suddenly malevolent now that it had a potential name.

Magic, Bookbinder thought. He thought of his house in Arlington, his wife and children, his retirement check just a few years away. After that, an easy job as a defense contractor, the double-dipping ensuring smooth sailing for Julie and the girls. Then golfing, summers in the RV at national parks, and long weekends at the seashore. Maybe grandkids if he was lucky.

Magic did not fit into that equation. Even those who didn't go Selfer were ostracized.

Get ahold of yourself, he thought. *It's like 1 percent of 1 percent who actually come up Latent. It's like the doc said—panic attack.*

He suddenly found himself hoping the doctor was right.

He punched up the SOC liaison on his dashboard phone during the drive home.

The voice that answered was grainy and distorted. "SOC. Talon."

Bookbinder paused at the lack of phone courtesy, then reminded himself that the SOC didn't follow protocol like the big army.

"Hi, this is Colonel Alan Bookbinder, I'm the J1 for AMC."

"Sure, sir." The voice became friendlier, he guessed in reaction to his rank. "How can I help you?"

"I feel ridiculous even calling you, but I've been feeling really weird lately, and the doc couldn't find anything wrong with me. But he said I have to report to you."

"Uh-huh," Talon said.

"So," Bookbinder went on, filling the uncomfortable silence that followed. "I'm reporting."

"Drowning sensation?" Talon asked. "Like you're in the middle of a river that's flowing through you?"

A sick chill settled in Bookbinder's gut and began to work its way up his spine. The current intensified.

"Yes. . . that's it exactly," he croaked.

Talon didn't react to the change in his voice. "You have a nightmare, sir? Or a really vivid dream just before the sensation came on?"

Bookbinder nodded at the speaker before remembering that Talon couldn't see him. The car behind him honked, and he realized he had slowed to a crawl. He put on his blinkers and pulled over.

"Yes," he said again.

"But you obviously haven't Manifested or you'd be on your way here in person instead of calling me." Talon's voice was calm.

"Yes," Bookbinder said. Panic drowned him. "Do you. . . oh my God, do you think I might be Latent?"

Talon chuckled on the other end of the phone. "Hell, sir. You're not Latent. If you had actually come up Latent enough to feel the flow, you'd have Manifested. If you were Rump, you probably wouldn't feel anything at all. And on the odd chance that you are Rump, you're no threat to yourself or others."

"But . . . but you knew about the nightmare . . ."

"That's a common symptom, but it doesn't always happen that way. I Manifested in the middle of the afternoon, taking a shower. It's okay, sir. You want me to send a Seer over to your house now to see if he can pick up a current? Or I could swing by myself . . ."

Relief replaced panic, drowning all. "No, no, it's fine. God, I feel like a damned fool. I'll come by tomorrow morning. Let me at least get a good night's sleep and see how I feel when I wake up."

Talon laughed again. "Roger that, sir. I'm usually in around 0700, we're on the . . ."

"Fifth floor, A ring, I know." You couldn't miss it on all the posters encouraging those who suspected they might be Latent to self-report. "Okay, I'll see you tomorrow."

See? Damned idiot. No way you're Latent. Relief and embarrassment churned in him. He felt the current rising, as if in response. Damn, but that was weird. Oh well, panic attack it was. He would go home, take the pills, and get some sleep.

But not before he kept his promise to Kelly.

He swung into the convenience-store parking lot and jogged through the entrance, pausing as he reviewed the signs swinging over the aisles looking for the breakfast cereal. He spotted a line of purple boxes peeking off one of the metal ledges and made his way toward them.

And stopped short.

The tide that drowned him was suddenly crossed by another;

strong and foreign. His eyes wrenched off the cereal boxes and moved unerringly toward the current's source.

A young boy, no more than sixteen, stood at the end of the aisle. Ripped blue jeans draped over wide sneakers. A black hooded sweatshirt masked most of his features, but not his eyes, wide open in shock and fixed on Bookbinder's uniform.

The sick feeling rushed back into Bookbinder's gut, bullying away the sweet relief. *He can feel my current, too.*

Panic attacks didn't facilitate that kind of communication.

Only magic did.

The kid yanked down the shelf, sending an avalanche of cereal boxes cascading between them.

He turned and ran.

Bookbinder went after him.

CHAPTER II
SEA CHANGE

The Danish Hekseri Corps took a different tack. They recognized Russia as the primary threat and understood that weather dominance was the only way to beat a numerically and financially superior enemy. Every Danish Trollmann is focused primarily on impacting flight paths and sea-lanes, and their Aeromancers are the best in the world. This single-minded focus changed the balance of power in Northern Europe in the course of a decade.

—Avery Whiting
The Great Reawakening and the Rebalancing of Power in the Postmodern World

Bookbinder vaulted the pile of cereal boxes. He landed a foot short, his slick-soled dress shoe skidding sideways and sending him sprawling. The kid dashed around the aisle, racing for the exit.

"Wait!" Bookbinder called after him, scrambling to his feet. "I'm not going to do anythi . . . I'm not . . ." *Not going to what?* he asked himself. *Why are you chasing him?*

I have to know, he answered himself, *if I'm like him.*

He spun, pushing off against the crushed boxes and chasing the kid through the store doors, ignoring the clerk, who was threatening to call the police.

"Kid! Stop I . . ." Bookbinder called. The kid pumped his arms, the hoodie flying back to reveal a shock of unruly black hair. He rounded the corner of the store and tore down the alley, knocking down trash cans.

Bookbinder pursued him, his wind up now, vaulting the obstacles smoothly. A chain-link fence topped with a coil of barbed wire blocked the exit, but the kid leapt up it. He tangled his sleeve in the barbed wire and struggled, entangling himself worse. He looked over his shoulder at Bookbinder, his eyes wide and unseeing, a panicked animal.

Bookbinder slowed, kept his distance. "Kid, it's okay. I just want to talk to you. I'm not SOC."

More scrambling. Bright lines of blood blossomed on the kid's face and arm.

"Jesus! Stop messing around." Bookbinder tugged gently at the kid's ankle. "You're going to hurt yourself."

Bookbinder could feel the kid's current pulsing erratically against his own. Where Bookbinder's tide felt like a steady soaking, the foreign tide was wild, mounting to crescendo.

"Fuck you!" the kid screamed. "I'm not going anywhere!"

"Nobody's taking you anywhere. I'm not SOC."

The kid paused, a glimmer of hope on his face, then he focused, and a snarl overcame his features. "Bullshit, man! I can feel you! You Latent motherfucker!"

The sick feeling he'd had when talking to Talon returned. *You have your answer, now get out of here.*

"Wait," Bookbinder said. "How do you know I'm Latent?" *You know how he knows.*

The kid's sleeve tore free, and he fell, landing a couple of feet from Bookbinder. He could hear the shouts of others at the end of the alley. The kid's eyes widened in terror as they looked over Bookbinder's shoulder. He leveled a hand at the colonel's chest.

"I can fucking control it, man! I can fucking fry you!"

Bookbinder felt the wild seesawing of his current and knew the kid was lying. "It's okay, son. Don't do anything stupid. Nobody's trying to hurt you here."

"Back off!" The boy's current spiked madly. "Just back the fuck off!"

Bookbinder took a few steps backward. The boy frowned, then gritted his teeth as his current spiked again. He raised his hands to his head, shrieking.

The boy doubled over, his current so strong that it blinded

Bookbinder's senses. The colonel lurched forward, reaching out. "It's okay! Calm down! You're going to be okay!"

"Oh Christ," someone said from behind Bookbinder. "Kid's going nova. Run!"

But Bookbinder didn't run, he knelt before the boy, his hands on his shoulders, trying to soothe him. "Listen to me, son. Focus on my voice. Concentrate. You can beat this. You just have to calm down."

The kid whipped his head from side to side, skin smoking, tendrils of gray vapor wafting from inside his sweatshirt. His hair began to smolder, then burst into flame. He screamed.

The boy threw his head back. His eyes shot wide, then disappeared in puffs of smoke as flames shot from his skull. His skin went black, curling and flapping away from his head. Bookbinder scrambled away on his hands, his eyebrows singed, as the kid writhed on the ground, burning brightly.

Bookbinder got to his feet, panting. He dusted off his uniform instinctively, hands moving involuntarily while his mind grappled with the sight before him.

The kid lay, a smoking ruin that was hard to imagine had once been alive.

That's magic. That's what's in me.

He spun, but the alley was empty; any onlookers had fled at the sight of the boy's fiery death throes.

He ran, the smell of cooked meat and the echoing screams driving him to his car.

Talon answered the phone on the first ring. "I'm definitely Latent," Bookbinder said. "I can feel the current."

Talon sounded exasperated. "Sir, we discussed this . . ."

"No! I met a kid! He just fried himself! I'm outside a grocery store and . . ."

Talon's voice went flat. "Sir, calm down and listen to me. I need you to be very clear. Are you saying you met a Latent individual and he went nova?"

"Yes! Right in front of me! Just a minute ago!"

"Are the police there?"

"Not yet, but some people saw, and I'm sure they called them."

"Sir, I need you to get out of there right now. Do you know where the POAC is?"

"The . . . what?"

"The Pentagon Officers Athletic Club. There's a loading dock underneath it. I'll make sure it's cleared. You drive there right now, is that clear? Do not speed. Do not get pulled over. Do not interact with the police in any way."

Bookbinder's stomach tensed, but he felt an odd sense of relief at having commands he could follow. "Got it."

"Okay, now give me your exact address. What's the name of the grocery store you're at?"

After Bookbinder told him, Talon asked, "So, what makes you sure you're Latent? Did you Manifest?"

"No, but I could feel it," Bookbinder said, starting the car and heading back to the Pentagon. "And this kid could sense it, too. He said he could tell."

"I highly doubt it, but we can't be too careful. Get here as quickly as you can, sir. Stay away from other people. Do not go home. Do not talk to anyone. Got it?"

"Okay. See you soon." Bookbinder's calm surprised him as he pulled back into traffic and began to retrace his route to the Pentagon. The uncertainty that had dogged him was gone. The thing inside him had a name. The authorities were on top of it, they would take him and . . .

. . . They would take him.

The current intensified in time with his rising panic. What if they threw him in jail? Or did tests on him? Bookbinder was pretty sure that since he had self-reported, he wouldn't be punished, but he didn't know for sure. What if they quarantined him? What if it was years before he saw his wife and children again?

Talon had told him to come straight in, not to go near anyone.

But Bookbinder found himself turning the car around, gunning the engine, and heading for home.

Bookbinder paused outside the door of his home, smoothed his uniform again, and wiped the panicked tears off his face. His wife and children were inside. He had to be strong for them. *Because this may be the last time you see them.* Bookbinder knew what happened to Selfers. There was no way he would run.

He took a moment to survey the neatly manicured lawn, the crisply pressed American flag flapping from a pole bolted to the doorjamb.

He took a deep breath and pushed through the door.

Julie stood at the table, unpacking a bag of groceries.

"Hi, sweetheart." The tremor in his voice was undeniable. Julie looked at him, her eyes wide with concern.

She placed her hands on his cheeks. "Oh, baby! What happened to you?"

The tears came. He collapsed into her arms, cursing his weakness.

"Alan!" He could hear his own panic transferred to her, now rising in her voice. "Alan, what's wrong?"

"Oh, bunny," he sobbed. "I'm sorry. I didn't mean for this to happen."

He felt Julie's throat work against his shoulder as she swallowed. When she spoke again, her voice was calm, possessed of all the command he lacked. She pushed him back and met his eyes. "Alan, you're scaring me. I need you to calm down and tell me what's going on. What didn't you mean to happen?"

"I'm Latent. I'm sorry, baby. I didn't mean for it to . . ."

"Latent?" Julie smiled. "Oh God, Alan. You're not Latent!"

"I am, baby. I really am. I can feel it."

"Alan." She laughed, kissed his forehead. "What has gotten into you? You had me scared half to death!"

"I saw a boy die, he burned to death. I felt his . . . I felt his magic. It's in me, too."

"Are you serious? Where? When?"

"Just now, I stopped off to get cereal for Kel . . . I didn't even get it. I'm sorry."

"It's okay," she said. "Tell me what happened. Did you call the police?"

"No, I called the SOC."

She pushed back from him, white-faced. "The SOC?"

Bookbinder nodded miserably. "They told me to come in. I'm not even supposed to be here. I had to see you."

She nodded firmly, showing all the resolve he lacked. "You did the right thing. You can't get in trouble if you report up front."

He tried to pull her back into an embrace, but she pushed him away. "Sweetie, you should get to them right now. If you just tell them everything and let them examine you, then you won't get in any trouble, and you can come home."

"Not if I'm Latent! What if they have to keep me for tests?"

She touched his elbow. "Honey, I'm hardly an expert, but you're not . . . showing any magic. That's what happens when people come up Latent."

"Julie, I'm serious. I can feel it. I have a magical . . . pulse, like a river flowing through me."

Julie put her hands on her hips. "I believe you feel something, but you were sick this morning, remember? Did you see the doc today at work?"

"He said I was having a panic attack."

"Well? Maybe that's all it is. You don't want to make trouble with the SOC over something like that. Stop playing around and get over there."

Bookbinder nodded but didn't move.

"The boy, you didn't . . ." Julie began.

"I had nothing to do with it, I just . . . We could feel each other's magic, then he went nova."

"Oh God," Julie said. She hugged him again and kissed his forehead. "Now. If you go now, they won't know you came here."

The kids, as if on cue, appeared at the top of the stairs. "Daddy?"

He knelt, holding out his arms, and they ran to him. He lifted them up and embraced them tightly, kissing them hard on the tops of their heads. "Daddy! Ow! You're squeezing me!" Kelly squealed.

"It's okay, sweetheart," Julie said. "Daddy just got scared is all."

"I save you, Daddy," Sarah said.

He put the girls back down. *You should say good-bye,* he thought. *Once you report to Talon, you don't know if you'll ever see them again.*

But something in the certainty of Julie's tone held him at bay. He had failed to be strong for her, but he could do it for his girls. "Mommy's right. Everything's fine. Daddy forgot something at work and has to run back for a minute, but I'll be home to tuck you in." He winced inwardly.

"Where's Harvey?" he asked. If he was saying good-bye, he wanted to cover all the bases.

"He's out back," Julie said. "Leave him be, you'll be home soon." She sounded so sure.

He kissed Julie, swept her into a tight hug. "Good-bye, bunny."

Julie's voice was worried, but she gave the right lines. "No dramatics, Alan. Go report yourself, get this straightened out, and come home."

They don't understand. This is as much good-bye as you get.

One more hug, and he was out the door. He knew if he looked back, he would lose his nerve.

So he didn't.

The phone was already ringing when he got in the car. "Where are you?" Talon asked.

"I'm inbound. I got . . . stuck in traffic. I'll be there in . . . ten minutes."

Talon's silence was pregnant with incredulity. Bookbinder sank into his seat under the weight of the unspoken accusation. "Get the lead out of your ass, sir. This isn't a game."

By the time Bookbinder arrived at the Pentagon parking lot, two police cars with flashing lights were waiting for him. At first, his stomach clenched, Talon had warned him to stay away from the police. But the cruisers were the gray and black of Pentagon police, not Arlington, and they waved him past through their windows, then fell in behind his car. The escort peeled off once he passed beneath the footbridge outside the POAC and turned into the loading dock.

The normally unending traffic of loading and unloading stocks of supplies was gone. Instead, a young SOC captain waited for him on the edge of the concrete platform, flanked by two Pentagon police officers in tactical gear, body armor, helmets, carbines slung across their chests.

Bookbinder reached for the door handle and paused. He looked back through the windshield at the short, dark-haired captain who he assumed was Talon. *Once you open that door, your life will change forever. Don't think about it. If you turn back, you'll lose your nerve, you'll run. Then, whatever life is left to you will be over.*

A part of his mind clung to Julie's dismissal. *Maybe she's right. Maybe this is a panic attack.*

If so, he'd apologize to her on his knees. He'd accept any derision she, or Talon, or anyone else cared to heap on him. And then Bookbinder, not normally a religious man, found himself praying. *Please, dear God. I've been a good husband, father, and soldier. I've done my job. I never cheated or stole or fooled around on my wife. I never hit my kids. Please, if you can make this cup pass from me, please do it. I don't want to be Latent. I don't want to lose everything I've built.*

"Sir!" Talon called to him. "Get out of the car right now!"

Bookbinder was soldier enough to follow orders. He reacted instinctively, opening the door and pushing out into the cool evening air.

He immediately felt Talon's current, tight and disciplined, eddying from him. Talon must have felt his as well, because he crouched, his eyes widening.

"Jesus!" Talon said, and stretched out his hands. Bookbinder felt his flow pass into Talon's, then roll back from it. He could still feel it flowing through him, but the drowning sensation had ceased.

"Colonel Bookbinder, I presume?" Talon asked, jumping down off the raised platform and walking toward him. "You're Latent, all right."

The sodium lights that lit the dock swayed momentarily as Bookbinder grappled with the truth. "Maybe it's a Rump Latency?"

Talon shook his head firmly. "Hell, no, sir. It's the strongest current I've felt in a long time."

Bookbinder bent over, hands on his knees. "Oh, shit."

Talon put his hand on his shoulder. "It's okay, sir. You reported yourself. It's fine. Don't worry about that kid, sir. Magic sinks happen. That's not on you."

"What happened to him?"

"The kid? Don't worry about that. We're taking care of it."

"I just. . . I thought that maybe it was a panic attack."

Talon laughed. "No, sir. I'm afraid not. You're Latent. I've got you Suppressed right now."

Bookbinder looked at Talon. The man's eyes were kind, older than the rest of his face. A silver Aeromancer's pin shone from his lapel. "Sir, a lot of guys have this reaction when they pop. It's really okay. You did it right. You lose nothing, not rank, not pay. It's a change, but we're going to help you through it. I came up Latent my first week at West Point. Believe me, you get used to it."

Bookbinder sagged against the wall. "What about my family?"

Talon's expression went hard. "I'm not sure, sir. You'll have to speak to one of our integration counselors."

Bookbinder looked into Talon's eyes, open and receptive just a moment before, and knew he was lying. He swallowed and shut his eyes. But the feel of the current, even Suppressed, wouldn't allow him even a moment of self-delusion.

"The problem, sir," Talon said, "is that you didn't Manifest. You've felt the current for how long?"

"Since last night. . . I mean, this morning technically. Maybe 0200."

Talon clicked his tongue. "Man, that's weird. That never happens."

"So, what's going to happen to me?"

Talon was silent for a long time. Finally, he sighed. "Honestly, sir? I have no idea. For one thing, you're field grade. For another, you're not Manifesting. That's a double whammy. Any call on this one is going to be made miles above my head."

CHAPTER III
STRESS TEST

In some very rare instances, powerful Latencies will fail to Manifest. The reason for this is a matter of continuing debate, but many believe it has to do with deficiencies in the limbic system. Indeed, the few documented Auto-Suppressed or "Stifled" Latencies are loners, usually males without family and few friends. They exhibit difficulty expressing emotion and are reticent to a fault.

—Avery Whiting
Modern Arcana: Theory and Practice

Talon bundled Bookbinder into a black van and produced a drawstring bag from his cargo pocket. "I need you to put this over your head."

"Are you serious?" Bookbinder asked.

"As a heart attack, sir."

"Do it, sir," said one of the police officers, climbing in on the van's opposite side.

Bookbinder shrugged and pulled the bag over his head. It was hot and close inside, but he could breathe well enough. Unable to see, he closed his eyes and tried to relax.

"I'm going to give you an injection in your thigh," Talon said. "It's Limbic Dampener. Everybody in the SOC uses it. It'll help you control the magical flow. You ready?"

Bookbinder nodded, wincing at the stab in his leg a moment later. Another moment passed, and he felt suddenly calm. The stress of his new Latency, the pain of losing his family, the anxiety over his uncertain future, all receded. He was aware of the emotions and their intensity, but they no longer rattled him.

"My wife," he began.

"We're getting word to her now," Talon said. "As soon as we're able, we'll arrange for you to speak to her."

The van drove for an hour, then finally slowed and stopped after bumping over what Bookbinder guessed was a field or unpaved road. He could hear the dull thudding of a helicopter's rotors as he was ushered out of the van, felt the wind whipping over him as he was hurried on board, a rigger's belt cinched around his waist and a carabiner clipped in place. A hand grabbed Bookbinder's wrist, guiding his hand to a support bar.

Then, the stomach-wrenching vertigo as the helo jumped skyward. Bookbinder grasped the bar hard as the helo banked sharply, then leveled off. They flew in silence for what felt like several hours. About halfway through the trip, Bookbinder's mouth began feeling like the Mojave Desert. He smacked his gums, trying to work up some saliva.

"Relax," Talon yelled over the pounding rotors, "it's the Limbic Dampener. Gives you bad cottonmouth. You want some water? We're almost there."

"I've gotta piss," Bookbinder said.

"On the ground in a moment, sir. Just hold it another bit."

When the helicopter finally jarred to a stop, Bookbinder heard the carabiner unclip and hands shoved him forward. He stumbled a few feet out of the helicopter, the rotors spinning down and the wash against his back abating. He took a few steps on what felt like dead leaves.

"Can't hold it," he said.

Talon laughed beside him, jerking the hood off his head.

"Go for it, sir. There's nobody here but us girls."

Bookbinder squinted against bright starlight. He unzipped and let go as his eyes adjusted to the darkness. Two long, low barns loomed in the distance, massive and solid.

"Where are we?" he asked, shaking off and zipping up.

Talon shrugged. "Welcome to LSA Portcullis."

"Logistical Staging Area? Where are we staging to?"

"Need to know, sir. For now, you need to know that you're expected inside and that we're going to run some tests."

The interior of the barn had been converted into an operational staging floor, gigantic and buzzing with men and equipment. The stars and stripes and the SOC arms were prominently displayed, hanging from the ceiling. PORTCULLIS—US ARMY LOGISTICAL STAGING AREA was written across the American flag.

A bull-necked Suppressor with a craggy face and a dark crew cut stood waiting for them, leaning against a chipped folding table. Talon nodded to him. "Sir, this is Lieutenant Plug. He's going to get you set up here."

"When do I get to call my family?" Bookbinder asked.

Bookbinder felt his current surge momentarily as Talon dropped the Suppression, then roll back again as Plug stepped forward, concentrating. "I've got it, sir." Plug said.

"We can't let you get in touch with your family from here, sir," Talon said. "Bad operations security. But the good news is that you won't be here long. It's just a place for you to get checked out and integrated into the service. Once you're assigned and settled, we'll figure out how to get you back in touch with them."

"You said I'd see them again," Bookbinder said.

"And you will," Talon assured him. "But you probably won't see me. It's been a pleasure, sir. Welcome to the Corps and good luck to you." He extended a hand.

Bookbinder shook it, and Talon left without another word.

Plug kicked a metal folding chair up to the table and tapped a clipboard there stacked to bursting with papers.

"Let's get the admin knocked out, sir. Transfer papers, non-disclosure agreement, personal statement . . . Should take you about an hour to get it all done, then we've got your medical inprocessing and psych eval. I've got to keep you Suppressed until the head doc pronounces you fit to go off Suppression. Talon says you're a Latent Grenade, so I don't think that should be a problem."

"Latent Grenade?"

Plug smiled. "It's what we call folks who aren't Rump Latents but don't Manifest, 'cause, you know, any second you could go off."

Bookbinder started in on the paperwork while Plug sat beside him, playing a handheld video game. After his hand cramped from signing his name, checking boxes, and reading words that blurred together, Bookbinder stood, trying to work blood back into his fingers.

"Army's the same wherever you go." He winced.

Plug led Bookbinder through the far end of the room and into a sterile-looking examination room, where three doctors waited. Unlike Doc Thompson, these three wore billowing blue plastic suits instead of white coats. They were businesslike, waving Bookbinder to a cold-looking metal table.

"Please remove your clothes, Colonel."

Bookbinder hesitated. "Look, I . . ."

"Sir," said one of the doctors, "the sooner we get this over with, the sooner we can get you cleaned up and fed, please cooperate."

Bookbinder sighed, and the tests began.

The doctors weren't gentle. Blood pressure, temperature, three different scans. Lights were shone into every orifice and he was poked and prodded for so long that he went numb at his joints.

After he dressed, Plug fetched him back to the same metal chair before the table, on which was a new sheaf of papers.

It turned out to be a multiple-choice bubble sheet attached to a battery of over five hundred questions—all true or false. After a while, all the questions began to blur together, and he filled out bubble after bubble until his hand cramped again.

At last, he stood, stretching as Plug arrived and collected the papers. "Appreciate your patience, sir."

Bookbinder nodded. "How about a shower?"

Plug sighed. "Just one more round, sir. I know you're tired, but there's some concern about the strength of your current and the fact that you haven't Manifested. The brass wants to be sure."

"Sure of what?"

Plug shrugged. "Just sure." He passed Bookbinder a bottle of water and a nutrition bar.

"Hopefully, this'll tide you over until the test is complete. Follow me, please."

He led him back outside the barn structure and around back to a clearing in the pines. Dawn was cresting the treetops and illuminating tall, straight trunks and thick clusters of lustrous green needles. The air had a sharp, metallic bite. Wherever they were, it was north of Washington.

Two more men met them in the clearing, both in digital camouflage uniforms. One of them, a thin major with thinner hair, wore the unit patch of the Judge Advocate General Corps. The other was a muscle-bound infantry sergeant.

"This him?" the lawyer asked. Plug nodded.

The lawyer handed Bookbinder a clipboard with yet more paperwork attached. "We need to give you a stress test, sir, one that we hope will help you Manifest your abilities. Shouldn't take more than ten to fifteen minutes. I'll need you to sign this consent form before we get started."

"Stress test?"

"The docs are thinking that you might be an Auto-Suppressed Latency. These are rare, but they happen from time to time. Magic is conducted through the emotional center in your brain, and in order to break the block and bring your current out, we're going to need to put you under some emotional stress. Don't worry. If your magic does Manifest, Plug is right here to roll it back."

The forms were several pages thick, and the sprawling legal-speak was impossible to read by the rising sun. Exhausted, Bookbinder signed and initialed each page and handed it back.

"So, what do we do . . ."

The breath exploded from him as the sergeant stepped forward and slammed his fist into Bookbinder's stomach. Bookbinder collapsed, retching. His current surged as Plug's Suppression dropped away. He drowned in the tide, unsure if it or the blow to his gut kept him from breathing.

The sergeant slapped him, rocking his face to one side. "Get up, you fucking pussy."

Bookbinder gasped, "What are you do—"

The sergeant's boot slammed into his balls. Bookbinder vomited in earnest, sprawling on the hard ground, sucking up pine needles as he gasped for breath.

The tide roared, drowning out the sergeant's next words to a high buzz. Something struck Bookbinder in the back of the head, bouncing his cheek off the ground and leaving his ears ringing.

He lay, waiting for the next blow to fall. When the buzzing finally cleared, he heard the lawyer speaking to Plug. "Nothing?"

"Nothing, sir. His current is completely pegged, but there's nothing doing."

"Okay," the lawyer said. "Get the dog."

Boots crunched, and someone stepped over him as Bookbinder scrabbled on the ground. "Not . . . I can't believe . . ."

"Shut up," said the sergeant, his voice growing distant.

Bookbinder got to his knees as the boots crunched back. He looked up, meeting the watery blue eyes of the lawyer.

When he looked back down, the sergeant stood before him, holding a beagle puppy, much younger than Harvey, on a leash. The little dog cowered.

Bookbinder pushed himself to his feet, knees shaking. "Look, I don't know what the hell you think you're doing here . . ."

"We know exactly what we're doing, sir," the lawyer said. "Now if you can just hold on for a moment, we'll be done."

The lawyer unsnapped his holster and pulled out his pistol, proffering it to Bookbinder handle first. "Take this, sir."

"What the hell do you expect me to do with . . ."

Bookbinder heard the cocking of a pistol hammer. The barrel touched the base of his skull. "We really need your full cooperation, sir," Plug said from behind him. "Now. Take the fucking gun."

Bookbinder began to tremble. The rumors were true. The SOC really was crazy. He took the pistol, the thick metal handle heavy and unfamiliar.

"Now," the lawyer said, "shoot the animal."

The beagle whined, cringing and straining against the leash, its dark eyes huge.

"Are you fucking kidding me?" Bookbinder asked. "It's a puppy. I'm not going to shoot it."

Plug shoved his head with the pistol barrel. "You're going to do exactly as you're told, or I'm going to fucking shoot you, sir."

The tide surged. He struggled for breath. "You people are fucking crazy! You can't do this!"

"Sir, you've got three seconds to put a round through that animal, or I am going to put you out of all of our misery," Plug said, driving the pistol barrel forward again.

Dear God, he's serious, Bookbinder thought.

"One," Plug said.

"Wait, just give me a . . ."

"Two!" Bookbinder swore he could hear the trigger spring creaking backward. The tide swamped him.

"Okay! Okay!" he shouted, he raised the pistol, his hand jerking wildly. His aim flopped like a beached fish, covering the dog, the sergeant, the space between.

He screamed and pulled the trigger.

Click.

Bookbinder stood, his jaw hanging open, tears welling in his eyes. He sniveled, swallowed hard.

"Well?" the lawyer asked.

Plug shook his head. "Nothing, sir. And his tide is the highest I've felt in a very long time."

The lawyer sighed and nodded to the sergeant, who scooped up the puppy, kissed it on the muzzle, and trotted back inside the barn.

"You son of a bitch," Bookbinder stuttered.

The lawyer patted the air with his hands. "I understand your distress, sir, but your psych profile indicated your biggest limbic triggers were violent confrontation and harm to animals. In order for the test to be effective, we have to respond accordingly."

"I'll have your fucking oak leaves." Bookbinder lunged forward. Plug seized his arm and hauled him back as easily as he would a child.

"No, sir. You won't," the lawyer said, waving the clipboard. "You agreed to this test in advance and hold us all harmless for any results. I have your signature right here."

"You fucker." Bookbinder seethed. "I'll remember this."

"Begging your pardon, sir"—the sergeant's voice came from the barn, gently menacing—"I'm sure you'll feel better waiting inside." Plug's grip tightened on his elbow, and Bookbinder knew he had no chance against the larger men. *They're real soldiers and you're a paper pusher. Being right doesn't make you any tougher.* The thought drained the strength from him, and he allowed himself to be led back inside.

He was left waiting for a long time. A female sergeant checked him over and determined that the drubbing he'd taken hadn't done any lasting damage. After a while, he drowsed. He had no idea how long he slept. When he awoke, a grizzled-looking lieutenant colonel with a broken nose and lantern jaw stood before him.

"How are you feeling, sir?" the lieutenant colonel asked.

Bookbinder cuffed the sleep from his eyes. "Let me guess, this is the patience test?"

The lieutenant colonel smiled. "My name is Seitz. I command here."

"Well, this is the most fucked-up command I've ever seen."

"We get that a lot from folks just coming out of the stress test. The good news is that you don't have to deal with my fucked-up command anymore, sir. We have to get you out of here."

"What's the bad news?"

"No bad news, sir. You self-reported. You keep your rank and position, but I'm afraid that you've been officially diagnosed as what we call an Auto-Suppressed Latency. Your magical tide is stifled."

"I'm a Latent Grenade."

Seitz's smile widened. "We don't like to call it that, sir, but yes. You could Manifest at any moment, and your current is very strong. The results could be dangerous for you and those around you. You need to be in a facility where we have the resources to properly monitor you and respond quickly in the event of a sudden Manifestation.

"There's some serendipity here, because we've got just such a facility that's in desperate need of a J1. I just got off the phone with General Dernwood, and she's approved a lateral transfer. She's also approved the award of a commendation medal for the great job you've done for her at AMC. So the sum total of your Latency is a new job and a positive mark on your record."

Bookbinder's stomach went cold. "What's the bad news? Where the hell are you sending me?"

Seitz handed him another small sheaf of papers. "That's compartmented information, sir. I just need to get you read into the program first." The cover sheet of the papers was bordered with blue-and-orange stripes. SPECIAL ACCESS PROGRAM: FRONTIER, it read.

The thought of any more reading made Bookbinder nauseous. "Cut the crap."

Seitz smiled again. "I guess we can just show you, sir. This way please."

Bookbinder grabbed Seitz's shoulder. "My family. I need to talk to them. Wherever I'm going, are they going to be able to join me?"

Seitz looked at Bookbinder's hand, and Bookbinder jerked it back instinctively, then cursed himself inwardly. He outranked this man, and a hand on the shoulder was hardly out of line under the circumstances.

Seitz seemed satisfied that Bookbinder was cowed. "You'll be able to get messages to your family biweekly, and we'll see what we can do about reuniting you at some point. Please try to understand, sir. It's for their own safety."

Bookbinder saw the lie for what it was and supposed he should have been devastated, but after the past few hours, all he could muster was numbness. The lack of agony made him feel like he was failing his loved ones, and he conjured their faces in his mind, even tried to picture Sarah crying, but there was nothing but the constant thrumming of his magical tide in thrall to Plug's Suppression.

Seitz provided him with a plastic badge already bearing Bookbinder's photo and reading LSA PORTCULLIS—GATE ACCESS. The badge warmed at the press of Bookbinder's thumb, leaving a permanent impression. He signed the signature block on the latest round of paperwork and followed Seitz through a pair of double doors into another room of the same size divided into an armory and firing range on one end and a vehicle park on the other. They stopped before another set of white and diagonal red-striped doors. A sign above read: RESTRICTED AREA—VISUAL INSPECTION OF CREDENTIALS REQUIRED—21-FOOT APPROACH ZONE RIGOROUSLY OBSERVED. DEADLY FORCE IS AUTHORIZED. YOU ARE RESPONSIBLE FOR YOUR OWN SAFETY AND COMPLIANCE! Two SOC Pyromancers guarding the door inspected Bookbinder's badge before a rotating yellow light above the door began to spin, and they were ushered through.

Beyond the doors was another warehouse-sized space, completely dark save for a circle of light illuminating a fat, pale man in a blue hospital gown. Cords snaked from beneath the gown and off into the darkness. A kindly-faced, elderly woman stood behind him, her hair in a tidy blond-gray bun. Her arms were around the man's neck, whispering soothingly into his ear.

A towering rectangle shimmered into view, unrolling like a

window shade. Static light danced across its surface, rippling through the darkness like waves lapping on a shore. Through the portal, Bookbinder could make out a muddy track. Three armored Humvees stood astride it, machine guns peeking from the camouflage netting draping their turrets.

Several soldiers, armed and armored for imminent battle, clustered around him. One of them handed a tactical vest and helmet to Plug, which he donned before accepting a carbine.

"Your protective security detail, sir," Seitz said.

Bookbinder couldn't take his eyes off the portal. "What is this?"

"This," Seitz said, "is the new frontier. If you don't mind, sir, let's get this convoy under way. The sooner we have you safely at Forward Operating Base Frontier, the better."

With a nudge from Plug, Bookbinder took a step forward, letting the static light wash over him and feeling his soles crunch on foreign ground.

CHAPTER IV
ORIENTATION

Magic is an incredibly powerful force, to be sure. But so is military technology. A fire-breathing dragon or a giant roc is definitely a thing to be reckoned with. But put it up against an Apache Long-bow? Or an F-22 Raptor? Or even a dedicated scout-sniper with a clear line of sight and plenty of ammo? No contest at all.

—Lance Corporal Jimmy "Gonzo" Gonzales
Thirteenth Suppression Lance, Second Marine Expeditionary Force

Bookbinder stepped out of the Humvee and nearly sank to his knees in the muddy lane. Where most of the other structures were makeshift trailers and tents shielded by piled sandbags and concrete blast walls, here the Seabees of the navy's construction battalions built a shingled awning supported by wooden posts and a swinging screen door keeping out a cloud of weird, vari-colored bugs. A suggestion box was nailed next to a hanging sign reading FORWARD OPERATING BASE—FRONTIER. CAMP COMMANDANT'S OFFICE. The font was rustic, evoking a state park rather than a military command post.

Two soldiers awaited Bookbinder. The first was another colonel. His gray hair was immaculate, his posture perfect. He had the face of an older movie star or a politician—chiseled jaw, serious brow. His combat infantryman's badge was prominently displayed. The lieutenant colonel beside him was stern-faced, ugly, and shorter. His combat uniform was so mud-spattered that his SOC patch and Pyromancer's pin were barely visible. He cracked a sharp salute as Bookbinder approached, but Bookbinder was too stunned to return it, his head still reeling from the briefing he'd been given during the Humvee ride from the Landing Zone to FOB Frontier.

Yesterday I was a trapped behind a desk in the Pentagon. Now I am Latent, on a secret base in an alternate magical universe.

Bookbinder managed to put a smile on his face and shake the hand that the sharp-dressed colonel offered him. "I'm Taylor, Camp Commandant," the colonel said. "Welcome to FOB Frontier." He gestured to the rugged looking Pyromancer. "This is Lieutenant Colonel Allen. He goes by his call sign, Crucible. He runs all the SOC operations on the FOB. He also heads up our Sorcerer's Apprentice Officer Leadership Combined Course. I understand that you must be rather tired and more than a little bewildered by your arrival here."

Bookbinder nodded, finally returning Crucible's salute and internally wincing as the lieutenant colonel gratefully dropped his right arm. "That's putting it mildly," Bookbinder said. "There were always rumors of a place like this floating around, but I never believed them."

Taylor forced a smile. "Well, I don't need to remind you that the existence of this base and all of the operations here are strictly compartmented, and that your nondisclosure agreement is lifelong."

Bookbinder bridled. Nondisclosure agreements were second nature to a man with the amount of time in grade that Bookbinder had, and Taylor would know that. "I'm fully aware of my obligations, Colonel Taylor."

"Outstanding," Taylor said. "I also want to warn you that this is a combat outpost, and we're frequently subjected to indirect fire and sometimes direct attacks from the local indig. We employ many of them as contractors out of necessity, but I've got my concerns about them. I know you're anxious to get cleaned up and grab a nap, but I'm going to insist that you have a force protection briefing first. Without direct combat experience, you're at risk during the initial adjustment period."

As he spoke, he picked at an imagined speck of mud from his uniform, his hand brushing the combat infantryman's badge. Bookbinder had been through this ritual before. *One of us has seen action. We both know who that is.* Bookbinder felt his face redden.

"Let's get this out of the way," Taylor continued. "You're the highest-ranking officer we've had on post in . . . well, barring visits, since I got here. That could potentially cause some confusion for the troops. The smooth operation of this base is my responsibility, Colonel, and it's of the utmost importance to me that nothing interfere with it, so I want this up front and understood—I command here. I will not have my orders questioned or countermanded in front of the men. I trust we're not going to have any conflicts over that issue?"

Bookbinder suddenly felt very alone and very tired. The strangeness of his new surroundings and the sudden change in his life had left him disarmed for dealing with the kind of territorial challenges that were his stock-in-trade back in the Pentagon's halls. He nodded.

Satisfied, Taylor nodded back. Crucible smiled. "How're you holding up, sir?"

"I guess you could say I'm a bit overwhelmed."

Crucible laughed. "Yeah, you could say that. How 'bout a cup of coffee? Might get your head right."

"I'd be much obliged, Colonel."

Crucible opened the swinging screen door, creaking on its hinges, and showed Bookbinder inside. Crucible, coming behind him, took a full minute wiping his feet, making Bookbinder feel rude as he looked down at the mud he'd tracked in.

Taylor's secretary sat behind a cherrywood desk outside his office door. She was older, dark-haired, and crisply professional. Her desk was strewn with all the knickknacks of life on the Home Plane—pictures of her children, a teddy bear wearing a FOB Frontier T-shirt, miniature American flags. In this sprawling camp of jury-rigged plywood and sucking mud, the sense of normalcy she provided was disarming.

"Hiya, Crucible," she said.

"Ma'am." Crucible tugged off his patrol cap. "This is Colonel Bookbinder, he's going to be the new J1 for the FOB. Also new to the Corps."

"Carmela Santiago," she said, shaking his hand. "Congratulations on joining us! What school'd you get?"

Bookbinder stammered for a moment before Crucible cut in. "We're still working on that," he said. "Would you mind running a couple of cups of coffee in for us? We're setting him up in Major Breffel's old office."

"Sure thing," Carmela said, putting a pot on a stainless-steel coffeemaker behind her desk. "I'll make extra. Fitzy's waiting in there for you."

"A cup for me too, thanks," said Taylor, coming in behind them and tracking mud across the floor to his office door, which he closed behind him without another word.

Carmela and Crucible exchanged sympathetic looks.

"You'll get used to him, sir," Crucible said. "He's not so bad after . . . well, he is so bad, actually. But he's fair and competent. He's just kind of . . . uh . . . challenging."

"I'm not saying anything," Carmela said.

"Well, let's show you your office," Crucible said, opening the door opposite Colonel Taylor's. Bookbinder's new office could have been lifted straight from the Pentagon's E ring. Dark wood paneling lined the walls, matching the expansive desk. An American flag stood beside the SOC arms on gleaming stands topped with shining brass eagles. Someone's family, Bookbinder guessed the previous occupant's, a Korean wife and two beautiful girls, grinned from inside a shifting photo frame. The image shifted to one of the girls throwing a ball to a golden retriever.

The room's occupants drew Bookbinder's attention away from the decor. The first was a short, muscular, bald-headed man. His mouth was a humorless line topped by a brief rectangle of moustache, his eyes hidden by mirrored sunglasses. He wore a black compression shirt and cargo pants and a black baseball cap featuring the striped bar of a chief warrant officer. The Suppressor's armored fist, supplemented by a star and laurel wreath, stood beside the SOC arms on his chest.

The other occupant was the size of a small child, its gnarled brown skin hidden mostly behind a blue jumpsuit. Long, pointed ears jutted from a bald skull. It knelt over an outlet, long fingers working to screw a gang plate into place.

Bookbinder stared. He had caught glimpses of the creatures during the bumpy Humvee ride from the LZ, but in his exhaustion and confusion he'd mentally filed them away to be dealt with later. No longer: This thing was not human, and it was fixing the electrical outlets in his office.

The chief warrant officer stood, following his gaze. He removed the sunglasses and jerked his chin toward the creature. "Don't worry about the goblins, sir. They're no threat so long as you don't let them get behind you." He extended a hand, "Chief Warrant Officer Fitzsimmons."

"Goblins? Are you serious?" Bookbinder asked as he shook Fitzsimmons's hand. The creature by the outlet turned to look at the new arrivals, revealing large eyes and a long, hooked nose.

"Yes, sir," Crucible said. "They're the indigenous civilization here. It's a tribal society, with some welcoming us and some fighting us. You're looking at one of the welcomers, or 'Embracers' as they call themselves. They contract on the base in exchange for commodities they can't get out in the wild, refined sugar, mostly, but also some medical supplies."

"I don't believe this," Bookbinder breathed.

Chief Warrant Officer Fitzsimmons jerked his head at the goblin again. "Get out of here," he growled. The creature sighed and got to its feet, resignation on its face, and departed.

"He seemed to understand that much," Bookbinder said.

"Oh, they've got a lot more English than they let on, sir," Fitzsimmons said. "But I wasn't kidding that they can't be trusted. The Embracers embrace us insofar as it gets 'em inside the wire to spot for indirect or steal guns and ammo. Begging your pardon for speaking freely, sir." He addressed the last to Crucible.

"Chief Warrant Officer Fitzsimmons heads up one of our most important programs here on the FOB," Crucible said. "It's one of the J1's biggest responsibilities here, as Congress has to approve the special appropriation that funds it on a month-to-month basis. We're constantly fighting to keep it running, and we think it's critical that it continue."

Bookbinder's head spun. "Can I sit down for a second?" Fitzsimmons gestured to the chair he'd just vacated and moved to the wall, arms folded across his substantial chest. Bookbinder slumped in the chair, rubbing his head.

"Let me get this straight. I'm in an alternate dimension. I just saw a goblin, a real and literal goblin, working in my new office. I am now in charge of a program so important and controversial that it is going to go from my desk straight to a congressional appropriations committee on a monthly basis?"

"Senatorial committee, sir," Crucible said. "But otherwise, that's pretty much on target."

"You'll forgive me if I'm somewhat overwhelmed."

Crucible smiled. "That's a common reaction when folks first arrive here, sir."

"With all due respect, sir," Fitzsimmons said. "This is the most critical program we've got running here, and I can't stress enough how important it is that our new J1 continue to support it."

"I hear and appreciate your concern, chief," Bookbinder said. "I'll do my job. Beyond that, the program is going to have to stand on its own."

Fitzsimmons's jaw clenched, and he looked as if he would say more. Bookbinder tried to hold his gaze but ultimately failed, looking around the room.

"All right," Bookbinder said, as Carmela arrived with the coffee. "I've got my coffee now, so you may as well give me a tour and show me this superimportant program."

"You don't want to grab a shower first, sir? Some rack time?" Crucible sounded concerned. Fitzsimmons moved toward the door immediately.

Bookbinder sighed. "Fresh as a daisy, Colonel. No point in putting off the inevitable. Maybe you can explain how I get in touch with my family while we walk?"

Crucible looked at his feet. Fitzsimmons cut in. "There's a mandatory weeklong comms blackout for all new arrivals, sir."

Bookbinder's stomach turned over. He felt his magical tide surge and interlace with both Crucible's and Fitzsimmons's flows, tugging at them, reeling their currents toward him.

Fitzsimmons frowned at the intersection, leaning toward him. "You all right, sir? You need me to Suppress you?"

"You tell me," Bookbinder said. "Nobody seems to know what the hell is going on with my magic other than it's super, critically important to prevent me from talking to my own damned wife and kids."

"I know it's stressful, sir," Crucible said. "But trust me, the SOC is used to handling sudden separations like this. I can assure you we have counselors on the Home Plane making sure that your wife and children know you're safe, and answering as many of their questions as they can."

"You got any children, Crucible?" Bookbinder asked.

Crucible paused. "One, sir, a boy."

"And do you honestly think it'd be enough for your son to talk to a counselor when he didn't know where his father was?"

Crucible and Fitzsimmons were both silent. Bookbinder instantly regretted the sharp words. "Forget it, guys, let's get this show on the road. What's this super program I'm in charge of funding called?"

Crucible and Fitzsimmons both spoke at the same time.

"Coven Four, Umbra," said Crucible.

"Shadow Coven," said Fitzsimmons.

By the time Fitzsimmons was halfway through his explanation of the Shadow Coven program, Bookbinder was completely overwhelmed. "An entire Coven of Probes? A Portamancer? And that's who we're going to meet?"

"That's right, sir. Britton's a pain in the ass, but he's coming along. I'm confident Shadow Coven will be operational within two weeks at the most. I just need a little more time to bring him into line."

"Oscar Britton," Bookbinder said. "I'll be damned. I saw that guy's face on the FBI's Ten Most Wanted List every day at work. You had him here the whole time."

Taylor had fallen into step with them as they made their way toward a plywood guard shack standing beside a giant corrugated metal gate on wheels. A sign hung from it, bearing the SOC arms. RESTRICTED AREA: APPROPRIATELY BADGED SOC PERSONNEL AND CONTRACTORS ONLY. ABSOLUTELY NO FOREIGN NATIONALS OR SOURCE-INDIGENOUS CONTRACTORS PERMITTED WITHOUT ESCORT.

The sky darkened. Thick clouds suddenly formed unnaturally low over their heads. An air raid–style siren wailed. A voice began to repeat, "All personnel, take cover, take cover, take cover."

Bookbinder felt the hairs on his arms stand on end as a powerful magical current eddied somewhere nearby, followed by a crack of thunder that shook his bones. The smell of ozone and churned earth filled his nostrils, and he caught a glimmer from the corner of his eye that looked like a column of lightning as thick as a tree trunk. He dove to the ground, covering his head with his hands and pressing himself against one of the concrete blast barricades. The thunder sounded again two more times, each more distant than the last. He realized he was trembling and forced himself to be still.

"Oh, come on now." Taylor's voice dripped with scorn.

Bookbinder rolled over and got to his knees, looking from the mud that now plastered his uniform to the men standing around him. Taylor shook his head. Crucible and Fitzsimmons looked uncomfortable.

"You're going to have to get over that," Taylor said. "We get several of those a day, and the men will be watching you."

"What the hell was that?" Bookbinder asked, blushing. The difference between his administrative role and the real soldiers surrounding him was plain enough without his groveling in the mud at the first thing that went boom.

"Lightning strike," Fitzsimmons said. "Conjured by some indig Aeromancer. Goblins come up Latent more often than we do and tend to have stronger magic."

"You'll get used to it after a while, sir," Crucible said. "Just remember with indirect fire that it's a small target zone and a big base. Odds are slim you'll get tagged."

"Hell, that one wasn't even danger close!" Taylor said.

Bookbinder stood, dusting off his uniform and avoiding Taylor's scolding gaze. Crucible coughed uncomfortably and patted his shoulder. "It's okay, sir. Just remember, small round, big base."

Yes, I'm fine, Bookbinder thought. *And whatever little respect I had in the eyes of these men is now gone.*

They kept on in silence until they were intercepted by a group of MPs, who waved them back. "Sorry, sir," said one, "gate to P-Block got hit. We've got the whole place locked down."

"That's all right," Taylor said, sounding relieved. "The colonel's got everything he needs on the program to authorize funding. He doesn't need a face-to-face with the operators. Wouldn't you agree?"

Fitzy was impassive, and Crucible looked like he didn't agree at all, but both men nodded and chorused, "Yes, sir."

The gate to P-Block was sliding back, a small group stepping outside as electric carts piled high with repair gear and goblin contractors filtered in to work on the damage. One of the group was a black man with a shaved head, built like a linebacker. He wore the same uniform as Fitzy with what looked like an archway on his chest. A smaller, pale man with thick glasses stood beside him, sporting the same uniform with a grinning skull in place of the archway. Both men went rigid at the sight of Fitzy.

"Here you go, sir," Fitzy said. "May I present Keystone and Rictus, two of my lambs."

The bigger man turned and immediately snapped to attention at the sight of Bookbinder's rank. "Sir," he said, soldier's habit evident in his tone.

Bookbinder's eyes widened. "Oscar Britton. I can't believe I'm meeting you."

Britton looked askance at Fitzy. The chief warrant officer nodded almost imperceptibly.

"Conditional pardon, sir," Britton said. "I'm a proud Entertech employee now."

"Enter . . ." Bookbinder began.

"It's the main contract manpower provider here," Fitzy said. "All of the goblins and some of the Sorcerers work for 'em. Most of the maintenance and special skills work, too."

Bookbinder turned to Taylor. "But I heard he was a Warlock or something. Isn't that Probe magic? Shouldn't he be . . ."

Britton's expression went sympathetic. "I'm still getting used to it myself, sir."

"Secure that," Fitzy barked. Britton shut his mouth, and his eyes snapped front.

Bookbinder turned back to Britton. "Public enemy number one," he said, then realized he could feel Britton's flow. "You're not even Suppressed!"

"We're making an omelet here," Taylor said. "I'll explain everything once we get back to the office." He nodded to Fitzy, who in turn growled at Britton and his companion until they followed the electric carts back inside the gate. Bookbinder watched Fitzy's demeanor soften as soon as Britton was out of sight. He'd seen men be nasty to train people before, but this looked more like genuine hate.

On the way back to the office, they nearly ran into a man standing in the muddy track, one corner of his mouth upturned in an impudent smile. He was thin, his skin unnaturally corpse gray. His slick black hair was plastered to his head. He wore black cargo pants bloused over hiking boots. A dirty, rumpled long-sleeved polo shirt sported the Entertech logo on the right breast.

"Gentlemen," he said. His voice cracked as if he wasn't used to using it.

Taylor's expression went hard at having his way blocked until his eyes reached the man's face. Then he melted into the most disingenuous smile Bookbinder had seen in a long time. "Hey!" Taylor said. "How's the camp treating you?"

"It's a mud-caked shit hole, Taylor," the man said. "No doubt thanks to your expert oversight."

Bookbinder sucked in his breath, but the colonel only grinned. "Yeah, it takes some getting used to, that's for sure.

"Let me introduce you to Colonel Alan Bookbinder," Taylor said, draping an arm over Bookbinder's shoulders. "Alan here's our new J1. Hopefully, he can get some of the contracting snaggles sorted out. Alan, this here's the Sculptor. He's our most valued Entertech consultant."

"Great," the Sculptor said, not looking at Bookbinder. "Maybe now that you have a manpower expert, you can get my bonus pay unfucked."

Bookbinder shrugged off Taylor's grip. "Now, wait just a minute—" he began, but Taylor's hand settled on his shoulder, gripping painfully. Taylor laughed loud enough to cut off Bookbinder's retort. "Alan's new here. Still learning the lay of the land."

The Sculptor's dark eyes settled on Bookbinder, narrowing. Bookbinder opened his mouth, but Taylor's grip tightened.

"New, huh," the Sculptor said. "Well, I know you'll get him schooled."

"You bet we will," Taylor said.

"Got a chopper to catch," the Sculptor said. "I'm heading back to the Home Plane, but I should be back around in the next few weeks. I'll call when I'm ready."

"Have a safe trip," Taylor said.

The Sculptor turned and stalked off. Taylor's death grip on Bookbinder eased with every step the contractor took away from them. When Bookbinder finally broke free, he noticed that the colonel was sweating.

"What the hell was that?" Bookbinder asked.

"Alan, I'm going to say this once," Taylor said. "I don't give a rat's ass if you're a full bird or the J1 of this post. Don't you ever, *ever* get into it with that particular contractor again."

Bookbinder felt the blood rush to his face. "Is the whole SOC out of its mind? You've got me shooting puppies, dodging magical indirect, and now I'm supposed to be deferring to contractors? Last time I checked, those guys work for us!"

Bookbinder felt the breaking point. If he was going to stop Taylor's treating him like an inconvenient stepchild, he was going to have to lay down the law. He put on his best command voice. "I also don't care that you're SOC and do things differently. The army is still the army, and I'm not going to let a contractor treat me like that."

Taylor turned purple. A vein throbbed redly in his forehead. Crucible and Fitzsimmons took a step back, and Bookbinder's courage fled as quickly as it had come. They waited in tense silence, Bookbinder fighting the panicked urge to apologize.

At last, Taylor smiled indulgently and spoke as if to a child. "Oh yes, you will. With this contractor you most certainly will. You have never seen a Physiomancer who can do what he can. Next time, I'll let you get into it with him and see how you like it. You're like a goddamn newborn babe. You don't even realize when someone saves your life."

CHAPTER V
CLOSED SESSION

To be honest, I'm not a fan of the term "Rump Latent." It's dismissive and unfair. The proper term for them is "Unmanifested Latencies," and they play an important role in the SOC. Our Unmanifested make up the bulk of our Suppressing Corps, and their ability to sense magical currents in others makes them an invaluable tool in tracking and identifying Selfers. Those are mission-critical roles in this organization. There's nothing "rump" about them.

—Lieutenant General Alexander Gatanas
Commandant, Supernatural Operations Corps

As it turned out, life on a secret base in an alternate magical dimension was much like life back home. Bookbinder spent his days with his butt planted in a swivel-backed black chair identical to the one in his office on the Pentagon's E ring doing paperwork. While goblins, rocs, and God knew what else cavorted outside the wire, Bookbinder stared at his computer screen until his head ached, poring over spreadsheets documenting everything from shipments of Meals-Ready-to-Eat to unfilled personnel billets. Oscar Britton, the most wanted criminal in the country, worked for him, but only to the extent of authorizing his budget line and operating costs. The world he knew was miles away, but Alan Bookbinder's world hadn't changed a bit.

Except for one thing.

He missed his family so much he ached. He made his calls from a darkened squad bay, via a specially rigged state-of-the-art Single Channel Ground and Airborne Radio System.

When Bookbinder first arrived to use the system, the Radio

Telephone Operator handed him the handset, then sat, folded his arms, and stared at the ceiling.

"You're going to hang around? This is a private call," Bookbinder said.

"Sorry, sir. You're calling through a Portamantic Gate. Security rule. I have to supervise the equipment."

"I'm talking to my wife!"

"And I've got to answer to my first sergeant. Respectfully, sir, I have to stay here."

Bookbinder turned his back on the private. There was a long silence. Bookbinder was just about to tell the RTO it wasn't working when the handset issued a series of clicks that materialized into Julie's voice.

"Hello? Alan?"

"Bunny? Bunny! How are you doing?"

"Alan? I can barely hear you. It sounds like you're down a well."

"Never mind that. How are you? How are the girls?"

"What?"

"The girls! Can you . . "

"The girls. Well, Sarah made a picture of . . . *bzzz* . . . Kel . . . *bzzz* . . . acting out becau . . . *bzzt*."

"What? Kelly's acting out? What about?"

"She's just having a hard ti . . . *bzzzt* . . . so I think that's all that . . . *bzzzt* . . . Her teacher says she . . . *bzzt*."

"What? Oh, Jesus fucking Christ!"

". . . *bzzz* . . . did I do? You don't have to yell at . . . *bzzzt*."

"No, bunny! I'm not yelling at you. I'm sorry. I didn't mean it that way. I was just cursing this damned comms system. I can barely hear you. Bunny? I'm sorry. I wasn't yelling at you. Can you hear me?"

". . . *bzzz* . . . hear you."

Despair rose in his stomach. "Oh God, bunny. I miss you."

Silence.

"Sorry, sir," the RTO said. "Window's closed."

Bookbinder looked down at the plain gold band of his wedding ring, turned it on his finger. With every call, Bookbinder felt his family slipping away. He pounded on his desk and left his office. Carmela looked up, her smile never slipping, which only made him feel more powerless. "What's up, sir?"

He nodded toward Colonel Taylor's office, the door shut tightly as usual. "I need to speak to him."

"He's in a meeting right now, sir. Is there anything I can help you with?"

Bookbinder knew it wasn't her fault that Taylor was impossible to get ahold of, or that the comms were so spotty. But it did nothing to cool his anger.

"This is unsat! He's always at a damned meeting. I haven't been able to talk to my family at any length, with any fidelity or any privacy, for weeks now. The comms are so spotty that we can barely understand one another! I need it fixed. We're losing touch . . . with each other." *You meant to say "I'm losing her."*

"I'm really sorry to hear that, sir. I know it can be frustrating with loved ones back home." Her tone was sympathetic, but her words so disingenuous that his anger burned even hotter.

"You don't have the first idea! If you did, you'd get me a damned appointment. It shouldn't be this hard to get to talk for five minutes with my own boss!"

Carmela coughed politely, her eyes dropping to the framed picture of her three smiling boys.

Bookbinder's shoulders sagged, and his cheeks burned. "I . . . I'm sorry. I didn't think about . . . When did you last speak to them?"

"It's been about two years now, sir. This was a comms-dark tour for me, and I knew that going in. It's still hard, though; I really do know how you feel."

However broken and spotty, he got to talk to his family once a week. Carmela didn't get to talk to hers at all. What a bastard he was. "How do you . . . manage it?"

She shrugged. "I have everything I need out here. Food, clothing, shelter, medical. My entire paycheck goes into an account back in the Home Plane. By the time I wind up this tour, all three of them won't have to worry about college tuition. When I miss them, I try to think about that."

"Carmela, I know it's . . . just the way things are out here, but it would really help if I could just get a little more time on the channel, or be alone, or . . . well, anything. I just need five minutes of his time."

"I'll do my best, sir. I promise you I will."

And he believed her. But that didn't mean it would do a damn bit of good.

The only break in the monotony was the near-daily testing. Bookbinder would walk to the bustling tent city that made up the FOB's Combat Surgical Hospital, or "cash." The huge operation was a testament to the military's ability to deal with trauma in a forward position. The army had come into another world and, using only what they brought with them, had managed to cobble together canvas sheets, stainless-steel poles, and ingenuity to create a world-class hospital in the middle of a mud pit.

On the other hand, that hospital was overwhelmed with activity day and night, which was a testament to how dangerous the Source was. Between the range of native fauna that were just plain predatory or deadly (birds that barked sonic booms, snakes that spit poison, giant flying things with beaks that could swallow a car), to the sentient indig that hated them, there were more than enough ways to get killed out here.

But not all the indig hated them. The goblins were divided into warring tribes that were spread across hundreds of villages that dotted the landscape around the FOB. Some of these tribes were Defenders, who saw the humans as interlopers. The Defenders grossly outnumbered the few Embracer tribes, who believed the humans had come home when they entered the Source, and that it was their duty to assist, even protect them. Many of the Embracers worked as contractors on the FOB, and the cash was full of them in blue jumpsuits and hospital scrubs, carrying trays of medical equipment, binding blood-pressure cuffs, or reading thermometers.

He made his way from the trauma ward to another tent under a sign reading ASSESSMENT/SUPPRESSION. He paused and sighed, shoulders slumping. *Remember they're trying to help. The sooner you get a handle on what's going on with your Latency, the sooner you can be through with this.*

The tent could host more patients, but they'd cleared it for Bookbinder's appointment. Two Suppressors lounged at the far end of the long room formed by the canvas walls, playing cards.

Not that one was needed, let alone two. Bookbinder's Latency remained fully stifled.

A white-coated army doctor stood beside a gurney piled with medical equipment. "Morning, Colonel. How are you feeling?"

"Lonely. Pissed off."

"Well, I'm sorry to hear that, sir. But it'll help you call the magic. You ready for the next round?"

"Let's get this over with. I have to get back to my desk." *So you can fill out more spreadsheets?*

The doctor motioned to one of the Suppressors and picked up a black plastic Taser from the gurney. He thumbed the trigger, sending a short arc of blue electricity between the electrodes.

"No way, Doc," Bookbinder said.

"It's just a little shock, sir. I have it at the lowest setting. We have to get the magic called up."

Bookbinder motioned the doc back. "No."

The doctor took a step forward. "This is standard, sir. You said you wanted to get this over with so . . ."

"Stand down, damn it! That's an order!"

The doctor froze, as did the Suppressor. *Nice going. You're going to lead men by screaming at them?*

"I'm sorry . . ." *Don't apologize, you idiot! You haven't done anything wrong!* "What I mean is, I don't need it."

"What do you mean, sir?"

"I mean I can call the current on my own. I figured out how to . . . what do you call it?"

"Drawing, sir?" the Suppressor asked.

"That's right," Bookbinder said. "I can Draw, and I can push it back."

The doctor cocked his head to one side. "How can you tell?"

Bookbinder shrugged. "I can feel it . . ."

The doctor and the Suppressor exchanged glances, then the doctor turned back to him. "Show me."

Bookbinder leaned into his frustration and sorrow. He missed his family, Taylor wouldn't see him, this doctor wanted to tase him first thing every morning. He felt the current respond to the spike in his emotions, the tide pulsing in his veins, making his temples throb.

The Suppressor arched his eyebrows. "He's pegged, Doc. I'm not doing anything."

The doctor turned back to the gurney, making notes on his tablet computer. "How long have you been able to do this?"

"Not long," Bookbinder said. "I think I figured it out in my office a day or so ago."

"Why didn't you say anything?"

"I'm sorry, I know I should have." *Damn it! Stop apologizing.* "I wanted to wait until I was sure."

The doctor put the tablet down. "With all due respect, sir, it's important that you share any development in your Latency with us at the earliest—"

Bookbinder cut him off. "I wanted to be sure of what I was feeling. I'll be sure to let you know about developments when I feel it's appropriate." *That's not the way to lead. You don't exert authority by being a dick.*

"All right, sir," the doctor said, making more notes. After a moment, he looked back up at the Suppressor. "You're not doing anything?"

"Not a thing, Doc. He's pegged."

"What's it Bound to?"

"I have no idea, Doc."

"What are you talking about?" Bookbinder asked.

The doctor ignored him. "Can we grab an active Sorcerer real quick?"

The other Suppressor put down his cards and disappeared through the back flap of the tent. He reappeared with a SOC captain, a subdued flameburst pinned to the right breast of his uniform.

"I already told you, Doc," Bookbinder said. "I don't need to be tased. Or burned for that matter."

The doctor continued to ignore him. "Captain, can you feel a current off the colonel here?"

Bookbinder could feel the Pyromancer's current. He felt his own current grasp it, the tendrils intertwining, tugging at it. The Pyromancer frowned, taking a step back. "Sir, he's . . ."

Bookbinder's current intensified, his head throbbing with the force of it. It was as if it were buoyed, doubled by the Pyromancer's magic. He broke out in a sweat. "Um," Bookbinder said. "I don't think this is good."

The Pyromancer took another step back. "What are you doing?"

Bookbinder's ears began to ring, his veins felt thick with power. "Not really sure," he groaned. "A little help here?"

The Suppressor raised his hands and Bookbinder felt his tide roll back. He breathed a sigh of relief. "Thanks."

"What the hell just happened?" the doctor asked.

"It was like . . . it was like he was stealing my magic. I felt this pull on . . . like he was pulling on it."

"What?" The doctor's voice rose an octave.

"You're a Pyromancer," Bookbinder said in amazement.

"What?" the doctor asked. "Of course he is."

"No, no. I mean, I can *feel* it. I know what school he is. I can feel it in his flow. Or, at least I could before you Suppressed me."

"That's impossible."

"No, I can tell. It felt . . . hot, caustic. I could tell he's a Pyromancer."

The Pyromancer rolled his eyes. "I've got my pin on, sir."

"Damn it, Captain, I'm not lying!" Bookbinder said.

The Pyromancer blanched. "I meant no disrespect, sir."

Bookbinder turned to the doctor. "I'm serious. I can feel his school. I don't know how I can, but I can."

The doctor tapped frantically into his tablet, then jerked his head toward the Suppressor. "What about him?"

Bookbinder paused for a moment. "Weak. That's all. It feels weak."

"Let him go," the doctor said to the Suppressor. "Take the Suppression off."

"Now, wait a second—" the Pyromancer said.

The doctor cut him off. "Captain, can you go get another Sorcerer for us? Any school will do. Please ask him to remove his school pin before coming in."

"Roger that, sir." The Pyromancer nodded and made a hasty exit.

"What the hell is happening?" Bookbinder asked.

"I have no idea, sir," the doctor said, "but we'll chip away at it until we figure it out."

A largish black man entered, slightly overweight, with a day's stubble on his chin. Captain's bars were Velcroed to the center of his uniform, and a dark patch showed where he'd removed the pin that marked his magical school. "You wanted to see me, sir?" he asked the doctor.

"Yes, Captain. Thanks for coming. Just need you to hang tight for a moment." He turned back to the Suppressor and arched an eyebrow.

"You're clear to go, sir," the Suppressor said.

Bookbinder Drew the magic and felt for the new captain's current. He found the flow instantly, and felt the same sense of intertwining, of tugging on the tide. The captain's eye's widened. "You sure this is okay, sir?" he asked.

"It's fine," Bookbinder said, gritting his teeth. He felt the current suffuse his own, his pores shot through with the magic, low, calm, solid.

Earthy.

"You're a Terramancer."

The captain's eyes narrowed. "How'd you know, sir?"

The doctor cut him off as the Suppressor rolled Bookbinder's magic back. "That'll be all, Captain, thank you."

"Sir," the captain said, and left.

"See?" Bookbinder said.

"He was a big guy," the Suppressor said. "Terramancers usually are."

"So? Get someone else," Bookbinder groused.

The doctor nodded. "That's exactly what we'll do."

They repeated the experiment five more times, with a Hydromancer, an Aeromancer, and three more Pyromancers.

Bookbinder nailed it each and every time.

Bookbinder's diagnosis remained the same: "Stifled Latency," which Bookbinder knew meant, "We have no idea what the hell is going on." He experimented on the way back to his hooch that evening, trying to sense the schools of other Sorcerers, only looking at their pins after he'd had a chance to wrap his current around theirs, reeling it in long enough to get a hint of their magic. He had to stop after three tries, as his subjects began looking wildly around as soon as his current began to pull against theirs, forcing him to let it go to prevent being discovered.

He lay awake that night, stomach twisted with loneliness.

Was this his power? He could tell what other Latents' schools were? What was the good in that?

That couldn't be it. He felt something more. His current wrapped around the magic of others, pulled it into him. It doubled his own power, swelled the reservoir until he felt the outpouring would overwhelm him. Identifying the school was the tip of the iceberg.

He tried to lay out the events of the test, then stopped himself. Everything bled together. It seemed that so much had happened so fast. He couldn't focus. His fingers strayed instinctively to his wedding band, twisting it on his finger.

Bunny. Oh God, I wish you were here. You would slow me down and talk me through it.

But his wife wasn't there. Alan Bookbinder was alone.

Just calm down and try to figure this out.

But his mind was full of Julie and the children. No matter how hard Bookbinder tried, he couldn't stop feeling sorry for himself. Frustrated tears began to flow, initiating a new round of self-loathing when he couldn't stop them. Some colonel, crying into his pillow. Bookbinder was still cursing himself when he drifted off to sleep.

And awoke to the sound of explosions.

At first, he thought it was the standard run of goblin magical indirect fire, but even as he rubbed the sleep from his eyes, he knew he was wrong.

Boom, boom, brakabrakabrakabraka.

Those weren't magical strikes. Those were conventional rounds. Small-arms fire, crackling frantically.

The sound of the good guys.

Somewhere in the distance, he could hear the loudspeaker public address system." . . . action stations. I say again, action stations."

They were under attack.

Bookbinder leapt out of his rack, cracking his head against the pressboard wardrobe. He cursed, rubbing the injury as he yanked on his uniform, racing out of his hooch still buckling on his gun belt, bootlaces trailing in the mud.

He heard the whine of rotors as helicopters raced overhead, searchlights beaming out toward the perimeter, their underbellies lit by the flickering of distant fire. Whistles and whumps sounded as mortar rounds impacted somewhere. Boots pounded in the mud around him as soldiers raced every which way.

In the distance, he heard the growl of fighters launching airborne. Whatever was going on, it was big.

He had no helmet, no go bag, no ammunition, and no idea what the hell he was supposed to do.

He was caught up short by a couple of MPs outside the office, who pushed him back gently, but firmly. "Sorry, sir. It's off-limits until we get this situation resolved."

"What the hell are you talking about?" Bookbinder asked. "My office is in there!"

"Sorry, sir. We have our orders."

"Well, I'm giving you new orders! Now get the hell out of my way!"

The MPs didn't budge.

"At least tell me what's going on?"

The MPs shared a look before shrugging. "Goblins breached the perimeter, sir. Suitability Assessment is overrun."

"The SASS?" His stomach turned over. That was where Oscar Britton trained daily and next door to Shadow Coven's quarters. "What about P-Block? Is that intact?"

"Sorry, sir. We don't know."

"Damn it! Let me talk to Colonel Taylor!"

The MP was about to say something when Taylor emerged from the office in full battle dress. He made for an electric cart idling in the mud.

Bookbinder lunged forward, but the MPs held him back.

"Colonel Taylor!" Bookbinder shouted. "Where do you want me? I can help!"

Taylor jerked toward Bookbinder's voice, his eyes rolling in disgust.

"I can help!" Bookbinder shouted again, straining against the MPs.

"The hell you can," Taylor said. He turned to the MPs. "Keep him here. I am not sending back to Washington for another goddamn J1!" He jumped on the cart and rumbled off toward the fighting.

Bookbinder shook off the MPs. "I'll have your goddamn stripes," he growled.

The MPs looked unimpressed. "Why don't you head back to

your hooch, sir? I'm sure Colonel Taylor will let you know if there's anything you can do to pitch in. For now, it's important that you keep yourself safe."

Bookbinder opened his mouth to curse them, then felt ashamed. They were following orders. Good officers didn't take their setbacks out on their people.

He returned to his hooch and sat on his rack, listening to the staccato of gunfire and the occasional whoosh-pop of heavier ordnance. Every so often, the crackle of energy indicated magic's presence in the fight raging nearby.

The fight that had no need of him.

Should he circumvent the MPs? Find a way to get into the battle? And then what? He could barely shoot. Christ, he hadn't shot in so long, he wasn't even sure if he knew how to take it off safety. Besides, he was a colonel. He wasn't supposed to be shooting. He was supposed to be commanding.

Bookbinder could command brigades of soldiers to process paperwork or fund operations. But he had no idea what one soldier was supposed to do in a firefight, much less a brigade.

He would be a hindrance.

Taylor was right. He was better off here.

The thought set him to feeling sorry for himself again, and this time he managed to stave off the self-pitying tears as he drifted off to sleep.

And was jolted awake for the second time that night.

The door to the hooch slammed open, jerking Bookbinder out of sleep and banging his head on the wardrobe again. Taylor stood in the doorway, his uniform smeared with dirt, his helmet gone. His body armor looked burned and splashed with long streaks of dried blood.

"You want to help? Now's your chance. Meet me at my office. I need you on station in ten minutes."

And he was gone, leaving Bookbinder wondering if he'd dreamed it.

He'd fallen asleep in his uniform this time, so he clomped down the short flight of stairs out of his hooch and down the muddy track toward the office. The night was eerily quiet, broken only by the short reports of single shots and the occasional shout. A single helicopter made lazy loops over the smoking ruins of the SASS, searchlight sweeping beneath it. A small unit of Aeromancers circled behind it, occasionally illuminating the sky with bursts of flickering lightning. This was clearly the battle's aftermath, and it looked like they'd won.

Carmela greeted him at the office, hair and makeup perfect, as if she'd been awake and at her desk all night. "Evening, sir," she said. "Colonel Taylor's in the huddle room."

"Thanks," Bookbinder said, trying to sound confident, and headed toward the door.

"Sir." She stopped him, then handed him a pad of yellow paper and two ballpoint pens. *How could I forget? The tools of my trade.*

Colonel Taylor, Chief Warrant Officer Fitzsimmons, Lieutenant Colonel Crucible, and two other officers sat gathered around the table, poring over a map of the FOB. They were talking in low tones that stopped when Bookbinder entered. They looked up at him, their brows furrowing, as if unsure of why he was here.

"Colonel Bookbinder," Taylor said. "I'm not sure if you've heard. We had a significant breach tonight. Goblins overran our Suitability Assessment Section. There have been significant losses, but we've beaten them back and secured the breach."

He talks like I never got out of my rack to try to fight.

"I heard," Bookbinder said.

There was a brief silence as the officers looked at one another, as if trying to decide if they should say anything further to him.

"Gentlemen," Bookbinder said, "you got me out of the rack, and it looks like the fighting is over, so I doubt you want me to lead anyone into the thick of anything. Why don't you tell me how can I help?"

Crucible smiled, Fitzsimmons's face was stone. Taylor nodded.

"Oscar Britton has escaped." Fitzsimmons said.

"The Portamancer? The one from Shadow Coven?"

Fitzsimmons nodded.

"I thought he'd raised the flag," Bookbinder said. "Come around to our line of thinking?"

Taylor looked daggers at Fitzsimmons. "I may have overestimated his degree of commitment to the mission, sir," Fitzsimmons said.

"Wait. Didn't you have a beacon in his chest? Some kind of a bomb?" Bookbinder asked.

Fitzsimmons nodded. "We detonated it once we realized he was running. Took out half the cash. It turns out one of the Physiomancers in the SASS with him helped him to get it out."

Bookbinder racked his brain, trying to remember the names of the SASS inmates from their personnel records and funding lines. "Therese . . . Therese Del Aqua?"

"That's the one," Fitzsimmons said. "They fled in the company of a goblin spy, Mardak Het-Parda, but Britton and his flunkies called him 'Marty.' I don't need to tell you how serious it is to have an ability as unique and dangerous as Oscar Britton's in goblin hands."

Bookbinder sucked in his breath. "No, I guess you don't. Who else got out?"

"Don't remember their real names, sir. They give themselves nicknames that they go by. There's an Aeromancer called Swift, a Terramancer called Peapod, a Hydromancer called Tsunami, and a Pyromancer called Pyre."

Bookbinder shook his head, making a mental note to update the personnel database on the missing, once he'd figured out their real names.

He sucked in his breath. "Wait . . . what about the Witch? The superdangerous one . . . Scylla?"

"Gone," Fitzy said, shaking his head.

"Jesus," Bookbinder breathed. "What can I do?" *Is it my magic? Is there something I can do with it?* His heart leapt.

"You can sign this. We need a special line of funding authorized to enable a special asset we've put in place to handle this kind of contingency." Taylor pushed a ream of papers toward Bookbinder.

As quickly as the hope flared, it died. They wanted him to do what he'd always faithfully done—push paper.

"It allows simultaneous operations both on the Home Plane and here in the Source. It needs authorization at the J1 level. In the past, I was the acting J1, so I'd just do it myself, but now you're here so . . ." Taylor didn't look pleased.

"So, now you need me to do it." Bookbinder slumped in one of the folding chairs and rubbed sleep from his face.

Taylor looked uncomfortable. "It's just a formality."

"No, Colonel Taylor. Funding authorization is not just a formality. It's an important aspect of financial oversight that ensures that taxpayer dollars are being spent appropriately. I can't just rubber-stamp something because you're in a hurry. I need details."

Fitzsimmons's mouth quirked. Crucible turned white. Taylor gritted his teeth. He spoke very slowly. "You're not authorized for details."

"Then you're not authorized for funding. I have an obligation to . . ."

Taylor leapt out of his chair, fist pounding the table. The map jumped. "We don't have time for this bullshit! We have an unsecured Portamancer running amok with half the damn SASS in tow! I can't delay getting this under control because you need to feel like you have a job!" He stabbed a finger at the stack of papers, knocked askew from his pounding on the table.

"I am in command, here!" He seethed. "Now. Sign. The. Fucking. Authorization."

Bookbinder stood and met Taylor's eyes. His heart and stomach were doing cartwheels so severe that he could barely distinguish one from another. *I will not be cowed. We are the same rank. I am done being pushed around. For all I know, I'm authorizing this guy to fund an addition to his bungalow in Hawaii.*

He gathered his courage and opened his mouth to reply . . .

Crucible's hand on his shoulder silenced him. He turned to face the lieutenant colonel, whose kind eyes were deep with concern. "Please, sir," Crucible said. "I appreciate your desire to do your duty, and I promise I will go over this with you later to the extent that I can. We'll get you read on if at all possible, but for now we've got a real situation here. We need to get this moving right now."

Bookbinder's anger evaporated. Taylor was an arrogant blowhard, but Crucible was competent and kind. Besides, what did Bookbinder really know about contingency operations? Signing paper was all he'd ever done, and now, when he was really needed to do it on an emergency basis, he balked.

Flushing to match Taylor, he grabbed the pen and signed.

Disgusted with himself, he sighed, then turned to go.

And almost rebounded off the glittering chest of a thing out of a B-movie.

The giant creature was bent nearly double to cram itself below the nine-foot ceiling. Its enormous chest was practically the size of the table. At least a dozen pairs of muscular arms draped to its waist, which stretched into a snake's tail, trailing out of the door. A forest of snake's heads bent to consider Bookbinder. He could see the shining, jewel-like scales flickering in the fluorescent light as some of the heads reached past him to look at him from behind. The array of colors was dazzling, contrasting with the glinting silver of a veritable butcher block of knives and swords held to its waist by a red silk sash.

Bookbinder had seen a wide array of strangeness since he'd arrived in the Source, but he was unprepared for this. He stumbled backward into his chair, knocking it over and almost falling on the table.

The creature reached out with one of its arms and caught him, lifting him as easily as if he were a dry twig, setting him back on his feet. It hissed at him in a singsong cadence that sounded vaguely like language.

"My apologies for startling you, sir," said a man beside the creature. "I assure you that His Highness is not a threat." The man's thick accent was Indian or Pakistani, with a lilt of an English formal education. He was young, with coffee-colored skin and eyes that danced with amusement. He smiled under a neatly trimmed beard. His muscular body was covered by an olive uniform faced with red edging and gold buttons, the Indian flag stitched onto the shoulder. His hair was hidden by a white turban.

Bookbinder straightened his uniform as the creature dusted him off, hissing something to the Indian man which made him chuckle. "Umm, sorry. I'm just not . . . not used to . . ."

"Of course," the man said. "The naga are impressive on first meeting. May I present His Highness Vasuki-Kai, who is my *Bandhav* and a prince among his people. I am Subedar Major Dhatri."

"Subedar Major Dhatri is the Sahir Corps liaison here, on behalf of the government of India," Crucible said helpfully.

"That's the Indian SOC?" Bookbinder asked.

"Where the hell do you get off barging in here without notice?" Taylor demanded.

The naga made a burst of angry-sounding hissing, but stopped when Dhatri placed a hand on one of its many elbows.

"Colonel Taylor, sir. Please accept my apologies for the intrusion," Dhatri said, his voice not sounding the least bit apologetic. "His Highness is greatly concerned in the aftermath of the battle that took place this past night. He respectfully requests to know why he wasn't alerted to the altercation and why we were not included in this council."

The naga hissed over Dhatri's words, not looking like it was respectfully requesting anything. Its cluster of heads stretched over the table, fixing Taylor with an array of golden eyes. One of the hands yanked a punch-dagger from the sash and cleaned the fingernails of another.

Taylor bridled but responded in more respectful tones. "Please tell your *Bandhav* that I appreciate his concern and apologize for any inconvenience." Dhatri translated into what Bookbinder assumed was Hindi. The naga nodded its understanding with those heads currently not occupied with glaring at Taylor.

"But," Taylor went on, "I must remind His Highness that the United States of America is a democracy which has relations with the government of the Republic of India, and not the Naga Raja. If His Highness wishes to file a request through you, Subedar Major, on behalf of your government—"

Vasuki-Kai cut him off with a wave of his hands.

"Yes, yes," Dhatri translated. "His Highness is abundantly familiar with your insistence on protocol. He assures you he will register complaints through the proper channels, and he also assures you that he has no faith at all in a response. He asks me to remind you that you are in the presence of royal blood that extends back more than five thousand years, and that you are guests in the Raja's domain. The Raja is master of all he surveys and tolerates your presence here only out of consideration to his more respectful children." Dhatri gestured to the Indian flag on his shoulder.

Taylor blushed, and even Fitzsimmons stirred at the words. The colonel looked as if he would retort, but Crucible cut him off, saying, "I know I speak for the colonel when I thank His Highness for his reminder and assure him that we will inform him of any news as it becomes available through normal channels."

The naga looked slightly mollified as Dhatri translated. It clapped Bookbinder on the shoulder and turned to go, turning sideways in an effort to fit through a doorway built to accommodate humans. This caused it to trip over its tail, which evoked a hiss that could only have been the naga equivalent of a curse. Finally, Vasuki-Kai gave up and took the doorframe broadside, his giant shoulders smashing the sides as easily as if it were made of paper.

He slithered out, Dhatri in tow, leaving two half-moons in the wood and drywall, Taylor muttering in his wake.

"The naga," Crucible explained to Bookbinder over Taylor's steady stream of profanity, "have rather grandiose ideas about their position in the Source."

"They think they fucking run the place!" Taylor said. "They're supposed to be our allies! Hell, the Indian Army uses *our* Portamancer to get their envoys over here to meet with them in the first place! I will not be talked down to like that on my own post! I swear to Almighty God if I wasn't . . ."

"Colonel Taylor is right," Crucible said to Bookbinder, as Taylor fell into another fit of rage. "But as you can see, Vasuki-Kai is kind of hard to argue with."

Bookbinder thought of the giant snake creature and nodded. Now he could add diplomacy with monsters to his list of new experiences.

He slumped back in his chair, staring in amazement at the shattered doorjamb, all the evidence that remained of the naga's passage.

CHAPTER VI
SHORT RATIONS

*It was Napoleon who first said that "an army travels on its stomach,"
an early nod to the all-important role of logistics in military campaigns. Armies that cannot feed themselves cannot fight, and armies
that cannot move critical assets to flash points rapidly and in good
order find themselves throwing in with too little, too late. US Transportation Command is proud to have embraced magic as a tool of
logistical dominance. Our Aeromancers calm storms, our Terramancers secure bridges, our Hydromancers ensure clean and abun-
dant drinking water no matter the terrain. Our Pyromancers clear
vegetative obstacles in seconds. The long-standing partnership
between USTRANSCOM and the SOC ensures that our warfighters
are rested, fed, and where they need to be, right on time.*

—Colonel Thomas Burge
Public Affairs, US Transportation Command

Bookbinder figured it out. With the comms so spotty through
the gate, there was no way he could to talk to Julie properly. But
maybe the same pipe would allow a short burst of data? He could
compose a thoughtful message and tell her how he felt without
fear of interruption.

It took him a full hour to say everything he needed to; how
much he missed her and the kids, how he was safe, and she
shouldn't worry. He repeated the all-important bottom line: that
he loved her and he loved her and oh, God, how he loved her.
No matter what he'd ever said, through every stupid fight and
thoughtless moment, that he loved her was the only thing he'd
ever meant. He loved her and the girls so much and *please* don't

forget to tell them. He added another short line asking Julie to send back her own video message. It might be one-way comms, but it would be better than the inadequate voice line.

At last, he copied it onto a thumb drive, stuffed it into his pocket, and made his way to the squad bay, heart rising in his chest. He was a fool not to have thought of this earlier. This would help bridge the gulf that had been growing between him and Julie since his assignment here began. He fought to keep from jogging to the squad bay, a smile stretching across his face.

That smile faded when he saw the RTO at his desk, playing video games. The SINCGARS system was turned off.

"Good afternoon, sir," the RTO said, not looking up from the screen.

"It's morning, Private. It's my comms window. Why isn't the system powered up?"

The RTO paused as the game took a turn that demanded his full attention. "Yes, sir. There's been a comms stand-down ordered. Some kind of communication trouble."

"What? Why?"

"Don't know, sir. I'm sure they'll get it squared away by your next window."

"Well . . . nobody told you anything?"

"No, sir. Nobody ever tells me anything."

And by the look of it, you like it that way.

Bookbinder stepped out into the sunshine and stood on the frozen mud, his stomach churning. *Just calm down. You're talking across two separate worlds here. There's bound to be glitches. This channel is entirely dependent on Portamantic magic. If only we had another Portamancer.*

His heart rose. *We did, didn't we? Maybe we've recaptured Oscar Britton.*

He quick-stepped it back to his office. Carmela looked up as he hurried inside. "That was quick, sir."

"Some kind of comms problem," Bookbinder said. "They wouldn't let me get a window. Where's Chief Warrant Officer Fitzsimmons? I need to talk to him. Did they net Oscar Britton yet?" *They should inform me when they do, but I'm just the paper pusher.*

"I'm sorry, sir, Chief Warrant Officer Fitzsimmons is on leave."

Bookbinder froze. "What? Now? With Britton on the run? That's crazy."

"I'm sorry, sir. That's all I know. I think the fight at the SASS really knocked him out. He probably had to take some R&R."

Bookbinder didn't know Fitzsimmons well, but the man struck him as highly unlikely to crack under the pressure of combat.

He turned toward his office, then swung back to Carmela. "Leave, right?"

"Yes, sir."

"I don't recall seeing a DA-31 on him. He's in a special-programs billet. You know I have to approve all leave chits for that."

"I don't know, sir. You get tons of chits across your desk every day. Maybe you just approved it and moved on."

She's lying. But Carmela was also one of the very few friends he had on the FOB, and he wasn't going to start a fight with her. He retreated to his office to think.

He stared at his screen saver, hiding the spreadsheets that his making of the video for Julie had put him behind on reviewing. Bookbinder might not be a "real" soldier. He knew he had all the leadership capability of a wet sock.

But when it came to pay and personnel matters, he was an absolute master. He knew every piece of paper and email that crossed his desk right down to the file and control number.

There had been no leave chit for Fitzsimmons.

He suddenly felt very tired. Whatever this was, it would end in yet another showdown with Taylor. He wanted to avoid that, but he didn't see how he could. There was one way, of course. He could be a good boy and sit at his desk and process paper like he was expected to, like he had all his life. *You've gone nearly three decades accepting what was fed to you, why is it a problem now?*

He pondered that question. *Because I'm Latent now. Because things have changed.*

Because whatever the hell is going on here is keeping me from talking to my wife.

The thought steeled his resolve. He would pound himself against whatever obstacles Taylor put in front of him until they broke or he did. Wasn't that what officers were supposed to do?

He stepped out of his office and put his fists on Carmela's

desk. "Carmela, you and Crucible have been the only people who have been even remotely nice to me since I got here. I want you to know that I really appreciate that."

Her smile was forced, her eyes guilty. "Thanks, sir. You seem like a nice guy yourself."

"So, I don't understand why it is that you're keeping something from me."

She looked away; at the desk, the computer, anywhere but at Bookbinder. His own stomach was doing cartwheels. *Am I being intimidating? Will she hate me now?*

"I know that Taylor puts a lot of pressure on you, and I know that the one thing he wants more than anything is for me to shut up and stay in my office. But that's never going to happen. I was put here to do a job, and I intend to do it. I am in charge of funding authorization for special programs. That means I have to approve all leave for officers on said programs. I never received a DA-31 for Chief Warrant Officer Fitzsimmons."

"Like I said, sir, maybe you just—"

He cut her off. "Carmela, I have been pushing paper for my entire career. I do not miss forms. Not. Ever. As far as I'm concerned, Chief Warrant Officer Fitzsimmons is AWOL. I want him front and center right now."

"I'm sorry, sir, but I—"

"I'm done wasting my time. Who runs the MP detachment here?"

She stammered.

"Who, Carmela? I'm not playing around here!" He hoped he sounded commanding without yelling. *God, I am so far out of my element here.*

"Captain Heerling, sir."

"Get him in here. I want an APB out on Fitzsimmons as a possible MIA or deserter." He took a deep breath, and went on, "And I need to talk to Colonel Taylor. Not get on his calendar, not wait. Now."

She stared at him. Bookbinder pointed at her phone. "Tell him I need to talk to him right now."

Carmela nodded and toggled the intercom to Taylor's office. As she spoke, Bookbinder breathed a sigh of amazement. What the hell was he doing? If he went too far with Taylor, who knew what the colonel could do in reprisal. Cut off his comms entirely? Charge him with insubordination? *Let him. If you don't like who you are, you have to change. I'm going to find a way to talk to my wife if I have to spend the rest of my life in the stockade to do it.*

Carmela's voice brought him out of his reverie. "I'm sorry, sir. He says he's very busy right now, but I can put you on his calendar for . . ."

Out the window, Bookbinder saw Taylor storm out his office back door, making for the FOB's main plaza.

"Goddamn it!" Bookbinder raced out of the office, running to intercept him. "Colonel Taylor! Colonel Taylor!" he shouted. "I need to talk to you."

Taylor ignored him, picking up his pace, but when it became clear that he'd have to run to get away, he stopped, clenching his fists. "What?" he grunted, looking at the sky.

"Colonel Taylor, I have to know . . ." Bookbinder was interrupted by a young captain. An MP's sleeve was slid over his upper arm. His name tape read, HEERLING. He jogged to a stop and saluted. Bookbinder paused to return it, but Taylor only turned his angry gaze on the new arrival. "Colonel Bookbinder, sir? You wanted to see me?" Heerling asked.

"Heerling!" Taylor interrupted. "What the hell are you doing here?"

"Colonel Bookbinder called for me, sir. He said that Chief Warrant Officer Fitzsimmons was MIA, and wanted me to conduct a search."

Taylor's face turned a deep purple, bordering on blue. "Stand down, Captain. Fitzsimmons is on leave, and you're not to conduct so much as a safety inspection of his electrical outlets. Is that perfectly clear?"

"Crystal, sir," Heerling said, saluting again.

This time, Taylor returned it. "And you will not mention this conversation to anyone. Dismissed." Heerling executed a crisp about-face and jogged off.

"Goddamn it, Taylor!" Bookbinder said as soon as the captain was out of earshot. "I demand to know what the hell is going on!"

Taylor stepped so close the brims on their patrol caps touched. "I am fucking *done* with you, you little shit. I have afforded you every opportunity to make yourself useful and stay the fuck out of my way. But you are just too goddamn *stupid* to do that. So, I will say this one more time. If you do not mind your fucking business. If you do not stay in your goddamned office. If you do not do. As. You. Are. Told. I will not call the MPs. I will not write up an Article 15.

"I will take you to a secluded portion of this mud pit and I will kick you until your teeth fall out. And then I will keep kicking you, until you piss blood for the rest of your natural life. And if you ever get back to that precious wife of yours, you won't be able to fuck her, because I will have kicked your nuts so hard they will have to be surgically removed and replaced with prosthetics. And nobody will say a thing about it, and do you know why? Because this is a combat fucking outpost, and we don't have time to indulge nosey, little fucking paper pushers who don't know their place and I *fucking command here*!"

With the last word, Taylor took a further step forward, his saliva spraying across the bridge of Bookbinder's nose and his chest bumping him back. The man was much bigger than Bookbinder, muscles hardened by years of combat training. Bookbinder had no doubt that, should Taylor follow through, he could easily hurt Bookbinder as badly as he had described. In all his years in the army, Bookbinder had never seen a commander lose it so completely. *Something has this guy on edge. It's making him crazy.*

Taylor was beyond out of line, but they were miles from civilization. Taylor did command here, and in a combat outpost, a commander's word was law. Bookbinder knew his way around the air-conditioned halls of the Pentagon. Here in the Source, he was utterly out of his element, and this situation was about to spiral wildly out of control. Right or wrong, he was outmatched physically, lacked Taylor's combat experience, and was on Taylor's home turf. He thought of a few retorts, but found himself looking down at his boots.

"Am I making myself perfectly fucking clear?" Taylor asked.

"Crystal," Bookbinder said, Heerling's word rising to his lips before he knew he'd spoken.

"Then we're done here. Now, fuck off back to your playpen, and I don't ever want to have a repeat of this conversation again."

Bookbinder moved woodenly, his fear and shame so palpable in his muscles that his veins felt stuffed with mercury. *You should have said something. Stood up to him!* But what if Taylor had truly gone off the deep end this time? What if he hit him? Bookbinder had no friends on this post. If the MPs came running, who would they back and who would they cart off to the stockade?

Bookbinder knew the answer to that.

He was already sitting in his chair before he realized that he'd gone there automatically, his body instinctively complying with Taylor's orders, kowtowing to Taylor's hysteria, even if it meant never seeing his family again.

Bookbinder still burned with humiliation when he went for breakfast the next morning. He kept his eyes on the dirt floor of the chow hall, ashamed to meet anyone's gaze. *You're being ridiculous,* he screamed at himself. *Hold your head up!* But every look seemed to hold an accusation.

The hot line was crowded, so Bookbinder headed for the cold-food section, piling his tray with fruit amid the relative quiet. *This is stupid. You want bacon and eggs. Go get on the damned hot line!*

I can't bear to look at anyone right now. Besides, this will help me lose weight.

You don't need to lose weight, you fucking coward! Go get the breakfast you want!

But while Bookbinder's mind raged, his body moved with the same wooden rote that it had when he'd gone to his office after Taylor threatened him. He took a foam bowl off the stack, filled it with bran flakes that he didn't even like, then opened the minifridge to get a container of milk. But the minifridge door didn't budge.

The unexpected resistance brought Bookbinder out of his reverie. He looked up to note that the fridge was locked and unplugged. A paper sign was taped to the front. NO MILK UNTIL FURTHER NOTICE.

Bookbinder had eaten in military DFACs his entire career. In all that time, none of them had ever run out of milk. He looked at the juice case. It was powered, at least, but three-quarters empty.

Bookbinder turned to one of the goblin contractors wrestling a stack of cardboard boxes from behind the refrigerated cases. "What's up here?" he pointed at the fridge.

The creature gave him a blank look, then turned to a navy non rate, who stuffed his clipboard into his armpit as he approached the colonel. "Can I help you with something, sir?"

"Yes, what's up with the milk and the juice? I'm the J1 here, and I didn't see any reduction in the standard food order."

"I know who you are, sir. There's been a rationing order put out for all perishables, effective immediately. Came down last night at 1800."

"A rationing order? Why?"

"I don't know, sir." He gestured to the fruit and salad bar. "That's starting to run low, too."

The comms blackout. Fitzsimmons's sudden vacation, and now this.

"Who runs food services here?" Bookbinder asked. "It's Major Holland, right? I didn't tell him to ration anything."

"No, sir. He got it straight from Colonel Taylor himself."

Taylor. That meant if he was going to get any answers, it would involve yet another confrontation, and Taylor had made it clear what he could expect from another one of those.

Something is very wrong. Supply issues are your problem. You have to find out what's going on. Even if it meant facing Taylor? He was terrified of the man's threats and rage. But he was angry that he had to worry about either one.

Bookbinder threw his tray down on top of the minifridge in disgust and stormed out.

As he moved through the entryway, he noted the corkboard clustered with slips of paper thumbtacked over one another, advertising the various events on the FOB. Announcements for the perimeter 5K run and the Sunday morning prayer breakfast were crowded out by the official notices, warning FOB residents of the dangers of Source flora and fauna (IF YOU DON'T RECOGNIZE IT, DON'T TOUCH IT! REPORT TO YOUR FIRST SERGEANT IMMEDIATELY), reminding them to report suspected Latency or negligent magical discharges.

But one sign dominated the board's center, stopping him dead in his tracks.

BY ORDER OF THE CAMP COMMANDANT: ALL NONESSENTIAL RANGE USE IS CANCELED UNTIL FURTHER NOTICE. WAIVERS

WILL BE EXTENDED ONLY FOR WEAPONS REQUALIFICATIONS.
UNIT ARMORERS ARE TO REPORT TO SFC SCOTT FOR INSTRUC-
TIONS ON AMMUNITION CONSERVATION AND DISPENSING.

It was dated that day.

*Perishable food. Ammunition. I don't care if he does kick my
teeth in. We've got a severe supply problem here.*

Bookbinder marched out onto the plaza, looking for Taylor.
With each step he took, his legs grew heavier as the cloud of fear
around him coalesced into molasses. *And then I will keep kicking
you, until you piss blood for the rest of your natural life.*

Of course, Taylor was trying to scare him. But fear robbed
Bookbinder of all perspective. All he could smell was the sour
taint of Taylor's breath, all he could feel was the pulse pound of
the man's tangible anger.

He was almost glad when the indirect hit.

A deafening bang rocked the plaza, as a pillar of flame shot
up over one of the blast barricades not fifty feet distant. A loud
succession of booms sounded in the distance. Bookbinder could
see a far-off cloud of circling rocs. The giant eaglelike birds
looked small from here, but he knew up close they were bigger
than a tank.

The SASS perimeter again. The goblins were launching
another attack, maybe hoping to break through before the
defenses were fully repaired.

The siren began to wail, calling all personnel to action stations. Men and women raced past him, pulling weapons off their
shoulders and checking magazine wells. The low growl of helicopters spinning up echoed in the distance.

*Well, you were going to get in a fight anyway. Might as well
get in one where you actually stand a chance.*

Since the last attack on the SASS, Bookbinder carried
three loaded magazines as he was supposed to do at all times.
He drew his pistol. It looked unfamiliar in his hand—heavy,
thick. He took the weapon off safety, kept his finger off the trigger, and raced in the general direction of the chaos. En route, he
spotted an electric cart heaped with helmets and body armor,
two goblin contractors jogging behind, keeping the heap from
tumbling off.

"You! Stop! I need gear!" he shouted. The driver stopped the
cart, hopping out and saluting. The soldier sized him up, pressed

him a vest and helmet, saluted again, then jumped back on the
cart. "Good luck, sir!"

Bookbinder donned the gear, still amazed at what a little
yelling had done, and followed behind. The crowd jostled as he
moved closer, pushing through a wall of dark smoke, blanketed
by noise; screams, gunfire, explosions, the sizzle and crackle of
magic. In the midst of the press, choking on the brimstone stink
of powdered concrete and cordite, all the people blended
together. In this darkness and confusion, there was no branch,
no rank, not even faces. There were just people, lots of them, all
moving toward a common goal. Here, Bookbinder wasn't an
administrative colonel, he was just another grunt, doing his part.

The peace it gave him would have been shocking if it weren't
so soothing. He was smiling as he stepped out of the cloud of
smoke.

And into hell.

He'd thought the indirect fire had hardened him. He'd shuddered through loud explosions, smelled the ozone stink of
impacting magic, heard the screams and even seen the charred
corpses of the dead.

It was nothing.

The SASS perimeter was a broken jumble of cracked concrete barricades and burning heaps of razor wire–topped fencing. The newly erected guard tower had collapsed, igniting the
magazine of the Mark 19 grenade launcher. The crew's remains
were strewn about the wreckage, hands, half a torso, smoldering
boots.

Two SOC Terramancers crouched in the wreckage, calling
up a shelf of earth that provided much needed cover from the
sea of goblins surging beyond. Bookbinder hadn't known that
so many of the creatures existed in the entire Source. They
trooped forward, many mounted on enormous, snarling wolves.
Their sorcerers came with them, skin painted chalk white, hands
crackling with magical energy. The horde hummed with rage, a
drone so loud that it competed with the steady stream of gunfire
mounting from the defense. Clouds of arrows, javelins, and gunfire erupted from the goblin throng, undisciplined bursts of fire
that were effective through sheer volume. A woman beside
Bookbinder coughed blood and collapsed.

A SOC Aeromancer streaked overhead, lightning arcing

from his fingers and plowing into the goblin mass, setting scores of them alight before a roc crashed into him, sending him spinning, and caught him in its beak, cracking his spine.

The rocks in the earth barricade glowed red-hot as a goblin Pyromancer arced a pillar of flame across it, sending one of the Terramancers and three other defenders screaming, beating at the flames.

A Stryker crested the rubble behind Bookbinder, the gunner letting off a brief stream of rounds from the fifty cal, then pausing as Colonel Taylor appeared, climbing the Stryker's standoff armor and yelling at him, waving frantically.

And then Taylor's eyes widened. He dove off the turret just as the gunner tried to duck below. A massive chunk of a barricade wall, rebar jutting from its jagged edges, knocked the turret clean off, sending it tumbling through the defenders, eliciting a chorus of screams. The dull thudding of approaching helicopters was momentarily drowned out by a roar of rage.

Taylor scrambled to his feet as Bookbinder turned.

Two huge creatures advanced through the goblins, each taller than any of the FOB's low buildings. They looked much like the goblins that barely reached above their shins; the same brown, gnarled skin. The same pointed ears and hooked noses. But there the similarity ended. Where the goblins were lean, these things were as thick as iron girders.

One of them roared again, swinging an oddly shaped club. Bookbinder realized it was the shorn turret of an Abrams tank.

One of the helicopters swooped low, miniguns opening on the creature, then began to spin as a summoned wind knocked it in a tight circle, a goblin Aeromancer rising over the creature's head. The giant snatched the helo's tail boom, stopping it in midair, leaning dramatically to avoid the spinning rotors. The pilots and crew tumbled out the side, screaming, disappearing in the horde of goblins beneath them. The giant roared and cast the helicopter into what remained of the Terramancer's barricade, flipping it over and tumbling into the defenders, who fell back.

"Come on!" Bookbinder shouted, striding forward. He leveled his pistol and squeezed off a few rounds, certain he wasn't hitting even the massive targets presented by the giants. "You scared of a couple of big goblins?" *You sound like an idiot. A scared idiot.*

But a small company of soldiers looked up at him, shame-faced, then took to their knees, finding cover in the broken rubble, firing into the approaching mass. An arrow whizzed close enough that he felt the fletching cut across his cheek. *Get down!* his mind screamed, but he forced himself to walk among the defenders, shouting encouragement. What would Patton say at a time like this? Oh Christ, he had no damned idea. "Pour it on, people!" he tried. He was terrified, but the wooden feeling in his limbs was gone. *Well, at least if the goblins kill me, I don't have to face Taylor.*

Pillars of flame erupted in the goblin ranks as SOC Pyromancers secured positions in the wreckage. A figure rose out of the ground and wrestled with one of the giants, some Terramancer's automaton, taking the drubbing from the swinging tank turret, but re-forming just as quickly, its rock fists giving as good as it got.

Bookbinder tried to keep his shoulders back, his chin up. He fired more shots in the enemy's direction. "You're going to let a bunch of pointy-eared rats overrun your position? Show 'em what you've got!" Could they hear the quaver in his voice? Around him, knots of defenders were coalescing. Here was a group of Suppressed Marines setting up a belt-fed grenade launcher. There was an army sniper team, picking targets quickly, the need to aim obviated by the enemy's clustered formation. Were they actually taking heart from his theatrics? He heard Taylor shouting at some unfortunate soldier. "Conserve your ammunition, damn it!"

Conserve ammunition? In the middle of this?

Suddenly the world spun around him. Something slammed into his head, rattling his teeth. A moment later, he realized it was the ground. The stink of ozone and blood filled his nostrils. Sound vanished, replaced by a ringing whine. He scrambled in the mud, his vision gone. Was he blind? No, he could see light, make out shapes. *Get up! Get up!* But his limbs moved as if through thick water, and he was hot . . . so very hot. The brimstone smell gave way to the acrid stench of burning plastic and hair.

His vision returned, and he rose to his knees, bringing one arm into view.

It burned brightly. He was on fire.

Bookbinder screamed, rolling on the ground, beating at the flames.

"I've got you, sir," someone said. He saw a navy sailor running toward him, shouldering his rifle and pulling a water bladder off his back. There was a whoosh and a blazing ball of fire caught him in the chest, sending him tumbling in a heap.

The heat subsided as Bookbinder rolled in the mud, until he bumped against the shins of a goblin. It was painted entirely chalk white, it's wizened features contorted with hate. It bent over and gripped the front of his smoldering body armor, hauling him to his knees. The goblin's magical current eddied out from it, so strong that it nearly overwhelmed him.

Well-done, he thought. *You were the only one walking around while everyone else was taking cover. You were so brave, you managed to attract one of their Sorcerers.*

The creature's fist ignited in a ball of flame. It spit something in its own language, raising its hand.

Bookbinder's current surged forward, borne on his panic. It interlaced with the goblin's. Where it tugged at other magical currents during testing, now it wrenched, and Bookbinder felt the creature's magic break free, funneled away from it. The goblin's eyes shot open in terror, and it dropped him, jumping backward, its fire fizzling out. Bookbinder felt its current passing into him, threatening to tear him apart. He pushed with everything he had, channeling the foreign current out of him, forcing it into a chunk of concrete barricade that he was braced against.

And then the current was gone. There was an odd silence. The goblin stared at him, its expression horrified, as if to say, *How could you?*

Bookbinder raised his pistol and shot it.

For all his lack of practice, he caught the creature in the middle of its forehead. Its look of horrified violation turned to surprise, then emptiness; then it fell over on its side, shuddered, and was still.

Bookbinder looked down. The chunk of concrete he had leaned against now smoldered with Pyromantic fire. It began to flake apart, the rebar inside glowing a dull red. Magical flame danced across its surface, dusting the air with black smoke.

Bookbinder could feel the dead goblin's current, now coming from that chunk of wreckage. His own tide vaguely flickered through him, pulsing toward it.

He furrowed his brow and rolled the tide back. A moment later, the sense of the goblin's current ceased, the fire flickering out, until it was just an ordinary chunk of masonry again.

And then Bookbinder noticed that the tide of battle had turned.

An avenue of gore opened through the goblins, wide as a two-lane road. The ground churned to mud beneath a carpet of lead, chunks of earth the size of a man's fist bouncing skyward to mix with the shredded flesh of goblin, wolf, and giant alike. The sky was dark with summoned clouds and drifting smoke, but Bookbinder knew that an A-10 Warthog had gotten airborne and begun its strafing run.

The withering fire added to the mounting defense, raining bullets on the attacking horde. At last, they began to buckle. First in ones and twos, the goblins sprinted back into the fields, falling under carpets of Aeromantic lightning. Bookbinder could practically feel the fear sweeping over the attackers. In moments, the trickle became a flood as the enemy fell back to the cheers of the defenders, fleeing.

Bookbinder watched them run. He lightly patted his hands over his body. His gear and clothing were melted and smoldering, but apart from what felt like a bad sunburn, he didn't feel too badly hurt. He turned back to the barricade chunk. What the hell happened?

You stole that goblin's magic. You siphoned it away from him and funneled it into this concrete and rebar. You're not a Latent Grenade.

What sort of parasite Latency stole the magic of others? Did Bookbinder truly have a school?

You have a school. It's just one nobody has ever seen before.

The scuff of boots in the dirt in front of him brought him back into focus. He looked up at a battered Marine staff sergeant, his gear streaked with dust and blood.

"You all right, sir?" The man asked.

"Um, I think so. How do I look?"

The man smiled. "Like a steely-eyed dealer of death, sir. Oorah." He saluted, then headed off.

Bookbinder stared at his back. A *real* Marine, the kind that ate nails for breakfast, had just complimented him. After a battle. Bookbinder's mind swirled; the smoke, the terror, the goblin standing over him, all threatened to overwhelm him. *Later.*

But a notion was leaping in his gut. Colonel Alan Bookbinder, fit only for processing spreadsheets and pay statements, had just fought in a battle and held his own.

Taylor's voice cut through his thoughts. The colonel held an army private by the collar and shook him vigorously. "Full auto!" Taylor screamed. "You're firing on full fucking auto! Did I not expressly order you to conserve rounds? Is that how you treat government property? Is that what you do with the taxpayer-funded ammunition entrusted to you?"

The scream was not the low growl of rage Taylor had confronted Bookbinder with before. It was high, bordering on hysteria.

Bookbinder was amazed at Taylor's lack of control, amazed at his revelation about his ability, amazed he had survived a real battle. Another amazement overshadowed them all.

Bookbinder was amazed that he no longer feared this man who was big but thick around the middle. Who was angry, but screaming with the whining hysteria of a man succumbing to panic.

Before he knew it, Bookbinder had crossed the intervening distance. "Colonel Taylor, I think this young man has had quite enough."

Taylor turned to face Bookbinder, hysteria yielding to surprise. His eyes widened as he let go of the private, who immediately saluted, grabbed his weapon, and jogged away.

It took a moment for Taylor to put on an authoritative expression. "Just what in the hell are you doing here?"

"Same as you, rallying to the defense of this base."

"I thought I told you—"

"You told me a lot of things. And now I need you to tell me something else. What the hell is going on here? There's some kind of supply issue, and all I know is that it's sudden and severe. We've got sundries issues at the DFAC, and you're shaking down a private, a fucking *private*, instead of leaving it to his first sergeant. And for firing on the enemy? Now quit fucking around and tell me what's up."

"I fucking warned you . . ."

"Then do it!" Bookbinder screamed, mashing his forehead against Taylor's, driving the bigger man back a step. "Go ahead and kick me in the blood piss, or whatever stupid shit you were going on about before. But you better fucking *kill* me, because if you don't, I will keep coming back until you won't be able to get a lick of work done because you'll spend every hour of every day fighting me."

Taylor gaped. Some predatory instinct deep within Bookbinder surged, carrying the magic with it. He struggled as he fought it down. Taylor stood in shocked silence.

"Now, there's two ways we can do this," Bookbinder began again, anger yielding to fatigue. "You can bring me into your confidence, and we can try to solve this problem together. Or I can order a complete inventory of all ammunition reserves, which is well within my authority as the J1 here. This will tie up all ammunition distribution. Nobody will get a single round without my say-so. That won't be a problem if new stores are inbound, but they're not, are they, Colonel Taylor?"

Taylor's shoulders sagged, the fight totally gone out of him. *I can't believe it. I was so certain he would crush me. Is this all he is?*

"Are they?" Bookbinder asked again through gritted teeth.

Taylor looked at the ground. When he spoke, his voice was barely above a whisper. "No, Alan. They're not."

The predatory sense of victory melted away at the sound of that voice. Bookbinder the alpha male was gone, replaced by Bookbinder the father and husband. He put his hand on Taylor's shoulder.

"Why?" Bookbinder asked. "What's going on?"

"We lost contact three days ago," Taylor said. "I'm not sure if it has to do with Oscar Britton's escape or not. All I know is that Billy's not opening the portals anymore. We've got no comms with the Home Plane. Nothing is coming through—no food, no ammo.

"We're cut off."

TAKING HOME

When you took Chatto, you thought you'd finished us, cut off the snake's head. I won't lie, it hurt. Chatto was a great leader, a great man. But he was just a man. The Reawakening has brought our gods back to us. The *Gahe* of the mountains, the gods of the four directions. They remember their children and they will lead us to victory.

—"Jimmy" Dahana
Tribal Council, White Mountain Apache

CHAPTER VII
LAST RITES

The "goblins" (the colloquial term the military uses for them) call themselves Heptahad On Paresh "Flow Children" or "Current Born." They believe that the magic essence of the Source has created all life. Life is born from the magical current, some at the heart, some on the edges. The current itself has a source (the source of the Source) that goblinkind envisions to be heaven, but not in the Judeo-Christian mode. It is viewed as a recycling back into the wellspring that feeds the world. They don't have a reincarnation concept, but death returns you to the current and connects you to all existence, fueling its resonance and wonder. Goblins believe that the dead have a hand in the sunrise and the glow of the grass.

—Simon Truelove
A Sojourn Among the Mattab On Sorrah

Britton stood in the goblin village. He'd fled here, and defeated the SOC team that pursued him, but the center of the village was a smoldering ruin. Corpses lay tangled together in the helicopter wreckage, goblin, human, and wolf, butchered so badly that Britton couldn't tell if they were from the assaulting force or the fleeing refugees. Of the original group he'd led here from the SASS, only Therese, Swift, Peapod, and Tsunami remained. Pyre lay dead where Fitzy's bullet had punched through him. Downer and Truelove, Britton's former colleagues in Shadow Coven and now technically their captives, stood nervously apart.

The goblin villagers ringed the ruined ground. They were one of the Embracer tribes, friendly to humans, but many of them were clearly furious at Britton and his friends, blaming them for bringing destruction to their home. Britton and his companions would never have escaped the SOC without Marty's help, and the little goblin continued to protect them, hastily assembling a cordon of guards to keep the crowd back. The goblin villagers hiss-whispered in their own language, pointing with long fingers and staring with wide, yellow eyes. Britton saw shock in some of those eyes, confusion in others, rage and hatred in far too many. The scorched ground was a testament to what the goblins had suffered from the battle Britton had unwittingly brought to their village.

Britton assessed the situation. They'd won the battle but were unprepared for the aftermath. They were cut off in a village of creatures they didn't know or understand. Marty was the only goblin any of them had ever truly met, and only Britton, Downer, Truelove, and Therese knew him at all. Dead soldiers sprawled all around them, but there were many more where they came from.

This was his fault. Britton had freed the Witch Scylla, duped by her in his desperation to save Marty. Instead of helping him, she had slaughtered hundreds and set off the chain of events that had put them all here. Everyone knew that, most of all Therese. Every time he tried to meet her eyes, she looked away.

It wrenched his heart, but there was no time. The SOC would even now be learning of the defeat of their team and plotting another attempt. Many of the goblins around them were hostile. He had to make sure his people were safe.

Your people? How can you call them that?

The SOC had robbed him of his career, friends, and family. These were the only people he had left.

And he would take care of them.

Therese hadn't had time to use her Physiomancy to heal everyone. She'd done a cursory healing of Swift before moving on to Downer, still cradled in Truelove's arms, her chest smoking where Swift's lightning bolt had struck her. Downer was beginning to revive under Therese's ministrations, the second time the Physiomancer had saved her young life.

"Not her!" Swift shouted. "Don't you help her!"

Britton could feel his current gathering and moved to intercept him.

Therese whirled on Swift. Her beautiful hair had been frozen off in clumps by the spy Wavesign's magic. She'd killed him, using her healing magic to Rend though she'd sworn she never would. "What?" she said. "You expect me to let her die?"

"Why the hell not?" Swift shouted. "She and her little boyfriend there tried to kill us. Did you miss the whole part where they gated in here with the attacking force? They're our prisoners!"

"Then they're protected by the Geneva Convention," Britton said, "and that means we give them proper medical attention."

"Fuck that," Tsunami said. "They tried to kill us. Turnabout's fair play."

"And now you're suddenly in the fight?" Britton asked her. "Because during the battle you seemed content to not do a whole lot." Tsunami turned red to the roots of her ginger hair, then looked at her feet.

Swift's color rose, his current Drawing hard. The muscles of his lean body corded beneath his pale skin. Truelove gently set Downer down and stood. "I won't let you." The Necromancer sounded terrified. "There are corpses enough here to make an army." Britton felt Truelove's tide rise.

"No, bring it on," Downer said, rising up on her elbows. "Make your move, Swift. I could use the fuel." Swift hesitated. Downer could turn any magical energy into an elemental bound to her will.

"We just went through this, Swift," Britton said. "Let it go."

Swift pointed at Downer, still boiling with rage from having to let his hated enemy, Harlequin, go free. Therese and Britton had convinced him not to kill the helpless Aeromancer, and instead, Britton had gated him onto the White House lawn along with the survivors of the assault force. "You watch your fucking back."

Marty turned and shot them a concerned look. Britton caught his meaning. The infighting wasn't winning them any friends among a crowd of goblins that was already half-surly and growing worse by the minute.

He had to deal with this now.

"Lock it up, Swift," Britton said. "That's not how it's going to be." He pointed to Downer and Truelove. "I've run missions with these two. They're good people. They were following orders."

"Unlike you," Downer said. "Why the hell did you run? You had a place with us."

Britton opened his mouth to answer, but Truelove spoke over him. "No, he didn't. Fitzy was going to kill Marty. You did right, Oscar. I wish I'd had the guts to do that."

Downer whirled on him. "What the fuck are you talking about?"

"She's still loyal to the army," Swift said. "You can't keep her alive."

Truelove looked up. He was painfully thin, his eyes enlarged behind his thick glasses, but his magic thrummed potently. The normally timid Necromancer had found his feet when he'd confronted Fitzy, and it seemed to have stuck. "You're not going to hurt her."

Britton stepped between them. "Nobody's hurting anybody."

"Who the hell put you in charge?" Tsunami asked.

"I did," Britton said. "Because, rightly or wrongly, I got us off that FOB. The only reason you're not still watching propaganda videos in the SASS is because of what I did. I saw you in the fight, Tsunami. If you were running things, we'd be sitting around shivering right now. Swift would busy trying to kill more people and who knows what . . ." His eyes fell on Peapod, mannish face framed by her close-cropped hair, standing with arms folded.

"I'd go home," the Terramancer said.

"Home?" Britton asked.

"The Home Plane," Therese supplied. "Peapod, that's crazy."

"No," Britton sighed. "It's not."

"Oscar," Therese replied, "you think there's a safe place anywhere in the whole United States for us now? What do you think the SOC will do to us if they find us? We're Selfers on the run. And Scylla. I can't even begin to think about what you just let loose on the world. Even without her, we just killed . . . I don't know how many soldiers. Our very existence is illegal!"

Peapod snorted. "Fuck that. I've been running from the law since before I came up Latent. That's the real reason they threw me in the SASS anyway. For selling weed."

"What?" Britton asked. "I thought you were some kind of rugby champion."

"That doesn't exactly pay the bills," Peapod said. "I was running a six-figure business by the time I graduated college. The SOC doesn't take kindly to that."

"Bullshit," Downer said. "They don't throw you in the SASS for selling pot."

"They do when you grow it Terramantically," Peapod said. "You should have seen the mushrooms."

Britton shook his head. "I don't believe this."

"Believe it," Peapod said. "And while you're at it, believe that I've made a life out of staying one step ahead of these douchebags. I got sloppy is all. It won't happen again. Send me home. I am done with this fucking plane and I am done with army types and I am *not*"—she pointed a finger at Truelove and Downer—"hanging around within a hundred miles of those two."

"She's right," Tsunami said. "Get us the hell out of here. There's nothing for me here. I don't want to stay, and I don't want to take my chances out there. Send me back home."

"Tsunami," Britton said, "this is bullshit . . ."

"Stop calling me that!" Tsunami said. "I have a name, and it's Nancy. I don't want to play your stupid little games anymore. I'm not a superhero, and I'm not in a damned army!"

"Fine. Nancy. It's still bullshit."

"How is it bullshit?" She swept her arms across the smoldering village. "You want to live here?" She pointed to the waving saw-toothed grass beyond the palisade wall. "You want to live out there with the monsters? We have to go home!"

"So long as the McGauer-Linden Act makes us legal pariahs, we don't have a home!" Britton shouted. "We have to change the law. We have to find a way to make home safe for us again."

"And how do you propose we do that?" Nancy asked.

"We need to start a movement . . . We need to . . ."

"Oh, that's horseshit," Nancy snorted. "You want to go found a political party now? Stick to what you know, soldier boy."

"I just need time to puzzle it out," Britton said. "President Walsh and Senator Whalen talk about prohibiting certain schools of magic while they traffic in it. We know about Shadow Coven. We know about FOB Frontier, all of it. I can be anywhere, at any moment. I can spread the word. Hell, maybe I can confront Walsh himself! That's how systems change, Tsu . . . Nancy, by rallying the public to your side. We've got the ultimate weapon to do that now. We've got the truth.

"It's not safe for you back there. You're a Selfer. You've seen a secret military installation. There is no home for you anymore. I can keep you safe here. I'll make it okay, you just have to give me time."

She shook her head. "I've seen what you do. Whether you meant it or not, there are a lot of people dead because of you. I'll take my chances with the SOC."

"I'm talking about a chance to change things for *real*. Change them for *good*," he said. "Why would you walk away from that?"

"Because I have no reason to believe it will work. I'd rather take my chances on my own," Nancy replied.

"No," he said.

"What?" Peapod asked.

"No. I'm not doing it. It's for your own good. I'm not sending you back to the Home Plane to die."

Nancy gritted her teeth. "It's easy for you. You can just do it. Why the hell won't you?"

"Even if I was willing to, I have to see a place, fix it in my mind, to be able to gate to it."

"You're from Vermont, right?" Peapod said. "Put me there. I can find my way to where I need to. I'll take Nancy with me."

Nancy nodded. "You heard her . . . she's a criminal. She's got contacts. She'll keep us hidden."

Britton looked at Peapod. "Where will you go?"

Peapod snorted. "As if I'd tell you. You wanted to be the hero and save us. Well, you've done that. Thanks. I don't have a medal to pin on you, but I'd be much obliged if you'd get me out of here so I can get on with my life. I'll take care of Nancy. You're not the only one who can take care of people."

"I trust her more than I do you," Nancy added.

Britton shook his head. "I won't send you back to die."

"All right"—Nancy curled her lip—"then you're my fucking jailer. I want you to know that. We're not in the army. We're not under your command, and we're not fucking children."

"Oscar." Therese touched his shoulder. The firelight from the burning thatch reflected in her eyes, imploring.

"I only want to keep her safe," he said. "I want that for all of you."

"I know," Therese said, but her eyes didn't change.

He looked back to Peapod. "They'll experiment on you. They'll kill you."

"Only if they catch me," she replied. Her confidence almost convinced him. But when he thought of Nancy in the midst of the battle, crying and hugging her knees to her chest, that confidence flagged. He couldn't imagine her staying one step ahead of a deputy county sheriff, let alone the SOC.

But he didn't want to be anyone's jailer either. "Are you sure?"

Peapod nodded. "Do it now."

"You know Route 7, near Shelburne?"

Peapod shrugged. "I can figure it out from there." She retrieved a pistol from one of the fallen soldiers, expertly checked the chamber and magazine well before secreting it in the small of her back. "We're wasting time."

"If you're in trouble, if you need me, you should . . ." Britton began.

Peapod rolled her eyes. "Whatever. Get us the hell out of here."

Her shook his head. "Let me finish."

"You are finished," Nancy said. "We aren't going to need your help. We don't want it. Let's go."

Britton sighed and rolled open the gate. The rural route in Shelburne snaked off into the distance, the dew turned to frost reflecting the gate's static light. Somewhere down that road was his parents' house, maybe with his mother still in it. His father was dead and rotting in the wilderness around him, gated there accidentally before Britton had learned to control his magic.

"Anyone else coming?" Peapod asked. They all shook their heads, save Swift, who stared at her, eyes distant.

"Swift?" she asked again.

After a moment, he shook his head, and she shrugged.

"Be careful," Britton said.

Peapod didn't answer and didn't look back. She grabbed Nancy's wrist, and they walked through the gate together. Britton let it close, and they were gone.

Outside the cordon, the goblins surged. At the back of the crowd, Britton could see the huge spear bearer who had greeted them when they first came to the village. One of his arms was bandaged where a bullet had grazed it, and the rest of his body was covered with cuts where he had acquitted himself well in the battle against the SOC. The white dots that had marked his face had been scrubbed off. They adorned Marty's face alone now. From the look of it, the spear bearer wasn't happy about that. He divided his angry glares equally between Marty and Britton's group. Occasionally, he would pump a fist and call out to the crowd, receiving a chorus of affirming replies. The guards made no move to stop his rabble-rousing, but neither did they let any goblins into the plaza, the borders of which were dwindling as the cordon was pushed inward.

"They don't look happy," Truelove said.

"Because of you," Swift sneered. "You brought the SOC here. I can't imagine they're too thrilled to see you alive."

"For once, you're right," Britton said. "We can't stay here. This is going to get ugly, and who knows how much time we've got before the SOC goes for round two. We've got to get off the X before they come back for us. If we stay, it'll only bring more hell to Marty's tribe. They've suffered enough for our sake already."

Downer gestured to the carnage around them. "We can't just leave them like this."

"No," Britton agreed. "We can't. These are soldiers. Their families will want to see them laid to rest properly. They died following orders and fighting faithfully."

"They died fighting against us," Swift growled.

"That makes no difference," Britton replied. "They lost, but they were still doing what they thought was right. They deserve a decent burial. Arlington Cemetery. That's what I'd have wanted."

Swift rolled his eyes. Britton ignored him. "Simon, can you get them stood up and ready?"

"For what?" Truelove asked.

"I'm gating them into Arlington. Roll 'em through, lay them down respectfully, and we'll let the staff handle the rest."

Truelove nodded. "What about them?" He gestured to Richards and Fitzy, their corpses in pieces. Richards had been a contractor like him, and while Fitzy was a soldier, Britton still felt a jet of hot rage when he thought of him.

"Them, too." Therese's voice filled him with shame. "They loved their life in the army and their jobs, or . . . at least that was their choice. They wouldn't want to be buried here."

Britton nodded. *She's right.*

Truelove gathered his current. Britton suppressed a shudder as the corpses stood, then trooped together into two orderly rows. Richards and Fitzy came last, the first holding his trunk to his lower body, the second holding his head under his arm like some Dickensian ghost. The goblins outside the guard cordon pressed closer at the sight, the hum of their voices becoming a loud buzz.

Britton was too exhausted to concentrate fully. The only scene of Arlington he could call to mind was the stone disc that housed the Kennedy eternal flame. If he concentrated on his vision of rows of white crosses, he would be just as likely to open a portal on Normandy as Arlington. He opened a gate.

It was early, and the plaza around the eternal flame was empty. Truelove marched the dead quickly through, where they lay themselves in a military column of twos. Britton sighed as he closed the gate. Those men were American soldiers. They deserved folded flags, an invocation, mourning loved ones. This was the best he could do for them. "The army'll take it from there."

The goblins strained against the cordon, pointing and shouting. For now, the guards were holding, but it didn't look like they could for much longer. Marty shouted back, straining to be heard above the din. He shot a pleading look at Britton.

"Keystone"—Downer called Britton by his call sign—"I don't think we've got much time here."

Britton looked back to Marty. There was so much he wanted to say to the goblin: thanks, apologies. But the crowd continued to rage at the presence of the humans who had brought destruction down on their village, about to overwhelm Marty and his supporters. The sooner Britton got them out of there, the sooner things would calm down.

"We're not leaving Pyre," he said, kneeling beside the Pyromancer's corpse.

"I've got him." Swift shouldered him out of the way,

scooping Pyre up in his arms. "He was my friend." *He was a friend to all of us,* Britton thought, but didn't push the issue.

He opened a gate on the bowl of frost-kissed rose moss where they had fled when they'd escaped the FOB. Swift stepped through, the rest of the group close behind. Britton looked at Marty's back as he retrieved a spear from the ground and joined the guards in pushing against the crowd, who surged again at the sight of Britton and his companions leaving.

"I'm sorry," he whispered. Then stepped through the gate, shutting it behind him.

Swift had already laid Pyre on the ground. "It's going to get ugly back there."

"Maybe not," Britton said. "Marty is the legitimate leader of that village. The problem was us, and we're gone now. He can reassert himself. He didn't seem to have any problem taking charge from the big guy with the spear."

"The problem was them." Swift pointed to Downer and Truelove. "And it still is. All those goblin dead. That's on them."

"It's on me, too," Britton said. "I let her out. I let her go." Scylla, grinning balefully in the moonlight. The FOB collapsing around her, the screams of the soldiers as their flesh rotted off their bones, weapons turning to blowing dust in their hands, the perimeter gates worn to stubs, then gone on the winter wind.

"The FOB," he said. "Oh God, I've got to go back."

Downer visibly brightened. Truelove stirred. "I don't think that's . . ."

"The goblins stormed it after Scylla destroyed the defenses and we escaped. For all we know, it's a smoking ruin by now. If there are survivors, I can help get them out."

"Oscar," Truelove began, "that's crazy! They can . . ."

"It's *my* fault! All of this is my fault. I let Scylla out and . . . oh God. Scylla."

"She's still out there," Therese breathed. "Damn it, Oscar. What if she comes back?"

"I'm not going to let that happen," Britton said. "I'm going to find her."

"Find her?" Swift snorted. "First, she'd fucking kill you. Second, Scylla earned her freedom. She deserves to be left alone."

"Earned it?" Therese stuttered. "How on earth did she earn it? She killed hundreds . . ."

"Hundreds of *soldiers*," Swift finished for her. "Which, I've been told, happens in war. These particular soldiers had run her down, imprisoned her, denied her all rights. Are you surprised that she was a little pissed off?"

"Scylla is an insane monster," Britton said. "She *enjoyed* killing those people."

"They're dead just the same," Therese said. The words struck him to the core. *It's true. They'd be alive if it weren't for you. You owe for that.*

"I can't do anything for them now," he said. "Might be I can do something for those remaining, but we've our own dead to tend to first." He dusted the ash from Pyre's face. Therese knelt beside him. *I didn't mean for this to happen,* he thought. *I never wanted him to die.* But he didn't say it. She was right. Pyre was dead just the same. Even her magic couldn't bring the dead to life.

Pyre had wanted, above all, to break free from the bonds of the SASS.

"We made it," Britton whispered to the corpse. "We're out."

For now, his mind replied. *You beat one team, but the SOC will still come for you.* Britton had killed the only other SOC Portamancer he'd ever seen. He'd talked boldly to Harlequin, but the truth was that he didn't know if the SOC had another one, or, if they did, how long it would take them to pinpoint his location and try to take him again.

Nothing had changed. *Unless you can change it.*

He touched Pyre's forehead. "You rest in peace." *I'll keep them free from here on out.*

And more. I'll find another way, a better way, so that we can stop running. So that we can live in peace.

Swift laid a hand on Pyre's chest. "Rest easy, pal. I promise you they'll pay for this." *The man who killed Pyre already paid,* Britton thought, *and by my hand, not yours.*

"We just lost our Terramancer," Britton said. "We're going to have to bury him the old-fashioned way. I'll have to find a shovel and some food for us. I just need a minute to rest first."

"If you can get me a lighter, some source of flame," Downer said, "I can take care of it."

Swift's eyes blazed anger at her at first, then cooled. "We did call him Pyre, after all."

Britton nodded. "Don't think a fire'd be noticed all the way out here. So long as you can make it quick?"

Downer nodded. "Over in minutes."

"Okay." Britton looked up at what remained of his group: Swift, Therese, Truelove, and Downer. "I'll get some water, too. Winter clothing.

"I won't keep any of you here, you know. I'm not going to be anyone's jailer. If you've got somewhere to go, I'll help you to get there."

They were silent at that. Where could they possibly go? Nowhere would welcome them. Nowhere was safe.

"I'm surprised you're still here," Britton said to Swift. "Why didn't you go with Peapod?"

"You got me thinking," Swift said. "You're right about one thing. The problem is the fucking government and their laws. That's what kicked this whole thing off. That it's illegal to be who we are."

Britton nodded. "I'm going to change that. I'm going to find a way. I swear to God I will."

"You just need a movement."

"Or something like that. It's going to take time, but yeah. I need a way to get the word out to the public about what's going on, get people organized to change things."

"There's a movement."

"What?" Therese asked.

"There's a movement. There are Selfers, organized, hiding. I know who they are and where they are. You want to change the rules? That's where you start."

CHAPTER VIII
OUTSIDE THE WIRE

Where is God now? What does Jesus Christ say about this? Where in the Old Testament or the New or the Qu'ran or any other religious tract does it explain how to deal with the Great Reawakening? This is the problem with deistic religion. It has limited boundaries. It is a completed construction, a finished house. But life is what lives inside, and it is constantly multiplying, changing, and growing. And what do you do when you outgrow the house you live in? You move somewhere else.

—Mary Copburn
Council for Ethical Atheism

"What are you talking about?" Britton asked. "Are you talking about Mescalero? Because that's not going to . . ."

Swift shook his head. "Hell, no. The Apache have already committed so many atrocities on camera that people will never get behind them. The masks, the Mountain Gods. They're too . . . alien. People follow . . . you know, other people. People like them."

"What Selfer feels familiar to a non-Latent person?"

"Houston Street. The Tunnel Runners."

Britton rolled his eyes. "Are you kidding me? They're terrorists."

Swift stabbed a finger at Britton. "They're only terrorists to you and the other Homeland Security douchebags. To the rest of the world, they're an oppressed minority fighting for their lives. Plenty of people don't like them, but plenty of people do. They've got sympathizers in Hollywood, famous musicians, nonprofits, even some politicians. How do you think they've stayed around so long? It's not for want of the SOC's trying to thwack 'em."

Britton shook his head. "They've killed Americans."

"For the same reasons Scylla did. To defend themselves. To stay free. That's where I was headed when the SOC took me down."

Britton turned to the rest of the group. "Do you believe this cra—" He paused at the expressions on their faces. "You don't agree with him, do you?"

"There's a lot of debate about the Tunnel Runners," Therese said. "I never came down on either side. Do you remember when they fed that crowd at Saint Paul's? Or the time they put out that block fire in Flatbush? They do a lot of good, Oscar."

"So does Hizballah."

Therese's expression hardened. "I don't have a lot of patience with people who expect others to starve and die because they don't like where they get their help. Swift's got a point."

Swift got to his feet. "You can't have it both ways, man. You want a movement, a bedrock you can start from to change the law? Houston Street is it. Big Bear is a great speaker, he talks just like a slick shyster suit, which is what you're going to need."

Britton had heard Big Bear, through his anonymized Internet postings. The Selfer Terramancer's mountain-man appearance, broad shoulders, long dark hair, bushy beard gave the lie to Swift's description, but he was right about the man's gift for public speaking. Big Bear came across as honest and reasonable. Everyone assigned to SOC runs had to learn Big Bear's dossier as one of their primary High-Value Targets. The SOC cherry-picked videos depicting Big Bear at his worst moments, calling for peace and Latent rights but tinged with the threat of violence. *We deeply regret the loss of life on Beaver Street yesterday. Our prayers are with the families of the NYPD officers who were regrettably killed. Those same families should look to the SOC and the Mayor of New York City for recompense. Those deaths were completely unnecessary, and would never have occurred if Latent Americans were allowed their inherent, American right to freedom of choice, action, speech, and association, as guaranteed by the US Constitution.*

The words had seemed like slick justification for the murder of men serving in the line of duty back then. But now he was the one hunted for the crime of simply being who he was. He hadn't asked for his abilities, and neither had any of the Tunnel Runners.

"I won't help you take down Scylla," Swift said. "She's got every right to do what she did and . . ." Britton remembered the expression of shaking terror when the SOC finally dragged Swift out of the hole they'd forced him to share with her for a night, ". . . and that bitch scares the hell out of me. I'm not squaring up against her. No way."

Britton couldn't blame him. He had seen her magic shred a whole section of a military base. All the personnel, equipment, and structures turned to dust and rotting slime in minutes.

"But this I can do," Swift said. "I can get to Houston Street. I can tell them about you. You've got the one thing they need, the ability to put anyone or anything anywhere at anytime. They're not going to sneer at that. Sure, they'll want to negotiate, but it's a start.

"Put me in the New York subway system. I can find my way from there. I'll get word to you. You want a movement? That's where you start."

Britton attacked Swift's argument from every angle his exhausted brain could manage, and he kept coming back to agreement. Downer opened her mouth to say something, then shut it again as Therese put her hand on her shoulder.

"You can't get word to me across planes," Britton said. "We'll go with you. We've got a better chance if we stick together."

Swift started to reply, but Therese cut him off. "The hell we will. Scylla is still out there, Oscar. We have to try to catch up with her."

"And we will," Britton replied, "once we get a base of operations set up and . . ."

"No, Oscar." Therese's eyes flashed with anger. "You unleashed this particular hell. Hundreds of people died because of what you did. You have to make it right. Not later. Now."

Britton couldn't hold her eyes, looked away.

Therese's voice softened. "Swift's perfectly capable of making contact on his own. Aren't you?"

Swift nodded. "I can get it done."

"Then give him some time to do it. The rest of us need to

make sure that nobody else . . . suffers what those soldiers back in the FOB did. Nobody deserves that."

Britton swallowed his shame before turning to Swift. "Once we take care of Scylla, I'll come back to the Home Plane. Use Yippee.com. Set up a free email account on there." He tried to think of something unique and complicated. "!!!Lightning-Bug123!!! use a password of Flyh!$h!" He pronounced each character. Swift nodded and they repeated the codes back and forth until they both had them memorized. "Once you've touched base with the Tunnel Runners, send yourself an email on that account. I'll log in and check it once we're done with Scylla. Let us know your status and where to find us."

Swift grinned like a wolf. "You got it. We can totally fucking do this. We can change the world."

"Okay, I only know one location in the subway system under New York," Britton said. "It's a maintenance locker where we ran an op once. I don't know where it goes. You're going to be on your own from there."

Swift shrugged. "I'll figure it out. I played gigs in New York before. I know my way around. I look like a bum right now anyway, and unlike you, my face isn't plastered on every wanted poster in the entire country." Swift had looked the hipster with his black, unevenly cut hair and his tattoo even before the battle, and now he looked like one gone to seed. Britton guessed no one in the New York subway system would give him a second look if he curled up in a corner with his palm out for change.

"Okay," Britton said. "Repeat that email and password to me one more time." After Swift did so, Britton opened a gate back to the fields outside Marty's village, well distant from the palisade wall. "I'll be back in one second," he said, then turned to Swift. "Come on."

Britton couldn't open gates to bridge locations in the same world. He could only open gates between the Source and the Home Plane. He and Swift returned to the Source, then Britton closed the gate and opened a tiny sliver of a gate on the subway maintenance locker. It had been restored, the gap in the wall sealed and tiled over. Plastic yellow mop buckets stood beside coils of cable and a wheeled, multidrawer tool case.

"You sure you can do this?" Britton asked.

Swift tilted his head from side to side. "You're a sanctimonious, self-righteous douchebag. But you've got the power to junk this system, and I'm not missing my chance to be a part of that. Mark my words, I'm going to find a way to make Harlequin pay, whether you like it or not. But this way, I get a shot at President Walsh and Senator Whalen, too. So, yeah. I can do this."

Britton opened the gate full size. "Good luck, we'll check in soon." *I hope.*

Swift paused. "I don't suppose I can convince you to just wait until I get you word? Scylla is going to mop the floor with you, dude."

Britton thought of Therese's anger. "Not a chance. I have to tie off that thread."

"How are you going to track her anyway? You have no idea where she went."

"I'll go to the FOB first. That's the last place I saw her. From there, I'll . . . figure it out. I'll find her."

"Then you're the one who needs luck." Swift sighed and stepped through the gate.

Britton gated back to Truelove, Downer, and Therese. "It's done. Now I need everyone to sit tight for a minute."

"Where are you going now?" Therese asked.

"I'm off to do some shoplifting," Britton answered, opening a gate outside the goblin village again. "Just don't move for fifteen minutes. I'll be right back."

He stepped through, checked his surroundings for danger, then opened another gate on a sporting goods store in downtown Shelburne. The place was shuttered and dark in the early morning, but Britton still crouched in the half-light, painfully aware of the huge windows that opened out on the street. He moved quickly, selecting sleeping bags, pack-and-frames, and bundles of warm clothing. Flashlights, a camping stove, batteries, boxes of trail mix and power bars, a handful of campfire starters. He piled everything on the floor, then flattened himself as a car drove past the window. Once the car passed, Britton opened the gate back on the Source and shoved the whole pile through. *I should have left a note,* he thought, *apologizing. Promising to pay.*

The hell with that. The SOC can pay once you've changed the playing field. You're not a thief any more than a kid stealing a loaf of bread to feed his starving family is.

Back in the Source, he opened another gate on the bowl of

rose moss and pushed the pile back through. Therese, Downer, and Truelove gathered around.

"Gear," Britton said. "We're going to need it."

"Can you raid a gun shop?" Truelove asked.

"No need," Britton said, sending a gate skimming, slicing a cluster of frozen bushes neatly in half. "Got all the guns we need right here. We're not getting in a standup fight with the SOC. The guards at the FOB had all the guns in the world. Didn't help them much against Scylla."

He held up one of the campfire starters in front of Downer and nodded down at Pyre. "You ready?"

The Elementalist nodded.

"Anybody want to say any last words?" Britton asked. Therese bowed her head, crossing herself and muttering a prayer in Spanish. Truelove shrugged, and Downer scowled. "I was never a big fan of religion. That's the crap my mom used to justify treating me like shit."

My dad, too, Britton thought. Therese looked up and started to speak, but Britton cut her off before the fight started. "I never spoke about religion with Pyre, so I don't know what he believed. I can only tell you what I do know, that he was proud to be among you. Above all, he wanted us all to be free. That's why he never raised the flag. That's why he fought for you . . ." He paused. When he was able to go on again, he said, "If there was one thing that Pyre would have been willing to die for, it would have been to make sure that we'd never have to be back under the SOC's yoke. He did that, and it's as fitting an end as I can think of for anyone. If Pyre is looking down on us right now, I hope he sees that he accomplished what he set out to do. We're safe. We're together. We're free.

"And we're going to stay that way. We're going to stay together, and we're going to take care of one another. Because together we have a better chance of keeping ourselves safe if the SOC comes for us, and we all know they will never stop trying. Together, we beat them. Together, we can do it again. That's what Pyre would have wanted, and that's the best way we can honor him. We love you, Pyre. Rest in peace."

"He gave me constant crap," Downer added, "but he gave me the fire I needed to take down that Render in the sewers. So, I guess that means he saved my life."

"All of our lives," Truelove added.

All true, Britton thought. Pyre had been petulant and combative, a banner member of Swift's recalcitrant No-No Crew, but he had been true to his beliefs. He hadn't knuckled under to the army, right to the end of his life.

Britton pulled the trigger on the starter, sparking a tiny flicker of flame at its metal tip. Downer Drew and Bound her current, and the tiny flame leapt from the starter's tip and danced across the frozen ground. She kicked together a pile of drier leaves and twigs, and the fire took on the shape of a tiny flame creature, stubby arms and legs, line of a mouth, determined slits for eyes. It pounced on the pile of tinder and flexed little red-orange muscles, a look of strain on its cartoon face. Britton smiled in spite of himself. The flame turned white-hot, and the tinder caught. Downer added a few more pieces of wood until it was a healthy blaze. The elemental grew and stepped out of the fire, this time in the form of a beautiful woman, robed and hooded. The dancing peaks of fire that were her face were creased in sympathy.

The elemental knelt beside Pyre's corpse, the frozen ground smoking around her, and gathered him into an embrace. Pyre's clothing smoldered, then caught, his skin blackening. The elemental's form remained distinct from the rest of the flame, the cloaked woman embracing him as he burned.

Within minutes, all that remained of Pyre was ash and a line of greasy smoke drifting skyward. Downer rolled her magic back. The elemental raised its hands to the sky and vanished, the flames dying as the cold and wet ground fought against them.

"Thank you, Sarah," Therese said. "That was beautiful."

Downer shrugged, embarrassed. "Least I could do for him."

Britton found himself choked with emotion from the tender display but mastered himself quickly. If they were to catch Scylla, time was a luxury they couldn't afford. He opened a gate on the outskirts of the FOB. "I'm bringing us in close enough that we should get a good view of the SASS perimeter, but hopefully far enough out that they won't see us. Stay low. The grass is tall and, with luck, it'll cover us."

He opened a gate. After making sure it was clear, he motioned them through, duckwalking and finally going belly down in the dirt beyond.

They emerged in a burned crater, the remnants of a mortar or rocket strike. Mixed corpses, both goblin and human, lay all around them. The smoking remains of a crashed Blackhawk helicopter were a short distance off to their left. The fight had ranged far from the FOB. It must have been one hell of a battle.

Even from this distance, he could see the FOB's perimeter. The concrete barricade walls and razor wire were gone, rotted and blown away on the wind. But a tall, thick, earthen wall stood in its place. It sported solid-looking parapets and guard towers, patrolled by black dots Britton assumed were soldiers. SOC Terramancy was breathtaking in its speed and efficiency. Britton marveled at how quickly they'd managed to raise effective defenses. A pair of Apaches spun around the perimeter. Dust rose from the ground as a pair of Abrams tanks followed on the ground.

"I can't make it out that well without binoculars . . . but it looks . . ."

"It looks locked down." Downer sounded relieved. "They won the fight and sealed the breach. They're okay."

Britton rested his forehead against the ground, letting the waves of relief wash over him. The FOB hadn't been destroyed. That much, at least, was off his conscience. But he still had to find Scylla.

"Okay . . ." he said, then stopped as Downer got to her feet. "Sarah! Get down!"

She shook her head. "I'm going back."

"You're what?" Truelove got to his knees and resisted as Britton tried to drag him back to the grass.

"I'm not going after Scylla. Not unless it's as part of a SOC unit."

"Sarah," Britton hissed, "get down before they spot us! You're not going back."

"You saved my life, and I owe you for that. But I'm not a fucking turncoat. I never stopped being army."

"Sarah, please," Therese said. "You were never army."

"She's right," Britton added. "You were a contractor like me. You're a Probe, and you'll always be a Probe. You can never be one of them. Sarah, they put a bomb in my chest. They were going to murder Marty just for following his own customs. They forced people, you included, to join the military. That's what you're going back to.

"You want to belong to something? Belong to us. We belonged to each other on those missions. We can do that again."

"They never forced me to join," Downer said without much conviction. "I had a choice."

"What choice did you *really* have?" Britton asked.

Truelove caught her elbow. "Sarah, stay."

She froze. "Stay with me," he said again.

Downer sank to her knees, her eyes on the grass beneath her. When she looked up, tears streaked down her cheeks. Her voice was that of the young girl she was, all military professionalism leeched away. "Where am I supposed to go? Back to my religious nutjob mom? She thinks I'm dead and would hate me for being a Probe anyway. After we get Scylla, then what? You want me to live on the run, hiding in the sewer system under New York City? Like it or not, there's only one place in the world where I can be alive legitimately and legally"—she pointed at the Terramantic earthwork that sealed the perimeter beach—"and it's behind that wall. You blew that option. I can still go back."

She hitched back a sob. "I don't have anywhere else."

Therese wrapped her arms around her. "Yes, you do. You've got us."

Truelove put his hand on her shoulder. "Sarah, you're like a gun to the army. As soon as they're done with you, they kill you, or experiment on you. You saw what they did to that goblin village. What they did to Oscar."

"What they did to Billy and what they were going to do to Scylla," Britton added. "They were going to carve up her brain to make her compliant. That's exactly what they'll do if they capture her now, and all of her power will be at their disposal. And you know they won't stop until they do capture her.

"That's why we've got to get to her first. And you've got one thing she can't rot, elemental magic. Fire doesn't rot, Sarah. Neither does wind. We need your help to make this right."

Downer mastered herself, pushing back from Therese's embrace. "I'm tired of all this running and fighting. I just want . . ." . . . *to go home,* Britton finished for her in his mind.

"I know you are," Britton said. "But there's no home for you behind those walls, not the kind you want, anyway. I just need you to dig a little bit deeper and hold on a little bit longer. First, we fix this . . . thing I did. I know it's on me, but I need your help to set it right. Then, we link up with Swift and make the kind of home we all need. A way we can be safe and free, all the time, without having to look over our shoulders. If you still decide that you want to go back to them, you can say I captured you, forced you. And you can bring them the news that they no longer have Scylla to worry about, that you took her down. That should count for something."

"He's right, sweetheart," Therese said. "Can you do that?"

Downer nodded, sniffling, and lowered herself into the grass again. The others followed suit.

"What are we going to do with Scylla when we find her?" Truelove asked. "I mean, we have to kill her, right?"

"No," Therese said. "She deserves a chance at least. I've done some bad things in my time—"

Britton cut her off. "You did what you had to in order to defend yourself. That's nothing anyone would ever be ashamed of."

Therese paused. "I agree we can't let the SOC take her back, but we need to give her a chance to join us when we link up with Swift."

"That's crazy," Britton said. "You saw what she did to the FOB, Therese. That woman is insane."

"Still"—color rose in Therese's cheeks—"you just want to keep on adding to the body count, Oscar? Don't you think you've done enough?"

Britton swore under his breath. He couldn't get into this now. He would deal with her misgivings when they caught up to Scylla. For now, he had to keep the group together. He pointed over their backs, away from the FOB. "Last time I saw her, she went that way. If there's a trail to follow, that's where we're going to find it."

"You know how to track?" Downer asked. "They never taught me that in Shadow Coven."

Britton shook his head. "Me neither, but we have to try."

"And what if there's no trail?" Downer asked.

"Then we head back, link up with Swift. But we're not giving up until we've searched long and hard. Scylla was alone, without any gear or food. She can't have gone far. And while we weren't trained to track, she wasn't trained to hide either.

"We're going to low crawl in that direction for a bit; and then we can walk at a crouch. I think the FOB has its hands full cleaning up close to the perimeter, but we need to stay frosty. It won't be long before they've got some kind of helo patrol out after Scylla."

They turned, positioning their elbows and knees to carry them forward. He looked over at Truelove, gesturing to the corpses around him.

"Can you, uh, get these mobile? Have 'em stay down and crawl after us?"

Truelove frowned. "Now?"

"If we run into her, an army of corpses to soak up her magic are exactly what we'll need, and this is best stockpile of them we're likely to run into. Once we get out there"—he pointed to at the lightening horizon—"we don't know what we'll find."

Britton felt the tide of Truelove's magic coalesce and flow outward. The grasses around them stirred as wolf, human, and goblin corpses flipped over and low crawled into a cluster behind them. A dead man in an air force uniform crouched over to them and deposited four scavenged pistols before returning to the hastily assembled brigade of dead. "Thought we might need these," Truelove said, taking one. Britton followed suit. Therese and Downer wrinkled their noses and took theirs as well.

"Nasty," Downer muttered.

"War usually is," Britton said. "Stay low." He crawled forward. The group followed, and the army of corpses slithered along behind them, silent and determined, leaving only the gently swaying grass to mark their passage.

CHAPTER IX
TRACKING

After only an hour of searching, they picked up her trail.

Scylla had made no effort to hide her passage. Where dense clumps of grass or rock formations impeded her, she'd simply Drawn her magic and decayed them until they could be bypassed, not even bothering to take a step out of her way.

By the time Britton deemed they had gone far enough from the FOB to stand up, he smelled the sulfur stink of putrefaction. A few steps onward, the ground opened up. A gray-black dusting of powdered rock was strewn across bare soil. To either side, the grass was sheened with gray-black slime, the stinking remains of vegetation. In the center of the trail was a purple smear that might have once been a bird.

"Jesus," he breathed. Beside him, Therese crossed herself. Truelove brought a hand to his mouth, trying to filter the rising stink through his fingers. Behind him, the shambling line of zombies silently imitated his movement.

You did this, Britton thought. *You let her go.* The moment he'd freed her, Scylla had murdered hundreds, breaching the FOB's perimeter and inviting a massive goblin attack. In the resulting battle, Therese had been forced to break her vow never to use her healing magic offensively, tearing flesh instead of knitting it. Britton knew she still blamed him for that.

"Well," Downer said, "I guess we don't have to worry about tracking her."

Britton took a knee and gathered them around. "All right, we're on her, apparently. We need to be ready in case we find her. Remember, she's just one Sorcerer, and we're four. We do this by the numbers. I'll run Suppression. Truelove and Downer should swamp her with elementals and zombies, and Therese will run defense.

"Honestly, Therese, I'm not sure how your healing will match up against her . . . rotting. If I can't keep her properly Suppressed, then hopefully you can restore our flesh quicker than she can strip it down. Nobody will ask you to Rend, but if there's not need for your magic, there's no reason you can't walk over and punch her in the face, right?"

Therese smirked. "Got it."

"Everybody cool with that?" Britton asked. "Am I missing anything?"

"Sounds about right," Truelove said.

"It's four on one," Downer added. "What could go wrong?"

"Don't," Therese said. "You'll jinx it."

Britton grunted, and they pushed on. A pack of demon horses sniffed them out after the first few hours. Britton had encountered them before; they were blind and vicious, a weird combination between horse and hyena, with an unsettling ability to mimic any sound they heard, including human voices. He wasted no time, sending a gate sliding horizontally through them, cutting three in half and sending the rest fleeing, mimicking the wet slicing sound the micron-thin edge of the portal made. The ground rose as the sun dipped in the sky, fat and clearer than the one on the Home Plane, going from soft yellow to brilliant orange.

Britton froze as he heard helicopter rotors in the distance. He snapped open a gate back to the bowl of frozen rose moss and ushered the group through, the corpses dropping once

Truelove's magic left them, lying hidden in the tall grass. Britton and his group waited in the frozen bowl on the Home Plane. After fifteen minutes, Britton opened a pinhole of a gate, looked, listened and determined that the danger had passed. They moved back through the gate and took up the march again. The corpses were tugged to their feet by Truelove's magic, trudging along behind them, silent save for the dragging shuffle of their feet. Britton kept his eyes forward and tried not to think about it.

A cold breeze picked up, and Britton turned to Downer. "Sarah? Best to be ready." He nodded to Truelove's corpses. "Let's get something up and running."

Downer nodded, and a small column of whirling funnels of air appeared. They shimmered, visible mostly by dint of the leaves, pebbles, and clods of earth transiting their spinning cores. Britton had faced similar things when he'd fought Downer before he'd come up Latent.

Air elementals.

They forged on. Truelove and Downer lagged behind a few paces, talking softly. Britton turned to Therese. "Looks like they're searching for Scylla, all right."

No answer.

"Maybe they're just doing a patrol, not searching for her. Who knows why they're out?"

Still no answer.

Britton sighed. "Therese, please. I did what I had to. I got us out safe. They would have killed Marty. They would have experimented on those of us who didn't play ball."

Therese's eyes stayed fixed on the horizon. "Are you talking to me or to yourself?"

"I don't know. Both?"

"It's between you and God, Oscar. It's not for me to judge you."

"I feel judged."

"What do you want me to say? You let Scylla out. She butchered half the FOB. You killed Fitzy. You didn't lift a finger to save Harlequin. You left me to do that."

"Therese, that's not fair."

"Fair doesn't enter into it, Oscar. You made choices. You are responsible for them." She choked on her next words. "God, Oscar! I had to Rend! I swore I'd never do it again!"

"I know, but would you rather Marty be dead? Would you rather all of us still be prisoners? You helped me, Therese, you . . ."

"You tricked me, Oscar. Or, at least, you influenced me. I didn't know what was happening. I was trying to save you."

"And I was trying to save you! To save all of us."

"And you did that, at the price of Lord knows how many hundreds of others."

"Therese, please. I'm alone in all of this. I need some . . ."

"Some what?" she asked.

Some support. I've lost everything.

"I need some help. I can't do this by myself. Didn't we have something back there? Weren't we headed somewhere?" he asked.

"Maybe, Oscar. But that was before . . . all this. I'm here, aren't I? Besides, what is it exactly you're trying to do?"

"Take care of us."

"Nobody asked you to do that."

"We both know that nobody else is going to."

"God will, Oscar. He already is. You should try prayer. Maybe he'll find a way to forgive you, and maybe I will, too. But not now, Oscar. Not now."

Britton thought of his father, the only other religious person he'd ever been close to. Stanley Britton had advised his son to pray as well.

But Britton didn't try.

He thought of his mother, eyes wide and accusing. He thought of Billy's mother, screaming as her son's brains spattered her floral print dress. He thought of hundreds of soldiers, curdling to piles of purple slime under the baleful tides of Scylla's rotting magic.

How could he pray? Even if there was a God, there was no way he would listen.

Not to him. Not now.

He choked down hot anger. "I thought you Christians were supposed to believe in forgiveness, to actually imitate your God. When I was a kid, I almost bought that.

"I did what I had to, for all of us. It's not my fault it worked out the way it did, just as it's not your fault that you had to Rend your dad's friend for putting his hands on you. You want to show a little of that supposed Christian forgiveness?

"You can start with yourself. Then you can forgive me. Because you're not the only one who's alone out here, or the only one who's trying, and I could use some goddamn support."

"Oscar, I . . ." she began, then broke off as he dropped to one knee, raising a fist. The rest of the group followed suit, True-love's column of corpses joining them. The Necromancer drew his pistol, holding it in a two-handed grip, muzzle pointing at the ground. The zombies imitated him, hands clasped together around an imaginary gun handle.

Downer's elementals fanned out in front, ripping up the grass in small patches.

Britton pointed around a tuft of grass. The edge of a log pali-sade, much like the village they'd just left, jutted out. "Stay here," he whispered. "I'm going to take a look."

They nodded, and he opened a gate, jumping back to the rose moss bowl and back out to low crawl into the rough grass farther to his left, where he had a better view of the palisade.

It was some kind of goblin FOB, much smaller than Marty's village. The logs looked hastily sharpened and assembled, with crude, peaked huts beyond. A pole leaned drunkenly beside the gate, a red-and-orange-striped bird skull affixed to the top.

Britton paused, listening. Nothing. The place seemed de-serted. The wind suddenly changed.

The smell hit him like a wall.

The goblin FOB stank somewhere south of gangrene. He gagged, eyes watering. Drawing his pistol, he got to one knee, bringing more of the encampment into view. One whole side of it was simply gone. The palisade walked along the hard ground, then vanished into scattered black dust and glistening purplish slime that Britton had come to associate with Scylla's dark magic.

He walked forward at a crouch, keeping his pistol ready, and advanced on the encampment. By the time he was level with the decayed opening in the palisade wall, he was breathing only through his mouth. After a moment, even that wasn't enough, and he lifted the front flap of his shirt over his mouth and nose. It didn't help.

This must have been an outpost established by the Defender clans to supply larger groups of goblins reconnoitering and attacking FOB Frontier. Britton thought he could see the remains of a cistern and a corral for the fat, bleating creatures the goblins herded. The remaining buildings were puckered in on themselves, the wood wet-looking and sagging like overripe fruit, edges gone to powder or dripping slime. The frozen ground was plastered with purple and yellow stains, slick and viscous, here and there chunky with the remains of the goblins Scylla had worked her power over. There was the upper part of a skull, the eye still staring unseeing off into the distance beside a long, pointed ear. Here was an arm, the fist still gripping a spear shaft coated in the mucal ruin that had once been its owner. There had been sorcerers here as well, the scraps left of them painted chalky white in goblin fashion. Beyond the silent remains, the place was deserted. The trail of withered grass led off beyond the gap in the palisade wall.

Britton doubled over, retching. When he'd finally gotten control of himself, he jogged out through the front gate and called to the others. "It's clear."

They rose, but he waved them back. "You don't want to go in there."

"Why not?" Therese asked.

"Looks like Scylla got there first. It's . . . messy. There's nothing to salvage. No one left alive."

"No one left alive?" Downer asked. "Who was . . ."

"It was a goblin outpost," Britton said, "for the Defender clans attacking the base. They must have not given her a very warm welcome when she came through."

Therese took a step forward, and Britton put a hand on her shoulder. She shrugged it off immediately. "Therese," he said, "it stinks so bad, I practically puked. I swear, if there was anything you could do, I would tell you."

She relaxed. "Can you tell which way she went?"

"The trail continues on beyond the encampment." He looked up at the waning light. "I don't want to be traveling by night out here. It's safer if we spend the night in the forest back on the Home Plane. It's getting dark there, too.

"The . . . remains of the goblins. They're still . . . fresh." He shuddered. "She can't have come through here too long ago."

"We should press on," Downer said. "Maybe if we haul ass, we can catch her."

Britton shook his head. "No way. I've flown on night-vision equipment, and it's hard enough with that. With just flashlights? We'd just wind up breaking our ankles or running into something unhappy to see us."

"Or worse, happy to see us," Truelove added.

Britton nodded. "Scylla can't see in the dark either. She's got to be as exhausted as we are. She needs rest. So do we. Remember, we can't just catch her, we have to be able to beat her. We can't do that blind and at the limit of our reserves. Slow is smooth and smooth is fast. Let's do this right."

Truelove didn't look convinced at all. Therese looked uncertain. Only Downer appeared confident.

Britton knew the cost fear could have on combat effectiveness. He stepped back to address all of them. "I understand what Scylla has done is horrifying. Her magic seems . . . well . . . magical, but it is a scientific reality with limits. Scylla is a Negramancer. That power manipulates decay. It doesn't make her more powerful than four SOC-trained Sorcerers. Scylla can also manipulate fear. But that's clever acting and a strong personality, not magic. And it only works if you let it. She's dangerous enough without scaring the crap out of you. Don't let her."

They gated back to the bowl of frozen rose moss, still deserted and now cast in a darkness that rendered the night noises sinister; every frost-snapped twig or windblown leaf transformed into the footfalls of an approaching enemy. Britton wouldn't permit a fire, but they cooked instant noodles over a covered camp stove and slept in the sleeping bags and tent he'd pilfered from the sporting goods store.

He volunteered to stand the first watch. After Truelove relieved him, he crawled into the tent to find Therese stretched out beside Downer, her body heat lending warmth to the younger girl. Britton zipped into his sleeping bag and lay beside her. Therese's hair, uneven and broken from the fight with Wavesign, rested on the camp pillow, filling him with longing. She was so close, so warm.

He sighed quietly, but the action filled his nose with the smell of her hair. Before he knew what he was doing, he reached out a hand tentatively, and let his fingertips slide across it. Even now, in the dark, back to him, she was so beautiful.

She stirred. He jerked his hand back and froze, feeling

creepy. But she slid back into him nestling against his bulk, her hair brushing his face and her warmth enveloping him. He didn't move, terrified she was still sleeping, desperately not wanting to wake her.

She grunted, reaching backward and grabbing his arm, pulling forward until it was draped over her.

"Just to keep warm," she said softly.

"Yeah," he answered, his voice thick. "Just to keep warm."

Despite his exhaustion, Britton barely slept all night, drowning in the smell of Therese's hair and the closeness of her, almost crying out when Truelove finally nudged her awake and she took her turn at watch.

Neither of them spoke when Britton roused them after eight hours, the sky still dark around them. After they had breakfasted in silence and buried their trash, he opened a gate, putting them back on Scylla's trail, the withered edges of the grass guiding them on.

Truelove raised his arms, and the entourage of dead shambled into view, their gray skins tinged with frost. Some of them had been nibbled on during the night by the local fauna, but overall, they were whole. Britton still swallowed his gorge at the sight of them, and even Truelove looked uncomfortable at so many in one place. But they were one more thing they had to throw against Scylla should they meet her. Downer called up her air elementals again, the strong breeze providing ample fuel for the spell.

The encroaching winter gave the Source air a crisp, metallic bite that would have been pleasant if it weren't so cold, but it still carried the curdled-egg stink of the aftermath of Scylla's passage. With the sun beginning to brighten the horizon and shroud the unfamiliar constellations of the Source from view, they pushed on.

They came across the helicopter as the sun began to crest, and the day came on in earnest. It was a Blackhawk, nose down in the frozen ground, tail boom crumpled over an accordioned cabin. The cockpit was flattened, the nose practically inverted.

The engine and rotors were gone, the metal simply rusted away to nothing from the cabin upward. Britton pointed. "She rotted off the rotors and let it drop out of the sky."

Purple stains, still slick, dotted the ground outside the crushed cabin. "And killed the team on board as they crawled from the wreckage. Jesus. Those must have been some hard operators to crawl away from that."

He moved to the cockpit, then froze. He hung his head. "Oh, hell. Oh, that fucking bitch."

"What?" Therese asked. "What is it?"

He pointed at the shattered windscreen, the hands still streaked with dried blood trying to pull themselves through it, gone gray with rigor mortis.

"She left the pilots alive. They were crushed in there, probably broke every bone in their body, bleeding out. Maybe choking to death on the smoke. But she left them."

Therese lifted a hand to her mouth. Britton could feel the current of her magic reach forward, then recoil. Physiomancers could only manipulate living flesh, and there was none of that to be found here.

He turned to her. "Still want to give her a chance to join us?" Without waiting for an answer, he moved down the trail.

"Bring them," he called to Truelove, gesturing at the pilots behind the shattered windscreen.

"Are you serious?" Truelove called back.

"We're practically on top of Scylla now," Britton answered. "They died to serve. Let them serve a little longer. It's the closest thing to revenge we can give them."

But Scylla's trail grew colder as they went, the wet-looking patches left by the aftereffects of her magic beginning to dry. Somehow, she had begun to gain on them. Britton grimaced and put on speed. They kept on for another two hours as the sky fully lightened, and the landscape came to life around them. The night had been unusually cold, and the ground twinkled with fresh frost. It sparkled in the sun, transforming the landscape into a spray of crystal green, but it made footing treacherous as the ground sloped downward and their boots slid with each step. This was made harder by a grove of tall trees, which forced them to descend at an angle as the decline increased.

After a while, Britton found himself crab-stepping sideways, sliding every other pace as the edges of his boot soles failed to find purchase on the slick surface of thawing frost. Therese stumbled, and he put out a hand to steady her. Truelove and Downer latched on to her, and they descended in a human chain. The elementals fanned out in front of them, blowing air back toward them, trying to help them stay upright with no success. Britton heard a thump, and one of the zombies, less sure-footed than his human master, flopped on its face and slid past them, tobogganing on its stomach before coming to stop and trying to rise, slipping as it strove to mimic Truelove's careful descent.

A moment later, Britton felt his own feet going out from under him, and he sat down hard, his tailbone reporting the impact, and began to slide downhill. Therese scrambled for balance for a moment and pulled where he had pushed, clinging to Truelove, who clung to Downer. All of them went down in a heap, flying down the hill and slamming into Britton. They wound up in a tangle of arms and legs at the bottom, laughing hysterically.

Britton hissed. "Secure that. We are too close for this crap; Scylla could be anywhere around here." The mirth dried on the others' faces and they turned sullen looks on him. *God,* he thought. *I must sound like Fitzy.* But that didn't make him wrong. He was willing to be a killjoy if it meant keeping them safe. They could laugh all they wanted once they'd dealt with her.

"Come on," he whispered. "We just made a lot of noise here. We need to get off the X."

He stood, then froze.

The slick, putrid sheen of the grass marched in a narrow lane around the copse of trees, so fresh that it dripped. The wind blew toward them, bringing the faintest hint of what might have been muttering from off in the distance. With the wind toward them, Britton could hope that whatever was making that noise hadn't heard them.

"Hold here," he whispered. He pointed to himself, then to the trail of slime. Once again, he gate-hopped back to the Home Plane, then opened another gate farther out on the freshly cleared trail, just high enough for him to low crawl through. Once through, he lay facedown in the tall grass, slowly inching himself up onto his elbows, raising his head for a clearer look.

From his new vantage point, he could see beyond the edge of the copse of trees, to where the strip of bare ground continued in long patches mostly freed of frost by the risen sun.

Four sleek, black, horned things stood astride the strip. They stood between eight and twelve feet high, dagger claws hanging at their sides. White grins showed teeth as long and sharp as knives, the only contrast to the unbroken, liquid darkness of their bodies.

The "Mountain Gods," the *Gahe* of the Apache. Britton, with all of Shadow Coven at his side, had barely managed to defeat one before. Here were four.

One of them was missing an arm. In its stead was a tiny rope of black sinuous flesh, twining uselessly from a stump of a shoulder. It pulsed, oozing slowly. Britton's stomach fell. The fight at Mescalero flashed through his mind, his gate slicing upward as the *Gahe*'s frozen touch spread through his torso, slicing through its shoulder, sending the arm spinning in a cloud of black smoke.

He recognized the creature instantly; he had fought it before, and it had nearly finished him.

The four *Gahe* stood tensely, shoulders hunched, clustered around a woman. Her black hair was cut in a severe bob, the points sharp-looking. Her eyes were dark, remorseless.

Scylla was none the worse for wear. Her skin was still pale and smooth, her face still wise and beautiful. She'd traded her prison jumpsuit for thicker, warmer goblin leathers, but her boots were the same. Army-issue, black and mud-spattered.

A cloud of black smoke drifted behind the *Gahe*, the grass beneath it frozen solid gray. *That's their blood,* Britton thought. *That freezing smoke. She must have killed one of them.*

Pulses of shimmering air passed from the *Gahe*, clustering about Scylla's head. "Come now," she said to them. "Do you really want this fight?"

The creatures growled and inched forward, and Scylla gave ground slightly, raising her hands. More shimmering pulses moved between the *Gahe* and her. "Really, now?" Scylla responded to their silent communication. "Maybe so, but I assure you. I'll take a few more of you with me."

The *Gahe* flashed across the ground, spreading out to surround her. Scylla crouched, bared her teeth.

Britton had seen enough. He opened another low gate and scrambled through it, then opened another gate back to his companions. He motioned them through, and they came, standing in the bowl of rose moss. "It's her, she's just around those trees."

They were silent. Truelove's eyes went wide.

"She's in the middle of some kind of standoff with the *Gahe*. You remember them? The Apache Mountain Gods?"

Truelove and Downer had been with him on the mission where they'd faced the one and severed its arm, but Therese had only ever seen them in training videos before. "I remember them," she said. "They're monsters. The Apache worship them."

Britton turned to her. "Truelove, Downer, and I have fought them before. They're fast. They move by short-teleporting. One second they're five feet away and the next they're on top of you. Their touch will freeze you, and they bleed smoke that's just as cold. We're talking hypothermia in minutes. You got all that?"

Therese nodded, her confusion and fear vanishing as her training took hold. "Got it. Same plan?"

Britton nodded. "Those things are doing us a favor. If we're going to get her, now is the best time, while she's distracted. We head back, collect Truelove's corpses, and rush her. Ignore the *Gahe*. They're not our fight. We take her down and get the hell out of there. Everyone square?"

Truelove's voice was tinged with panic. "Can't you just gate in next to her and take her out?"

Britton shook his head. "And risk getting cut off alone? If she takes me down, you're all stranded. Bad idea. We go as a unit. Your corpses and Downer's elementals up front. She'll be pinned between our expendable element and the *Gahe*. Safest course."

"We're wasting time," Downer said.

Britton nodded and gated them back to their original position. Truelove raised the line of corpses, fallen flat in their absence, and they moved around the edge of the copse, where Scylla whirled to face them. The *Gahe* stood behind her. Whatever differences they'd had with Scylla, they appeared to be reconciled.

CHAPTER X
QUARRY

We've impressed ourselves upon magic, tried to shoehorn it into human limitations. We've given it taxonomy, ontology, category. But it's the nature of magic to ignore all that. It's not interested in making us comfortable. It doesn't care what we think is a "school" or which element we think it controls. Magic is wild and new and free. The idea of "schools" is an inadequate way to get our heads around a force that we're only beginning to understand. Magic can do many things that we can only dream of. We're chipping at the tip of an iceberg that runs very deep and very, very wide below the surface.

—Professor Andre Sinnawa
"The Magic Behind the Magic"
Journal of Modern Arcana

"Hello, Oscar," Scylla said. "You're just in time to meet my new friends." She gestured to the settling cloud of freezing black smoke. "We've just come to a mutually beneficial understanding."

The *Gahe* shrieked, the one-armed one's shoulders hunching, its recognition of Britton written clearly across its posture.

Britton reached out for Scylla's current. He felt it immediately, strong and rich, and wrapped his own around it, rolling it back.

Scylla cocked an eyebrow at him, smiling. She rolled her shoulders and, without a hint of effort, pierced his Suppression, his own current roaring back into him and hers surging through, unimpeded.

Britton cursed and threw open a gate.

Downer sent her elementals streaking toward Scylla, simultaneously drawing her pistol and squeezing off a round. The *Gahe* crouched. They stuttered forward until they screened Scylla, their position shifting like poorly advancing film, one second in one place, one second the next. Their shrieks went silent, and Britton saw the air shimmer between them, accompanied by a low thrumming. Downer's bullet disappeared into one of their dark bodies, swallowed as surely as if it had been fired into the cold void of space.

Britton sent the gate skimming across the ground at Scylla. The *Gahe* stutter-flashed out of the way, shrieking. Scylla reached forward and Suppressed Britton's own current effortlessly, and Britton's gate vanished long before reaching her.

Downer's elementals raced toward the *Gahe*. One of the *Gahe* swept its clawed hand through one of them, only to be caught in the elemental's whirling funnel and tossed aside. Another *Gahe* pulsed away from them, stuttering its position from side to side as they pursued. The remaining two *Gahe* howled again, then pulsed silent communication to Scylla.

Scylla smiled. "You know one another? I don't know if that's more surprising than your showing up at all."

Truelove gestured, and the corpses shambled toward her as quickly as they could, leaving parts of themselves on the frozen grass in their urgency. Scylla dropped her Suppression of Britton as the corpses closed on her. Therese and Downer pulled in behind the zombies, and Britton stepped out on their flank, opening another gate, which hovered over his hand.

Scylla sighed dramatically, spreading her arms. "Oh, let's not fight. You just got here. I was chatting with my newfound traveling companions, and you're welcome to join the conversation." She turned to the three snarling *Gahe* not busy with Downer's elementals, who had begun to spread out, two approaching from one side of the cordon of zombies, while the one-armed one circled to the other.

"Although," Scylla mused, "they don't seem to like you very much."

Her voice was syrup-smooth, her tone reasonable. Britton was almost tempted to negotiate with her. Then he remembered the crashed helicopter, the slick stains that had once been humans and goblins. And now she was linked up with *Gahe*. He'd been lulled by that voice before. A lot of people were dead because he had allowed it to convince him. "Now," Scylla began again, "what do you expect . . ."

"Therese!" Britton shouted. "Lock her magic down!" He dove to the side, sending the gate flashing toward her. She arced backward, face to the sky, back gracefully bent, the pointed tips of her bobbed black hair shorn off by the gate as it sliced a hairsbreadth above her nose. She straightened with near-boneless grace. "Now, that's no way to make friends." Her smile curdled. "I see you're still determined to be on the wrong side of history."

She Drew and Bound. The ground around Britton blackened. The grass wilted aside, the frost turning to sickened vapor. Britton vomited instantly. The sick agony he'd felt when Scylla had first put him in the grip of her Sorcery back in the SASS was nothing compared to this. The illness was an expanding fist in his gut. He felt the lining of his stomach contract, spasm painfully, as if it would rip itself from his body and hurl itself out of his throat to eject the decay fostering within him. He felt something leaking from the corners of his eyes, not tears. Muscles across his body cramped in response, every atom of his rebelling against the disease that spread throughout his system.

In the same instant, he felt Therese's magic engulf him, the warm current of it repair his flesh as it came apart.

But it wasn't enough.

Britton pitched forward, unable even to cry out. He felt his jaw sag open, then cramp in position. Black fluid leaked from it, flecked with blood. He heard the *Gahe* shrieking off, heard Downer scream, the angry buzzing of her elementals, but there was nothing he could do.

He struggled to reach for the tide of his magic, but all he could feel was the wrenching of his body. The sick stink of rot filled his nose until the soft hairs in his nostrils and throat turned slick, then liquid, trickling out of him. Even as he fought to hang on to life, he awaited the mercy death would bring.

He felt Therese's hands fall to his shoulders, heard her grunt with effort behind him. Slowly, her magic began to get the upper hand. A spark of warmth flooded through him, stilling the muscles, knitting them. He could still feel the illness, but the agony of it was no longer so intense. He heard Therese's pistol crack as she fired at Scylla, forcing the Witch to dive to the side, breaking the torrent that washed over him.

He rose to one knee. Downer was crawling on her side, three long claw marks gashed down her chest. Her elementals still harried one of the *Gahe*, tossing it to the side only to have it stutter back among them, the speed of its passage dragging their forms askew. Downer's wound welled blood, was rimed with gray ice. She pulled herself along with one hand, shivering violently. Her lips were already turning gray-blue. One of the *Gahe* loomed over her for another strike. The other two were engaged with Truelove's corpses, knocking them aside with sweeps of their long, clawed hands.

Britton found his magic and summoned a gate, sending it sliding horizontally toward the *Gahe* just as the creature brought its clawed hand down. It turned just as the gate cut through its wrist. Britton arced it upward, slicing up through the torso and neck. The *Gahe*'s scream went silent, its upper body enveloped in black smoke that cloaked the ground around it. Downer disappeared underneath, crying out. The grass froze instantly, wreathed in twinkling gray as the *Gahe* vanished. One of her elementals sped to her side, its spinning funnel racing as it tried to blow the heavy, freezing mist away from her, with little effect.

The other *Gahe* snarled and flung themselves toward Britton. "Simon!" he managed before they were upon him. "Get Scylla!"

Then the first *Gahe* had stutter-flashed across the ground, horned head lowered. Britton threw himself to the side, missing the horn, but catching the side of the creature's head. It threw him sprawling in the grass, burning cold rippling through his shoulder.

Behind it, he could see Truelove's small army of dead charging Scylla. They lurched a few feet, then collapsed into puddles of rancid slime. Scylla rolled her eyes. "Are you serious? I can do this all damned day!"

The *Gahe* swung at him, and Britton kicked upward, his boot knocking its forearm back. His toes registered the cold through his winter socks as he used the kick's momentum to jump to his feet. He launched a gate toward the creature, but it flashed aside, its brother behind it moving in time so that the gate missed them both, cutting through the open ground until it split one of the trees at the edge of the copse, and Britton closed it, cursing.

Therese raced to Downer's side as Truelove knelt, concentrating. The corpses drew back from Scylla, running toward each other, the dead flesh fusing, running together. They began to ball into one another, even as Scylla rotted them away. From the midst of that ferment, a shape began to rise.

The *Gahe* circled Britton warily now, trying to bracket him, leery of his gates. Britton conjured one, darted it out toward one of them to gauge its reaction. It flinched, flashing backward. He spun to face the other, the one-armed creature he'd fought and wounded before, and opened his hand, causing it to dart back as well. Then he turned back to the original *Gahe* as it charged, too close to dodge, the gate catching it in the abdomen and slicing it in half. He felt the other *Gahe* collide with his back, tearing at his rucksack, filling him with cold.

The black mist from the *Gahe*'s bisected corpse washed over him. He burned with cold, but only for a moment, then all was numbness and he staggered forward, teeth chattering. He felt his rucksack tear away and the weight of the other *Gahe* break off. Truelove's army of corpses had melded into a huge creature, a giant golem of dead flesh. Its marbled flesh was a gray patchwork of shredded uniforms, dried blood, and jutting gristle and bone. It swung a dead fist at Scylla, who backpedaled, grinning fiercely, rotting it even as it came on. Britton could see it diminishing, withering beneath the tide of her decaying magic. It wouldn't last long.

He pivoted on his knee, snapped open a gate on the rose moss bowl, leveled it at the *Gahe*, who circled him, cautious without its partner. Therese, Downer slack in her arms, raced toward him. "Oscar!" she shouted. "Oscar!" Beyond her, the other *Gahe* still tangled with Downer's elementals, the stuttering, spinning dance continuing with no clear victor.

Bone-deep cold wracked Britton with shivers that threatened to interrupt the tide of his magic. The *Gahe* seemed to sense this and flashed to one side. He barely managed to keep up with it, the edge of the gate leveled between them. His arms felt like lead weights. A tooth cracked as he bit down in the effort to keep his tide focused.

Downer was . . . well . . . down, Truelove's undead golem eroding every second. Britton didn't think he could hang on much longer, and he wasn't leaving Therese to face Scylla and her new ally alone.

"Simon! Come on!" he shouted.

He upended the gate, turning it toward Therese. She raced through, Downer still in her arms. Truelove spun, and Britton sent the gate skidding toward him, nearly taking his head off. But Truelove ducked and let himself fall sideways through. Scylla cursed as Truelove used his last burst of magic to force the undead golem to leap onto her, knocking her to the ground and buying Britton a few precious moments.

The *Gahe* flew forward as Britton slid the gate back toward himself. Its good arm gripped his throat, sending him spiraling into chilly darkness. The other arm was still the pulsing tendril. The *Gahe* pulled him forward, opening its huge slit of a mouth, bright teeth long as knives.

Then it shrieked as its other arm fell away, sliced off by the gate's edge. Black smoke washed over Britton as he turned the gate and fell forward into it, shutting it behind him.

He lay, facedown in the frostbitten moss, shivering.

The cold wracked him every bit as much as Scylla's magic had. His body spasmed, muscles clenching painfully, his skin alternately registering burning and numbness. Beneath it all, he felt a slow, spreading warmth, not the gentle touch of Therese's healing magic. This was the succubus kiss of hypothermia, beckoning him down into the dark. He knew that, somewhere nearby, Downer must be enduring the same thing.

"Li . . . ligh . . . light a fire," he managed through chattering teeth. He heard Therese unzipping her rucksack, still on her back throughout the fight. A body nestled in beside him, cold as a block of ice. Downer. Therese spread her sleeping bag over them and then he felt her weight as she lay across them both, adding her body heat to theirs as her healing magic shored up the cell walls of their flesh, pushing against the ice crystals threatening to form there. Therese was no Hydromancer. She couldn't manipulate the water in their bodies. Nor was she an Aeromancer, who could heat the air around them. But she could make their blood pump faster, moving it to the areas worst affected by the cold, increasing their body heat, forcing their organs to push on where they would otherwise fail.

Britton caught a whiff of kerosene smoke as Truelove started a fire. He felt Downer's magic Draw around him as she made an elemental and set it to building the blaze higher and hotter. Britton blacked out. When he came to, he had been pushed up close to the fire. Downer's warming body was pressed against him, and Truelove and Therese now both lay across them. Their weight was smothering, the heat of the fire so close he felt his clothing smoldering, but he lacked the strength to protest.

He'd given all he had. Therese and Truelove had gotten them to this point. He would trust them to see them the rest of the way. His chest felt heavy. His skin stopped reporting pain, and he took a final breath and surrendered to exhaustion, following the trail of warmth down into darkness.

He awoke leaning against a tree, Therese beside him. She'd removed his boots and laid her hands against his feet. The warmth of her magic raced up his legs, causing tingling at his knees. Below that point, he could feel nothing. The hard, waxy surface of his skin had sprouted purple-and-yellow blisters, beginning to retreat under her ministrations.

He watched her work, grateful beyond measure. "I'm lucky to know you."

She shrugged. "It was touch-and-go with both of you. Moderate frostbite. I got to you before the flesh died. As the feeling comes back, it's going to hurt like hell, but you'll recover."

"Thank you," he said. Already, his hands and feet were throbbing painfully. They'd lost the tent with his rucksack, but the fire Truelove had built was blazing brightly now, fed by a couple of big logs he'd dragged over. The flames lit up the gathering night. It might alert authorities, but Britton was too weak to deal with that now. Downer's elemental was gone, and he couldn't sense her magic at all.

"Sarah?" he asked, trying to sit up.

"She's okay," Truelove said. He pointed to what Britton had assumed was a log beside the fire. It was Downer, bundled into a sleeping bag, unconscious.

"The wound in her chest is . . . infected somehow," Therese said. "I was able to get it closed, but it's going to need further treatment. The *Gahe* have some kind of poison, I think. I've tried everything I know how to do. Boosted her white blood cell and lymphocyte activity, but it's not helping enough. Back in the cash, we'd sometimes use Terramancers to root out serious infections. Bacteria are just tiny plants, right? They respond to Earth magic. But this feels . . . different. Nastier. Whatever the *Gahe* put in her, it's sticking around."

"Will she die?" Britton asked.

"Not anytime soon, but I need help here. She's resting for now. Was frostbitten worse than you. She lost a couple of fingers. I've regrown them as best I could, but she won't be playing guitar again."

Truelove pressed a hot plastic canteen into Britton's hand. "It's soup. Salty. It'll warm you up."

Britton shook his head and pressed the hot bottle into his armpit. "Didn't they give you field medical?"

Truelove shrugged. "We escaped before graduation. They probably saved that crap for last."

"After exposure to severe cold," Britton said, "hot liquid is more likely to put you in cardiac arrest. Don't give any to Sarah either. We need to wait a few hours until we're sure our core temperatures have stabilized. You're sure she's okay?"

Therese shook her head. "She's tough as nails, Oscar. I'm as sure as I can be. How do you feel?"

Britton's body felt as if it were on fire, and began to itch horribly, but he knew better than to scratch. He'd done cold-weather training in the army and knew exactly where that road led. His head felt clear and his heartbeat steady. He leaned forward, and the world swam slightly, but his focus returned quickly.

"I think I'm okay," he said. "I'm a little worried about that fire. Nobody's supposed to camp out here, and nobody in their right mind would at night in the cold season. Anybody sees light, they're going to assume it's a forest fire and come running."

Therese nodded. "Just a few more minutes, Oscar. For Sarah if not for you. We have to risk it."

Britton sat up. Therese and Truelove moved to support him, but he shook them off. "Thanks, but I'm okay."

"So," Truelove ventured, "that didn't work out so well."

"No," Britton replied. "It didn't. They say no plan survives contact with the enemy, but that was beyond the pale. I thought she was fighting the *Gahe* when I saw her, but she was either putting on a show, or I just caught the tail end of it." He watched their eyes, looking for blame, but for now at least, he found none.

"They definitely recognized us from the Mescalero op," Truelove said. "Might be they just hated us more than her."

"I think it's fair to say we got our asses handed to us," Britton said. "I couldn't Suppress her at all. She's far too strong. I don't want to go up against her and the *Gahe* together again. Not without a better plan, anyway. We barely made it out of there."

"Scylla was . . ." Therese trailed off. "We can't go after her, Oscar."

Britton pursed his lips, then grimaced as the movement sent needles of pain through his mouth. "No, we can't. Not right now. I promise we'll try again, Therese. I'm not just dropping this, but we can't—"

Therese cut him off. "I know, Oscar."

Britton stood. He'd unleashed Scylla on the world, and now he'd failed to make good on his promise to bring her down. The guilt gnawed at him. He swallowed and tried to focus on what could be done. "What we need is a safe place. Somewhere we can get warm and fed. We've also got to figure out what's going on with Downer.

"We've got to find Swift. Maybe he can help."

Therese nodded.

"Once you're sure that Sarah is warm, put extra clothing on her and get that fire out," Britton said. "I'll be back as soon as I can." He handed the hot canteen back to Truelove. "Give this to her once she's up and coherent, *not* before. Do it too soon, and she could have a heart attack."

"Not while I'm here," Therese said.

Britton nodded. "Therese, can you . . . uh . . . mix up my face a little? Don't ruin my good looks forever, but could you make me a little harder to recognize?"

"I think so. It's going to hurt, though."

"Can't be worse than what I've got going already," Britton answered, wincing at his burning hands and feet. "Let's get it done."

Therese placed her hands on his face and he bit down to keep from screaming. The warmth of her magic flooded him, but where the tendrils of her current touched, they wrenched his flesh. He felt his nose bending, his cheeks rising, his lips spreading horizontally. One ear bent back until he swore it would be torn away.

At last it was done, and he fell back, sweating. "How do I look?" he asked. The words came out slurred, his lips feeling tight against his face.

"Like someone beat your ass and set you on fire," Truelove said, wrinkling his nose.

"Can you tell it's me?"

Therese shook her head. "I better be able to fix that."

"Where are you going?" Truelove asked.

"To check my email," Britton answered. "Sit tight. Shouldn't take too long."

Britton gate-hopped back to the Source, then to the town of Brattleboro, Vermont, where'd he'd once visited with his father during a brief flirtation with the possibility of boarding school. After making sure his destination was clear, he stepped through the gate beside the trash-strewn Dumpsters behind the coffee shop where he'd stopped with his father to grab lunch. Britton thrust his hands in his pockets and hugged his coat tightly to him, before walking around the front of the building. Brattleboro was hours away from his hometown of Shelburne, and he doubted anyone would recognize him here. With Therese's mangling of his face, he felt doubly secure in his anonymity.

He pushed through the glass front door. Posters extolling the virtues of good books and good coffee lined the walls, circling wooden tables covered with newspapers, food, and laptop computers. A few people were scattered around, chatting, reading, or typing. The shop was warm and inviting, the smell of sandwiches and coffee filling the air. Britton had to fight the urge to pull up a chair and sit down for a while. Nobody noticed his entry, and he picked out a young man, probably a student, with thick black-framed glasses and a bulky gray sweater, hunched over his laptop.

Britton walked over to him, head down. "You get on the wifi okay?"

The young man nodded absently, not looking up from his work.

"Then I'm sorry I have to do this." Britton reached over and yanked the laptop away from him, ripping it free from his power cord. "I'll make good on it, if I ever can," he said to the man, who fell backward off his chair and began to scramble to his feet, shouting. Britton opened a gate back to the Source and stepped through.

He paused in the grass outside Marty's village long enough to cast a glance toward it. It was quiet, torchlit, seemingly peaceful. If Marty had been unequal to the crisis Britton had stirred up, it didn't show from this distance. Britton added making it up to Marty to the long list of things he needed to do if he could ever get his feet under him, and opened a gate on a dark corner beside the elevator bank in the Brooks Memorial Library, just a little way from the coffee shop he'd just visited.

The library was shuttered and dark. Britton could see lights in the offices upstairs, hear voices and footsteps, but the stacks and desks on the ground floor were empty. He stepped through the gate and into the shadows pooling by the elevator shaft. He listened to the voices overhead, making sure he was alone. His eyes adjusted slowly to the darkness, and he traced the outline of the reference desk, the silent monitors atop it. Nothing moved.

He slid down to a sitting position and opened the laptop. He toggled the wifi and connected to the library's network, opening a Web browser, careful to avoid looking at anything else on the machine. Just because he was a thief didn't mean he needed to be a snoop. He couldn't avoid seeing the photograph the owner had put on the desktop. It was a shot of the young man he'd stolen the computer from sitting at a desk in front of an empty classroom, looking over his shoulder, grinning at the camera. A banner hung on the wall, depicting a stylized white steeple on a green background with the letters UVM beneath. *Probably a graduate student or adjunct professor at the University of Vermont,* Britton thought. The campus was just a fifteen-minute drive from the house he'd grown up in though he'd never considered going there, his desire to get away from his father far too strong. Britton doubted the poor guy could afford a new laptop and briefly considered leaving it behind once he'd finished, with a note to return it to its owner. He bet the folks working at the library were honest enough to do that.

But the SOC was clever enough to perform electronic forensics on it as well, maybe skillfully enough to figure out where Swift was. He couldn't risk it.

A thief then, and a real one. Hopefully, that guy had rich parents or renter's insurance. He sighed and did a quick Internet search on the words "gate" and "White House." A number of stories came up, and he clicked on a campaign video by one of President Walsh's front-running opponents in the upcoming election, Senator Ahmad Fareed.

Words scrolled across the screen. SENATOR AHMAD FAREED competed with ghosted text reading HONESTY, INTEGRITY, and STRAIGHT TALK. Fareed's photograph appeared, a sallow, craggy-faced man with a genuine smile and earnest brown eyes.

The film cut to Senator Whalen, Chairman of the Reawakening Commission, standing behind a podium. General Tommy Arrow, the Air Force Chief of Staff, stood at the microphone.

THE GOVERNMENT LIED ABOUT WATERGATE AND NANNY GATE. HERE'S WHAT THEY SAY ABOUT GATE-GATE. The film cut to cell-phone videos of wounded Supernatural Operations Corps assaulters, led by a battered Harlequin, limping onto the White House lawn. Behind them stood the gate that Oscar Britton had opened after defeating them. White-shirted Secret Service police milled around them, unsure of what to do. Crowds pressed against the lawn's iron perimeter fence, snapping photos. Britton turned the volume down so that only a whisper of sound reached him.

Then he chuckled. Gate-Gate. That was a nice touch.

General Arrow's voice cut in, flinty and commanding. "What you're seeing is nothing more than air force experimental technology that deals with the logistical challenge of transporting large bodies of troops. Arthur C. Clarke once said that 'any technology, if sufficiently advanced, is indistinguishable from magic.' What you're seeing here is just that, advanced technology, not magic."

DO YOU BELIEVE HIM? Scrolling text asked.

Senator Whalen's voice came in. "Portamancy remains a Prohibited magical school, and the United States government does not traffic in it."

DO YOU BELIEVE HER?

The film showed a sober-looking man in a gray suit and red tie stepping up to the microphone. HOWARD HAND, the text read, CEO—ENTERTECH CORPORATION.

"I'm afraid that this incident is the fault of a few negligent and overly enthusiastic contract engineers," Hand said. "I want to assure you that the responsible parties have been disciplined, dismissed from Entertech, and are facing prosecution for unauthorized disclosure of classified information. Entertech remains committed to an ongoing and productive relationship with the military. 'Serving those who serve' has always been our motto."

DO YOU BELIEVE HIM?

The video cut to Fareed, seated behind a cherrywood desk against a backdrop that unmistakably evoked the Oval Office.

"I don't believe a word of it, and neither do you." Fareed's voice was honest, endearing. "It's time for the Walsh administration to stop treating us like we're fools. No technology can do what thousands of people saw on the White House lawn that day. If the military is using prohibited magic, then it's time that Senator Whalen and her inner circle of spooks came clean and faced punishment for their actions. With the Selfer insurgency raging and spilling off the reservations, can we really afford more lies? Can we afford another four years of incompetency covered by secrets?"

The screen froze, Fareed's winning smile against the backdrop of an American flag. "Senator Ahmad Fareed," an announcer said, "straight talk, clean government. Now that's *real* magic. Paid for by Senator Ahmad Fareed for President."

Britton smiled. *I really did it. I gave Walsh a bloody nose.* Hope surged in his chest. Maybe he really had a chance here. Maybe a weakened and defensive Walsh administration would negotiate with a dynamic and well-organized Latent-rights movement.

He logged onto Yippee.com, navigating to the search engine's free email service. He wracked his brain for the email account and password he'd agreed on with Swift. He swore under his breath, digging into the depths of his mind and finding only fatigue. If he'd forgotten it, he'd never find the Aeromancer again. And who could blame him? He'd just barely escaped with his life from one of the nastiest Sorcerers in creation. If only

Swift had been there. He could have used his lightning in that fight . . .

Lightning. His memory made a sudden leap and brought the account to the surface. Britton breathed a sigh of relief and typed !!!LightningBug123!!! into the LOGON ID field. The password came quickly once he remembered the user name, and he only had to hold his breath for a brief moment before the screen flashed and opened to his email account.

There were two messages waiting. The first was from Yippee.com, welcoming users to its free email service. The second from Bug, Lightning. The name associated with the account. Sent to itself.

Britton could feel his pulse pounding as he clicked on the message.

Better than expected. You're a legend to these people, Oscar. Waiting for you.

Below that were instructions on how to find them.

Britton allowed himself a long sigh of relief, finally admitting to himself that, if he hadn't gotten this email, he was out of ideas, had no clue where to go next.

But that was no longer a problem.

It would be good to keep the email account, just in case he needed to get in touch with Swift again. But the SOC was all over the Internet. Britton had to assume that any hint of their location would be found sooner or later. He couldn't risk it.

He read the message until he had it memorized. Then, he deleted the email, then the entire account. He opened a gate back into the Source, took a long last look at the library's soft darkness, the comforting, familiar sound of people at work, and stepped back through.

CHAPTER XI
TUNNELS

Some have theorized that the American creative spirit and unre-strained imagination made them "early adopters" of organized magic, which has given the US a decided advantage. There's a ker-nel of truth to this, but it shouldn't be overstated. The Taiwanese "Seven Sages of the Willow Grove" have changed the cross-strait balance of power. India's rapid development of the Sahir Corps effectively ended the Kashmir conflict overnight. Sudan is both reunited and purged of Islam because of the military applications of their animist magic users. It is the unique blend of military hard-ware and a defense budget greater than the next ten nations com-bined that makes US magical operations so unstoppable. But that is not the same as a pure magical edge, and policy makers need to keep this in mind when engaging with foreign partners on a contin-gency basis.

—Li Kuo
"American Magical Dominance in the New Century"
Foreign Policy Magazine

Britton smashed the laptop to pieces against a rock, then ground the fragments under his bootheels until there was little left of it but powder. If the SOC was somehow able to locate the broken remains of that computer, they'd have a devil of a time getting anything out of it. *Sorry, pal,* he thought to the young man he'd stolen it from. *I needed it more than you did.*

He opened another gate and stepped back into the rose moss bowl in the Green Mountain National Forest, less than a three-hour drive from the library he'd just stood inside.

The fire was out, the blackened logs sending streamers of smoke up into the night sky. The tall trees blotted out the stars, and he paused until his eyes adjusted. He made out Truelove and Therese, crammed into the sleeping bag alongside Downer, huddled under a pile of every spare scrap of clothing they could find. Britton grunted, satisfied. They looked warm.

The sleeping bag rustled as Therese rolled over at the sound of his boots crunching toward them. "It's me," he said quietly. "I've got good news."

Swift's instructions were clear. The Canal Street subway station had a "chamber" formed by a construction project that had never been completed. It was just off the platform edge on the Brooklyn-bound side. The Houston Street gang would take care of the security camera and send someone to check on the space every night around midnight for the next two weeks. They'd check less often after that. *He must figure if we don't make it by then, we're not going to.*

The problem was Downer. She emerged from the sleeping bag, pale and groggy. Therese's magic had sealed the wound across her chest, but all was clearly not well. "I'm fine," she said, but her teeth were still chattering, even after he rubbed her wrists and felt that she was perfectly warm.

"Did you try again to help?" Britton asked. He winced at his tone; his voice sounded harder than he intended in his concern for Downer.

If Therese noticed, she didn't react. "The *Gahe* . . . put something in her. Something from the Source, something foreign. I can heal her flesh, and I've boosted her immune system to fight it, but this is . . . different."

"What? How is it different?"

"I don't know," she said. "The Source is a new world. That means new bugs. You have to figure there are bacteria over there, maybe living on the *Gahe*'s claws, that we haven't encountered before. Whatever it is, it's powerful and resistant to magic. If I had a strong Terramancer to work with, that might help. Who knows? Maybe she'd respond to conventional antibiotics."

"Is she going to be okay?"

Therese smiled wanly. "I hope so, Oscar. Hanging out in the woods here sure isn't helping."

Britton nodded. "Okay, we know where we need to be, so let's get moving."

"Let me fix your face, first. It'll hurt again, but . . ."

"Leave it, I'm the most recognizable of all of us. I can stand being ugly a little while longer until we know we're in a safe place.

"Or are you missing my pretty face?" He smiled, aware of how horrid the sight must be from the sensation of his lips stretching tight across his altered features.

Therese's smile was genuine this time. "Maybe just a little."

Britton felt the smile expand, then a cough from Downer wiped it away. He was wasting time. "Do you know the New York City subway system?"

She shrugged. "A little. I can get around. We're going to need money to buy a fare."

Britton grimaced. "I had to steal some poor guy's laptop just to check the email account. I don't want to start robbing cash registers now. Let's just get there, and I'll figure it out. There's got to be a way I can gate us in."

Therese thought about it. "This is the great thing about New York. There's so many people and so much craziness that we're not going to stand out at all, even messed up as we are. We just need to get to a deserted platform late at night and jump the turnstile. People do it all the time."

"Well, I only know one way in," Britton said. "So that's where we're going to have to start."

He called to Truelove and Downer and opened a gate back into the Source. Downer stood quickly, swayed a moment, then shook her head and walked through straight-backed.

"Leave your packs. It'll only draw attention," Britton said once they stood outside the palisade wall of Marty's village.

"Maybe we could spend the night there," Truelove said, pointing to the village. "Maybe Marty could help Sarah? Maybe they have someone there who knows how."

"No way," Britton said. "You two are persona non grata with those goblins. You almost started a riot the last time you were there. I don't think a couple of days have made much of a difference. Marty had his hands full as it was dealing with the aftermath of that fight, and I don't want to go making the trouble any worse. If we're going to find help, it's going to have to be with the Houston Street gang." *Besides, Swift said that I'm a legend to them. If he's telling the truth, we can expect a warmer welcome there.*

Truelove started to say something, then stopped.

"What?" Britton asked.

"It's just . . . Oscar, it's Swift."

"I know," Britton sighed.

"He's . . . he's kind of nuts."

"No, he's not nuts. He's pissed and irrational and grief-stricken. But I never thought he was crazy. I think we can trust him to act in his own self-interest."

"He's not crazy," Therese agreed. "Just hurting."

"He's just an asshole," Downer added.

Truelove smiled at her, then turned back to Britton. "Yeah, but what's his self-interest in this case? All he wants is to kill Harlequin . . . and that's just a start. Then he wants to bring the whole government down. Walsh, Whalen, all of them."

"Right. And he knows he's got a better chance to do that if I'm in his corner."

Truelove looked doubtful.

"Anyway, what other options do we have?" Britton asked. "We can't sit out here freezing our asses off, and I'm not going after Scylla again right now. It was wrong of me to ask you to come along for that. That was my fight." He looked over Truelove's shoulder at Downer.

"I've got no regrets," Downer said, shivering. "That crazy bitch needs to be put down."

Therese said nothing, only looked over at Downer, eyes wide with concern.

"We've got to get shelter and proper food and rest," Britton said. "And if we've got a chance to really change things, Houston Street is as good a place to start as any. I'm open to ideas if you've got any."

After Truelove was silent, Britton looked to Downer. "Any ideas, Sarah?"

Downer hugged herself. "Let's get this show on the road."

"We need to get out of the cold, Oscar," Therese said.

Britton nodded and opened another gate.

They stepped into the subway maintenance locker where he'd

run the mission against the Selfer and later dropped off Swift. The interior was pitch-black. Britton opened another gate to give them a little light and gently tried the handle. It opened on a well-lit platform entrance, just inside the turnstiles. There was an empty attendant's booth on the other side, the bulletproof glass scratched with graffiti. Britton began to open the door farther and step out of the locker, then suddenly jerked back, raising a finger to his lips.

"What?" Therese whispered.

"There's a cop," Britton said. "Just standing guard. In . . . tactical gear. Looks like SWAT."

Therese nodded. "They've got them at all the stations now. It's a reaction to Houston Street. They know they're in the tunnels and at least want to make a show of trying to do something about it. Is it just the one?"

Britton peeked back out the door. The cop leaned against the turnstile, helmet tucked under one elbow, using the edge of his body armor to prop up his double chin. He looked bored. Britton pulled back into the locker. He risked a glance in the other direction. The platform looked empty.

"Just the one."

"I've got this," she said, pushing Britton aside and gently peeking out the door. She concentrated, and Britton could feel her magic gathering. A moment later the cop lit up a streak of curses, hand flying to the small of his back. "Goddamn it!" he swore. He lurched around the turnstiles for a moment, trying to massage his lower back through the body armor before giving up and making for the staircase out of the station, calling into his radio.

"Let's go," Therese said. "I don't know how long it'll be before they replace him."

"I thought you swore to never . . ."

"Relax, Oscar. I just tweaked some muscles around his sciatic nerve. Figured a guy that out of shape would have back problems already. It'll hurt for a while, but they should be loosening up already. He'll be okay. Let's go."

They walked quickly to the train platform's far end, out of view of the booth and the staircase, clustered around a map on the wall. It turned out they were on Manhattan's east side, a few stops away from the Canal Street station. Once they confirmed where they had to go, they spread out, sitting on the dirty bench or the dirtier tiled floor. Britton jerked his hood up and kept his head down. Therese and Truelove looked ordinary enough, sitting on the bench chatting softly. Downer didn't have to work hard to look down on her luck. She hunched beside Britton, shivering and sweating, her clothing filthy. Britton put an arm around her, and she leaned against him. His heart leapt into his throat as other passengers arrived on the platform, but they were veteran New Yorkers and didn't spare the homeless couple or the commuters on the bench a second glance.

Britton looked up at the ceiling and spotted the steel housing with scratched plastic plate that held the security cameras. A tiny light flashed red at regular intervals. He bit down on the panic the sight raised. There was no reason to think that anyone watching camera footage would think any more of Britton and his group than the other passengers did.

They boarded the train and spread out, making occasional eye contact. None of the other passengers batted an eyelash all the way to Canal Street, and Britton breathed a sigh of relief as they exited the train and made their way to the platform Swift had indicated. This late at night, there were few people there, but Britton knew they'd have to wait for the platform to completely empty before they could make for the rendezvous location. If this station had a cop, he was out of sight, probably by the turnstiles and attendant booth upstairs.

The platform was broken up by a series of ceiling supports, wide steel I-beams broad enough to hide a person behind. He sidled up alongside Therese. "Keep spread out and on the platform, I'm going to find our entry point. Once I signal you, gather by me, but loosely. Let's try not to give the impression that we're together." Therese nodded silently, thrust her hands in her pockets, and made her way down the platform.

Britton began to run his eyes along the ceiling, looking for security cameras. He saw one immediately, on the edge of the platform, just before the darkness of the tunnel's edge. He was about to move closer to it when something stuck to the tile walls caught his eye.

It was a small black sticker, about five inches across. Someone had made the effort to scrape it off and given up after rendering it mostly transparent. Dirty patches of dried adhesive around it showed him that this was the last of over a dozen stickers that had already been removed. The sticker's center was a black-and-white mug shot that he had to squint at to make out. But after a moment, he was certain.

It was him. The photo was from his military Common Access Card, the same one the police had been using on his wanted posters.

Above it, Britton could make out the words: WHY IS THIS MAN RUNNING FOR HIS LIFE?

Below it, almost illegible, were the words FREE OSCAR BRITTON.

His breath caught in his throat, his heart raced.

He was looking for a movement, but he'd never thought that a movement might be looking for him.

Therese sidled alongside him, followed his gaze, then squinted. He was turning away when he heard her catch her breath. "Oh, wow. Is that what I think it is?"

Not now. Stay focused. "Leave it," he said. "Don't draw attention to it or to us."

The sticker had kicked off a string of emotions. Excitement, fear, honor, worthlessness. None of them would help him examine that camera. He let it fill his attention, pushing the butterflies in his stomach away.

The camera had a good view of the entire platform, its view only obscured by the steel columns. It was precisely like the other cameras he'd seen at the last station. Except for one difference.

The red light was out.

Britton caught Therese's eye, then moved behind one of the columns. Truelove came next, supporting Downer, who slewed drunkenly against him. Therese was just behind. They stood in a small circle, making a show of tending to Downer, a friend who'd had one too many. Britton and Therese detailed opposite sides of the column, casting glances down the platform length, waiting to see if it cleared.

After nearly an hour of agonizing waiting, the train pulled up, the last passengers on the platform stepped on, and nobody got off.

Britton tapped Therese and raced off the platform's edge, dropping into the darkness beyond. He fell about four feet, his boots crunching on packed gravel and wood fragments. Three separate thuds told him the rest of his group had joined him. The inky blackness covered them. Smells reached him, trash, rank water, creosote. He heard scrabbling, and squeaking as rats protested his intrusion into their domain.

"Put Downer in the middle," he said. He opened a small gate, using its light to get his bearings. The gate's uneven light glinted off the train rails to his right. He guessed that they had enough room to flatten themselves against the tunnel wall if a train were to pass, but he couldn't be sure and didn't want to find out. "We hug this wall. The chamber should be a couple of hundred feet in."

He shut the gate and followed the wall along, the rest of the group coming behind him, each person with a hand on the shoulder of the person in front. Downer kept up, though Britton could feel her pulling at his coat at times, letting him drag her along.

Twice he felt the wall on his left open up into alcoves. He opened the gate both times, using the light to find only long strings of incandescent bulbs, now dark and unused. He moved on, straining to hear the sounds of rumbling wheels that indicated a train was headed their way. At last they came to another alcove, and he opened the gate again, expecting another lighting niche.

But the back of this alcove had been knocked out. Old sawhorses stood in front of it, strung with tape that had probably once been yellow before it, like everything else in this filthy tunnel, had been completely covered with black residue. Britton pushed one aside and led them in. The empty back opened into a tiny, bare chamber. The floor was broken earth and rocks, the walls layer upon layer of ancient, long-dried mastic and mortar. The musty smell of old concrete drove out all other scents. There was enough room for all of them, but not much more, and no other exits but the one they'd just used.

"Do you think this is the right place?" Therese asked. Britton scanned the walls, running the gate's light over the broken surface of the desiccated stone before finding what he was looking for. Near the ceiling of the wall to the left of the entrance, was a fist-sized red X. Red letters had been marked into the triangles formed by the X's intersecting lines.

North to south read: HS.

East to west read: NY.

Britton nodded. "This is the right place. We wait here."

"Did we beat midnight?" Truelove asked.

Britton shrugged. "I have no idea, and none of us have a watch. We wait as long as it takes. If maintenance crews or anyone else discovers us, I'll just gate us out of here." He turned to Downer. "You going to be okay?"

"I keep telling you, I'm fine." She hugged herself, shivering. "I'm just a little tired, is all." She leaned against the wall and slid down to a sitting position, heedless of the filth tracking along her back and the ripping of her coat against the sharp and uneven surface of the wall.

Britton nodded, then looked at Therese. *She's not fine,* he mouthed. Therese nodded back and nestled up alongside Downer, warming her with her body heat. Britton could feel the current of Therese's magic eddying around them. Truelove took up position alongside the entrance, lowering himself more carefully to the ground, knees up to his chin. "I hope we're doing the right thing."

"We are," Britton said firmly. "And if we're not, I can get us out of here. Either way, we've got to try. Try to get some shut-eye if you can. There's just one entrance. I can keep it covered."

Truelove nodded and was silent.

Britton had no idea how much time passed. The darkness was total, and the only sound was Downer's labored breathing and the occasional rustle as someone shifted position or rats scurried past the entrance. After several trains had roared by, Britton cursed himself for not keeping count of them. He guessed that this late at night, they were running every half hour, and he could have used their passage as a clock. His mind raced, with things he wanted to say to Therese, worry about the gang they were about to meet, nuclear-winter scenarios about Downer's illness. At long last his mind was overwhelmed by the tide of worry and went numb. He focused on the entrance to the alcove. Overwatch was simple. Overwatch was something he could do.

He was brought out of his reverie as Therese moved to his side, her hands finding his face in the darkness. For a moment, he leaned into her touch, raising his hands to hers. She hesitated before stammering, "Let me fix your face, Oscar. If the gang comes to find us, we want you recognizable."

He jerked his hand away, embarrassed. "Of course."

"A little light to work by? It helps if I can see what I'm doing."

He opened a pinprick of gate again, closed his eyes, then bit down on agony as the magic did its work, his features melting back into their original positions. After what seemed an eternity, the pain stopped, and he opened his eyes. Therese's hands still cupped his cheeks, the warmth of her skin tingling against him. Her eyes were deep orbs of black, reflecting the gate's light. Her lips were parted slightly.

"All fixed?" he asked. "How do I look?"

She kept her hands pressed to him. "You look great, Oscar."

He raised a hand again, taking hers.

A rhythmic scraping, crunching sound reached them. At first he thought it was another rat, but it was heavier, more regular.

And drawing closer.

He dropped Therese's hand and hissed a warning, closing the pinprick gate and opening a full-sized one back to the Source. Anyone coming would surely see the shimmering light, but he would rather have the ground prepped if they needed to make a hasty exit. Around him, Therese, Downer, and Truelove got to their feet and moved closer to the portal, ready to run.

The crunching materialized into obvious human footfalls, approaching easily, making no attempt at stealth. They paused just outside the alcove entrance, probably altered to the gate light inside.

"Hello?" a voice called. Thick New York accent. "Anybody in there?"

Britton motioned Therese, Downer, and Truelove through the gate. He could always bring them back later. If it was the SOC, and they Suppressed him, he didn't want the rest of his people going down, too. He strained, feeling for a magical tide. Even Suppressors had currents. He couldn't feel anything from this distance. He put half his body through the gate. Waited.

"Hello?" The voice came again. "I'm comin' in. Don't do nothin' stupid."

A magical current reached him from the alcove entrance. Moderate, but not particularly well controlled. It felt nothing like the disciplined, tight eddying of the tides of SOC operators.

He relaxed slightly but stayed ready to leap through the gate the moment he felt that tide touch his own.

A man ducked into the room. He was young, powerfully muscular, wearing blue jeans and a black, thermal, long-sleeved shirt. The shaved surface of his head reflected the light from the gate. His height, build, and bald head reminded Britton of Fitzy, but that was where the similarity ended. Where Fitzy's expression was hard and suspicious, this man looked on with delighted surprise. His face and scalp were covered with stylized flames, red, yellow, and orange, whether tattooed or painted, Britton couldn't tell.

He stopped, put his hands on his hips, and arched his eyebrows. "How do ya like that? Oscar Britton. I bet you wouldn't show. You just cost me twenty bucks, you know that?"

When Britton didn't answer, he smiled. "Yeah, well. Worth it, I guess. Welcome to New York. Let's get out of here."

CHAPTER XII
MEET THE GANG

I will not publicly comment on intelligence applications for magic. Anyone with a functional imagination can speculate on the vast benefits the arcane offers us in the prosecution of intelligence collection and analysis. Suffice it to say that the intelligence community has been doing its best to leverage all available assets to keep policy makers and military commanders equipped with information as timely and actionable as possible. No further questions, please.

—Nicholas Steering
Director of National Intelligence (DNI)
Speaking at a press conference following the Bloch Incident

They'd been across the tunnel the entire time, no more than one hundred feet away. The thought made Britton smile as they pushed through the alcove on the tunnel's opposite side, filing through a narrow passage that ended at a collapsed pile of rock and broken tile.

The man made sure everyone was with him, then searched the pile. At last he found what he was looking for, a tiny bit of wire, barely visible, sticking out from the heap. He tugged it gently, then waited.

Britton felt the faintest edges of another magical current from beyond the pile, then the rock slid aside, the edges running together to form a solid mass. The man gestured to the small tunnel it formed. Light flickered faintly from the inside. Britton paused, saw the same worry in his companions' eyes. They'd come this far, and willingly. But that didn't change the fact that they were about to walk into a camp of known criminals, whom many considered terrorists. Swift was down there, Britton guessed, but he'd never called the man a friend.

The bald man frowned at the hesitation. "Look, Oscar," he said, "we don't like to keep this passage open longer than we got to. Nobody's gonna jump you. Just go ahead."

Behind him, Downer coughed wetly. There was nowhere else to go.

He ducked into the passageway, feeling his way along. The gentle light grew as he made his way, and after a moment, he came out into a wide chamber, lit and heated by rocks magicked to glowing resonance by clumsy but powerful Pyromancy. The chamber was an old, vaulted room, the walls made of crumbling brick. The ceiling was supported by worked-stone arches, stretching up into near darkness, architecture of a bygone age.

Five people stood in a loose semicircle, watching as Britton and his group filed out of the tunnel and into the room. All emitted strong magical currents, but only one showed the kind of measured discipline that Britton had come to expect from military operators.

That one was Swift, hands in his pockets, smiling. "Knew you'd make it."

The next three were ordinary-looking. A young black man, basketball-player tall and thin, in jeans and a hooded jersey. Beside him stood two women, both beautiful. The first had dark hair in ringlets and olive skin. The other was as blond and pale as a heroine from a Norse saga. Both wore fine, businesslike skirts and blouses under expensive-looking winter coats. Their soft leather boots matched. As Britton and his group entered, they held hands, leaning closer together.

The last figure was even bigger than Britton. His broad shoulders strained his thick, longshoreman's sweater. A voluminous black beard fell to his navel, his long hair just as thick and dark. His features were craggy, wise. Large, long nose, jutting brow, deep green eyes. He smiled, genuine, welcoming.

Britton recognized him from a dozen posters and videos. Big Bear.

"Oscar Britton." Big Bear's voice was rich and dark, earthy as the magic that had driven him out of society. "I have to admit we didn't think we'd see you. This is an honor indeed."

The blond woman opened her jacket and blouse to reveal a black T-shirt printed with Britton's mug shot. FREE OSCAR BRITTON, it read along the bottom.

Britton smiled. "You've got to be kidding me."

"Nope," the woman said. "You're a legend here. I can't believe we're finally meeting you. When you suddenly disappeared from the FBI's Most Wanted Web site, we figured they'd taken you, or killed you. We were going to launch a publicity campaign. Then you reappeared."

"That's when we figured you might have escaped," Big Bear added. "And then you sent Swift to us. I can't tell you how delighted we are about that." He stretched out his hand. Britton shook it, looking past him to his companions. Their expressions were delighted, awestruck. The blond woman was captivated by Britton, but her companion's eyes were locked on Therese, staring unabashedly. Therese, Downer, and Truelove all stared back at Big Bear. Therese with curiosity, Truelove with trepidation, and Downer with what open hostility she could muster in her weakened state.

"I saw a sticker on the subway platform. Was that you, too?"

The woman smiled. "I'll never tell."

"I'm—" the big man began.

"Big Bear," Britton said. "Your reputation precedes you. Thanks for taking us in."

"Your reputation precedes you as well. Or, your actions do. What you did on the White House lawn has advanced our cause greatly. We knew it was Portamancy, but we didn't know it was you until Swift gave us the full story. The SOC has been very careful to paint you as a Negramancer in all of their wanted posters and news clips. I always knew they feared the truth, but I didn't understand exactly why until now. But we're going to make sure the truth gets out, Oscar. I'm excited to do just that."

Britton nodded. "First, I've got a sick camper here." He gestured to Downer.

"I'm fine," Downer said. "I'll get over it."

Big Bear looked concerned. "We have a Physio—"

"So do we." Britton gestured to Therese. "SOC-trained. The best. She ran afoul of some Source creatures. They wounded her. The infection isn't anything we've seen before, and it's not responding. We'd be glad to see if your Physiomancer can help, but as I said, Therese is fantastic at what she does, and she's not making much headway."

"We may have work for you then," Big Bear said to her. "I'm very glad to meet you."

"My pleasure," Therese said. "It's amazing to meet you. I've been reading about you since before I came up Latent. I honestly wasn't sure you were real."

"I'm real," Big Bear said. "Ask the gang."

"He's real," snorted the curly-haired woman.

"Too damned real," her companion chimed in, smiling.

"They tolerate me," Big Bear said. "I haven't gotten them killed so far."

"This is the whole gang?" Truelove asked.

"Not by a long shot," Big Bear answered. "But we don't gather together in large groups in one place for obvious reasons. Especially when we're meeting new folks."

"It's an infection." Britton brought the subject back around to Downer. "Or a disease. But it's . . . otherworldly. It's not responding to Physiomantic magic."

"You're a Terramancer," Therese began. "Do you think you could . . . ?"

Big Bear shook his head firmly. "Coax bacteria integrated with the human cellular system? I'm nowhere good enough to risk it. What if I caused a bloom? I could kill her. Might be the SOC has Terramancers that skilled, but we don't have half the training they do."

Britton sighed. "Is there a regular doctor among you? We need to try antibiotics, or something."

Big Bear paused, looked over at the tall black man, who shook his head. "No," Big Bear said slowly. "But we have many contacts on the outside. We can get her help. I just need some time to make arrangements."

"I'd appreciate that."

Downer shrugged. "Okay, thanks." She sat down suddenly, drew her knees up to her chest, and shivered. Big Bear started forward, taking her by the elbows and looking into her eyes. She jerked back from him. "I appreciate it, but I'm fine."

"We don't like to stay this close to the maintenance walkways," Big Bear said. "Let's move deeper in, and we can talk there."

"Someplace warm?"

Big Bear nodded. "We'll take care of it; come on."

The old brickwork of the chamber continued into an arched passageway that reminded Britton of the old tunnels in which he'd taken down the Russian Selfer. Stylized stone eagles appeared at regular intervals over chiseled American flags. He caught an inscription with a date in the nineteen thirties, but they had moved on before he could make out the specific year.

The tall man took up the rear. Truelove kept looking over his shoulder at him until he finally couldn't bear it any longer. "You're Deshawn Williams, aren't you?" he asked.

The tall man nodded, looking resigned. "Haven't gone by that name in a while."

"Wow, man." Truelove looked momentarily boyish, like he had when he'd first discovered that Britton had flown helicopters. "I used to watch you when you were with the Spurs. You were amazing. I was wondering what happened to you. I kind of thought I'd see you in the SASS. When you weren't there, I just figured . . ."

"That I was dead," the tall man finished for him. "Good. That's what I wanted."

"Get up to any b-ball down here?" Truelove asked.

The tall man only looked at him, his eyes cold. Truelove swallowed and faced front.

"What's the SASS again?" the bald man asked Swift.

"It's the gulag where the SOC takes you once they capture you," Swift answered. "Though I think it's rubble now. Rubble and slime. Like I told you, Scylla completely wasted the place."

"I don't think so," Therese said. "We went back, and it looked like they shored it up pretty well."

The worked brick ended and packed earth began, narrower and looking less stable as they continued to descend. Britton guessed this was Terramantic construction. Britton instinctively liked Big Bear, but he kept his magic ready and occasionally brushed his palm against the butt of his pistol, secreted in his lower back under his coat. He'd trusted the farmer Nelson, too, and he remembered keenly how far that had gotten him.

"Swift tells us that you took names in the SASS, your own call signs, like the SOC. We do the same thing here," Big Bear said.

"Not all of us did that," Therese answered.

Big Bear ignored her. "He goes by Spur now, on account of his basketball days." He gestured to the tall man. "The ladies are Guinevere and Iseult, and our scout who picked you up is Flicker."

Britton nodded to Guinevere. "I still can't get over that T-shirt."

Guinevere laughed. "Isn't it great! My idea. Not a lot of Self-ers top the FBI list. Most get taken down and quickly, or aren't important enough to rate that kind of publicity. We knew you were special right away. And all the press! We've been wanting to talk to you forever."

"You said this Witch, Scylla, destroyed the SASS?" Iseult, the curly-haired woman, asked. Her voice had a trace of a New York accent though softer and more genteel than Flicker's. "Swift's described her to me. Did any of you ever get·her real name?"

Britton shook his head. "We didn't know anything about her other than that she's completely crazy."

"Crazy smart," Therese said. "A good speaker. Smooth. You could tell she was educated, used to power. Belonged in a cor-porate boardroom."

Iseult laughed. "That's because she spent most of her life in a corporate boardroom. We worked together before she came up Latent though she was miles over my head. Pale, jet-black hair, about this long." She chopped her hand along her jawline. "Really hot?"

Britton nodded in time with the rest of them.

"That's Grace."

"Huh?" Britton asked.

"Her name was Grace. I saw what happened to her when she ran. Like everyone did with Spur, I assumed the SOC had killed her. They took her down in the boardroom right in front of everybody. It wasn't until I heard Swift's story that I realized they'd captured her instead."

"They did the same with Downer," Britton added. "What was her last name? Grace what?"

Iseult shook her head. "Sorry," she said. "I still work there. It's hard enough keeping my magic secret from everyone on the outside, so I'm extra careful about security, even here. I'm going to keep that to myself."

"Iseult and Spur did rather well financially on the outside," Big Bear said. "We have come to depend on that generosity to fund our operations. In Iseult's case, it's an ongoing effort. Not everybody runs. It's a precarious existence, keeping your Latency secret, but we're grateful to those willing to make the sacrifice."

The tunnel gave out into another large, vaulted chamber, this one obviously constructed entirely via Terramantic magic. The high walls were completely smooth earth, seamless and plastic-looking, notched throughout with flat stones covered in slick plant life that glowed with an eerie blue-green color. Aeroman-tically warmed air kept the chamber at a pleasant room temperature. The room was furnished like a comfortable office. Several well-appointed desks and swivel-backed chairs were arranged against one wall, beside a row of fine, leather-upholstered couches and reclining chairs. A giant flat-screen television was mounted to one wall, the electric cord snaking into the ground through a hatch. Britton could hear the hum of a generator be-neath it. The floor was covered in overlapping and tastefully chosen deep pile rugs. He even spotted a couple of vases full of fresh-cut flowers.

He gaped. "I don't . . ."

"Not what you'd expect from a bunch of terrorists, eh?" Big Bear smiled. "We're a movement, Oscar. We're organized and well funded. Contrary to what the SOC would have you believe, we don't make rash decisions, and we don't live like animals. Welcome to our lower Manhattan council chamber."

"How the hell do you keep hidden here? I mean, doesn't the SOC come after you?"

"Constantly." Big Bear motioned to one of the leather couches. Downer slumped into it immediately, stretching out. Therese sat down beside her, cradling her head on her lap. Iseult joined her, squeezing in to sit uncomfortably close. Guinevere pursed her lips. "I'll get the girl some water."

"New York is one of the oldest cities in the country," Big Bear went on. "Around three centuries old depending on when you count the founding. It's actually several cities, when you get down to it, each built on top of the other. When you add in some Terramantic renovations, the SOC has more ground to cover than they think. The entrance you saw is just one of many. And every chamber"—he pointed upward—"has a rockfall that allows us to collapse it if we feel it's going to be compromised. Add to that the ongoing jurisdictional dispute between the SOC and the NYPD, and we do all right. We're Sorcerers, too, you know."

Something in Big Bear's argument didn't hold water. He'd seen the SOC go after targets in the past. They'd be more likely to level the entire city than let a Selfer gang like Houston Street run underneath it unchecked. But Mescalero still boiled in open revolt, and that had been allowed to fester, so maybe things were more complicated than he thought. Big Bear's claims to Sorcery didn't impress him either. The SOC mantra of "skill beats will" had been proved too many times for him to doubt it. Big Bear's tide was far more disciplined than the other Selfers around him, but it was nothing compared to what Britton knew the SOC could do. Wild magic was far less effective in a stand-up fight. Spells were more likely to fail, Sorcerers more likely to go nova.

Big Bear dragged an office chair over and motioned for them all to sit on one of the empty couches. Guinevere returned with a pitcher of water and a stack of plastic cups. She was followed by another man, of a size with Big Bear, but solid muscle. He wore black jeans and a black T-shirt. His long brown hair was tied into a waist-length ponytail, bound in several gunmetal rings. His face was a storm cloud, his eyes possessed of the heightened awareness Britton had come to know in the most seasoned military operators. He clearly recognized Britton, but where Iseult looked at Britton with worship, he was decidedly unimpressed.

Britton recognized him immediately from a dozen familiarization video clips and wanted posters. He knew his voice from twice as many Internet messages and recordings distributed across the entire East Coast.

Render. Houston Street's most famous member besides Big Bear. Britton tried to recall the number of confirmed kills of police and SOC operators to his tale. He stopped at around twenty-five.

Downer emerged a bit from her fog, eyes widening.

Britton sat forward in his chair, pulling his magic around him, readying for a fight. He knew that Render was part of the gang but hadn't been prepared to meet him so soon.

The reaction wasn't lost on Render. His smile never reached his eyes. "The pleasure's all mine."

Downer sat back, Truelove sliding closer to her. "What's he doing here?" she asked.

"I was planning on checking you out, making sure you're okay, but all of a sudden I'm having second thoughts," he said, looking over at Big Bear.

Big Bear frowned. "Render is our Physiomancer," he said. "I asked him to be ready to assist in case you were injured."

"I can handle that," Therese said, standing. She was practically shaking. Britton wasn't surprised. He knew how she felt about the use of offensive Physiomancy. He could only imagine how she felt confronted by a person so proud of that capability that he had taken it as a nom de guerre.

"Render is a talented Healer," Big Bear said.

"Which is why he calls himself Render," Therese responded.

Swift tried to break in. "Guys, what the fuck . . ."

Big Bear shrugged. "We are free to choose whatever monikers we like in this organization."

Render rolled his shoulders and eyes in time. He dropped a black bag at Therese's feet. "Whatever. I'm not going to argue with you. Especially when, to hear Swift tell it, you fuckers worked for the SOC for ages. I'll put my body count up against yours any day. At least mine were in self-defense." He pointed at the bag. "That's stocked with sports drinks and nutrition bars. Not sure what you've been eating while you were on the run, but bland stuff like that will help restore your vitals without making you sick. We can put you back on regular food once we're sure you're all right."

"Render was an EMT . . ." Iseult began.

Render chopped his hand through the air. "Save it," he said. "I don't need this bunch to like me."

He stopped, met Therese's stare. "Why don't you take a fucking picture, it's cheaper."

She bridled, trying to find her words.

He smiled. "Saw some videos, huh? My reputation precedes me? You think you're the first new arrival who knew who I was?

Why don't you go ahead and get your judgmental speech over with. Then I can dissect all the bullshit in it and we can get on with more productive stuff."

"You . . ." she began.

"Kill people," he said. "In absolutely horrible ways. Last one was a Port Authority cop. By the time I was done with him, he looked like he'd been through a blender set on frappe."

"Jesus. You sound proud of it."

"Goddamn right I am," Render replied. "That was some grade A prime Physiomancy at work there."

"No it wasn't," Britton said, annoyed at his arrogance. "You lack training. I can feel it in your current. I'm not saying you're not doing something, but you've got a long way to go compared to the SOC."

Render looked at Britton, the long ponytail jerking with the sharp motion of his head. "Tell that to the SOC-hoppers I've got ground into my boot soles. I've lost count of how many of those douchebags I've taken down. If they're so good, how do you explain that?"

"I'm not sure," Britton answered honestly. "Still trying to get my head around that, but my friendly advice is not to get cocky. I've fought Physiomancers before, and so has she. It was a hell of a lot nastier than you, and we still took care of it."

"It?" Render asked.

"It was a monster." Therese shuddered. "Not even human anymore."

Render and Big Bear went suddenly silent, eyes on the ground. *They know,* Britton thought. *They knew that thing, maybe they even helped it.*

He was opening his mouth to answer when Render turned to Therese, his voice cracking before he got it under control. "Have you ever even Rended before? You make it sound like you're some kind of saint."

She nodded. "Once. I promised I'd never do it again. Then I had to. It was . . . horrible."

Britton winced, knowing she blamed him for having to give a repeat performance.

"How is it more horrible than cooking someone with Pyromancy? Or frying them with Aeromantic lightning? Or using Terramancy to suck them underground? Killing's killing, and the tool at hand is the one you use. You might as well swear off knives because guns are the cleaner instrument," Render said.

"You call yourself 'Render,' " Therese answered coldly. "You wear it like a medal."

"Pinned on me for killing my sworn enemies? For reducing the number of scumbags who can bully innocent Latents for the crime of being born? For reminding Walsh and Whalen and this dictatorship that there are people who aren't going to stand idle while they ruin the world? People who keep them awake at night, worrying about their precious safety while they destroy that same peace for others?

"Yeah"—he leaned in close—"I'd take a medal for that."

Britton tapped his shoulder. "You can say that from about a foot farther back from the lady. I'm proud of a few things myself, and I'd be happy to show them to you."

"I don't need your help." Therese glared at Britton. She turned back to Render. "You think you're the first loudmouth I've tangled with?"

Big Bear broke in. "Render, enough. The girl is ill. She's been infected by something from the Source, and it's not responding to normal Physiomancy."

Render's eyes fell to Downer, and he bit his lower lip, then looked back up at Therese. She swallowed and nodded. "Please . . ." She choked on the words. "I . . . I need help."

Britton felt Render's tide reach out and touch Downer. "You boosted her immune system?"

Therese nodded. "Whatever it is, it's breaking down her organs. I've kept them repaired. I also jumped her white-blood-cell and lymphocyte counts, but I'm just holding whatever it is in check."

Render's eyebrows rose. "You can do that? Directly manipulate her lymphocytes?"

Therese looked confused. "Can't you?"

"No," he said flatly. "We don't all have the benefit of SOC training." He turned to Big Bear. "If she can't help the girl, then I can't either. I haven't spent the last few months being trained to use my magic by the fucking United States military."

Big Bear sighed. "Thank you for trying."

Render looked furious. "That all?"

"I wanted to have Mr. Hoy see if he could help," Big Bear

answered. "Maybe conventional medicine will work. Can you ask him to meet us at the hothouse in an hour or so? As soon as he can make it."

Render cocked an eyebrow, hesitated. "You want to call that chit in?"

Big Bear looked back at Downer, slumped back in the couch, sweating freely, bruised purple patches shadowing her eyes. "Yes," he said. "I do."

Render nodded. "Okay, I'll let you know what he says." He turned to go, then turned back to Therese.

"I'm sorry," he added. "For the girl. I wish I could help her."

Therese smiled tensely as he left, then knelt and rummaged through the bag he'd left, passing out the contents to the rest of them. Downer gulped greedily at the drink, sighed. "Better," she said. "Needed that."

"We'll get her the help she needs," Big Bear said. "Mr. Hoy has access to conventional antibiotics and might have some other tricks up his sleeve."

"You're sure you don't want to try Terramancy?" Britton asked.

But Big Bear was already shaking his head. "You'll forgive me, Oscar, but that's some incredibly intricate work. Not all of us have the benefit of the kind of military training you've enjoyed. It's something I was hoping you could bring to the rest of us."

"It's less the training," Britton said. "There's a drug . . ." though he had to admit, Big Bear's current wasn't nearly as wild as the other Selfers he'd met.

"Limbic Dampener," Big Bear said. "We know it. We've even managed to secure a few doses here and there. It's amazing stuff."

"Maybe you could take some and try?" He gestured to Downer.

"And risk making whatever it is worse? Maybe if we get desperate, but we're not there yet. Let's see what Mr. Hoy has to say."

Britton bit down on his disappointment and cast a worried glance at Downer. She looked revived by the electrolytes in the sports drink and was sitting up now. Therese pressed her palm against Downer's forehead. "Slight fever." She looked at Britton, the corners of her mouth stretching slightly. "Should be okay for a while. Relax."

And just like that, he did. In spite of everything, alternately fighting and running for his life, his place in the world utterly unmoored, future uncertain, in spite of all of that, he did relax. His shoulders eased, the tension melted out of his back. He turned to face Big Bear, confident that he had made the right call, that whatever was coming, he could handle it.

Therese made him feel that way with a look.

"Okay," he said.

"To business," Swift said. "No reason we can't get moving while the rest of them get Downer what she needs." He said the last hesitantly. Britton could tell he still trucked with Downer and Truelove only with the greatest reluctance.

"Get moving? Where are we going?" Britton asked.

"Your friend is . . . eager . . . to get things started," Big Bear said. "Your plan, Oscar. To change the law and the world. It's our plan, too. We're excited to start figuring out how you can help us to make it a reality."

"Damn straight," Swift said. "You can be anywhere you want, whenever you want. That's the key."

"So, what were you thinking?" Britton asked.

"Actually, I wanted to hear what you're thinking first," Big Bear replied. "This is your ability, Oscar."

Britton turned back to Therese. "What are you looking at me for? You're a big boy," she said.

Britton smiled sheepishly and turned back to Big Bear. "I actually did have an idea. We need to amend the McGauer-Linden Act. We could license magic use on an individual basis. We set up a board of reviewers or something who can approve people at NIH to come out from Suppression and use their magic freely."

"You set up a SASS at the National Institutes of Health?" Therese asked.

Britton nodded. "Something like that, only without the indoctrination. Just teach people to get control of it and handle it safely. Then, when they're ready, they can pass a test, a demonstration. Then you get a safety license, and you can go free. Oh, and we make Limbic Dampener free and available to everyone."

Big Bear was pensive. "That could work. The SOC could still nail you if you went wild of your own free will after you got out."

"Right," Britton said.

"So, who would be on the board?" Therese asked.

"One rep from the SOC," Britton replied, "and everyone else would be civilians. They could be elected, or maybe appointed by the Reawakening Commission. I haven't got that part figured out yet. It would be slow and cumbersome, but it could happen. Latency is rare. For folks who blow it, have minor slip-ups, they could assign you a probation officer or something, you could check in once a . . . whatever . . . a month. Pain in the ass, but still freer than the SASS or having to join the SOC. People who have their abilities locked down, are law-abiding, are left to get on with their lives."

"No way," Big Bear said. "They will never just flat-out let people live their lives unmolested. The government views magic as a loaded gun. People aren't just allowed to walk around with loaded guns. They might allow that probation idea you just described, but it would have to be for everyone, forever.

"And the government would have to want to do it. This would be a major change, Oscar. Those things don't happen quickly or easily. You're underestimating how much magic scares people. The idea of people, even licensed people, just running around . . ."

"The SOC just runs around," Britton said. "That's what the SOC is, licensed people with magic, out in public."

"It's different," Therese said. "That's the military."

"Military is still people. Heck, Therese, I was in the military when I came up Latent."

"That's not how people will see it," Big Bear said. "The government isn't going to give up that kind of control."

Britton smiled. "But we've got a trump card to convince them, the one thing they're terrified of."

"The truth," Therese breathed.

Britton nodded. "FOB Frontier, the Shadow Coven program. All of it. It's an election year. I'll tell the president that if he doesn't make changes, I'll take it public, or to his opponent. I watched a video when I was looking for Swift's email. Fareed is already using what I did as a club to beat Walsh with. I gated

Harlequin and his guys right onto the White House lawn in plain view of a ton of people. That stirred up a hornet's nest right there. This would be the two in the one-two punch."

"You're going to threaten him? The president? That's crazy," Therese said.

"I'm not threatening his life, just his job."

"What if he turns you down?" Big Bear asked.

"Then we make good on the threat. Go to the papers. Go to Fareed. Let the world know that the same government that forbids Probe magic traffics in it."

Big Bear was quiet for a long time. "That's not precisely what we'd had in mind."

Britton didn't like the pregnant silence behind the long pause. "What did you have in mind?"

"You want to offer Walsh this deal," Big Bear said.

Britton nodded.

Swift could no longer stay silent. "That's it?"

"That's enough," Britton replied.

"Walsh just gets voted out of office? Senator Whalen, too?"

Britton narrowed his eyes. "For starters. Walsh'll probably be impeached when the truth comes out. He might wind up in jail, or at least spend the rest of his life fighting civil suits. Latent people will get a real choice. That's what matters."

"That's bullshit! Walsh'll walk. He won't do a day of time, and if he does, it'll be in some country-club facility where the hardest thing he'll have to endure is when the dining facility runs out of caviar. He's the fucking President of the United States! Do you honestly think he'll really be punished? When does anyone at that level ever really pay for anything?"

Swift's face had taken on the wild look he'd had when he'd stood over Harlequin and been forced to let him go.

Big Bear nodded. "You also have to keep in mind that Walsh might find a way to beat it, Oscar. He's got an army of media specialists who can run propaganda of their own."

"Damn right," Swift said. "He needs to pay. Pay for real."

"I'm not in the punishment business, Swift. This isn't about revenge, it's about what's right," Britton said.

Swift spit. "What's right is making that son of a bitch *pay*. Don't go to Fareed. Or go to Fareed later, I don't give a flying fuck. But first you open a gate and you *get me to him*. That's all I'm asking for, Oscar. Put me in Walsh's pocket, just for a minute. You owe me that much."

Now it was Britton's turn to spit. "Owe you? For what? I know you've been through a lot, Swift, and you have my sympathy. But I've done everything I could to help you, and you insist on cleaving to the same bullshit act you were running back in the SASS. You're a human being, and we were in the suck together. We fought side by side when the SOC came after us. I'll never forget that. I will stand by you when it's right. But now? Now it's not right. So you can fucking forget it."

"What the fuck is wrong with you? This isn't about revenge! It's about justice! If fuckers like Walsh and Harlequin are able to do whatever the fuck they want to whomever they want, whenever they want, and never *pay* for it, then the next crop will be no better. Fareed doesn't care about Latents! He just wants to expose the FOB to get in office! Once he's there, it'll be hello to the new boss, same as the old boss. You know that! They hate you, Oscar! You're not part of that world anymore. You can never go back, and they'll never take you. Stop trying to be their dog!"

Britton's voice dropped to a growl. "I'm nobody's dog."

Big Bear cut in. "This isn't helping. We've got enough on our plate without fighting among ourselves. Your friend is passionate, Oscar. But I think that passion is obscuring his main point, and it's one that not just I, but the rest of our group, largely agrees on. Walsh and Whalen are far too entrenched in their positions. They have long since lost their grip on the central concept that their job is to uphold and defend the Constitution of this country. They are despots in all but name.

"They have to be brought down, Oscar. They have to go. You can help us to do that."

"You mean they have to die."

Big Bear sighed. "How many innocent people have died as a result of their desire to hold on to power? Bin Laden had to die, Oscar. So did Pol Pot."

"That's a bullshit comparison, and you know it," Britton said. "I'm not a fucking assassin. So you can just put that out of your mind right now."

"This isn't assassination, Oscar," Big Bear countered. "It's war. Undeclared, to be sure, but what war is these days?"

"You know who talked like that? Scylla," Therese said.

"Your buddy Grace." Britton nodded to Iseult.

"She has a point," Iseult said.

Big Bear waved his hands. "Everyone calm down. We're just talking here."

"Well, I don't like what we're talking about," Britton replied.

"Consider this, Oscar. You're not just trying to change a law," Big Bear said. "You're trying to uproot a culture. Fear of magic is so deep-seated in the American psyche that people will do almost anything to defend themselves from it. If you're going to unseat that, make public, open Latency a fact on the ground, you're going to need a dramatic event. Otherwise, people are going to cleave to safety, to the illusion that law enforcement and the military will protect them. The change you're seeking won't come easily, Oscar, and I'm sad to say it won't come peacefully, either."

"You're talking about a revolution."

Big Bear nodded. "Every major societal shift has required one."

"Blood in the streets, chaos."

"Not necessarily, the Arab Democracy Movement . . ."

"Resulted in thousands dead," Britton answered. "We just didn't see it here. Well, we didn't unless we bothered to look, then it was all too obvious."

Big Bear looked exasperated. "Will you listen to yourself, Oscar? Do you honestly think that a change as major as what you're proposing will simply happen? This is a democracy. The majority has to want to make it a law. I don't know if you've lost touch with the goings-on here in the Home Plane while you were over in FOB Frontier, but the majority of people in this country think Latency is a scourge and that we're monsters. It's tyranny of the majority. If we want this to change, we're going to have to force the issue. Sometimes, that means that blood has to be spilled, fires lit. You can't avoid that."

"Maybe," Britton said. "But I have to try."

Big Bear opened his mouth to argue but stopped when Render appeared. "We're in luck," he said. "Mr. Hoy's free now. He's waiting for us."

"We'll talk more about this," Big Bear said. "Your friend's health is the most important thing, and I don't want to delay that a moment longer. Let's pick this up later. I'm confident we can figure out a mutually agreeable position."

Britton wasn't confident of that at all, but he nodded and helped Downer to her feet, following Big Bear out of the room.

No, he decided with a sudden certainty that surprised him. *I'm not confident of that at all.*

CHAPTER XIII
BAIT AND SWITCH

Not all Latent folks are the same. There are intensity levels involved. Certain people have highly developed limbic conduction that makes their magic more powerful than others. But even in Rump Latencies, that can be mitigated somewhat with training. Control is, and always has been, the key factor. Some people are just gifted at it as well, more in tune with what's required to make magic work. You've heard people say of athletes and artists "that guy's a natural." Goes for Sorcerers, too.

—Colonel Jess Demetreon
SOC Liaison, US Army Training and Doctrine Command (TRADOC)

Big Bear hadn't been lying about the extent of the tunnels. They walked for over an hour, the narrow passages twisting and turning so many times that Britton quickly lost his bearings. He stopped counting after the tenth branching archway they passed. Many were lit, and while they never saw anyone else, Britton felt magical currents more than once, alerting him that another Selfer was nearby, just out of sight.

They were silent as they went, the tension of the last conversation still hanging over them. Britton tried to put it out of his mind, focus on his surroundings, but he couldn't shake the growing unease in him, the feeling that he had fallen in with the wrong group. *What did you expect? That they'd just appoint you leader and do whatever you said?* He shook his head and put the thought out of his mind.

Big Bear stopped. "I'm sure we can make it the rest of the

way on our own," he said to Flicker, who had accompanied them thus far. "The forage element should be back by now, and I'm concerned they might need some help. Would you mind checking back at the Sixth Pool? I'll radio-relay if we need anything." He tapped a small radio on a belt at his waist. "Just stay on channel two."

The Pyromancer hesitated, stumbling over words as he tried to come up with an excuse to stay.

Big Bear smiled like an indulgent father. "Do you honestly think they mean to do me harm? Come on, I'm fine. You know Hoy doesn't like meeting large groups of us anyway. Therese is a Physiomancer if there's any call for that. I'll radio you if you're needed."

"I'll be on channel two." The Pyromancer sounded worried. He didn't move.

Big Bear clapped his shoulder. "I know you will. I'll be fine, it's okay."

He turned and led the group onward without looking back. By the time Britton cast a glance over his shoulder, the Pyromancer was gone.

"You have to forgive him," Big Bear said as the narrow earthen tunnel once again widened into a brick-walled edifice. A stone catwalk angled steeply upward as water flowed below. Britton spotted more worked-stone decor, tangled vines and flowers instead of eagles this time, but no less beautiful. The catwalk's incline increased as they went.

"This is what comes of living as hunted people," the Terramancer went on. "It's a bone-deep fear. The kind that comes from never being able to settle, from having no safe place in the world. It hardens people."

He stopped suddenly, looked across their faces, then flashed an avuncular smile. "Listen to me. I've forgotten who I'm talking to. You know all about that, don't you?"

"I'm afraid we do," Britton said. The warmth of the smile allayed some of his worry.

"That's what it does to people. When I first met Render, he was a medieval reenactor. He played role-playing games. The SOC made him like he is now. I get so angry . . ." He paused, mastered himself with an effort. "It's unnecessary. We grow less human every day the SOC hunts us, and they've been hunting us for so long that I can barely remember a time we weren't running.

"I'll tell you the truth, Oscar. I do believe certain figures need to be removed, but you've heard me speak out against those who want a straight-up violent revolution." He gestured to Swift, who had folded his arms across his chest, watching the big Terramancer with a mild smirk on his face.

"But it's not because I don't agree with them. Do you remember when Kim-Jong Il died? In peace, in repose. Rich, fat, and happy. He never paid for what he did. There was an end to the crime, but there was no justice. It is so often the case with the truly great evils in the world, the ones committed by those in power. That burns me, Oscar.

"But your instincts are right. Revolutions don't change the world. Not in the lasting ways we need here. That only comes when the majority of the people become so comfortable with a thing that they're willing to make it the law of the land. It has to become a part of the culture, a fact of the ground.

"That's why I'm so glad you're here. Because I think we finally have what we need to make that happen. Flicker's wondering why I trust you enough to be alone with you and three of your friends. I guess it's because if you're an enemy, if I can't trust you, then it means that hope is all for nothing. And I can't live with that, Oscar. I really can't."

The sincerity in his face held Britton, made him ashamed of having doubted the man. He looked at the ground, no longer the bear of a Terramancer who led the most wanted band of Selfer terrorists outside of Mescalero. He was a tired old man, displaced. Sick of running. Desperately wanting a home.

Just like Britton. Just like all of them.

"I don't know what to say," Britton said.

"Don't say anything for now. Let's go see Mr. Hoy and get that infection treated." He pointed at Downer. "Then you can say that, no matter what crap Render or Flicker flings your way, and there will be more and not just from them, count on it, that you'll stick with me. Together, we'll find a way to start sorting out this mess. Remember what Gandhi said . . ." He frowned, searching for the expression.

"We have to be the change we wish to see . . ." Therese offered.

Big Bear's smile took years off him. "I'm done with skulk-
ing around tunnels. It's time to change the world."

Britton's heart swelled. "Let's go," he said, gesturing up the
tunnel. They went on, even Downer stepping more lightly in
the wake of Big Bear's words.

The tunnel sloped up at a sharper angle until they were
almost climbing stairs, sidestepping up cracks in the concrete
surface. It finally let out into a small, arched chamber about six
feet across, the walls painted a deep forest green streaked with
rust and graffiti. In the center was an ancient-looking spiral
staircase, the scrolled iron looking much like the detailed carvings in the surface walls—a beautifully worked relic long gone
to seed. The linseed oil had flaked away, black showing patches
of rust. Britton wondered if it would hold.

"What's up there?" he asked.

"Hope." Big Bear grinned. He mounted the staircase and
made his way up. It shook but held. Britton motioned Downer
and Truelove up first, then Therese, wanting to spare his heavy
weight for last. The stairs lurched sickeningly at each step, but
he could feel the strength of their anchor at the top, and they held
as the group pushed through the hatch in the ceiling and out into
bright electric lights.

Britton blinked, letting his eyes adjust after the soft magical
phosphoresce of the tunnels. The light was harsh and piercing,
but he could still tell that they stood in an enormous abandoned
hothouse, the Victorian sweeps of rusting metal frame housing
ancient glass of uneven thickness. The ground was flattened dirt,
long gone to weeds and scrub grass, smelling of old cigarette
butts, spilled motor oil, and rotten food.

A man stood about twenty feet away in a poorly tailored business suit. He looked bulky, lumpen, like a football player in his
pads. He waved to Big Bear. "You made it! Great to see you."

Big Bear moved around behind Britton. He could hear the
Terramancer sliding a hatch into place over the hole they'd just
come through. He glanced from Big Bear back to the man in
front of them, blinking again as the figure came into focus.

The suit flapped off him, pin-striped, ridiculous-looking over
the man's huge frame. Then Britton's eyes settled on his neck
and face and narrowed. His head was too small to match that
giant body.

He wasn't bulky beneath that suit. He was wearing body armor.

"Hello, Oscar," the man said, smiling. "I see you've met the Sculptor."

Britton spun back to Big Bear. The Terramancer grinned, then melted.

His flesh re-formed with breathtaking rapidity, the color draining from his skin, the long beard dropping away, the huge form narrowing, width turning to height. He groaned at the pain, but the grin never changed.

In Big Bear's place a thin man now stood, taller, his skin corpse gray. His black hair was slicked to the top of his head, looking greasy. He was already shrugging off Big Bear's clothing, suddenly many sizes too large. Beneath, a skintight black bodysuit hugged his narrow frame, the Entertech logo blazoned on the chest. His face was blade thin, all nose and jutting lips. His dark eyes narrowed as he grinned wider.

Britton caught his breath. Not a Terramancer. A Physiomancer. And the most talented one Britton had ever seen. "Sorry, Oscar," the Sculptor said. "They told me you were dumb, just not how dumb."

Then Britton's magic rolled back, and the glass around them exploded.

Cloth-wrapped ropes pivoted against the hothouse's metal frame, bending inward as the men clinging to them kicked out the glass, sliding down their length to the ground, weird, bulky guns leveled. Their body armor, helmets, and weapons were a uniform black. The only contrast came from the subdued American flags on their shoulders and the unit patches on the opposite, bearing the familiar motto: OUR GIFTS FOR OUR NATION.

The SOC.

The first round caught Truelove in the side of his head, sending him reeling in a cloud of spraying clear mist. Britton caught a whiff of it even as he spun to keep it from spraying in his eyes. Hot, spicy. Military grade pepper spray could incapacitate an angry bear. Truelove was already screaming, clawing at his face, as Britton ducked another stream of pepper spray–filled paintballs. Swift cursed and fell back, a soldier grabbing him from behind, pinning his arms.

At least they want us alive. Britton rolled beneath the stream of paintballs and kicked the shooter in the chest, feeling his boot impact solidly on the interceptor plate of his body armor. The operator fell backward, but Britton seized his weapon, elbowed him in the throat, and arrested his momentum with the sling. The operator pivoted between sling and elbow, flipping sideways and landing face-first in the dirt as Britton spun to face the Sculptor, pulling his pistol from his waistband. "You fucking sneaky son of a . . ." The Physiomancer was impersonating Big Bear the entire time. Had the real Big Bear been killed and replaced? Britton cursed and fired .

The Sculptor made no attempt to dodge. His body oozed sideways, sucking the bodysuit inward so that the bullet skimmed harmlessly by. Britton felt his magic flood back into him for an instant while the Sculptor dropped the Suppression to work his own magic, but he blocked Britton's flow again in an instant. Britton had never seen such precision. "Now, Oscar," the Sculptor said. "That's not very nice, is it?"

The operators advanced, screaming at them. "Get on the ground, right now! Get your hands in the air!" Truelove already crawled in the dirt, howling, his eyes pinched tight. His glasses were gone. Swift had gone slack in the grip of the soldier behind him. Downer crouched beside Truelove, trying to help. Therese spun to face Britton, whose attack on the operator had carried him away from the rest of his friends. Apart from the magical tide Suppressing him, Britton could feel dozens of others, all around him. But they were no fools; even with Downer sick, they knew better than to give her material she could use against them.

Therese was another matter. A pepper-spray ball had exploded against her abdomen, soaking her hips, but the vapors didn't seem to be doing more than causing her to sniff and blink. She reached the Sculptor in three strides and fastened her hands around his neck. "Call them off," she said. "Call them off, or you turn into mush."

He chuckled. "Seriously? You going to Rend, Mother Theresa? Thought you'd sworn off that. Even if I hadn't heard that whole chitchat with you and Render, I still got the pleasure of reading your dossier. Real sob story. Do your worst."

Therese gritted her teeth, and Britton couldn't tell if her magic was Suppressed or if her expression reflected frustration at the Sculptor's accurate call. Either way, nothing happened. The Sculptor slowly pried her fingers apart. "That's better."

Britton planted his boot on the operator's neck as he tried to rise, scanning with his pistol. The cordon of SOC operators tightened. There were over twenty of them. The hatch they'd entered through was closed.

"Give it up, Oscar," the man in the suit called to him. "You don't want to shoot anybody. Let us get your friends some help, and we can go sort this out."

But Downer, for the moment at least, didn't look like she needed help. Her forehead was beading sweat, but her eyes were scanning the room with every bit of alertness he'd seen on the missions they'd run together.

"Sarah! I've only got ten more rounds!" he shouted, pointed the gun into the crowd of operators and pulled the trigger. The soldiers dove as the gun sparked, spitting out the round, a small tongue of flame jetting from the muzzle. Britton felt flows drop and adjust as the operators focused on diving for cover over Suppression. He yanked the trigger again and again, the poor control causing the shots to drop crazily, all accuracy gone.

But that didn't matter. The bullets careened off the metal struts of the hothouse structure, pulsed fire from the gun's muzzle.

Elements in motion, hot kinetic energy.

Britton hoped to hell that Downer wouldn't let him down.

She didn't.

By the time the magazine had emptied, and the slide locked to the rear, two small elementals had risen at the far side of the chamber. One blazed dirty, cordite-laden fire. The other sparked static electricity from a rust-chipped metal strut. They moved with blazing speed, lighting among the SOC team, ignoring the men with guns across their chests, diving instead for the ones with metal fists emblazoned on their body armor, each clutching a bundle of lightning bolts. Their size didn't detract from their blazing energy. The Suppressors swore and dove again, beating at the little balls burning and sparking around their heads.

"Good girl," Britton whispered, and lunged for the Sculptor. He stumbled on the operator's body, his right cross turning into a wild haymaker that caught the Sorcerer's throat in the crook of his arm. The Sculptor coughed, his head lurching. A fleshy knob erupted from his back, knocking the wind out of Britton, launching him back to land on his face. Britton felt his magic return to him as the Sculptor dropped the Suppression and engaged his own magic. Britton struggled to Draw, but his hitching lungs and bruised belly forced him to focus simply on breathing.

"Stupid, fucking . . ." The Sculptor seethed, his head twisting all the way around. He leered at Britton, his suddenly elastic neck supporting his head while his body remained facing forward. A moment later, the flesh oozed, reversed, and he was whole again, solid and facing Britton. "You don't get it, do you?" he said as he resumed Suppressing Britton. "You can't fight city hall, Oscar. We will always find you. We will always make you pay."

Britton recovered his wind and tried to Draw again. His magic railed against the Scultpor's disciplined tide, utterly impotent. "You fucking work for them. I was coming here to help people like you."

"Pshaw. I don't need your help, silly boy," the Sculptor said, taunting him. "I'm doing just fine."

His head suddenly lurched forward, greasy black hair flying up, teeth clicking together. Spit flew from his mouth, and he slewed sideways, eyes shutting and jaw going slack.

Behind him, Therese shook her fist, her knuckles bleeding. Whether or not she was willing to Rend, there was nothing stopping her from putting her fist in the Sculptor's ear. Britton felt his magic rush back to him as the Sculptor's Suppression failed with his consciousness.

It wouldn't take another Suppressor long to figure out that Britton's tide was free. He opened a gate across the hothouse floor, just before Therese and the rest of them. It opened on the wooden palisade wall of Marty's village.

"Go!" Britton shouted. "Right now, go!"

The sight of the gate energized Swift. He howled in rage and raised the hand of the soldier pinning him to his face, biting down hard, his teeth penetrating the thin fabric of the shooter's glove. Bone crunched, and the man screamed, giving Swift enough leverage to free a hand, which dropped to the operator's pistol, yanking hard. The butt caught on the drop holster, and the pistol held fast, but the soldier had to release Swift to keep him from stealing his weapon, and in the next moment Swift was free, pelting across the ground and diving through the gate.

Therese pulled Truelove up from the ground and spun to face Britton. Her eyes were wide.

"Go!" Britton shouted again. "I'll slide it here once you're through!"

She nodded and leapt through the portal, Truelove wailing in her arms, as three more paintballs smacked into her chest and abdomen.

"Sarah, damn it!" Britton shouted again, on his feet now, pushing the gate toward her.

Downer looked at him, at the soldiers around her, her eyes clear. Two operators tried to dash between her and the gate, but Britton flickered it forward, and they dove to avoid being cut by its edge.

"Go, Sarah," Britton said, hope fading in his breast. "Don't . . . Just go."

But Sarah Downer looked back to him and shook her head, once, firmly. She dropped to her knees clasping her hands behind her head. Britton could see the elementals flicker out in his peripheral vision, the small sparks of their resistance quenched as Downer's magic rolled back of her own accord.

He swore and slid the gate toward himself, but another current drove into his own, batting it aside and suffocating it. The gate flickered and vanished, leaving Oscar staring at the barrels of a dozen submachine guns. The Sculptor pushed his way through them, the bruise forming on his head already beginning to heal as he turned his magic to it.

"Open the gate," he said. "Open it right now and show us where they went."

Britton shook his head. "No way."

The Physiomancer pointed, the tip of his finger stretching into a bone spike that hovered in front of Britton's eyeball, so close he could see the pores in the bone, flecked with glistening red. "Are you fucking stupid? Do you have any idea how much I can hurt you? Do you want to die?"

Britton remembered Harlequin, diving from the flight-line tower to save him. The one thing he could count on the SOC to do was try to preserve his power, bend it to their uses. He knew the Sculptor's threats of torture weren't idle. But his threats of death were.

"Do you want to kill me?" Britton mused. "Because that's what you're going to have to do to get me to open another gate anywhere, ever." He strained to see Downer, but the girl was screened by the legs and boots of soldiers and SOC operators, crowding around her. He thought of calling out to her, then remembered the expression on her face as she'd dropped to her knees. *I don't have anywhere else,* she'd said. He hadn't been able to make her see that she did have somewhere else, and now she'd made her choice. Failure choked him.

The Sculptor cocked an eyebrow as one of the operators moved behind Britton, his voice firm and low. "Hands behind your back. Spread your fingers." Britton thought briefly of fighting, then considered the array of weapons pointed at him. He complied, wincing as the cuffs cinched tight.

"All right, let's go." They began to walk him toward the rear of the hothouse, where a pair of metal-framed double doors stood open. As he passed the Sculptor, he twisted toward him, glaring.

"Be nice," the Sculptor said, meeting his eyes. "I Rend as well as I disguise. We have a lot of questions to ask you, Oscar. And I'm going to be helping out in that regard, so you'd do well to be kind to me."

Britton was forced out onto a cracked concrete driveway, beside which he could see an unmarked white van. Beyond it, a river reflected the lights of assembled skyscrapers, straining skyward like glittering concrete teeth. Police cars blocked the street at both ends, sirens spinning, yellow tape keeping pedestrians well away.

They stopped him, and the Sculptor came forward, raising a black hood. "You know the drill." He held it over Britton's head, meeting his glare. The Sculptor's eyes were pale gray and filmy. The eyes of a dead man. Pitiless.

Sick fear churned in Britton's stomach. His heart fluttered like a caged bird.

"Oh, you and I are going to be spending some quality time together from now on, my dear Oscar Britton," the Sculptor said. "I am so looking forward to it."

The hood came down, and Britton drowned in darkness.

CROSS-PURPOSES

The "Embracer" faith centers around the belief that magic is the wellspring of life. All those who live outside the faith are thought to have become "lost," wandering from that pivotal origin. It is the duty of all rightly minded goblins to bring all living things back to that flow. Success in this endeavor will bring about some kind of heralded golden age. Bringing the "lost" home is a matter of dogma among the Embracers, and the defense of those they choose to embrace one of the few things that will move them to violence. The Mattab On Sorrah exist in a constant state of war with the neighboring Defender tribes that wish to fight against humans.

—Simon Truelove
A Sojourn Among the Mattab on Sorrah

CHAPTER XIV
IN COMMAND

Working with the indig is . . . I guess it's productive. They do a lot of work around the base. We use 'em as 'terps and scouts sometimes. They know the country, and that helps. Some of 'em learn English, and that's great. But the truth is that I don't ever turn my back on 'em, not for a minute. When I was in Afghanistan, even the "good" muj were still muj. They liked us, they loved America, yadda yadda yadda. But we all knew they'd shoot us in the back if they thought it'd get 'em somewhere. Goblins' the same way. This is their home, not ours, and we both know it.

—Staff Sergeant Byron Pointer
212th Suppression Lance, Third Marine Expeditionary Unit
FOB Frontier

Bookbinder was awakened by explosions and shrieking gunfire. He rolled into a sitting position, blinking and rubbing his eyes. He felt the hair on the back of his neck rise as Aeromantic magic drove what must have been a massive column of lightning into the ground just outside his hooch. The converted container shook, and the smell of ozone filled the tiny room.

He yawned, shook his head, and buckled on his gun belt, strapped on his body armor and helmet, tied his boots. He opened the door and made his way outside, not hurrying. Why should he? Repulsing the attacking goblins bought them two days of peace. The attacks had come roughly every other day since then, increasing in intensity. It was as if the local tribes knew they were cut off and running low on supplies. Or maybe they had seen the interior of the FOB when they'd first overrun the SASS and gone mad at the thought of plunder.

Soldiers raced pell-mell on the muddy track. The attack seemed to be on the flight-line perimeter this time, a bad call by the attackers, as air support didn't have far to go to get in the fight.

Bookbinder saw an MP standing in front of the hooch across from his rocking back and forth like he was wrestling with something. Bookbinder stared until the man drew back his fist and began punching, then he jogged over. As he drew closer, he could see the MP had a goblin contractor pinned against the side of the hooch. The creature's face was bruised and going bloody under the blows. The MP's battle buddy stood to one side, watching impassively.

Bookbinder noted the man's stripes before shouting, "Damn it, Sergeant! What the hell is going on here?"

The man turned and saluted, his knuckles bloody. His other hand still held the goblin by its skinny throat. "Sorry, sir. I caught this little fucker spotting for the enemy."

"What was he doing?" Bookbinder asked. "Drawing a map?"

The MP's partner, an army private first class, replied. "You know how it is, sir."

"No, I do *not* fucking know how it is. You're going to explain it to me right now."

The PFC might have rolled his eyes, but it was impossible to tell in the half-light, smoke, and chaos around them. "He was pacing off, sir, to guide in the indirect."

Bookbinder gestured around him. "Here? A bunch of residential hooches that are far apart and sandbagged out the ass? They might get three people if they're lucky. Spotters would be working the crowded areas, like the DFAC or the cash."

The PFC shrugged, and the sergeant began to look irritated. "He was pacing off, sir. They give that to their Sorcerers to call in the magical strikes."

"I know how they do it. And what you're telling me is that he was *walking*."

The sergeant's eyes narrowed, "Pacing, sir. We're taking him in."

"Take him in, question him. That's your job. You know what's not your job? Beating the living shit out of him."

"He was resisting, sir," the sergeant said. He was at least double the creature's size and kitted out in full battle rattle, while the goblin was unarmed and only semiconscious.

"Uh-huh, looks like a real threat. Let him go and let me see your ID. We're going to have a little chat with your—"

Bookbinder was cut off by the deafening howl of one of the air-defense systems engaging. It popped from its nest of wire and concrete gabions, the radar in its white dome tracking something, and let loose a volley of twenty-millimeter rounds. Bookbinder looked up just in time to see a smallish dragon, its dark blue hide almost invisible in the night sky, dodging around the vicious column of fire. A goblin, skin painted white and nearly as big as the flying creature, clung tightly to its back, legs wrapped around its underbelly, arms around its long neck.

As it passed over them, the goblin howled something in its own language and pointed downward. The ground beneath Bookbinder's feet rolled like an ocean wave. A fist-sized chunk of rock careened off his body armor and spun past his head with enough force that it would have decapitated him had it been just a few inches closer. It collided with the white radar dome of the air-defense system, shattering the plastic and sending a spray of sparks showering over Bookbinder. The gunfire stopped immediately.

Bookbinder heard a shriek and cursing from the MPs. He shut his eyes against the sparks as the air-defense system coughed and died. He flailed for his pistol, unable to get his footing on the rolling ground.

Boot tips brushed the top of Bookbinder's helmet and, suddenly, the ground steadied. He yanked his pistol from his holster and jerked it skyward, just in time to see the goblin sorcerer winging away from him, two SOC Aeromancers in close pursuit, a summoned storm cloud belching fist-sized hailstones, pummeling the little dragon that served as its mount.

"Fuuuuuck! Oh, fuck!" someone wailed.

Bookbinder looked down. The sergeant and the goblin were gone. The PFC remained, swallowed by the earth from his waist down. His helmet and goggles were gone, and blood trickled from the corner of one eye. His face had gone white.

Bookbinder ran to his side and knelt. "Are you okay?" *You*

idiot. Does he look okay? "You're stuck?" He thrust his hands into the PFC's armpits, trying to haul him up.

"No! No! No!" the PFC shrieked. "My . . . I'm all smashed up down there! Stop! Stop!"

Bookbinder jumped to his feet. "Okay . . . Hang on, I'll go for help."

He bolted for the cash. "Medic!" he shouted. "Need a medic here!"

The farther he got from the flight line, the quieter the FOB became. Before long, the muddy pathways were completely deserted.

That all changed once he reached the cash. Lines of wounded stretched out of the entrance flaps, some draped over gurneys, others sprawled in the mud, their buddies trying vainly to help them. The cries and moans reached Bookbinder long before he reached them. A few white-coated doctors, assistants, and orderlies buzzed among the wounded, engaged in desperate triage.

Bookbinder's stomach fell as he realized that PFC would have to linger in agony or die until this assault passed. There was simply no help to spare.

I can at least get him a syringe of morphine. The PFC had been involved in what was likely the illegal beating of an innocent contractor. But that was no reason not to help the man. He was a soldier, and Bookbinder was a leader of soldiers. That PFC wasn't the only one who had begun to look askance at the sizeable cadre of goblin contractors who worked on the base. Many had disappeared following Britton's escape. The hostility and distrust of the indig skyrocketed with the increasing pace of attacks.

Bookbinder knelt beside an orderly in scrubs so blood-soaked they were a shade between rust and purple. Though he already knew the answer, he said, "I've got a guy about a quarter klick east hurt bad. I need a medic."

The orderly shook his head without turning. "Sorry, we're all hands on deck here. There's a map in the trauma tent. Mark his location there and fill out a casualty card. We'll get to him when we can."

Bookbinder nodded and stood. "Think they'd let me take him some morphine? He's in a lot of pain."

But the orderly was already moving down the line to the next group of wounded, pointing those that could walk to one stretch of freezing mud, calling on others to attend to those who didn't look mobile.

Bookbinder sighed and went to look for the map, nearly rebounding off Colonel Taylor's chest. The bigger man looked wan, exhausted.

"Colonel Taylor! What are you doing here?" Bookbinder asked. The tension between them had been palpable ever since their confrontation, but it simmered beneath a surface of polite respect. Taylor answered Bookbinder's questions, and Bookbinder let Taylor do his best to resolve their increasingly desperate plight. They agreed not to make a formal announcement to the FOB, though Bookbinder figured they could only go another day before having to make some kind of public statement.

Taylor actually looked glad to see him. "I sent a runner to your hooch. Looks like you read my mind. I need you to take over here. I have to get in the fight."

Bookbinder nodded, glad to have something he could do to help. "Sure thing. What's the situation?"

"Pretty much what you see. Overwhelmed and undermanned, and now supply problems: saline, hemostatic agents, clean syringes. I've got Pyromancers cauterizing wounds. We're in the dark ages. Come inside, I'll hook you up with Lieutenant Colonel Dacic. He could use a full bird to give his orders some weight."

Bookbinder followed him into the tent. "The pace of the attacks is increasing. I think they have an idea we're in trouble here."

Taylor grunted. "Concur. It's not sustainable. We've got to find a way to button this up." He stopped walking, and Bookbinder had to check his stride to avoid running into him. Taylor turned toward him and sighed. "This is a goddamn mess, Alan." He had begun calling Bookbinder by his first name consistently ever since the confrontation. Bookbinder didn't want to risk damaging the fragile détente that had built between them by reciprocating.

Taylor shook his head. "I was hoping to hold off on this, but I'm going to initiate Emergency Plan Tiger Smile as soon as I get you settled here."

Bookbinder groaned inwardly at the ridiculous code names these combat types used.

"What is that?" he asked, trying not to let his reaction show on his face.

Taylor looked embarrassed. "Classified."

Bookbinder didn't want another fight with Taylor, but he was not about to lose all the forward progress he'd made. "Come on, Colonel. I thought we were in this together. I can help here, but you've got to give me the tools I need to do the job."

Taylor grimaced. Bookbinder waited for the color to rise in his face, for his bullying petulance to return.

But Taylor only pursed his lips. "I know, Alan. I know. Read-on for this one's a pain in the ass. Let me double-check a couple of things, then I'll get you up to speed. Just give me a few hours to cover my ass, okay?"

Bookbinder was a master bureaucrat. He had hidden behind regulations and "covering his behind" hundreds of times when he didn't want to deal with an issue. He could hardly begrudge that particular dodge to Taylor, especially now. "Sure thing. Just don't forget me, okay?"

Taylor nodded and turned back into the tent, Bookbinder following.

The chaos outside was nothing compared to the charnel house within. The stink of burned flesh and congealing blood hit Bookbinder like a wall, mixed with the high, chemical odor of rubbing alcohol, iodine, and latex. The tent seethed with activity; white coats and blue scrubs flew past him in a blur, covering goblin and human alike. The low buzz of medical conversation—diagnosis, triage, and treatment—was punctuated by the occasional agonized howl. Despite the encroaching winter, the heat inside was damp, oppressive.

"Jesus," Bookbinder said.

"Tell me about it," Taylor responded, then began waving to a white-coated officer over a sea of bobbing heads. "Colonel Dacic! Dacic!" He turned to Bookbinder. "Come on."

Taylor began pushing his way through the hot press of bodies. He made good progress for a few steps, then came up short against a couple of goblin contractors who couldn't get out of his way quickly enough. They looked comical in their baggy blue scrubs. Their surgical masks were made for human features, and stretched to the limit over their long noses. The press of bodies was so close that Bookbinder's chest thumped against Taylor's back when they stopped.

"Damn it!" Taylor cursed at the creatures. "Get the lead out of your asses!"

The goblins jostled, bumping into Taylor's knees, chattering angrily to one another in their own language.

"What the hell is wrong with you?" The angry edge that Bookbinder used to fear leapt into Taylor's voice. "Get out of my way!"

The goblins suddenly stopped, facing one another. All of the jostling disorganization vanished. They tapped their eyelids synchronously, then turned.

One of them grabbed Taylor's knees and drove its bulbous head into his stomach.

Taylor doubled over, his face slack with shock.

The other goblin reached into its waistband and produced a surgical scalpel. With a shout, it plunged it into Taylor's throat, driving it in so deep that the handle nearly disappeared.

Gurgling, Taylor fell backward as the first goblin swarmed up his legs, planted its foot on his chest and vaulted over him, screaming, reaching for Bookbinder.

Bookbinder's existence split in two. The first part stood in stunned horror as the scene unfolded. Taylor slumped to the floor, blood fountaining from the wound in his neck with such ferocity that it sprayed Bookbinder's boots to midshin. The goblin reached for Bookbinder's face, screaming curses in its own language.

The second part simply reacted. Bookbinder grabbed the goblin's face, his fingers gripping the long nose, one punching into an eye socket. His other hand dragged the pistol from his holster, fumbling as it came so that he found himself clutching the barrel. He drove the smaller creature into the dirt floor, putting his full body weight on top of it. The second goblin scrambled after him, but he extended one boot, punting the thing backward. "Rogue contractors!" he heard the second part of himself shout. "A little help here!"

The first part watched in amazement as the second part lifted the pistol and slammed the butt into the first goblin's head, brought it up and down again, up and down again, a carpenter hammering a nail. After the third stroke, the hard surface of the goblin's head went soft. After the fifth, Bookbinder was tenderizing meat.

The soft contact of the blows brought him back to himself, and the two Bookbinders merged into one—horrified, frightened, exhausted. He looked up.

The controlled chaos of the cash had spilled its banks. All work had stopped. A wide circle had emptied around him, filled only with Taylor's still and pale body, Bookbinder, and his assailant. The second goblin was pinned beneath a burly patient, who had thrown himself off his gurney and was busy choking the life out of it. Outside the circle, people rushed to and fro. They tripped over one another, toppling heart monitors and oxygen tanks, pulling plugs and IV tubes. They were on the verge of a stampede in the middle of the worst possible place for it.

Bookbinder dropped his pistol and reached toward Taylor. His hand came into view, stained red to the wrist, flecked with tiny yellow-white pieces of the dead goblin's skull. That couldn't be his hand; it wasn't the hand of a paper pusher. And yet, here it was, reaching out to take Taylor's pulse, finding nothing, closing the staring eyes.

Bookbinder stood, shouted. "Everybody needs to calm down! Let's try to get some order in here! Why isn't someone securing the exits? Where the hell are the first sergeants?"

A few people paused, looking at him in obvious relief. A white-coated physician's assistant ran to him, first sergeant's diamonds stitched above his name tape. "You need to get those exits secured," Bookbinder said. "Maybe get MPs to round up the goblins. Do *not* harm them. Just get 'em separated out, I can't have fights breaking out. We need to get this cash running again, stat!"

"Sir!" the first sergeant said, and took off, shouting orders. Some semblance of order returned to the cash, but not nearly enough. Across the room, Bookbinder saw two Marines lighting into a group of goblin contractors pushing a cart of medical supplies, punching them indiscriminately.

"Hey!" he shouted. "Cut that the hell out! Somebody stop those men!"

The Marines couldn't hear him across the din of the surging cash. A couple of goblins leapt into the fray, trying to assist their comrades. The stampede was threatening to become a full-scale brawl.

"Damn it! We need order in here!" Bookbinder shouted. "Someone give me a hand!" He began to wade through the surging mass of people toward the fighting.

"Goddamn it!" he screamed, his voice finally cutting through the din and bringing some relative quiet as all turned to face him.

"Enough of this jackassery!" Bookbinder shouted. "Who the hell is in command here?"

The first sergeant who'd been helping him turned, his face pale and sweating. "You are, sir," he said, his eyes sweeping past Bookbinder to Taylor's cooling corpse.

"You are."

CHAPTER XV
LEAD FROM THE FRONT

Sorcerers are still officers. SAOLCC teaches you how to use magic, but it also teaches you to lead. And how do you lead? From the front, of course.

—Lieutenant Colonel "Crucible" Allen
Chief, Sorcerer's Apprentice/Officer Leadership Combined Course
(SAOLCC)

Bookbinder sat in Colonel Taylor's office. His office now. He'd have to get used to that concept sooner or later. It wasn't much bigger than his old office, with the same decor, imposing cherrywood desk, crossed flags. He had gathered all of Taylor's personal effects—his challenge-coin collection, pictures of his family, a signed baseball from a World Series a decade ago—into a cardboard box, which now sat on the floor in the corner. With the FOB cut off, there was no way to get it home anyway, or even report Taylor's death.

Cold panic crept up his spine, tying his stomach in knots. He was the ranking officer on post. With Taylor dead, the command of the sprawling, division-sized base, with all its operations, fell to him. Fifteen thousand servicemen and -women from all five branches of the military and all the supporting government civilians and contractor personnel. Roughly thirty square miles of fortified ground, all of it under siege almost daily. Low on supplies, cut off from home.

I can't do this. I'm a bureaucrat. Even a hardened commander would balk at this.

Stop it. You have to do it. Everyone is looking to you. Dig deep and find a way.

But the deeper Bookbinder dug, the hollower he felt. Where he looked for a reserve of confidence and ideas, he found only more questions. Where did he even start? Who did he talk to first? He looked down at his fingernails. He had washed his hands dozens of times since that horrific night in the cash, but he still imagined he could see the faint brown streak of Taylor's blood on them.

Dig deep, damn it. Find a way. There's a division's worth of people looking to you to lead them. You will not let them down.

He swallowed as Carmela appeared in the entryway. "Sir?"

He willed his face to take on hard contours, a firm gaze, resolute mouth. He would act the part of a commander and hope he eventually felt it. "Carmela."

"Lieutenant Colonel Allen is here to see you, sir."

"Very well, thank you. Please send him in."

Crucible entered, his helmet under his arm. One of Bookbinder's first orders once he took command was for all FOB personnel never to leave fixed structures without helmet, body armor, and at least a sidearm. The short man's hair was matted to his head, a day's growth of stubble on his face. He looked like he hadn't showered in several days. But he took a formal step to Bookbinder's desk and stood at attention. "You wanted to see me, sir?"

"At ease," Bookbinder said, gesturing at the chair opposite his desk. "First, take a load off. Second, call me Alan."

"Sir?" Crucible looked puzzled as he sat.

"Alan. It's my name. I want you to start using it when we're alone together, okay?"

Crucible looked uncomfortable. "Alan."

"Thanks. You know, you SOC guys always go by your call signs. I never got your first name."

Crucible gaped. "Um, we just go by the call signs, si . . . Alan."

Bookbinder sighed and bowed his head behind his steepled fingers. "Crucible, please. I'm alone in this."

There was a long silence. Bookbinder was about to go on when Crucible said, "Richard. People call me Rick."

Bookbinder looked up in surprise. "Rick. Thanks."

"No problem."

"The meeting is set up?"

Crucible nodded. "All officers O-3 and up not on critical assignment will be assembling in the plaza at 1400, sir, per your orders. I'll have one of our Aeromancers do some air vibrations so that you won't need to use a microphone."

"Senior enlisted, too. I want all the command sergeant majors and master chiefs."

"Of course, sir."

"And I'd like you to move into my old office, Rick. I need you close by."

Crucible paused. "Sir . . . Alan, if it's all the same to you, I'd prefer to remain where I am. SAOLCC needs—"

Bookbinder cut in. "It isn't all the same to me. I don't think you fully appreciate what's going on here, Rick. Keeping SAOLCC running is on the absolute bottom of my priority list right now."

Crucible sat back in his chair and cocked his head to the side. "Excuse me, sir?"

"I'll explain it all during the address. Just make sure we double the perimeter patrols during the meeting. The last thing I want is for all of our leadership to be taken out at a stroke."

Crucible was silent. Bookbinder's comment about reprioritizing Crucible's main program was not scoring any points with the man.

Bookbinder sighed. "I'm sorry, Rick. I know that program is your baby, and it's important to the army, but we're going to have to make some big changes here. It's a shame, really; I could have used some of that leadership training. Especially now."

Crucible met his gaze, inscrutable. Bookbinder felt his magic current across the desk, disciplined and muted. He resisted the urge to use his own magic to reach out and tug it toward him. After the man made no reply, Bookbinder sat back in his chair. He hoped to make a friend here today, to feel like he had someone in his court. That clearly wasn't happening. "All right, you can go."

Crucible stood stiffly and headed to the door. Bookbinder went back to his computer and had woken it up from the screen saver when Crucible's voice reached him. "You can do this, sir."

"Excuse me?"

Crucible looked so uncomfortable that Bookbinder thought he might crawl out of his own skin. "I'm just saying, si . . . Alan. You can do this. I know you've never been in combat before you came here. I think that's a lot less important than the army makes it out to be. From what I've seen since you arrived, you know when to hold and when to fold. That makes a big difference. I'm not happy Taylor's gone, but nobody's kidding themselves that he was a great leader. Most of us hated him. I guess what I'm trying to say is that I think you're going to be fine, sir."

Bookbinder nodded, a tide of relief flooding his gut. His throat swelled, and it took him a moment to speak. "I don't know what to say."

Crucible's mouth quirked. "That's fine. I mean, it's fine now. It won't be fine at the meeting this afternoon. But I'm confident you'll get it worked out by then.

"I'm with you, sir. I guess that's what I'm trying to say."

And then he was gone, leaving Bookbinder to master his whirling emotions and the magical tide that surged along with them.

A Terramancer raised an earthen platform with a short flight of rock steps leading up to it. The full range of officers and senior enlisted stood around it in a sea of green, tan, and gray. Bookbinder began to wade his way through the crowd, uttering polite excuse me's as he went. At first, the men and women pushed back against him, glaring. Then a few pairs of eyes lighted on the eagle stitched to the front of his helmet liner and whispers began to spread. By the time he mounted the platform steps, the throng was silent. He crested the platform and looked over the hundreds of people covering the plaza and streaming around the DFAC, MWR, and surrounding structures. Necks strained expectantly toward him, battle-hardened operators, medical personnel stained to the elbows in the blood of their comrades, technicians and logisticians, police officers and pilots. Professionals, all.

Looking to him to lead.

Panic gripped him, and his vision grayed. He felt sickness rise in his throat. Every fiber of his being wanted to run, to crawl into a hole. Anything but having to address the crowd before him. He swayed on his feet.

No, damn it. By God you will not faint. Not now.

He gritted his teeth and blinked hard. When he opened his eyes, he felt a bit steadier, but noted some cocked eyebrows in the audience. A hushed whisper was building. Somewhere out there, Crucible was standing, watching him.

"Okay," Bookbinder said. The Aeromantic magic surrounding the platform carried his voice to the farthest reaches of the crowd, silencing the buzzing whisper. His voice thundered in his ears.

"I want to thank everyone for coming, and I also want to keep this short, not least because I've got the entire leadership of this FOB in a single, easily targeted location."

There was a ripple of nervous laughter. Bookbinder saw a few smiles spreading through the crowd. Well, it was a start.

"I'm sure the rumors have been flying thick and furious throughout this base, and I want to lay out for you exactly what's going on and what you're going to be dealing with in the coming days. Now, some of you may be of the school that thinks, 'What the troops don't know won't hurt them.' That's not how I run things. Nothing we're discussing here is classified, and you are ordered to fully disseminate what I'm about to tell you in detail and with a sense of urgency to the men, women, and Source-indigenous personnel serving under your command.

"That's right. I said, 'That's not how I run things.' From that statement you have likely deduced that I am now in command of this Forward Operating Base. Which brings me to the first piece of information I have to disseminate. Colonel Taylor was murdered by rogue goblin contractors."

The buzz swelled and broke into a stream of near shouting. Faces turned away from Bookbinder as the officers began to confer with one another, asking if it could possibly be true, if anyone had heard differently, if there were more assassins among them. Bookbinder raised his voice to shout over them, then reeled it back as he realized that he didn't have to. The Aeromancer adjusted the magic, ensuring that his most timid whisper carried to the farthest reaches of the plaza despite the din.

"Taylor will be buried with full military honors at the parade ground at sunrise this coming Wednesday. Of course, I won't require any of you to attend, but field-grade officers would set a good example for their troops by being present.

"And let me be clear on something else. This was the action of a couple of goblins obviously loyal to the Defender clans. The vast majority of Entertech contractors on this post are Embracers and our friends and allies. You will not seek retribution. You will not refuse to work with goblins on this post or in any way undermine the work they are currently doing. I assure you that my force protection staff will be hard at work discovering and rooting out any threat to the security of this base. But we have enough on our plate and cannot begin to address the problems at hand if we're turning on one another. I am instructing my Provost Marshal General to be enthusiastic in the investigation and prosecution of attacks on goblins on this installation that he believes may be motivated by paranoia or a desire for revenge. Is everybody tracking?"

The buzz receded into silence.

"I just asked you a question," Bookbinder said, cocking an eyebrow.

A ripple of "yes, sir" and "aye aye, sir" swept through the throng. Heads bobbed.

"Good. I'm not playing around here. I will have order on this FOB. We've got some tough times ahead, and I'm going to need each and every one of you to pull together in helping to get us through them."

He stared out over the audience, making eye contact with hardened veterans of multiple campaigns, men and women who'd soldiered in this hostile dimension since the FOB had first been stood up. The gazes returned to him looked serious, respectful. *My God. Am I actually pulling this off?* His next thought was of his wife. His fingers instinctively brushed against his wedding band. *Oh, bunny. I wish you could see this.*

"So, what are we up against? Well, let me get to that in a roundabout fashion. I'm appointing Lieutenant Colonel Allen, Crucible, as my XO and Deputy Camp Commandant. That should tell you that he is being relieved of command of SAOLCC. Why is that? Because I'm shutting SAOLCC down. In fact, I'm shutting down every activity not specifically related to the protection and sustenance of this base. Nothing of a non-defensive nature gets built, and nothing that isn't feeding, caring for, or protecting the people here gets done. Now, I'm sure you've noticed there's been a dwindling of sundry items over the last few days, ever since the attacks started stepping up. Range days have been canceled. The DFAC is running out of milk and fruit. Unless you live under a rock, you've picked up on this. Am I right?"

Silence. The feeling of faintness passed utterly. Bookbinder stepped to the edge of the platform. "Jesus, people. A little help here. Am I right?"

"Yes, sir!" the crowd responded in almost one voice, crowding forward. *They're hungry for answers. They want someone to lead them. And you're standing up here making them believe you're it.*

"Well, it's time you were let in on why that's happening. This FOB is entirely dependent on Portamantic magic for access to the Home Plane. Every single one of you gained access to the LZ at LSA Portcullis via a magical gate.

"A few days ago, those gates stopped opening. Worse, our backup plan took off with the aid of what looks like an organized conspiracy hatched in the SASS with the help of another rogue goblin. What does this mean? It means we're cut off. It means there is no resupply and no way home."

He paused to let that sink in. A chorus of whispers, half-fearful, half-angry, swept over the crowd. *I will not lie to these people. They are adults and officers. If we're going to beat this, we need to do it together. All of us, with eyes wide open.*

You idiot, another part of him screamed, a part of him steeped in military tradition, trained to release as little information as possible. *You're killing their morale!*

He ignored that voice and pressed on. "That's the bad news, and I won't sugarcoat it. We're in deep kimchee here, and things are going to get worse before they get better.

"But here's the good news, they can and will get better. In the short time I've served with you, I've come to know you as the most locked-on, squared-away, high-speed, low-drag, wind tunnel–tested group of men and women I've ever met. The enemy we face are numerous and magically powerful, but they are factious, tribal, and functioning at a medieval level of technology. We're Americans—disciplined, smart, experienced, and well equipped even without constant resupply. We're trained and specialized. We're tight. We're competent. If we can hold on to those things, if we can keep cohesion as these attacks come on, and, rest assured, they will keep coming on, then we can hold this FOB until we can find a way home.

"And remember, the enemy aren't the only ones with magic. FOB Frontier is the heart of the SOC, the best of what it has to offer. If we harness that, we can't fail to find our way through this.

"I know the level of leadership you deserve, that you'd come to expect from Colonel Taylor. I want to assure you that I'm going to do the same. I will not fail you. The primary focus of my command is to secure this base, keep us sustained, and get us resupplied and relieved. It is my one purpose, and I will carry it out with everything I have.

"I'm proud to serve with each and every one of you. Thank you for the chance to show you just how much."

Bookbinder realized he had edged slowly forward as he spoke, and now stood directly at the platform's edge, bent forward at the waist, his eyes sweeping over the assembled officers and senior enlisted.

Silence. A sea of faces looked back at him, expressions blank. He had blown it. Honesty was not always the best policy. They were standing in stark horror, stunned into silence by the gravity of what faced them. Sometimes it paid to sugarcoat it, and he had just run headlong into one of those times. *You can't get it right every time. But this time, this time, you really needed to.*

Trying not to let the defeat show, Bookbinder turned and made his way toward the back of the platform. The pressure of their eyes and their silence fell away, leaving him exhausted. Having single-handedly drained the morale of an entire division's worth of officers, he could now safely crawl into his rack and sleep. Maybe he'd let Crucible run things. The man could hardly do a worse job than he was.

A sound stopped him, a sweeping brush, a thudding smack. It was faint, light at first. Then it was joined by others, light pats that became a rhythmic chorus. Bookbinder stood still as his brain registered that he was hearing hands clapping.

Applause.

He turned back to the audience as the trickle of claps became a flood. The faces stayed serious. There were no catcalls of praise, no hoots. But the steady thunder of palms on palms told Bookbinder all he needed to know.

The approval made him feel faint all over again. "Thanks . . ." he managed. "Thanks, everyone. Okay. Okay. I'll need all quartermasters and supply officers to get on my calendar. Please see Crucible about that. I'd like to have the first meetings today. I'll send word about who I want to see next." The Aeromancy notched up again in an effort to carry his voice over the thunder of clapping.

"Okay," he said, feeling his heart swell along with his throat. *I have to get off this platform before I choke up in front of everyone.* "Thank you again. Dismissed."

The applause followed him all the way back to his office, though whether it was a lingering trick of the Aeromancy or the sheer volume of it, he could not tell.

Crucible brought the first of the supply officers twenty minutes later. Bookbinder sat behind his desk, still too stunned to wrap his head around what had just happened. He munched on an MRE that Carmela prepared for him. He'd ordered her not to bring him any fresh food. If he was going to force his men to ration, he'd have to lead by example.

Crucible entered without knocking, a soft smile on his face. Behind him, three supply officers, two navy and one air force, trailed along, helmets under their arms. Bookbinder could feel a current off the female air force officer. Her school pin was hidden by her body armor, but Bookbinder's ability told him she was a Terramancer, though he reminded himself not to let her know that he knew. He didn't need the uniqueness of his magic adding to the complications here. She stared at him, her broad face weathered and lined. Her eyes were sunken and shadowed. She looked tired but confident. The big woman's glossy black hair was streaked with gray, tied into a braid that was further tucked into a bun. All business.

"Alan," Crucible said. "Sorry to bug you while you're eating."

"Not at all," Bookbinder said, wiping his chin. "Come in and sit down."

There was a moment of awkward silence as he realized that

he had two chairs for four people, but one of the supply officers, a fresh-faced navy lieutenant commander, threw him a bone. "We're fine standing, sir."

"These are our three section heads," Crucible said. "Lieutenant Commanders Pierre and Roche"—he indicated the male sailors "and Major Woon" he gestured to the air force officer.

"Thanks for coming," Bookbinder said. "I'll try to keep this short. I'm afraid a lot of the burden of the coming days is going to fall heavily on you. Supply is the most critical element to our holding out here, and we're going to have to be awfully creative about how we make do."

"We're with you, sir," Pierre said with a hint of a Caribbean accent. Bookbinder missed a beat while he absorbed those words and the look on the young man's face. *My God, he really means it.*

Bookbinder mastered himself more quickly this time. *You're going to have to get used to the good as well as the bad. You can't be going to pieces every time somebody expresses confidence in you.*

"Very well," he said. "The first thing we've got to do is implement austerity measures. I have no idea how long it's going to be before we're resupplied. No doubt they're scrambling to find a way to reach us on the Home Plane," he said with a confidence he didn't feel. "And we're going to come up with a plan on this end. Until then, I want all perishable food strictly rationed. If you think it's going to go bad, get it eaten right away. Work from the bottom up; fresh vegetables, milk, and stuff like that goes to the lowest-ranked first, with priority given to those in perimeter security and medical roles."

The supply officers produced notepads and began to scribble furiously. "Roger that, sir," Woon said.

"Ammunition rationing continues as per Taylor's instructions. Strict fire discipline. Nobody puts their weapon on full auto or burst mode unless specifically authorized. Only shoot at what you can hit. Get Pyromancers on regular patrols. If we're going to need suppressing fire, I want it to be of the magical variety. No range days, no practices. I want negligent discharges rigorously prosecuted. You catch someone hoarding ammo, you make them pay and pay publicly."

"Aye aye, sir."

"Next, we need to get used to the idea of supplying ourselves via magic. We might not like it as much as cold cereal and whole-wheat toast, but it'll do in a pinch. I want Hydromancers detailed to set up a freshwater pond in the plaza. Get it walled off and guarded twenty-four/seven. Feed it with summoned rainfall or an underground spring. Just make sure it's full and fresh."

"Respectfully, sir?" Roche said.

"Speak freely."

"One pond isn't going to cover everyone. You're going to need at least ten."

"Outstanding. Make it happen. Just make sure of this: that there's enough magically produced freshwater *under guard* at all times. Make damn sure that the cash and the DFAC are adequately supplied. Since you're the idea man on this one, Roche, if you can figure out a way to get it piped or transported to where it needs to be, I'll write you up for a commendation. Ditto if you can get it bottled and distributed."

Roche smiled. "I've got some ideas, sir."

"Outstanding. The bottom line is that nobody on this post should want for clean, potable water at any time. Run a river through here if you have to, just make sure it's clean and safe. How can we handle heating it? Is that a Hydromancy or Pyromancy issue?"

"Both, sir. But fortunately, it's fairly easy. Same thing for climate control. We've got Aeromancers who can make sure nobody freezes or overheats if the AC goes out."

"Great. Sanitation is another issue. I'm assuming Terramancers can have the latrine pits mulch the waste we put in them?"

Woon nodded. "I'm a Terramancer, sir. We can do that."

Bookbinder smiled. *I already knew that, young lady.* "Okay. That's on you, then. Make it happen. No sanitation issues and no odors. Quality of life is a concern if we're going to keep morale up. You can also handle chow. I need Terramancers detailed to gardening. I need space cleared for that immediately. Make sure it keeps everyone here in fresh fruits and vegetables."

Woon pursed her lips as she wrote. "Seed stock might be a problem."

"Requisition whatever you need from the DFAC. I assume a Terramancer can turn one rotten cucumber into a field of them?"

Woon nodded. "Got it, sir. There are some native species I know are safe to consume, too. We'll take care of it."

Bookbinder leaned back in his chair. "Okay, now here's the part you're not going to like. I need you to pick out a handful of promising Terramancers and order them to learn to Whisper."

Crucible alone showed no reaction. The supply officers sucked in their breath as one. Woon frowned. "Sir, I'm not sure . . ."

"I wasn't asking for your opinion, Major. I was giving you an order."

"Sir, respectfully, that's an illegal order. Whispering is prohibited under the . . ."

Okay. Time to play the part.

Bookbinder tried to project some of Taylor's angry authority into his own voice. He stood, putting his knuckles on the desk, and raised his voice. *Easy, don't overdo it. Nobody liked Taylor very much.*

"Don't presume to lecture me on the law, Major. I'm well familiar with what I'm asking. This is my call, and I'll take whatever flak comes when we finally make it back to the Home Plane. For now, we're cut off and under fire, and we need every advantage we can take to stay alive. Our troops are going to need meat, and we're going to need animal scouts to reconnoiter enemy positions without risking valuable fuel, equipment, and personnel.

"If it makes you feel any better, I'll write a damned memo saying it was my idea, and you can give it to the Office of Special Investigations when you get home. But, for now, I need you with me on this. Are we clear?"

Woon straightened. "Crystal, sir."

"And you're going to carry out this order? I can't have you fucking around on this, Woon. I need you with me."

"I'm with you, sir. I'll see to it, and I'll make sure my people understand the gravity of the situation."

Bookbinder relaxed, letting some of this relief show. "Thanks. I appreciate that."

"Respectfully, sir. I don't know that my people can figure out how to Whisper."

Bookbinder rolled his eyes. "That's horseshit, Major. Plenty of Terramancers learn how to Whisper on their own. We wouldn't have had to outlaw it if it was difficult to do."

Woon looked chastened, but not humiliated. "Sir."

"Okay. That's a start. Any bright ideas, you run them to Crucible. We've got a lot of hard work ahead of us, but I have total confidence that we can sustain ourselves here indefinitely if we're smart about conserving resources and using magic efficiently. You all have the premier role in making that happen. It's an important job, maybe the most important job on this FOB. Can you handle this?"

They smiled at him, young, eager, inspired. "No sweat, sir."

"All right. Get out of here and make me proud."

Once they were gone, Bookbinder slumped in his chair, rubbing his temples. He felt weak from the tension of having to act the boss he just couldn't bring himself to feel like. "How'd I do, Rick?"

"Convinced the hell out of me," Crucible said. "They'll follow you into hell if you ask them."

"I only hope that's not what I'm asking them."

"Time will tell. You're off to a good start." Crucible looked uncomfortable.

"What?" Bookbinder asked. "What did I fuck up?"

"Nothing, sir. It's just . . . I just thought of something."

"Well? Out with it."

"Our foreign partners, sir. You didn't invite them to the address. The FOB's a combined op."

Bookbinder sighed. "Don't we have a protocol officer, or someone who handles that crap?"

Crucible slapped his forehead. "Yes, we do. Damn it. It's Major Constance, and she's something of a prima donna. Damn it. I'm sorry, sir. I could have anticipated that. I should have been covering your six."

"Don't beat yourself up. We've both been under a ton of pressure since this whole thing . . . went south."

"Ugh. Still. Damn it."

"Well, shit. Who's on the FOB?"

Crucible looked at the ceiling as he thought. "Before we got cut off, I know we had the Swedish *Trollkarl Kar*, the Indian *Sahir* Corps, and the Russian *Spetznaz Vedma*. Oh, and I think there was one of those Saudi *Djinn* wranglers."

"Saudi? I thought Muslims outlawed magic."

"They do in public, sir. But we supposedly outlawed Probes, too, didn't we?"

"Fair point. Okay, can you put your nose to the ground and find out why the hell this Major Constance is asleep at the switch? Get her unfucked and fast, Riok. Things are tight right now. We can't afford mistakes like that."

"Roger that, sir."

"And once we get Constance online, maybe we can reach out to these foreign partners. Might be there's something they can do to help?"

Crucible, about to answer, was cut off by the light rapping of knuckles at the door. A moment later, Carmela poked her head in. "Sir, sorry to disturb you, but the Indian attaché is here to see you, he says it's urgent."

Bookbinder and Crucible exchanged glances, arching their eyebrows. "That's good timing. Send him in."

Carmela paused. "Would you be willing to meet him out by my desk, sir? He's got his . . . partner with him."

Bookbinder nodded. The naga was enormous. It had barely fit through the door of the ready room. His office door was even smaller. He stood, brushed himself off, and motioned Crucible to go ahead of him.

The sight of Vasuki-Kai still made him nervous. The huge creature looked impatient, its many heads darting back and forth, multiple pairs of arms crossed over its broad chest. Dhatri stood beside it, smiling and relaxed as ever. His formal uniform had been replaced by creamed spinach–looking camouflage under body armor decorated with the subdued Indian flag and what Bookbinder assumed was an indicator of his rank, a black national emblem with a stripe. A carbine was slung across his chest, and a pistol nestled in a holster on his thigh.

Once Vasuki-Kai noticed their entrance, he began to gesture angrily with several sets of hands while his heads darted toward Bookbinder, setting up a chorus of vaguely Hindi-sounding hissing.

Dhatri placed a comforting hand on one of the creature's elbows, and it quieted, shooting a glare his way from several sets of serpentine eyes. "His Highness wishes to express his condolences for the loss of Colonel Taylor and to congratulate you on your assumption of command. He also demands to know why he wasn't informed of this immediately and invited to the change-of-command ceremony."

Crucible's jaw tightened, and Bookbinder swallowed. *Remember, the naga think they rule over all humans, and this particular naga is a prince among his own kind. You have to treat him like royalty.* He bowed deeply from the waist, motioning Crucible to do the same.

"Please extend my sincere apologies to His Highness. Colonel Taylor's death was sudden, and I'm not used to the protocol required in combined operations like this one. I trust that His Highness will understand that I meant no offense."

Dhatri translated in real time. Vasuki-Kai's arms crossed again, but much of the anger clearly subsided. Some of the heads drew upward into a regal pose. Others nodded.

There was a brief silence, then the naga issued another burst of hissing, this time more moderate in tone. "His Highness wishes me to inform you that he is concerned about the increased pace of attacks on the perimeter of this installation. He also notes that you gave a speech earlier—"

Bookbinder cut him off, patting the air with his palms. "Yes, I know. I apologize for not inviting you, it wasn't intentional. Like I said, I'm still finding my feet here."

Dhatri nodded. "His Highness says he is aware that this installation is cut off from the Home Plane and without resupply. He theorizes that you cannot hold out against the heightened pace of attacks. He notes that, without resupply, you will eventually be overrun."

Bookbinder's stomach fell. *Don't fall for it. Who knows what his agenda is.*

He took a deep breath, trying not to show how the naga's words affected him. "Tell His Highness that I am in the process of implementing security and austerity measures that will ensure our ability to hold this position indefinitely. I know I speak for my government when I say that we value His Highness's counsel and respectfully request any inputs he may have to boost our sustenance and force protection efforts." *Dear God, do all foreign exchanges sound this pompous?*

But while the corner of Crucible's mouth rose slightly, Dhatri grunted as if he'd expected that response. He translated in real time back to Vasuki-Kai, who issued another burst of hissing.

"His Highness says you misunderstand. The weather grows cold, ending the campaign season for the tribes. The intensity of the attacks you are experiencing now is nothing compared to what will come with the spring thaw. Any measures you implement will only buy you time. When the flowers begin to bloom in the pasturelands outside your gates, you will surely be overrun. His Highness says the Defender tribes are as numerous as plague insects. There are a hundred of them for each one of you. Even if they had no magic and no guns, if you are not properly resupplied, they will wash over this place like the sea."

Bookbinder traded looks with Crucible. "He's got a point, sir. They are a lot more active in the spring. We never had to worry about it before because of artillery and air support, but they're not exactly plentiful right now."

Bookbinder hung his head. "Well . . . shit."

He knew he shouldn't let the Indian liaisons see him like this, but he couldn't help himself. Every time he tackled one problem, a new one confronted him. He couldn't catch a break.

"His Highness asks what your plan to obtain relief personnel and resupply is."

Bookbinder sighed. "Well, I hadn't exactly gotten to that part yet."

Vasuki-Kai made a chorus of choking hisses that Bookbinder was fairly certain was laughter. One of his huge hands clapped Bookbinder on the shoulder. "His Highness says that he may be able to be of some assistance."

"Tell His Highness that I am deeply grateful for any assistance he may be able to offer."

Dhatri turned to Vasuki-Kai and chattered for a long moment in Hindi punctuated by hissing. At times, their conversation grew animated. After a moment, the naga thrust a finger into the Subedar Major's chest and hissed with some finality. Dhatri nodded, swallowed, and turned back to Bookbinder.

"Sir, His Highness directs me to inform you that the Naga Raajya has its own Portamancer."

Hope flooded through Bookbinder's chest, weakening his

knees. He paused for a moment before he trusted himself to speak. "And they can help us reestablish contact with the Home Plane?"

Dhatri and several of Vasuki-Kai's heads nodded simultaneously.

Bookbinder clapped his hands together and allowed himself a broad smile. "Please extend my profuse and sincere gratitude to His Highness. This is wonderful news. How do we make this happen?"

"My government has its own FOB in the Naga Raajya, this is the naga's own domain. The Naga Raja, their king, has permitted us to establish a base around his palace. It is some distance away."

Bookbinder frowned. "I thought we were the only country with a presence here . . ."

Dhatri blushed. "Yes, well . . . Sir, it wasn't a widely distributed piece of information. But it's true. His Highness has ordered me to share this information with you. He will not suffer this place to be destroyed with everyone in it simply so my government can keep a secret."

"Okay. How do we get in touch with them?"

Dhatri's British- and Hindi-accented English sounded embarrassed. "This is problematic. There are no satellites in the Source, and we have relied on SINCGARS communications with our FOB. Unfortunately, the Source's electromagnetic sphere is not well understood. There is frequent interference, and communications are not consistent."

"So, how do you keep in touch?"

"By envoy, sir. The trip is long and dangerous for a human. But nagas can do it, with some difficulty."

"You send . . . runners?" *I almost said "slitherers."*

Dhatri nodded. "I'm afraid so, sir. It's not efficient. Lately, we've been having a devil of a time getting in touch."

Bookbinder turned to Crucible. "Is this that 'Tiger Smile' thing that Taylor was going on about?" He doubted Taylor would have wanted the Indians to know that code word, but it seemed that secrets were becoming awfully inconvenient given the current crisis.

Crucible shrugged.

Bookbinder turned back to Dhatri. "So, Subedar Major, what

you're telling me is that there's a way out of this, but we're going to have to walk there. Through hostile country."

"Very hostile, sir, I'm afraid."

"And how far is it?"

"About twenty-one hundred kilometers, sir. Maybe a little less." Dhatri paused. "I'm sorry, I'm know you go by miles, but I'm not sure that . . ."

Bookbinder stopped him with a wave. Twenty-one hundred kilometers was around thirteen hundred miles. Over hostile terrain, with no roads and no ability to resupply.

Help was out there, and so far away that it might as well be in another world.

CHAPTER XVI
BOOTS ON THE GROUND

When you look at the Etymologiae *and* Physiologus *of Pliny the Elder and Isidore of Seville, you get a bestiary of fabulous creatures from manticores and goblins to the fish and birds we see every day. Before the Great Reawakening, these writers were dismissed as primitive fantasists. But they wrote roughly a millennium before our own time, which fits with planar orbital theory and the notion of a "Source" plane where magic exists as an elemental force. If that force could bleed into the Home Plane, then it stands to reason that the fauna of that place could find ways to cross over as well.*

—Avery Whiting
Modern Arcana: Theory and Practice

"You're not going." There was an edge of emotion to Crucible's voice that weakened Bookbinder's resolve. Crucible was competent, careful, kind. He trusted the man implicitly. Maybe he was right? *No. This is your task. You have to do this.*

"I don't recall asking you for your opinion," Bookbinder said, trying to sound authoritative and failing utterly.

"You can't have it both ways, *Alan*," Crucible said. "You can't be all buddy-buddy with me one second, then try to order me around the next. You wanted a friend and confidant. Well, you've got one. And I say you're not going."

Bookbinder rolled his eyes. "I don't suppose we can go back to me being the stern and imposing CO for this part, can we?"

Crucible snorted.

"Rick, I'm serious here. I have to do this. Me."

"No, you don't. You are in command here. You can send a team."

"To go out into that wilderness? It's practically a suicide mission, and you know it."

Crucible spread his hands. "I do know it. And since when is it a good idea to send the post CO out to die?"

Bookbinder pounded the desk. "Since that CO has been a CO for all of fifteen minutes. Hell, Rick, we both know you can run this base a hundred times better than I can. The troops know and respect you. Rank isn't the issue. Fuck, I'll brevet you to full bird if that makes a difference."

"Now is not the time to have a crisis of confidence, sir! You should have seen their faces when you gave that speech. You've made a good impression, and they're coming around. Those austerity measures were smart. You trust your people, you delegate. You're firm without being overbearing. You're a natural."

Bookbinder shook his head. "I'll admit that part went well. But it was one speech, Rick. I'll even give myself the credit you're extending to me. But the fact remains that even a natural talent still has to learn his trade. That's what's missing here. I don't have the track record. I don't know the right people. You, at least, ran the SAOLCC. Christ, look at the whole thing with the protocol officer! I had no clue whom to go to. If you hadn't known about Constance and her propensity for preening over labor, we would have been well and truly screwed."

He leaned over the desk and softened his voice. "You believe in me. I get it. But there isn't enough time for me to learn as I go here. This has to be done right the first time."

"And somehow you'll have the time to learn as you go leading a scout/recon mission?"

"It's more than that. It's an envoy to a foreign government's FOB, one that we're not supposed to know about." He tapped the eagle sewn on his uniform, signifying his colonel's rank. "The full bird will help some there."

"Christ, Alan. You're a Latent Grenade. What if you go off out there?"

Bookbinder paused. "Yes, well. About that."

"What?"

"I already went off."

Crucible's mouth fell open. He stood for a long moment before he closed it. "You're fucking kidding me."

"Nope."

"But, nobody even noticed! I mean, you never Manifested! What school are you?"

"No school. At least, none I've ever heard of. Jesus, sit down." Bookbinder gestured at the chair in the corner of the office.

Crucible kicked it. "Hell, no. What are you talking about?"

"Okay, don't freak out. All right?"

Crucible only stared.

"I may have to abort this, I don't have a lot of practice." Bookbinder Drew his current, reached out for the foreign flow of Crucible's magic and Bound it. He began to draw it into himself. Crucible's eyes shot wide. "What the hell is going on?"

"I'm not sure," Bookbinder said through gritted teeth. "It's some kind of parasitic thing. I'm a magic thief." He began to feel his veins flush with Crucible's magic, beginning to overwhelm his senses. The current was caustic, hot. Bookbinder glanced around his office, trying to look for a place to shunt the magic off to. There was no convenient chunk of blast barricade to use as a focus. He tamped down on the current, rolling his own magic back. For a moment, he worried that he would be unable, and would have to beg Crucible to Suppress him, but then he felt his magic obey him, releasing Crucible's current to flow back into him. A sheen of sweat broke out on Bookbinder's forehead as he slumped in his chair. "Damn it. I forgot that you're a Pyromancer. I don't want to set anything in this office on fire."

"Holy crap, Alan. I felt you . . . yanking my magic out of me."

"I know. I pull it into myself. It's like I have magic for two people inside me. I can only hold it for a short time, then I have to project it out into something else."

"Like what?"

"Like anything, I guess. I've only done it once before, during a goblin attack. I pulled one of their sorcerer's Pyromancy and Bound it to a chunk of concrete. The thing was on fire. We're talking concrete. Burning."

Crucible changed his mind and sat down. "Holy cow."

"I know."

"So not only are you . . . some kind of magic vampire, but you can create . . . magic stuff?"

Bookbinder shrugged. "That's what it looks like. I haven't had a lot of time to practice."

"Holy cow," Crucible said again.

"I know," Bookbinder said again.

"Sir, I've been with this program since its inception. I've never even heard of something like that."

"Well, we haven't been out in the Source long, maybe that's got something to do with it?"

"This has to be studied. Why the hell didn't you tell anyone?"

"I only found out once we'd already been cut off, and the attacks had started stepping up. You'll forgive me if the timing didn't seem exactly auspicious."

"But, if you don't know how to use it . . ."

Bookbinder raised a hand. "I've thought that over. If anything, I see it as an advantage. At a minimum, this power is stable. At best, it's the most diverse form of magic out there. If I can master it, it'll bring us every advantage once we're out there trying to reach the Indian FOB."

"Are you sure you know that's what this is? You can drain other people's magic and Bind it to inanimate objects? Maybe the stress of combat confused you."

Bookbinder pounded the desk, then uncurled his fist, extending a finger toward Crucible. "Damn it, Rick. Don't patronize me! I know what I'm talking about here. I'm a smart guy, and I'm handling things, so don't treat me like a fucking invalid."

Crucible patted the air. "You're right, sir. I'm sorry."

"It's okay," Bookbinder said, willing the color out of his face.

"How the hell do you plan to master it?" Crucible finally broke the silence. "I mean, even in SAOLCC we couldn't . . ."

"You couldn't help me in SAOLCC anyway. This is new. You don't know any more about it than I do. I'll either figure it out on my own, or I won't. I'll make sure I have someone along who can Suppress, just in case."

"You've already decided on a team?"

Bookbinder nodded. "More or less. I've been thinking about it. This base needs all hands on deck to weather the coming storm until either we find help or the government finds a way to reach us. I'm going to take as little as I can. I'm assuming a base like this doesn't have in-flight refueling capability?"

Crucible shook his head. "I'll double-check with the air boss, but I highly doubt it. That's a big air force thing. We never needed it out here. There's some fixed-wing capability on the flight line, but it's single-seater combat stuff. It's primarily a helo flight."

"I thought so. So, air-dropping us is not a real option. And I'm not sparing a helo, even a Little Bird, just to have it go bingo-fuel halfway to our destination, then ground it for the enemy to rip apart. Air cover is one of the bigger advantages we have over the Defender clans. The rocs and wyverns they throw at us don't really hold up. I need every swinging dick in the air, so to speak."

Crucible nodded. "Concur. Dhatri said their FOB doesn't have a runway, so there's no place for a fixed-wing to land anyway."

"And my guess is that the terrain between here and the Indian FOB doesn't even have unimproved dirt roads. It's broken by rivers, uneven ground, woods. Even a Stryker couldn't handle it."

Crucible kept nodding.

"So we're going to have to walk."

Crucible swore under his breath. "That's one hell of a walk."

"And we're going to need to move fast. We've got a lot of ground to cover. So, I want to keep the team small, light, and able to handle anything we come across. Now, I'm assuming that Sorcerers are at as much of a premium as aircraft?"

"More," Crucible said. "With supply cut off, magic is the only renewable resource this base has. Every Sorcerer you take lowers the survivability by an order of magnitude."

"Which is why I'll only take one. Well, apart from me. That'll be the heart of the team."

"And that would be?"

"Myself, Vasuki-Kai, and Dhatri. One Terramancer. Four enlisted. One medic, One NCO, two scout/snipers. I want you to pick 'em, Rick. The best we've got."

"Jesus. That's not even a platoon."

"It doesn't need to be. You've seen what I can do. I don't know about Dhatri, but Vasuki-Kai is probably good for ten to twenty goblins on his own. A Terramancer can make sure we're fed and have eyes around us. Rick, I know some of our people practice Whispering on their own. Find me one of those. They get amnesty. I don't care if it's illegal, I'm making the call. Find someone who understands that."

Crucible crossed his arms over his chest. "This is stupid, Alan."

"Fine, but it's also an order, and you're going to see to it. I am going to fix this, Rick. I am going to fucking fix this, or I am going to die trying. And you're going to help me."

Crucible met his eyes and held them. "Yes, sir."

"Um . . . there's one other thing," Bookbinder said into the silence that followed. He reached into his desk drawer, removed an envelope, and handed it across the desk to Crucible.

The Pyromancer made no move to take it. "What's that?"

"You know what it is. I'd save an email in my drafts folder if I thought there was a chance in hell we'd have comms back home anytime soon. It's for my wife and kids. If I don't make it back, see that they get this when you get reconnected to the Home Plane."

Crucible nodded, took the letter, and folded it in half, tucking it into a pocket on his cargo pants. "You're making it back, sir. You owe me."

Bookbinder cocked an eyebrow at him. "I owe you?"

"You want me to run this place so you can run off and play some combo game of diplomat-hero? Well, you drive the big car, and I drive the little car. But this is a shit job, and you're just sticking me with it so you can have an adventure. The least you can do is write me a weekend pass and put me in for a commendation. Hell, maybe a letter to the promotion board. If you're dead, you won't be able to put in the paperwork. That would just be wrong."

Bookbinder snorted. "Yeah, I guess it would.

"I'll see what I can do."

Crucible found Bookbinder standing beside one of the new Terramantic gardens that Woon had ordered set up, his head craned skyward. A roc circled overhead. A quarter klick away by the perimeter, booms sounded, indicating the start of another attack.

The lieutenant colonel jogged forward but stopped short of Bookbinder. "Sir! The air defenses . . ."

"I ordered them shut off here."

"Wha . . . why?"

"I'm practicing."

A goblin Terramancer snugged to the back of the roc's neck. The basket on its back held three goblins. One of them was painted fully white, his hands extended above his head, bursting into flame. As Crucible watched, the goblin Pyromancer extended his hands and a gout of fire arced earthward, scouring the garden, turning most of it to ash. The roc swept past and began to circle back for another pass. Soldiers gathered around them, pointing weapons skyward, clearly itching to shoot but under orders not to. Bookbinder could feel the tension in their trigger fingers as clearly as any magical current.

"Sir!" Crucible said again.

"One more pass," Bookbinder said. "Almost got it."

The roc came back around, descending. The Pyromancer leaned over the basket's edge, sighting down at Bookbinder and the growing knot of people around him. He pumped a fist, fire swirling about his head and shoulders.

"Christ!" Crucible shouted. "Incoming! Scatter!"

The Pyromancer reached forward, the flames forming another deadly pillar.

And then winked out.

Bookbinder threw his head back, the muscles in his back clenching. "Fuuuuuuck," he said, then threw his doubled current outward.

The roc, the basket, the goblins all burst into flame. The huge bird screamed in agony. One of the goblins jumped from the basket, beating at the flames, plummeting to the ground. The roc flapped madly, trying to gain altitude, trailing greasy smoke from its wing tips, throwing the Terramancer from its back. He followed his fellows to the ground, screaming all the way down.

"All right, that's enough," Bookbinder said, bending over, hands on his knees, panting. "Put 'em out of their misery." At least twenty carbines opened up, followed by the howling torrents of the air-defense systems. Within moments, the roc and its passengers were wet ribbons, slowly drifting earthward.

Bookbinder arched an eyebrow at Crucible. "Guess it works on more than just inanimate objects, huh?"

Crucible stood dumbstruck. "Guess it does, sir."

"Still worried about me leading the team?"

Crucible shrugged and gestured to the woman beside him. "You remember Major Woon, sir."

Bookbinder straightened and looked at the Terramancer, with her gray-streaked hair and serious expression. "I do remember. You've been doing a fine job with the gardens, Major. I'm sorry this one got a little cooked."

"That's fine, sir. We can regrow it."

Bookbinder's gaze traveled down to the ground. A small fox-looking creature sat there. It had huge ears and intelligent eyes. Its front legs ended in human-looking hands.

"Is that what I think it is?"

"We don't have a name for it, sir. But they're fairly common around the FOB," Woon said.

"That's not what I meant," Bookbinder said.

"I know, sir," Woon said. "Yes, I have it Whispered."

Bookbinder crossed his arms. "You are a very naughty major, you know that?"

Woon colored. "Sir, Crucible assured me that amnesty would be granted for . . ."

"At ease. He told you right. I just . . . I didn't suspect it from you."

Woon cocked her head. "Why is that, sir?"

"You seem so . . . by the book. Serious. I'd never pegged you as a lawbreaker. I mean, I'm glad you are, but I'm surprised."

Woon shrugged.

"You don't even go by your call sign," Bookbinder said.

Woon shrugged again. "I've been supply all my career, sir. When I came up Latent, that didn't change. Most Terramancers are guys, so I never really fit in anyway."

"What is your call sign, anyway?" Bookbinder asked.

"Branchmender, sir." Crucible answered for her.

"I hate it, sir," Woon said.

"Fair enough," Bookbinder said. "What can I do for you?"

Crucible cleared his throat. "Woon's your Terramancer, sir. For the mission to FOB Sarpakavu."

"FOB . . . FOB what?"

"The Indian FOB, sir. That's what they call it."

"Woon is . . .? No. I need you running the Terramantic austerity measures here," Bookbinder said.

"Major Woon has a talented XO, sir," Crucible replied. "A captain of real ability who she has fully briefed on your intentions regarding the austerity measures. Both Major Woon and I have complete confidence in his ability to get the job done and done right, sir."

"Sir," Major Woon added, "if there's a chance to save this installation, then I want to be a part of it. Not to glory-hound, but I am one of the most able Terramancers on this base, and definitely the best Whisperer outside of Umbra Coven."

Bookbinder stared at her, and some of Woon's nervousness returned. "Sir," she added.

"Sir," Crucible added, "Major Woon is following your excellent example of stepping up to the mission while simultaneously delegating authority to a competent subordinate."

Bookbinder chuckled. "Touché."

"You told me to get you the best," Crucible said. "This is it."

"High praise," Bookbinder said. "Very well. I guess you're hired."

It took Woon a moment to suppress the smile that spread across her face, transforming her from tired woman to young girl. "You won't regret it, sir."

"Here's your enlisted compliment, sir." Crucible gestured behind him at four men who looked as if they'd stepped out of an action film. Their leader, a sergeant first class, looked every inch the Spaghetti Western desperado, complete with flint gray eyes and a day's growth of stubble on his chiseled jaw. The next two looked like they could bend cold iron with their bare hands, their hair cropped Marine Corps short and their biceps straining the cuffed sleeves of their uniforms. The remaining soldier was noticeably shorter, had let his hair grow so long it bordered on insubordinate. He was thin in comparison to the rest, but his eyes were like his comrades', calm, alert, focused. Killer's eyes. All four men wore SPECIAL FORCES tabs on their shoulders.

"Sergeant First Class Sharp is your noncom, sir," Crucible said. "Specialists Fillion and Anan are your shooters." He gestured to the shorter man. "This is Specialist Archer. Best medic they've got. Sharp, Fillion, and Anan ran an op with Oscar Britton before he escaped. They got a little banged up, but are back on the line now. Like Major Woon, they requested this assignment as soon as I put the word out. They come with impeccable credentials."

Bookbinder nodded, noting their professional nonchalance. "They look tough."

"Toughest we've got, sir. If there are operators who can get this job done, they're it."

Sharp and his men said nothing. There was no bravado, no false modesty. They stood with folded arms, waiting for orders.

"All right," Bookbinder said. "I guess that's that. Now all we have to do is contact Dhatri and . . ."

"Sir." Dhatri's voice reached him. Bookbinder turned to see the subedar major, the towering naga trailing in his wake, hissing urgently.

He halted a few paces away and cracked a British-style salute, palm outward. Bookbinder returned it in American fashion and smiled. "Speak of the devil, Subedar Major. We were just talking about you."

Dhatri puffed, looking harried. Vasuki-Kai hissed loudly, pointing first at him, then at Bookbinder.

"Sir," Dhatri said. "I apologize for coming unannounced, but His Highness is most insistent. He says that time is growing short and demands that you outfit an expedition to FOB Sarpakavu immediately."

Bookbinder laughed. Crucible and Woon grinned. Even the corners of Sharp's mouth rose a bit.

Dhatri's expression hovered between shock and anger. Vasuki-Kai rolled his shoulders back, his heads darting upward, looking in all directions at once in apparent confusion. He hissed an interrogative.

"His Highness demands to know what it is you are finding so funny."

It was a moment before Bookbinder could answer. "Please apologize to His Highness on my behalf, Subedar Major. It's just that we were about to come find you to inform you that we have assembled a team and are preparing to depart for your FOB."

Dhatri looked mollified. "Very good, sir. Where is this team?"

Bookbinder swept an arm backward, indicated Woon, Sharp, and his men. "Here it is. I'll be leading it personally."

Vasuki-Kai paused before tentatively hissing.

"His Highness says this is a very small team."

Bookbinder nodded. "Which is why I respectfully request that His Highness and his *Bandhav* accompany us. We leave tomorrow at dawn."

Crucible met Bookbinder in his office long after dark. Bookbinder had been racing to complete preparations before departing, an act he apparently planned to accomplish on no sleep at all, despite Crucible's fervent protests. A lieutenant entered at Crucible's side. She was nervous, all of maybe twenty-three years old, her uniform looking a size too big for her.

"This is Lieutenant Ripple, sir." Crucible gestured to the young woman, who stood at attention.

"At ease, Lieutenant," Bookbinder said, and turned shadowed eyes to her. "Ripple a call sign or your name?"

"Both, sir," she answered. She gestured to her Hydromancer's lapel pin. "The guys thought it appropriate when I came up Latent."

Bookbinder chuckled. "Well, okay, I was—"

"You want me to be on the team, sir?" Ripple cut him off, then put a hand over her eyes. "Sorry, sir, I'm . . . uh . . . enthusiastic sometimes."

Bookbinder chuckled again. "It's fine, Lieutenant, but no. I need all hands on deck here, especially folks with your abilities. The FOB has to hold, and clean water is going to be critical to that particular mission."

"It's going to be critical to your mission, too," Crucible added. "I was thinking you'd decided to take a Hydromancer when you asked me to bring Lieutenant Ripple to see you."

"Yeah, about that," Bookbinder said, reaching behind his desk and lifting a plastic bucket of water with a grunt. "Heavy," he said, setting it on the desk. The water's surface was rank, with particles of mud and algae swirling across it. A foul odor wafted through the room.

Crucible wrinkled his nose. "What's this for?"

Bookbinder gestured to Ripple. "You can clean that up, right? Make it drinkable?"

Ripple didn't blink. "Certainly, sir."

"How? What exactly is your magic doing when you clean water?"

"It's hard to explain, sir. I don't mess with the dirt and bacteria, that's a Terramancer's job. I sort of . . . call the water itself forth from that, separate it out. What you wind up with is just pure water. No contaminants. That's the short answer, anyway."

"That's the answer I wanted," Bookbinder said, pulling a short piece of rebar from his pocket and holding it over the bucket. "Okay, use your magic to clean the water in this bucket."

Ripple shrugged and held out a hand. Bookbinder placed one of his hands over her own and shut his eyes, concentrating. The water in the bucket began to bubble for a short moment before petering out, the slime on the surface reconstituting.

Ripple's eyes widened. "Sir, what are you . . ."

"Keep going!" Bookbinder interrupted her. "Finish the spell. This won't hurt you, I promise."

Ripple's eyes remained wide and fixed on Bookbinder, but she complied.

After a moment, Bookbinder grunted in satisfaction. He hefted the piece of rebar, unchanged. "Well, let's hope this works."

He waved away Crucible's question and dropped the piece of metal into the bucket. He stared at it with folded arms, not breathing.

"Sir, enough of the dance-of-a-thousand-veils act. What's the point of this exercise?"

"The point," Bookbinder said, looking up, "is to leave you with as many Sorcerers as possible. And I do believe I have just succeeded in that very objective."

He gestured back down at the bucket, full to the brim with potable water, clear and sparkling under the fluorescent office lights.

CHAPTER XVII
MOVE OUT

Magic has been good to us. Kashmir is back where it belongs. Relations with the Chinese have warmed into the partnership we had always hoped they would eventually become. India has taken her rightful place as the major player in Asia that we have sought to be since we won our independence. But this is not the greatest thing it has done for us. The Great Reawakening has done nothing less than unite us with our traditions, and the deities that passed them along to us millennia ago. India is, quite literally, a nation that has at long last come home.

—Madhav Singh, Minister Arcane, Republic of India

Bookbinder sank into his body armor, letting the huge rucksack slung over his shoulders absorb the shuddering of the helicopter's airframe. Vasuki-Kai, Dhatri, Woon, Sharp, Fillion, Anan, and Archer all sat uncomfortably on the Chinook's long benches. The humans looked like camouflage-patterned cauliflower, bulging grotesquely with gear. Outside the helo's open cargo hatch, two door gunners scanned the airspace and the ground beneath them for threats. Fortunately, they didn't see any. If the goblins spotted the helo this far out from the FOB, they'd probably be under attack from the moment they landed. They needed time to get clear of the ring of hostile Defender tribes and into the territory beyond. After that, the helo would push them as far as its fuel would allow, saving only the reserves necessary for a safe return to the FOB.

Bookbinder tried to sleep, resting his helmet brim against the action of the breaching shotgun they'd given him to carry, but it was useless. The giant helo was sensitive to every gust of wind, jostling him awake the moment he thought he might be drifting off. Sharp and his people looked bored. Vasuki-Kai coiled toward the entrance to the cockpit, bent nearly double to accommodate his height, looking like he held court in helicopter cabins every day. Dhatri sat nestled in the coils of his giant tail, looking nervously out the open cargo hatch. Woon had put her goggles over her eyes, leaving the black cloth dustcover in place, hiding her expression. Bookbinder finally gave up on sleeping and sat blinking through his dust goggles as the helo shed speed and altitude, the roaring of the rotors dying down. Sharp and his men advanced to the cargo ramp, weapons at the low ready, while the rest of the group scrambled for their gear.

At last, the helo touched down with a jolt, and Sharp and his men advanced out of the hatch, guns tracking the perimeter, before taking a knee and giving a hand signal that it was safe to exit. Bookbinder, Woon, and Dhatri shouldered their weighty gear and stumbled out into the saw-toothed grass, rippling in the rotor wash like the green surface of an ocean. Vasuki-Kai followed leisurely behind.

Bookbinder was still taking in the landscape when he felt a tap on his shoulder. He turned to see the helo's crew chief, sun visor and helmet hiding the upper half of his face, lean forward to shout into his ear. "You're clear as far as we could see all the way down, sir! I wouldn't sit still any longer than I have to. Good luck and Godspeed!"

Bookbinder nodded, and the crew chief saluted, racing back into the helo. The huge airframe shook as it rose skyward again, circling the area once before disappearing back the way they had come, a slowly shrinking point in the early-winter sky.

Bookbinder took in their surroundings. There was almost nothing to see. As far as his eye could cover, knee-high saw-toothed grass waved in the cold air, patches of mottled brown the only break in the carpet of pale green. He felt a brief moment of disorientation, vertigo. There was no way to tell where they had come from, where they were going.

Sharp tapped his shoulder and pointed behind him. "Sir, it's that way. We need to get moving." Relief flooded him. Crucible hadn't been kidding that he'd found the best, in such company he would be fine. That's what the military was about after all, leaning on the person next to you.

The relief brought his command presence back. "All right," Bookbinder said. "We'll move out in a minute, I just need to check a couple of things. Who's got the comms?"

Archer raised his hand, producing a handset from his backpack. "Do a pulse check with the FOB," Bookbinder said. "I guess you're RTO for this run." Archer nodded and began speaking into the handset in hushed tones.

Bookbinder tried to meet the eyes of each member of the team and did fine until he came to Vasuki-Kai. After a moment, he picked one of the flurry of snake's heads and figured that would have to do. "Remember," he said, "if the comms pulses stop coming, the FOB will send out another team. Per my instructions, that team's objective is *not* to locate or rescue us. That team's objective is to reach the FOB Sarpakavu and secure assistance from the Naga Raja and the government of India. I want everyone to understand that. I'm not calling this a suicide mission. We're too squared away for that. But it is a do-or-die mission, and I want that understood. I hate stupid bumper-sticker slogans like 'failure is not an option.' But this is one of the rare circumstances where it's actually appropriate. Everybody clear?"

The entire team nodded concurrence with the exception of Vasuki-Kai, who hissed questions at Dhatri, who translated back in a low voice. Bookbinder recalled his last words to Crucible before boarding the helo out. *Even with the helo getting us partway, it'll take us the better part of a month to walk the rest of the distance. You have to hold until then.*

Crucible had nodded. *We'll hold, sir.*

"Okay," Bookbinder said. "Remember your fire discipline. Only shoot at what you can hit, and don't shoot unless you have no other option. Remember that Major Woon can Whisper if we run into hostile fauna. I'd rather have her violating the hell out of the McGauer-Linden Act than you wasting precious ammo."

Archer, who had just returned the handset to his pack, raised a hand. "Pulse check is good, sir."

"All right," Bookbinder said, mostly to himself. "Anything else . . . anything else . . ."

"Water-decontamination tablets," Archer said. "You want to distribute those now, sir? I'd feel better if they were spread across the team."

"That's right," Bookbinder said. He produced three pieces of rebar from his cargo pocket, handing one to Archer and one to Sharp and keeping one for himself. "Here ya go."

Sharp looked down at his palm in disbelief. "This is a piece of metal, sir."

Bookbinder nodded. "It'll do the trick. And unlike decontamination tablets, it doesn't run out . . . I think."

Sharp's eyes narrowed, but Woon crowded closer. "I can . . . I think I can feel a current off it . . ."

"You can," he agreed. "I've got tablets as backup, but those'll work."

"Are they magic, sir?"

Bookbinder tapped the side of his nose. "Call it experimental tech. I'm calling it a Bound Magical Energy Repository for now."

"BMER . . ." Woon mused. "Boomer?"

Bookbinder nodded. "Boomer it is. Just sling the questions for now. They work. That's what you need to know."

Woon frowned, and Dhatri and Vasuki-Kai exchanged conversation in their own language, but Sharp and his men shrugged. "What else, sir?"

Bookbinder looked down at the breaching shotgun slung across his chest. "I'm not even qualified on this stupid thing."

"You're just humping it, sir," Sharp said. "Not shooting it."

"You can have the SAW if you want, sir," Anan said, lifting the machine gun slung over his shoulder. It looked at least double the shotgun's weight.

Bookbinder pursed his lips. "Hmm. I think I'll hold what I've got."

Anan chuckled. "Suit yourself, sir. I'm just trying to provide options."

"I appreciate it. Anybody have any questions?"

Nobody did.

"All right, let's go."

Within the first half hour, Bookbinder began to see Crucible's wisdom in suggesting that he stay on the FOB. The rucksack and its straps were padded, and it was balanced as well as it could possibly be. The shotgun was cinched tight across his chest. His helmet, his body armor, his boots were all rigged tight. None of it mattered. The gear still jostled against him as he marched over the uneven terrain, occasionally stumbling as his foot found some hole that the tall grass had concealed. *Go ahead and roll an ankle now, you jackass. That's exactly what we need.* His high boots had supported his ankles thus far, and he stepped gingerly. Regardless, before long his helmet chafed the center of his forehead, his boots rubbed his shins raw. A knot formed over his spine right between his shoulder blades, and the straps of his pack felt like they were digging furrows in the insides of his arms. His breath came in labored puffs. Sweat soaked his helmet liner despite the cold.

"You okay, sir?" Sharp, moving so easily across the ground that he looked like he was floating in spite of his load, looked over at him.

Bookbinder glared back. "Fine . . ." he wheezed. "Fine, thanks. Just . . . don't want you . . . to feel like I'm making you look bad." If Sharp found it funny, he gave no sign. *You wanted to lead this little camping trip. Now suck it up.* But, oh dear God. The light runs he'd done all his life hadn't prepared him for this.

The only other one who seemed to be having a hard time of it was Dhatri, but the Indian officer didn't complain, his eyes eager, fixed ahead. Vasuki-Kai slithered along in the middle of the column, his many heads looking in all directions, towering over them. It somewhat made up for the fact that the naga, being royalty, refused to carry any gear at all, despite his large and powerful frame being capable of hauling more than any three of the humans combined. *Multicultural sensitivity,* Bookbinder thought. *Who'd have ever thought it would apply to other species?*

Bookbinder fell in alongside Fillion. The operator ignored him, eyes on the horizon, scanning for threats. Bookbinder appreciated his alertness, but Vasuki-Kai had all the angles covered, and there was clearly nothing around for miles. He figured now was as good a time as any to get to know his people. A leader should do that.

"Where you from?" he asked.

Fillion ignored him. He repeated the question, and the

specialist finally turned as if noticing him for the first time. "New York, sir." He spoke so quietly that Bookbinder could barely hear.

Bookbinder nodded. "Right. The city?"

Fillion's eyes had already gone back to the horizon. "No, sir."

Bookbinder sighed and turned away. Anan was covering the column's other flank with every bit as much intent silence, so Bookbinder gave up and fell in with Sharp again.

"Your boys are certainly dynamic conversationalists."

"Don't take it personal, sir. They're just focused," Sharp said.

"Focused," Bookbinder replied.

"That's why they call us the quiet professionals."

"Well, they've got the quiet part down."

"They just want to do their best for you, sir, and that means no distractions."

"No distractions, right." Bookbinder kept his peace and marched on.

They made good progress the first day. The only creatures they saw were a pack of what looked like horses, with shaggy-hyena-looking fur coats. They trotted toward the party, keening eerily, their eyeless snouts terminating in a single, sharp-looking tooth.

Anan sighted his SAW as they drew near. Bookbinder could feel Woon Drawing her magic in preparation to Whisper one of them. He hoped they wouldn't have a fight on their hands already. "Hold your fire," he said, waiting to see what the creatures' intentions were. He drew his own pistol and took aim just in case.

"Hud yur feer. Hud yur feer . . ." one of the creatures began to croon, circling them. The crude impression of Bookbinder's voice sent chills down his spine. Dhatri took a knee, aiming his carbine and whispering an oath in Hindi.

Vasuki-Kai hissed what sounded like exasperation, sank into his coiled tail, and sprang into the air. Bookbinder was shocked by how lightly and quickly the giant naga could move. He landed in the midst of the creatures, drawing six of the swords and knives he kept thrust into his sash and hissing a warning, puffing out his chest and shoulders, his heads lashing around him, snapping at the empty air.

The creatures howled, a few of them making shrieking

imitations of Vasuki-Kai's hissing before they scattered, tufted tails tucked between their legs as they raced away. The naga drew a bladed ring from his belt and cast it after one of them; it sliced through the creature's tail before gracefully arcing back to one of his hands. The creature shrieked and put on speed, forming back up with the pack and making for the horizon. Vasuki-Kai's many heads scanned the horizon for threats before he returned his weapons to the sash at his waist. He nodded in satisfaction, slithering his way back to the group and hissing smugly to Dhatri.

"His Highness says that we do not have time to play with animals," Dhatri translated. "He demands we continue along at once."

By the time the Source's big sun began to set, washing all in an intense, almost neon rippling of orange and bruised blue, Bookbinder could see the ground beginning to slope down toward a wide river. Beyond it, he could make out a stand of trees.

"What do you think?" he asked Sharp, as darkness began to cloak them.

"We're making good time," Sharp answered. "Night-vision equipment is good for short ops, but you don't want to be hiking in it, and I don't know what the big guy's night eyes are like." He jerked a thumb over his shoulder at Vasuki-Kai, whose eyes had begun to glow a dull yellow in the failing light.

"All right, let's make camp. I'd like to steer clear of that water until we know what's in it."

Woon conjured a small earthen hut while the rest of them grounded their gear and Bookbinder demonstrated his water-cleaning "boomer" to Sharp in a nearby half-frozen puddle. Sharp shook his head in amazement but didn't hesitate to drink the water out of his cupped hand. Dhatri and Vasuki-Kai watched with great interest, saying nothing.

"Tastes weird," Sharp said. "Like you boiled the hell out of it."

Bookbinder nodded. "It's completely sterile. Naturally occurring water, even filtered stuff, has some contaminants in it. This is totally pure."

Sharp shrugged and drank the rest of the water as Bookbinder turned back to the team.

"No campfire," he ordered. "Let's do MREs tonight and get some shut-eye. Up tomorrow as soon as the light allows. We'll need to set a watch." He lowered his pack to the ground, every muscle in his back and shoulders screaming at him. *You can lead, but you can't exceed your limitations.* "And I can't do the first shift, sorry."

Vasuki-Kai hissed something and Dhatri nodded, slinging his own pack to the ground and stretching gratefully. "His Highness says that watches will be unnecessary. You may all sleep, and he will keep an eye over the camp."

"Doesn't he need to sleep?" Bookbinder asked.

"He will sleep, sir. Naga do not close their eyes, even in sleeping. He will see an enemy coming while he rests."

Sharp cocked an eyebrow. "Can he see in the dark?"

"Not exactly," Dhatri replied. "He can see . . . he can see heat. Or he can taste it. It is very difficult to explain." As if to underscore the point, several of Vasuki-Kai's heads flicked out varicolored forked tongues, tasting the air before returning.

"Sir," Sharp said under his breath. "Are you sure you trust this . . . uh, guy?"

Bookbinder paused a moment, considering the naga. The creature had been willing to reveal secrets precious to the Indian government to help him. "Yes, Sergeant. I do. Implicitly."

That was good enough for Sharp. He shrugged, and his men joined him in stripping out of their gear, wordlessly coordinating their efforts with looks and nods. Within moments, they were disassembling their already immaculate weapons for another cleaning. Woon knelt in the grass beside the shelter, practicing her Whispering on small beetles, whom Bookbinder hadn't noticed because their gray shells were perfectly camouflaged to look like pebbles. Within minutes, she had orderly groups of them trooping up the side of the hut and back down again. Bookbinder smiled and gave her a thumbs-up as she glanced over. She returned the smile with a nod. "Crime pays, sir."

"No crime," Bookbinder answered. "Exigent circumstances. Duly authorized by your CO. Carry on."

Woon did, and Bookbinder wandered off, stripping off the wrapping of his MRE, his legs restless despite the grinding fatigue he felt. Before long, he found himself sucking on a pretzel stick, standing beside Vasuki-Kai. The naga prince stood still as a statue, its tail coiled around Dhatri's pack, heads fanned out in a near-perfect circle, illuminating the thickening darkness with its glowing eyes.

Bookbinder stared at the naga. Was he asleep? How could you even tell? The huge chest rose and fell evenly, but there was no sound of breathing at all though little clouds of warmer air puffed in and out of dozens of pairs of nostrils.

After a moment, one of the heads arced, turned sideways, and fixed him with a single yellow eye. It hissed briefly.

Dhatri's voice sounded from behind him. "His Highness asks why you are staring at him."

Bookbinder blinked. "Please apologize to His Highness. I was just trying to figure out if he was sleeping. With my people, you can always tell because our eyes are closed."

The snake's head hissed again. "His Highness is sleeping," Dhatri said. "But if you have any questions, he will permit you to ask them."

Bookbinder tried not to let his confusion show. He had many questions. For one thing, he hadn't seen the naga eat. Wasn't it hungry? "No, no questions. I'm sorry to have disturbed you . . . er . . . I'm sorry to have disturbed His Highness."

Bookbinder turned to go, but the single head hissed again. "His Highness asks why you chose to come on this mission."

Bookbinder turned back to the head, struggling to overcome his instinct to address Dhatri directly. "Excuse me?"

"His Highness is merely returning home, and it is the custom of princes to be envoys. But he understands that among Americans, you send an . . . what is the word? An attaché. You are a commander. This is not your custom."

Bookbinder thought for a while before answering, "His Highness is right. But . . . I guess I'm not a very good commander. I figured I'd be better off doing this."

The snake's head paused before hissing again, more urgently. "His Highness says he thinks you are an excellent commander. He says if you were a real . . . um . . . an Indian officer, you would be a brigadier, and he would request you lead our installation in the Naga Raajya."

Bookbinder was glad that the darkness concealed his flush. "His Highness is too kind."

"His Highness has never said a thing like that about an American before."

"I don't know what to say. How did . . . you two get together?" Bookbinder asked, trying to overcome the awkward silence his discomfort with praise had caused. "Your races . . ."

"The naga came to us," Dhatri said. "They had already done some reconnaissance of the Home Plane, and when the Great Reawakening took hold, they sent a delegation, but to see about their 'cousins' . . ."

"You mean snakes?"

"Just so." Dhatri nodded. "Of course, they were disappointed to see that they were still . . . animals. People, on the other hand, had come a long way since the last Reawakening. They had dealt with us before, but it was only now that we had evolved to the point where the *Bandhav* relationships could be implemented. We had certain modern technologies in which they were interested."

"Do any live with you in the Home Plane?"

Dhatri shook his head. "They do not even visit. That is through stringent agreement between my government and the Naga Raja."

"And Vasuki-Kai is your . . . *Bandhav*? How does that work?"

"It is complicated," Dhatri answered. "Naga princes will usually become fond of a human, we are somewhat like their children. They teach us their ways, and we teach them ours."

"It's one to one?"

"Yes, sir. One naga will take one human *Bandhav* for that human's entire life, for naga always outlive people. When we die, they sometimes take another, sometimes not. I am very fortunate to be the first one chosen by His Highness. I have taught him Hindi and he has taught me to understand his speech; they have a special version they use for us. A human could never hope to understand how naga communicate with each other."

"Why'd he pick you? I mean . . . you're a great guy and everything, I just . . ."

Dhatri laughed. "It's all right, sir. I am not offended. We don't know why naga choose their *Bandhavs*. They say they know when they have met the one."

Bookbinder cocked an eyebrow. "Sounds very intimate."

"It is," Dhatri answered seriously. "It is a love like family."

Vasuki-Kai hissed again and Dhatri translated "His Highness asks if you have eggs . . . He means children, sir. He is asking after your family."

"Two girls," Bookbinder said. "And a wife. I miss them very much."

"His Highness says that family is the most important thing in life. He says very few of his people get to make families, but he has had that honor. He proudly tells you that he has had three successful clutches. This is very unusual among the naga. His Highness has ninety children."

Bookbinder tried to sound enthusiastic. "You must congratulate His Highness for me."

The single head nodded, pride evident in the regal movement. "His Highness asks if you have word from your family?"

"No," Bookbinder said. "Not since we got cut off. To be honest, very little before then either."

The head hissed empathically. "His Highness says that once we reach his kingdom, he will speak personally to the Raja on your behalf about putting you in contact with your family."

Bookbinder swallowed hard, grateful for the dark as a tear tracked its way down his cheek. "His Highness is enormously kind," he said. "But I'm sure he knows I must first see to the welfare of my troops."

Dhatri nodded. "His Highness commends your concern for your people. He is certain the Raja will be moved by your compassion and assist. He is a merciful king."

Bookbinder looked up, meeting the snake's eyes firmly. "I dearly hope so," he said.

"I dearly hope so."

The river was wider than Bookbinder had thought. He could make out the far bank, but only just, mostly by virtue of some kind of long-necked birds congregating on the far side. Tiny insects, their vibrating wings making a sound like tinkling glass, darted to and fro in the dying rushes along the bank.

"Well, shit," Bookbinder said, staring through a pair of field binoculars. "I don't suppose we can go around it."

"Not without losing a whole lot of time," Sharp said.

"And I take it we can't ford here," Bookbinder said.

Sharp arched his eyebrows and said nothing.

"Well, shit," Bookbinder repeated. "Can you bridge it?" he asked Woon.

The major shrugged. "It's a hell of a stretch, sir, but I can try."

"If you can, I'll give you a . . ." Bookbinder paused. "Well, I don't have anything to give you. I'll pat you on the back."

"I'll take it," Woon said, making her way into the rushes. Bookbinder felt her tide gathering as she Drew, then focusing as she Bound the magic into the river mud. The river's dark surface rippled and broke as a dripping mud bridge, wide enough to accommodate two people abreast, lifted through it, slowly making its way toward the far bank.

"Outstanding," Bookbinder said.

"Not there yet, sir," Woon grunted.

The bridge continued to split the river, the current washing chunks of it away before Woon formed it into arches that allowed the water to wash beneath it. It marched forward, painfully slow, until it finally reached the other side. Woon tested the surface with her toe, and her boot sank into the soft mud, coming out dripping. "Save that pat, sir," she said and redoubled her efforts. She grunted, and Bookbinder watched as the mud dried rapidly, the bridge hardening, solidifying from one end to the other.

At last, Woon sat down, removing her helmet and mopping her brow. "Okay . . ." she gasped. "Pat . . . pat."

Bookbinder thumped her on the shoulder. "Outstanding, Major."

Woon waved at him and said nothing.

Sharp nodded to Anan, who stepped onto the bridge, SAW at the low ready. It supported the big man's weight with all his gear easily. He nodded back at Sharp and continued across.

"All righty," Bookbinder said. "Let's get a move on." He started forward.

Sharp's hand on his shoulder stopped him. "Let my boys get a look at the far bank first, sir, if you don't mind."

Bookbinder stopped short, embarrassed. "Of course, Sergeant. Good idea."

Anan crossed the bridge slowly, raising the SAW and sighting down it as he walked. He swept the muzzle left and right, shoulders tense, as he approached the waving grass and moved several feet into it before taking a knee. After what felt like an eternity, he finally raised a hand and beckoned behind him.

Fillion jogged out onto the bridge, his posture more relaxed with Anan covering the far end. Bookbinder felt some of the tension fall out of his own shoulders. If hard men like Sharp's operators were calm, then so was he.

There was a rumble, a huge sloshing sound, and a shadow fell across Fillion. It took Bookbinder a moment to realize that it had fallen across all of them, blanketing the bridge, the operators, both banks.

Bookbinder looked up and blinked.

An eighty-foot stretch of the river had stood, the water coursing down a concave back as wide as a mountain pass. A wedge-shaped head dripped rivulets of green water, coursing over scales in mottled shades of blue, green, and pale yellow. Eyes the size of truck tires slid toward them beneath nictitating membranes milky with algae.

Fillion took one look and bolted for the far side of the bridge where Anan had spun, raising his SAW, not bothering to fire, understanding that 5.56-millimeter ammunition would do little more than make a creature that big angry. Sharp raised his own weapon, then lowered it just as fast, turning toward Archer, who was already loading a round into the grenade launcher mounted to the underside of his carbine. Their movements were smooth, the only indication that they hadn't dealt with creatures like this a hundred times was a slight tenseness in their jaws.

The monster lunged forward, moving almost leisurely, the underside of its steam-shovel jaw driving through the bridge just behind Fillion's boot, knocking all of Woon's work into clods of mud as easily as a house of cards.

Anan grabbed Fillion by the handle on his body armor and dragged him back from the bank, keeping the SAW leveled at the monster with one hand. Bookbinder didn't think it would take a lot of aiming to hit the thing, for all the good it would do. He spun toward Dhatri and froze. Both the subedar major and his *Bandhav* were prostrate on the riverbank. Dhatri looked ridiculous, thumping his forehead against the ground, but it was nothing compared to Vasuki-Kai, hissing madly, his heads spread out like a fan, slithering in the mud, as low as possible.

Bookbinder was about to ask what the hell they were doing when a roar turned him away from the kowtowing and back to the monster, which had backed away from the wreckage of the bridge. Its huge bulk rose, six crocodilian legs flailing in the air. Dhatri and Vasuki-Kai bowed and scraped, Sharp and his men backed away slowly, weapons raised.

Woon! Where the hell is Woon?

Bookbinder felt panic race across his gut as the giant thing came back down. He felt the instinct to cringe and raise his arms to protect himself but overrode the habit with a will. Like it or not, he was the leader of this little expedition. If Sharp and his men could be cool under fire, then so could he.

The giant creature twisted in midair, its huge torso wheeling away from the shattered bridge and slamming back into the river, its huge tail whipping over the far bank. Anan and Fillion cried out and disappeared as it covered them. The monster grunted, the sound of air brakes on a bus, and began to reluctantly slosh downriver, each step strained, as if unsure of the direction it wanted to go, slowly lowering itself into the water as it went.

Vasuki-Kai and Dhatri continued their prostrations without looking up.

"Woon! Major Woon!" Bookbinder shouted frantically, racing toward the bank.

"I'm okay, sir." Woon sloshed her way up the bank, soaked to the waist. "I'm more worried about them." She gestured to the far bank.

"I think they're okay, sir," Sharp said, sighting through his carbine's scope. Bookbinder could see vague dark forms in the grass, moving. "Yeah, they're okay." Sharp said.

"That was the *Makara*," Dhatri said as he approached with Vasuki-Kai in tow, hissing. "The goddess of the river. We are fortunate to have escaped with our lives."

Bookbinder frowned. "That thing was female?"

Dhatri ignored the question as he translated for his *Bandhav*. "His Highness says you are very fortunate to have us along with you because we knew to behave with proper reverence and supplication. Only by observing the proper custom was disaster turned aside."

"Thank His Highness for me," Bookbinder said. "Please excuse me for a moment."

He moved into the longer grass down by the river's edge, where Woon was vainly trying to dry herself, shivering in the cold. "Are you okay?"

"I'll be fine so long as I don't freeze to death, sir."

"Well, get into some dry clothes. I promise not to look while you get changed." He cast a quick glance over his shoulder, to where Dhatri and Vasuki-Kai chatted animatedly. "You Whispered that thing away, didn't you?"

Woon nodded, smiling. "Never thought it'd come in handy before today, sir."

"Do me a favor, don't go mentioning that to our foreign partners, okay?"

Woon's smile faded. "Okay, sir."

Bookbinder tapped his temple. "Diplomacy."

"Stuff of kings, sir. What now?"

"Now you dry off. Then you make us another bridge."

They were clear of the woods beyond the river in a few hours. Bookbinder felt relief as they pushed out of the shadows and strange sounds. The Source was an unmapped, alien landscape. Could a brush against a flower petal give him a sickness that would kill him overnight? Was there some beast crouching in the branches overhead, waiting to spring on them? The FOB, for all its austerity, suddenly felt like the height of civilization.

The landscape beyond the woods returned to the endless sea of waving saw-toothed grass. A horned serpent's head rose above the grass, regarding them silently as they trekked past, joined a moment later by a second. Sharp sighted down his carbine at it, but Vasuki-Kai slapped the barrel down with an angry hiss. Sharp nodded, not needing Dhatri to translate the naga's affinity for snakes of any kind.

After a full day's march, Bookbinder became convinced that he smelled smoke. The odor strengthened as they marched over the next day, and he noted Vasuki-Kai's many tongues unfurling to taste the air with greater and greater frequency. The naga began to look agitated and conversed with Dhatri in hushed tones.

"Smell that?" Bookbinder asked Sharp.

"Yes, sir. Forest fire. Maybe a grass fire. But I don't feel any heat. Must not be close enough yet."

"No," Bookbinder said. "This smells like . . . other stuff burning. Maybe rubber? Metal?"

Sharp's eyes narrowed slightly. "You're right." He made a wide circle, sighting through his carbine's scope. "Nothing."

The smell worsened as they pressed on. At last it was so thick that Bookbinder began to cough. The air become hazy.

"Sir"—Dhatri tugged on his elbow—"we have to stop."

"Why?"

Dhatri pointed off to his left. "We need to go in this direction."

Bookbinder looked at Sharp, and the sergeant shook his head.

"That's not the way we're headed," Bookbinder said.

"I know, sir, but His Highness informs me that we are heading into very dangerous territory, and we will need to go around it."

Bookbinder sighed. "How far is this detour?"

Dhatri turned to Vasuki-Kai and asked a question in Hindi. The naga replied with a burst of hissing. "His Highness says approximately two weeks on foot."

"Dhatri, you know the FOB doesn't have that kind of time. I told Crucible a month, and we've already burned a quarter of that. Now, what's the problem?"

Vasuki-Kai gesticulated, but Dhatri put a hand on his elbow. "The Naga Raajya have a mortal enemy in the agni danav, whose own Raajya lies some distance from them. The agni danav are terrible monsters. I have seen them with my own eyes, sir."

Bookbinder shook his head. Just when he thought he was coming to grips with the Source's strangeness, something like this came along.

"Their territory must have expanded since we last came to the FOB," Dhatri went on. "His Highness is very troubled by this. We had hoped to skirt the Agni Danav Raajya, but I think that is not possible now. We must go around."

"How can you know this?" Bookbinder asked.

"His Highness's senses are keener than mine," Dhatri said,

indicating the naga's many flicking tongues. "But even a human nose can smell the damage from here. The agni danav only suffer that which does not burn to live."

Bookbinder turned to Woon and Sharp. "Well?"

Sharp shrugged. "Not my call, sir."

Woon nodded. "Sir, two weeks could make the difference between holding on and not holding on."

"Sharp? I want your input here," Bookbinder said.

"I'm not in the habit of going around dangerous spots, sir."

Bookbinder turned back to Dhatri. "I need your honest, bottom-line, no-bullshit assessment, Subedar Major. What are we walking into here? Is this going to be tough? Or is it suicide?"

Dhatri turned to Vasuki-Kai, and Bookbinder stopped him with a hand on his shoulder. "Um, I don't suppose you'd mind making that question a bit more polite before you translate?"

Dhatri smiled, then spoke to his *Bandhav* for a long time. At last, he turned back.

"His Highness says he has fought the agni danav before and defeated them. He is confident in my safety because I am his *Bandhav* and so, his blood. But he cannot speak for you though he does not doubt your courage."

Bookbinder looked back at Sharp and Woon. "We'll be fine, sir," they said in near-perfect synchronicity, then looked at each other in surprise and laughed.

Bookbinder turned back to Dhatri. "No detour. We press on."

After another few hours, the landscape began to change. The grass slowly gave up its green, ceding first to pale yellow and, finally, to withered brown. The stink of brimstone became overpowering, choking them until Sharp removed cloths from his backpack, soaked them in water, and passed them around. Tied over the nose and mouth, they made the trip bearable, but only just. They squinted through air becoming thick with gray smoke, first warm and finally hot. At last, all vegetation petered out, and they found themselves crunching across ground dusted with fine, gray ash. Within moments, it covered them from head to foot.

What the hell did I just get us into? Bookbinder considered turning back, and again decided against it. The FOB didn't have time. Bookbinder had told Crucible it would take them roughly a month. The loss of two weeks to a detour would leave his XO way beyond that window. They hadn't come out here to be comfortable. They'd come out here to save lives, at the expense of their own, if necessary.

A blue flash lit through the smoke before him. Bookbinder stopped, putting his hand on Sharp's arm. The sergeant raised a fist and signaled a halt, then sighted down his carbine into the smoking haze. "What is it, sir?"

"I thought . . . I could have sworn . . . There it is again!" Bookbinder pointed at another bright blue flash, then another alongside it. "You see that?"

"I see it, sir. Wait here." Sharp pushed into the smoke, disappearing for a few agonizing moments. Then his voice came drifting back to Bookbinder. "I think you should come take a look at this, sir."

Bookbinder walked into the smoke. Sharp materialized, standing beside the source of the blue glow.

It was a lizard, its thick, mottled skin softly emanating dull blue light, mysteriously free of the ash dust that coated the rest of them. "There's a bunch of 'em around, sir," Sharp said. "They don't seem scared, but they won't let me get close either."

Bookbinder took a step toward the creature and leaned down, extending a hand before jerking it suddenly back. The lizard scuttled away, skittish at his closeness.

"Jesus, Sergeant. It's cold. The air around it is freezing."

"Yeah," Sharp said. "I noticed that. Must be how they survive in this. I haven't seen anything else alive."

"Well, I'm going to call that a good thing," Bookbinder said. "Let's take a rest, grab some chow before we move on."

They did their best, gathering around a chest-high boulder that was the sole marker on the otherwise featureless landscape. The ash dust got into their rapidly dwindling supply of MREs the moment they opened them, and they raced to get the food in their mouths once they'd rinsed it off with the water in the portable bladders on their backs. They sweated in the oppressive heat, tugging at the collars on their body armor. "Feels like we're sitting too close to a campfire," Woon said.

Bookbinder put his MRE on his pack and stood up. "I've got an idea about that. Get clear of this rock."

"Sir?" Woon asked as the group gave the boulder a wide berth.

"Just trust me." He strode out to where more blue flashes indicated the presence of the ubiquitous lizards. He stood beside one and Drew his magic, Binding it to the weak but chilly current he felt washing off one of them. Once he felt his own being suffused with it, he turned and sighted the boulder, Binding it hard. The rock shook gently, then turned blue, the ridge tinged with white frost.

Bookbinder trotted back over, holding his hands over it, feeling the cold air wash over him. He sighed. "That's more like it."

He looked at the rest of the group, all eyeing him with wide-eyed amazement.

"I thought you were a Latent Grenade." Woon's eyes narrowed. "The boomers . . . the things you use to clean the water. I know what . . . your magic is now."

Bookbinder cocked an eyebrow. "Life's full of surprises," he said. "Grab some cold, and we'll get a move on."

CHAPTER XVIII
FIELD OF FIRE

Count on the US to do it completely wrong. The so-called "Selfer" commune the SOC shut down in Portland? They were making tomatoes the size of your head, stalks of wheat with triple the yield. They could have fed whole villages of starving Pakistanis. But that's not acceptable. Too dangerous, the government says. Using Terramancy to build better roads to move tanks or ammunition? That's just fine. Firming up the walls for armories and combat outposts? Good use of Terramancy. Growing superfoods to feed the world? Threat to national security.

—Amy Rutledge, Professor of Political Science, Harvard University
    Speaking before the Great Reawakening Commission, US Senate

The ground rose as they marched on, the added exertion of the climb exhausting them in the choking ash dust and heat. Bookbinder permitted them to loosen the straps on their body armor, but it was all he would allow. They were on dangerous ground, and he wouldn't have them caught flat-footed. They proceeded in silence, only the Special Forces operators giving no indicator of discomfort.

The ground continued to rise sharply for another hour, then at long last it stopped so suddenly that Bookbinder had to catch himself, pinwheeling his arms briefly as he recovered his balance.

The haze cleared, revealing a vista that Bookbinder could only describe as the traditional vision of hell.

As far as the eye could see, the plain was reduced to ash. It looked like the scoured bottom of a furnace, completely featureless save for cracked and broken rocks, glowing red-hot. Here and there, plumes of fire belched skyward, emitting tendrils of black, noisome smoke. The heat hit them like a wall. Bookbinder realized that the ridge they'd been climbing had blocked the worst of it, and now they were facing the furnace's full force. In an instant, he had soaked through his uniform, helmet liner, the padding beneath his body armor and rucksack.

Dhatri coughed. "This is bad, sir. The agni danav burn everything. Their Terramancy is nasty stuff. They raise . . . what is the English for a mountain that shoots fire?"

Bookbinder thought for a moment. "Volcanoes?"

Dhatri nodded. "They raise volcanoes that shower everything with ash. There must be a new one fairly close to have done this."

"Holy shit," Bookbinder breathed, then lapsed into a fit of coughing. Beside him, Sharp nodded.

Apart from the blue flashes of the cold lizards, Bookbinder thought he could make out large pillars of flame moving about, black cores gesturing. Bookbinder glanced down the sheer wall of the ridge to where it terminated in the field of ash. Some of lizards congregated there, their splayed toes carrying them across the surface much like snowshoes, leaving soggy pools of semiliquid ash in their wake.

"We've got to cross this, huh?" Bookbinder asked.

Sharp nodded, then pointed down the ridge. "There's a tumble there. Remnants of an avalanche, I'd guess. Should be able to scramble down."

"You . . . uh . . . you want to recon it first?"

Sharp looked at him, smiling beneath the cloth covering his face. "You catch on fast, sir." He gestured to Fillion, who nodded, slung his carbine, and began picking his way down the rock scramble, so steep that it was more of a climb. Anan took a knee along the ridge, covering his comrade with the SAW.

Bookbinder held his breath until Fillion reached the bottom. The operator coughed, patting at his gloves, which smoldered from the hot surface of the ridge side. He gave a thumbs-up, then turned to the smooth surface of ash powder before him. He tested it with his boot tip, then knelt and dabbed at it with a finger. At last he cupped a hand over his mouth and called back up to Sharp. "It's not hot!"

Sharp gave him a thumbs-up and moved to the top of the scramble. Fillion turned, planted his boot on the ash, and put his weight on it.

The ash swallowed him faster than Bookbinder could blink.

Sharp cursed and began descending the ridge side so fast that he fell rather than climbed down, calling for Archer. Bookbinder turned to Woon. "Get him up!"

"On it." Woon raced to the top of the scramble. Bookbinder could feel her current Drawing fast and hard.

Sharp paced at the edge of the ash sea, twisting his hands, muttering under his breath, "Stupid, stupid, stupid." It was the first time Bookbinder ever saw the man lose his composure. Bookbinder scrambled down to stand at his side as the ash began to churn before them. A moment later, a hardened platform of the stuff, roughly ten feet across, rose in response to Woon's magic. Fillion sprawled across it, his weapon, helmet, and pack missing. Covered in ash dust, he looked like a gray sculpture depicting a man in agony. His mouth was open, a small stream of ash pouring from it below twin trickles from his nose.

Sharp leapt to the hardened platform. Archer scrambled down and joined him. The two men knelt at Fillion's side for the briefest of moments before Sharp stood, his flinty demeanor returned. "He's dead, sir."

You should say something to comfort them. But all Bookbinder could say was, "Are you sure?"

Sharp nodded. He composed the corpse, laying Fillion gently on his back, crossing his arms over his chest. He ripped he American flag patch off his shoulder and pressed it into the palm of his hand, then he reached into the man's breast pocket and removed a small package wrapped in plastic. He tucked it into his pocket and glanced up at the ridgetop, where Anan nodded to him, making his way to the scramble.

Sharp and Archer retrieved what gear they could, then returned to the ash's edge. The sergeant nodded to Woon. "Send him back down, ma'am."

Woon hesitated. Bookbinder asked, "Is there something you'd like to do for him?"

Sharp shook his head, his voice barely a whisper. "We've done it, sir. We need to get moving."

Dhatri translated for Vasuki-Kai, who joined them at the

ridge's bottom. "His Highness says you should clean and cremate the body, so that he may join Yama Raja in paradise. His Highness will be glad to serve as a mourner for you."

Sharp shot the naga a dangerous look and said nothing.

"Please thank His Highness and inform him that this man must be laid to rest in accordance with his own custom," Bookbinder said quickly. He turned to Woon without waiting for a reply. "Send him back down, Major. Now, please."

Woon nodded and dropped her arms. The hardened platform went with them, and Fillion disappeared for the second time.

Vasuki-Kai bridled at the action and looked as if he might argue, but a number of his heads suddenly jerked to the side, tongues darting. He hissed a warning to Dhatri.

"They are coming," the subedar major said.

Bookbinder looked up. Two of the black, flame-wreathed shapes had ceased their roaming and angled toward them purposefully. Vasuki-Kai hissed again and drove his hands into his sash. They emerged with a bladed arsenal that weaved in time with his darting heads, a dancing cloud of threats.

"His Highness says there will be battle. Your Terramancer may wish to give us suitable ground."

Woon nodded and the ash around them solidified. Sharp pointed to Archer, who took cover in some of the rocks. Anan scrambled back up to the ridge, popping the release on the SAW's bipod. Feeling useless, Bookbinder racked the shotgun's slide. If Sharp had doubts about his ability to use it, he kept them to himself.

Dhatri took cover in the coils of Vasuki-Kai's tail, sighting down his carbine.

The shapes materialized as they drew closer. They were huge. Each one was at least eight feet tall, bigger even than Vasuki-Kai. Their bodies were human, cartoonishly muscular. Their hairless skin was a deep bronze, almost orange. A triangle of black hair marked their chests. Their heads were enormous, horned and fanged, a twisted parody of a buffalo. Orange eyes burned with rage, black pupils fixed on them. Their entire bodies, their black-furred heads, their wicked-looking maces, all were wreathed in wicked flame. The ground around them sparkled as they came.

Glass, Bookbinder thought. *They're melting the ash to glass. These fuckers must be hotter than hell.*

"Agni danav," Dhatri said. His carbine cracked.

A flash of fire on one of the creatures' torsos indicated the round's impact. The agni danav grunted, a bovine sound, and kept coming. From the ridgeline, Anan's SAW set up a rhythmic thumping. The ash around the agni danav exploded in dust and splintered glass. The flame cloud around the creatures exploded with white-hot pinpoints where the rounds impacted. Sharp and Archer added fire. A dull, thudding explosion burst just behind the creatures as one of Archer's grenades impacted.

The agni danav didn't slow.

Bookbinder felt Woon's magic Bind before him and the ash slammed upward into a hard wall. The agni danav lowered their horned heads and smashed through it, only paces away now.

Vasuki-Kai hissed a battle cry that Dhatri echoed in Hindi. *"Har Har Mahadev!"* He sprang from his coils, his forest of swords and snapping heads extending to meeting them. Bookbinder raised the shotgun and yanked on the trigger. It resisted solidly. *You left the safety on, idiot.*

The first agni danav met Vasuki-Kai's blur of attacks, parrying with its mace with blinding speed, leaning forward to snap at the naga with its fanged head. Within moments, the naga's weapons glowed dull red. The darting snake's heads snapped and hissed but couldn't land a bite, yanking back from the intense heat surrounding the agni danav.

An automaton of ash rose out of the ground, clenching its fists and delivering a double hammerblow to the side of the other agni danav, who lowed, doubling over, as it slammed its mace into the thing's head, shattering it and sending clouds of ash scattering over them. Woon snarled and the automaton fell back, the head re-forming.

The agni danav pressed forward, the withering fire from Sharp's and Anan's weapons incinerating on contact with the flames surrounding them. The first recovered from Vasuki-Kai's onslaught and began to beat the naga back. Vasuki-Kai's weapons glowed white-hot now as he traded blows with the creature. Dhatri backpedaled behind him, changing magazines and angling for a clear shot.

The second agni danav dodged Woon's re-formed automaton and leapt for her. Bookbinder jumped between them, finally thumbing the safety off and firing the shotgun at the creature's face. The weapon kicked like a mule, sending him sprawling. The frangible slug shattered and burned up in the agni danav's flame halo, the burning shards peppering its face. It blinked furiously, stumbling backward. It recovered quickly, shaking its head and raising its mace to crush Bookbinder. He backpedaled as fast as he could, racking the shotgun's slide, knowing that he wouldn't get out of the way of the descending ball of black iron in time.

And then the agni danav lowed, knocked to the side by a huge boulder that had tumbled down the ridge side. Anan knelt at the crest, SAW abandoned, having guessed that rocks could succeed where bullets were failing. The agni danav grunted and threw the boulder off, forcing Bookbinder to dodge. It struggled to its feet, clutching its ribs, then swept its mace at Woon's automaton. Off to his left, Bookbinder could hear Vasuki-Kai hissing and snapping as the other agni danav continued to push him back.

They couldn't sustain this. They were holding the monsters at bay, but they weren't hurting them.

And these were only two. A quick glance out at the sea of ash around them showed Bookbinder there were many, many more.

Bookbinder raised the shotgun and blasted the agni danav in the face again, stunning it. He turned, and shouted to Woon, "Forget the automaton! Get the lizards in the fight!"

Woon cursed and turned. Her ashen creation froze as the agni danav shook its head and swiped at its eyes, only to rock under another onslaught of popping rounds as Anan got behind the SAW again.

The agni danav threw its head back and roared, then swung toward Bookbinder. It flexed its shoulders, throwing out its arms and sending out a pulse wave of shimmering heat that blew him off his feet, beating at the smoldering shotgun sling, dangerously close to his face. It lowed again, then charged, raising a giant foot over his face.

Bookbinder struggled to get the shotgun around and fumbled it, smacking himself in the chin with the now-smoking-hot barrel. "Gaaaah!!!! Fuckfuckfuckyoufucker!" he shouted, squeezing his eyes shut as the agni danav's foot hurtled toward his head.

Gusts of chill air breezed over his face, the agni danav lowed in terror, and no blow fell.

Bookbinder opened his eyes. Three of the blue lizards

swarmed up the giant creature's thighs, leaving gray, smoking tracks where they touched it. It screamed, flailing at them, then jerking its hands away as they smoked on contact. The other agni danav had turned from Vasuki-Kai, its eyes widening at the normally skittish creatures, suddenly organized and on the attack. Vasuki-Kai pressed the offense, his blades whirling through the flame halo and scoring a half dozen deep cuts on the agni danav's chest. It shrieked and took off running, its companion took another halfhearted swipe at the lizards steadily climbing its chest, then its eyes rolled up to the whites, its mouth frothing, and it turned and ran, shaking the lizards off, following its partner into the distance.

Bookbinder glanced over his shoulder to see Woon, hands outstretched, a smug smile on her broad face.

He bent double, hands on his knees breathing hard. "You . . . are . . . getting . . . a . . . medal. If we ever . . . get out of this, that is."

Woon smiled, relaxing her magic as the agni danav disappeared in the distance. "I'll be sure to remind you of that, sir."

As Anan joined them, Bookbinder did a quick check of the team. Everyone looked sweaty and exhausted. No one looked hurt. Some agni danav circled in the distance, and a few broke off, moving toward their fleeing foes, but none approached closer. "I think we put the fear of God into them," Bookbinder mused. "I don't think these guys are used to losing."

"His Highness says your Terramancer is a great boon to you," Dhatri said. "He has never seen the agni danav run before."

Bookbinder nodded. "I'm very lucky."

Woon shrugged.

"When we arrive at the Raajya, His Highness will petition the Raja to grant your Terramancer the *Maha Vir Chakra*. It's quite an honor."

Bookbinder was too exhausted for formalities. He merely nodded thanks.

He pulled the water bladder feed from his shoulder and gulped at it hungrily, spitting the dust from his mouth. "Everybody drink," he commanded. A moment later he turned to Woon. "If we're going to cross this, you've got your work cut out for you. You're going to need to keep a bridge going the whole way. Can you do that?"

Woon nodded. "I think so, but if they decide to jump us, and I have to Whisper at the same time . . . that's going to be pushing it, sir."

Bookbinder nodded and thought for a moment, then turned to Sharp. "Sergeant, pass me a round?" Sharp looked askance at him and gestured to the bandolier of shotgun slugs built into his own rucksack's shoulder strap. Bookbinder shook his head in embarrassment. "Sorry." He eased a shell out and turned back to Woon. "Major, another lizard, if you please."

Woon glanced off into the distance and gestured. A moment later, one of the glowing blue reptiles came trotting toward them, stopping just short of Bookbinder's feet. The entire group moved instinctively toward it, grateful for the chill air wafting off its skin.

Bookbinder Drew his magic and siphoned off the magical cold from the creature's skin, then Bound it into the shotgun slug, careful to confine the magic to the projectile, away from the powder. His fingers went numb through the gloves, and he moved quickly to slam the round into the shotgun's magazine tube. The metal began to sweat as the cold inside it reacted against the heat around them. Bookbinder worked the pump action quickly, ejecting the normal shells to patter on the hardened ash around him. When he got to the bottom of the magazine tube, he shouldered the shotgun and aimed at the ridge side.

He pulled the trigger and the weapon boomed, kicking fiercely into his shoulder. The slug sped from the barrel, leaving a white-blue streak in the air. It slammed into the ridge side, sending chips of rock flying. An instant later, a frozen patch of ice expanded across the surface, growing until it was a few feet in diameter.

Anan whistled. Vasuki-Kai hissed in appreciation. "That might do it," Sharp said.

"Okay," Bookbinder said. "Take another five to gather your wits, then"—he turned to Woon—"let's get started on a road across this mess."

They pushed on at a near trot. Bookbinder wanted them beyond the edge of this wasteland as quickly as possible and was willing to drive them as hard as necessary to achieve it. Woon worked the bridge, keeping the ground firming up before them as fast as they could jog. At first Bookbinder was hesitant, fearing running off the edge and drowning in the ashen depths as Fillion had, but at last he learned to trust in Woon's magic and forged ahead with all the steam an exhausted, overburdened, middle-aged man could muster. Fillion's death lingered at the back of his mind. Whatever the man's experience, however hard-bitten, he was still Bookbinder's responsibility. The thought ate at him, and Bookbinder forced himself to turn his thoughts to the task at hand. When night fell, Bookbinder refused to make camp. "We push on," he said. "If we can get clear of this in forty-eight hours, we can sleep all we want on the far side." If others saw a problem with his reasoning, they didn't mention it.

The agni danav tried to take them after another ten hours of solid marching. A cluster of them, Bookbinder guessed maybe five or six, gathered together across their path and began to move forward in a deliberate line. Woon stopped the bridge without a word and Whispered one of the blue lizards over as Bookbinder gestured for one of the SAW's magazines. He magicked as many of the rounds as he could manage, drawing off the lizard's freezing magic until he felt the agni danav had come close enough. He handed the drum back to Anan, juggling it to keep the chill from penetrating too deeply through his gloves. The Special Forces operator slammed it into his weapon and took a knee, aiming carefully.

"Don't miss," Bookbinder groused.

"I'm terrible at missing, sir," Anan said, and pulled the trigger. A burst of three rounds arced blue over the distance, impacting in the distant flame columns that marked the agni danav's approach. Some of the fires went out, wafting black smoke skyward. Bookbinder could hear the throaty lows of agony even from this distance. Anan kept aiming but held his fire. After a moment, the agni danav dispersed, breaking to either side and vanishing into the distance.

Anan finally lowered his weapon and thumbed the magazine release, letting the drum drop to the ground.

He winced, pulling a hand back from the now-freezing gun. "This can't be good for the weapon, sir," he said.

Bookbinder chuckled. "Fortunately, it's not good for the agni danav either."

Anan looked at him and smiled.

They pushed on.

CHAPTER XIX
THIEVES

*Magic sure as hell hasn't changed human nature. We're every bit
as avaricious and nasty as we ever were. The only real difference
is now we've got shiny new tools to make each other suffer.*

—Dan Steele, Lieutenant
Seventieth Precinct, New York City Police Department

Bookbinder ran. The whole world narrowed, coalescing into the
bobbing of the horizon, the dryness in his throat, the steady
crunching of his boots across Woon's bridge. His vision wavered,
drifting in darkness that might have been his eyelids fluttering
in exhaustion, or the simple blackness of night. At last, he gave
up on sight, relying only on the steady crunching of his boot
soles and the labored rhythm of his breathing. He was grateful
for the fatigue, the unending rhythm of forward movement.
It helped keep his mind off the fact that he had just lost his
first man.

Crunch. Pant. Crunch. Pant. Crunch. Pant. Tap. Tap. Tap.

Bookbinder stopped. The sound of his footfalls had changed.
His body screamed at him to lie down, to gulp water, to do anything but keep moving. He fended off the exhaustion and looked
down. The ground was no longer an unbroken field of ash. He
looked over his shoulder. Grass, albeit brown and mottled yellow, had begun to populate the ground in small clumps behind
them, dawn slowly breaking beyond.

Bookbinder wracked his tired mind and realized he had no
clue how long they'd been walking, how they'd come here.
Somewhere in the fog of their march, they'd left the vast burned

landscape of the Agni Danav Raajaya and returned to a world where plants grew. He breathed deeply. The stench of brimstone was still thick, but nowhere near what it had been. He looked up and saw stars winking back at him, big and beautiful, largely unobscured by smoke.

The entire group stopped with him, swaying on their feet, asking no questions, simply grateful to bring an end to forward movement. Sharp alone looked lucid. Bookbinder turned to him. "What do you think?"

Sharp looked behind them, then back at Bookbinder. "I'd say we're clear, sir."

Forty-eight hours. We've been running with almost no breaks for forty-eight hours.

Bookbinder nodded. The next moment, he was sitting in the grass with his back propped against his pack, with no recollection of how he'd gotten there. When had he taken his helmet off?

He looked up at Vasuki-Kai, unable to read what passed for fatigue in one of his kind. "You've got . . . I mean you can sleep with your eyes open, right?"

For once, the naga did not ask Dhatri to translate. He merely bent down and patted Bookbinder's shoulder, a few of his heads nodding agreement. Then he straightened, the heads spreading in the fan posture he always adopted when standing watch, looking in all directions simultaneously, eyes glowing in the dark. Vasuki-Kai was so still that Bookbinder could have mistaken him for a statue of a naga rather than the real thing.

"Thanks," he managed. He realized that he could no longer see, and guessed his eyes had closed. He supposed that was all right. He couldn't keep them open anyway.

When Bookbinder blinked awake, the sun was high in the sky. He sat up abruptly, the rest of the team already up and bustling around him.

Sharp knelt beside him. "Two problems, sir," he said. "First is not so big, second is bigger, but pretty much expected."

"Okay," Bookbinder managed. His tongue felt like a dried sock in his mouth.

As if he could sense it, Sharp held out the feed line from his own backpack water bladder. He spoke as Bookbinder sucked on it. "First, we've lost a day. You slept for roughly ten hours, the rest of us slightly less."

A jolt of adrenaline brought Bookbinder fully awake. He struggled not to choke on the water he was drinking. *We can't afford that. The FOB can't afford it.* But he said, "I'm sure we all needed it."

Sharp nodded. "Second problem is that we've got no comms with the FOB. No more radio pulse checks." He gestured to Archer, who was tinkering with the SINCGARS with no apparent success. At last he stowed the handset in his rucksack and shook his head at Sharp.

"I'm no expert," Archer said, "but I'd bet it's something to do with the atmosphere over that burned patch we just crossed. Mucking up the signal."

Dhatri was pensive. "Perhaps that's why we were having trouble getting in touch with FOB Sarpakavu before."

"Maybe we can radio the Indian FOB as we get closer," Archer mused. "Although this thing is squirrelly as hell." He slapped his rucksack and the equipment inside.

Bookbinder shrugged. "I doubt it matters now. Has everybody eaten already?"

Nods from everyone on the team.

"Drank, too? Packed and ready to go?"

More nods, most of them sheepish.

Bookbinder stood. "Why the hell didn't anyone wake me?"

"You looked peaceful, sir," Anan volunteered.

Bookbinder looked askance at Woon, but the major only shrugged. "You did."

"What about him?" Bookbinder jerked his thumb at Vasuki-Kai.

"His Highness ate before we departed FOB Frontier," Dhatri said. "Naga can go for very long periods on a single meal. He will be sustained until we reach the Naga Raajya."

Bookbinder nodded and shouldered his pack, sucking at his own water feed now. "Surely you must eat, sir," Dhatri said, his voice concerned.

"I can eat while we walk," Bookbinder replied. "We've lost enough time to my cherubic sleepy-time appearance. Let's move."

The grass regained its health as they proceeded, the air gradually becoming clearer. By the time the sun began to set again, they felt refreshed by the simple act of inhaling clean air

without the aid of a wet scarf. Bookbinder set his goggles up on
his helmet, grateful for the lack of pressure around his eyes.
They even came across a stream in the morning where they
could restock their water supplies with the aid of Bookbinder's
"boomer." He noticed the enchanted rebar was beginning to lose
its charge. The water came clean, but not as fully as before, some
of the swirling particles still visible in it. He made a mental note
that the magic didn't last forever, pleased that he had brought
conventional water decontamination tablets with them as
backup.

Bookbinder spent most of the time replaying Fillion's death.
Why did he let that man go down the rock face? He should have
done it himself. He knew that Sharp and his men had the real
combat experience, but he was still in charge. It should have
been him drowned in that sea of ash. *That's ridiculous,* he told
himself. *You have to make it to FOB Sarpakavu to negotiate.
No one else in the team has the authority you do.* But he couldn't
stop replaying the scene in his mind; Fillion putting his boot on
the ash, then disappearing beneath it.

"Down to our last MREs, sir," Sharp noted, breaking him out
of his reverie. "We're going to have to hunt from now on."

"That should be easy with Woon's Whispering," Bookbinder
answered, but the thought didn't make him any calmer. Even
Whispering animals in to slaughter would take time, and they'd
just spent three days crossing the ash field and sleeping off the
exhaustion of the effort.

As the edges of the sky turned molten bronze, Sharp turned
toward him. "You about ready to pack it in for the night, sir?"

"Let's keep going," Bookbinder said, "at least until it gets
dark. I'm feeling pretty good."

The others nodded and pushed on as darkness gathered
around them.

After another half hour of walking, Bookbinder began to
hear a creaking, clinking sound ahead of them. Sharp brought
his carbine up, halted the team with a hand signal, and pushed
off slowly into the gathering gloom, Anan and Archer falling
wordlessly in beside him.

They hadn't gone ten steps when a small group of goblins
came out of the half-light, surrounding a wooden cart piled high
with something bulging under a burlap cover, yoked to one of

the shaggy beasts Bookbinder knew they herded back in
their villages. They were clothed in leather frocks, with only
one or two carrying weapons. Sharp and his men lowered their
guns.

A few seconds later, the goblins noticed them and froze,
drawing close around their cart. They stood in silence, staring.

Bookbinder figured the situation would best be defused
quickly. He waved and smiled, muttered, "Cover me," under his
breath, and walked forward. "Hello there, friends!" he said. "I
bet we're the last people you expected to see out here."

The goblins chattered to one another, relaxing a little.

Bookbinder stopped beyond spear range and waved again. "I
don't suppose any of you happens to speak . . . English?"

None of them did. They continued to stare, pressing closer
to the wooden cart. One of them stepped forward. He was identical to the rest of them, save that his brown leather frock had a
metal pectoral sewn into the center and he held a spear propped
over one shoulder. He spoke to Bookbinder with a mild authority in his voice, gesturing to the wagon, then back the way the
goblins had come. The team edged closer. At the sight of Vasuki-
Kai, the goblins recoiled, the one with the spear hopping on top
of the wagon.

Vasuki-Kai halted, hissing consolation. Archer trotted forward, and said, "Sir, if you'll permit me." He tapped his eyelids,
bowing slightly from the waist. The goblins paused, shocked,
before returning the gesture.

Archer then spoke to them in halting, broken goblin. The bigger goblin on top of the cart finally got off it, answering slowly
and carefully, as if to a young child.

Archer finally nodded and turned back to Bookbinder.

"I didn't know you spoke goblin," Bookbinder said.

"I don't, really. I just picked up a little from the contractors
we had working in our vehicle park. These guys are traders.
That wagon is full of goods for sale."

Bookbinder arched his eyebrows. "Well, what have they got?
I could go for some chow that isn't bagged or Whispered to its
death by the good major here."

Archer pointed at the wagon, nodding.

"Hell, I could have done that," Bookbinder said.

The goblin with the spear turned to a gnarled, smaller goblin. They talked for a moment before the smaller goblin nodded and gestured at the burlap covering the wagon. The goblin with the spear bowed, tapping his eyelids, then undid the cords, pulling the burlap back.

The wagon was piled high with goods; bolts of leather and woven cloth, bundles of some kind of pungent dried weed, strands of colored beads, stack upon stack of pelts. Bookbinder smiled as he stepped forward to inspect the wares.

Then he froze.

Scattered among the goblin-made goods were others that he recognized. A couple of pistol magazines, a gas-mask filter, a tattered helmet liner. Here was a small-arms field-reporting guide. There was a ruggedized, camouflaged copy of the Holy Bible.

Bookbinder felt Woon stiffen behind him and immediately raised a hand to her elbow. He smiled at the goblins, stroked his chin, and began turning over the goods in the cart, inspecting them. Woon started to speak, and he caught her eyes. "Not just now, Major."

She looked angry, but nodded. "Sir."

The goblins looked hopeful as Bookbinder made a great show of turning over a bundle of some dried spice, tied with a bit of colored yarn. He took another few minutes to peruse the trader's wares before he stepped back, shaking his head. "There's nothing we need here, Sergeant Sharp. If you'd please send them on their way with our thanks."

Sharp nodded to Archer, who spoke another burst of halting goblin. The traders frowned, gesturing to the cart and muttering, but Archer spoke again, and firmly.

Finally, one of the goblins stepped forward. Bookbinder's hand dropped instinctively to his weapon, but they were only prodding the animal yoked to the cart, turning it around. It bleated plaintively at the change of direction. They trundled away from Bookbinder's team. Bookbinder watched as the goblins faded into the gathering darkness, then finally let out his breath.

He stood in silence before he felt Sharp's presence at his elbow. "They're gone, sir. You okay?"

"You know what that was?" Bookbinder asked.

"I've got an idea, sir," Sharp said.

"That was US military gear in that cart. I'd bet you a silver dollar it was pilfered off American corpses.

Sharp was silent for a moment. "Could be legitimately acquired. Maybe it was excessed from the FOB."

"Do you really believe that, Sergeant?"

Sharp was silent again before answering, "No, sir. I don't."

"We should have said something," Woon said. "I was going to—"

Bookbinder cut her off. "I know, and that's why I stopped you. We don't need to pick a fight out here in the middle of the wilderness for no reason, Major. Our mission is to get to FOB Sarpakavu, not to bring corpse-robbers to justice."

"Could be they made the corpses in the first place, sir," Woon added.

"And there'll be a lot more corpses if we don't reach the Indian FOB," Bookbinder added. "Besides, if you wanted a fight, I think you're going to get one. They've seen how few of us there are, noted our gear. If they trade in stolen US military goods, we'll be far too tempting to pass up. If their village is anywhere nearby, I'd wager they'll be back. You saw how they turned around and headed back the way they came after meeting us?"

Sharp nodded. "I did, sir."

"I'd say we need to be extra alert tonight. I don't doubt we can handle even a sizeable goblin force, what with His Highness's help, eh? What do you think?"

Sharp didn't hesitate. "We can do for them, sir, in far greater numbers than what we just saw."

"Okay," Bookbinder said. "Let's risk moving on as long as we can tonight. I'd like to get as far from our original position as possible. When we finally bed down, we're going to have to be extra careful."

The dark came on fast, and they were only able to walk for a short distance before the gloom made the march treacherous, forcing them to set up camp. They ate in silence, casting worried eyes over their shoulders. Bookbinder imagined that every shifting shadow was an approaching goblin army, but after an hour, there was no sign of any enemy. Vasuki-Kai set his watch, assuring them he'd smell goblins a long way off. Bookbinder was uneasy anyway, but exhaustion won out in the end, and he drifted off to sleep curled around the shotgun's stock, the plastic against his cheek comforting despite its hard, cold surface.

Bookbinder was awakened by the working of a carbine's action and Vasuki-Kai's hissing. He sat up, rubbing his face and fumbling with the shotgun. "Whassgoinon?" he asked of no one in particular.

"Vasuki-Kai smells something." Sharp's voice was urgent, hushed. "You were right, sir. They're coming back. Just hang here, we're going to flank them. Check your fire that way." He pointed into the darkness.

Bookbinder nodded, slowly rocking to his knees and standing up.

"Sir," Sharp said again. "I need you to remember that. If you fire to the east, you're going to hit us."

"I've got it," Bookbinder said.

Sharp gestured to Anan and Archer, and they disappeared into the darkness.

Vasuki-Kai didn't draw his weapons, but his hands danced across the many pommels. Dhatri and Woon cradled their carbines close, ready to raise them at a moment's notice. Bookbinder felt Woon Drawing her magic about her.

A few moments later, he began to hear the tramping of many feet through the grass to their east. Goblins, attempting to be stealthy and failing miserably. By the sound of it, there were many more than they'd seen with the trading wagon.

Bookbinder's muscles began to cramp with the effort of making himself sit still as the goblins approached. At long last, they abandoned stealth and charged, shouting a war cry as they rushed the camp. Vasuki-Kai spun, drawing his blades, and Woon whipped her magic forward, Binding it to the earth around them.

Shots rang out, and the war cries turned to howls of agony. Bookbinder could hear Anan's SAW rumbling in the near distance. Two goblins burst into the encampment and the earth rose to meet them, formed by Woon's magic into yokes that seized their necks and slammed them down into the ground.

"Keep them alive!" Bookbinder shouted as he racked the shotgun's action and bolted in the direction of the gunfire. *You think you're actually going to help out three hardened Special Forces operators? Show some common sense!*

He stopped at camp's edge, warring with himself, and within moments heard the goblins racing through the tall grass away from them, giving up the fight. The operators' guns spoke some more, a shot here and there, but it was clear that the ambush had broken the goblins' nerve. Bookbinder stood and waited until they stopped firing, and an eerie silence crept over the camp, with only a few wisps of lingering gun smoke to indicate there had been anything amiss, until they, too, were swallowed by the darkness.

"Sir." Sharp's voice made Bookbinder jump. The man had crept up next to him. "They're routed."

Sharp's tone was morose, his eyes looked big. "What happened?" Bookbinder asked.

Archer appeared out of the darkness, shaking his head.

Bookbinder's stomach turned over. "Where's Anan?"

Sharp bit his lip and was silent. When he finally spoke he said. "Sir, we've already taken care of him. If you could get the major to walk about twenty paces that way and put him under the ground, we'd be grateful."

Bookbinder swayed with the force of the realization. *This is your fault,* he told himself. There was no accusation in Sharp's or Archer's eyes, but he could feel it flowing from their pores. *There had to be a way you could have avoided this. Maybe if you'd bought something from them? Made a show of your gun not working?*

Bookbinder found his hands twirling lamely at his sides. "I'm sorry," he rasped.

Sharp shook his head. "He knew the job. We all did."

"I'll get Woon," Bookbinder said. At least he could do that much.

Sharp said nothing as he headed back to the camp, Archer silently in tow.

By the time Woon returned from burying Anan, Bookbinder squatted on his haunches beside Archer, who sat in front of the goblin captives. To Bookbinder, they looked nearly identical, gnarled brown bodies, pointed ears and noses, long hands. The only real distinguishing markers were their clothing, a tight leather cape and trousers on one, sewn with metal discs. But the other wore a distinctive blue jumpsuit; its faded and threadbare surface couldn't conceal the patch still sewn over the chest.

Entertech.

Archer said a few words in goblin, then leaned forward. "I know you speak some English," he said. "You worked on the FOB, didn't you?"

The goblin looked at him, sullenly silent, even as Woon raised the earthen yokes until they stood the goblins up. "What were you after?" Archer asked. "You want our guns?" He tapped the carbine slung across his chest, then asked something again in a burst of halting goblin.

The creature barked an answer, pulling against the yoke that held it, then let out a cry of fear as Vasuki-Kai spread his arms behind Archer, his heads darting to and fro, hissing madly. Dhatri said "His Highness has little patience for traitors. He says he would just as soon eat these creatures though he is certain they will taste badly."

Archer's jaw muscles worked, suppressing a smile. He looked back at the goblin. "You hear that? That's a foreign partner. I can hardly refuse him, can I? Bad for diplomatic relations."

"Let . . . go . . ." the goblin in the jumpsuit said.

Bookbinder opened his mouth to say something, but Archer silenced him with a gesture. "He's got it, sir," Sharp whispered to him.

"Let go. We help," the creature said again.

"How will you help?" Archer asked, kneeling, till he was eye to eye with the goblin.

"Where go?" the goblin asked, his voice wheedling as Vasuki-Kai loomed larger over Archer's shoulder.

"You saw which way we're going," Archer said, pointing.

"Yes . . . I see . . ." He paused, searching for the right words. "What for go?"

Archer shook his head. "Nice try."

The goblin shook his head as well, pulling against the earthen yoke again. "No there," he said, his voice genuinely afraid. "There bad. Trouble. No, no." Beside him, the other goblin began to nod frantically, repeating the one word in English he apparently knew. "No, no, no."

"Calm down," Archer said. "Why is it bad? What's bad?"

The goblin in the Entertech jumpsuit struggled for a moment before spitting out several words in goblin that Archer didn't understand. "Man," the goblin finally ventured in English. "Bad man."

Bookbinder could hold himself back no longer. "What do you mean, 'man'?" he asked. "You mean a human? Like me?" He jerked his thumb at his chest.

But the goblin only continued its fear-maddened prattling, shaking its head violently. "Bad man. No go."

Bookbinder conferred with Sharp and Archer out of the goblin's earshot while Vasuki-Kai slithered back and forth before them, keeping them trembling.

"What do you think?" Bookbinder asked.

"You were right, sir," Archer said. "You were right about them. They're scavengers after human gear. They were probably hoping to take us unawares and pillage our stuff."

"No, I mean about the man. Do you think there's another human out here?"

Sharp shrugged. "I don't see how it's possible for anyone to survive out here."

Bookbinder was silent. "If there's even a chance, we need to take a look."

Sharp shrugged again. "If what the goblins were saying is true, it's right on our way, sir."

"Do you think we could handle having them along, just for a short while?" Bookbinder asked.

"We could swing it, sir. They seem pretty damned scared of the naga." He chuckled. "Ought to help keep 'em behaved."

Archer smiled. "They don't look big enough to eat much anyway."

Bookbinder nodded. "Okay." He led the operators back over to the prisoners and motioned to Woon to release them. "We're going to let you go for a bit," he said. "But if you do anything bad"—he pointed at the naga prince—"His Highness is going to eat you. Got it?"

He motioned to Woon and turned to Sharp. "You got a couple of extra pairs of zip cuffs in your—"

"Shit!" Woon shouted.

Bookbinder spun. As soon as she'd released them from the earthen yokes, the goblins had raced for Archer's grounded pack. The goblin in the blue jumpsuit dove on it and yanked one of the grenades from the shoulder strap. It spun, shouted triumphantly, and pulled the pin.

Sharp crouched, his hand a blur as it dropped to his thigh, yanking the pistol from its drop holster. It drove forward, the motion clean and fluid, slack coming out of the trigger even as he extended his hand. In less than three seconds, he'd fired twice. The first round punched through the throat of the goblin in the leather cape. The second holed the goblin in the jumpsuit directly between the eyes. The creature sighed and collapsed, the armed grenade spinning in the air above it.

"Down!" Sharp shouted, diving on Bookbinder, knocking him onto the ground with enough force that his head bounced, teeth clicking and stars exploding behind his eyes. "Is everyone o—" Bookbinder began to say but was cut off by a deafening boom. He felt a wall of heat slap his buttocks and legs, pushing him forward a few feet, his face digging a furrow in the earth. He lay silent, doubled over, his ears ringing as earth and rock rained down on him. After a moment, he felt Sharp's weight lift, heard the sergeant calling to him through as if down a long tunnel. Bookbinder stood, dusting himself, checking himself for injuries. He turned to the team, shouting, "Is everyone okay?" At least he thought he shouted that, he could barely hear his own voice over the ringing in his ears.

At last he visually accounted for them all. Each of them stood, nodding, uninjured. Bookbinder looked toward the remains for Archer's rucksack, now little more than a smoking hole in the ground. Tiny shreds of meat were the only indicator that goblins had ever stood over it.

Bookbinder put a pinky in his ear and wiggled it. The ringing had begun to fade, replaced by a headache that threatened to overwhelm him.

He looked over at Archer, who cursed. "Can't believe those little fuckers could be so stupid."

"Or so fast," Sharp added.

Bookbinder tried to shrug nonchalantly and found it hurt too much. "We're all okay, that's what matters. What did we lose in your pack?"

Archer's voice was bitter. "Some MREs, ammo, my medical supplies."

The only ones they had left. Bookbinder tried to look uncon-
cerned. "Is that all?" he asked archly.

There was nothing arch about Archer's reply. "No sir, that's
not all. The comms system was in there, and my 'boomer.'"

Bookbinder grunted. "Boomers were running out of magical
charge anyway. We've got regular decontamination tablets for
backup. and we don't need comms now." Inwardly, he screamed
at himself. There had to be a way he could have avoided that. A
piece of him consoled himself. *Sometimes you get in impossible situations. There's nothing you can do.* But that wouldn't
cut it if they were to reach the Indian FOB. He couldn't afford
mistakes. He looked back at Archer as the operator set about
inventorying his remaining gear. The man was stoic, but did
Bookbinder catch a disapproving glance? Fillion's open mouth,
the ash pouring forth, flashed in his mind, followed by Anan's
back disappearing into the dark grass from which he'd never
emerge. *I should have stopped him,* Bookbinder thought. *I
should have ordered Sharp to kill them when we first saw their
cart so they couldn't report back to their village.* He shook his
head, trying to clear the images, but they stuck with him. His
mind reeled, replaying each scene over in his head, wondering
what he could have done differently.

CHAPTER XX
BAD MAN

Why do you think the Geneva Convention was so quick to add an amendment outlawing Whispering? Any fool can see the range of military applications. It can only be because governments saw that the rights issue would cause a headache on a scale that would dwarf any benefit. What would we do when dolphins could finally tell us all that they didn't enjoy performing tricks for thrown fish? Or monkeys revealed that they'd rather live alongside us in luxury condominiums? What would we do when cows marched on Washington, demanding the right to keep milk for their own young?

—Arnold Dishart, Vice President
People for the Moral Treatment of Animals (PMTA)

The terrain dampened as they proceeded. Before long, they were trudging through a half-frozen bog, the tall grass giving way to rushes and puffed-up reeds that stretched over even Vasuki-Kai's height. Pools of stagnant water surrounded them, squelching beneath their boots. They paused, using their failing boomers to clean the water and refill their supply. The last of these finally gave out, the enchantment spent, so they switched to the decontamination tablets to finish the job.

The ground then began to rise slightly, a low line of rocky hills appearing in the distance. Bookbinder made for them, grateful to have a landmark to fix his sights on. The ground dried as the hills drew closer, the bog giving way to a stony plain.

Bookbinder angled along the line, making for a break in the rocky surface where the crossing looked easy. He had become used to the team naturally gravitating to his course. Even Anan, usually on point, seemed to feel his changes of direction and moved with him. This time, Bookbinder found himself walking alone. *He was your trooper, and you couldn't save him.*

He stopped, looking back over his shoulder to where Sharp was peering through his carbine scope at a point on the hillside farther down the line. "What?" he asked.

Sharp handed him the carbine. "Take a look, sir," he said, pointing. "A little more to the right . . . a little more . . . there."

Bookbinder stopped moving the rifle barrel and peered through the scope. The targeting reticle's red dot hovered over what looked like a cave mouth. "So? It's a cave."

Sharp reached over Bookbinder's head and adjusted something on the scope. "Maybe that's better. Look again."

Bookbinder looked back through the scope and didn't see anything different. He was just about to lower the carbine when something caught his eye. At the cave entrance were a couple of regular flat surfaces. "Are those . . . rugs?"

"Looked like it to me, sir." Sharp answered. "Now look a little to the left and right of the entrance. Those aren't natural growths." .

Bookbinder did as Sharp said. The sergeant was right. What he had assumed to be trees were sharpened stakes, planted in the hard soil. Two of them sported skulls, eyeless, with single teeth protruding from the snouts. A couple of the stakes appeared to have been topped in some kind of clustered blossoms.

Bookbinder swallowed hard. Not blossoms. Goblin heads, impaled through their necks. "Jesus," he said, lowering the weapon. "Whoever that is doesn't like goblins very much. Should we check it out?"

Sharp gave his characteristic shrug. "It's not the mission, sir. But I thought you should see it. Might be that bad man our prisoners were going on about."

"You're my senior NCO. Advise me."

Sharp smiled. "Your call, sir. I'm pretty sure we can do for anything out here. Even if it beats up on goblins."

Bookbinder paused. *You've already lost Fillion and Anan. You want to risk the rest of your team?* He turned away from the cave, then stopped. *But what if it really is a human in there? Can you just walk away from that?*

Bookbinder decided he couldn't. "Damn it," he said. "Take a look. Just you and Archer. Be careful."

Sharp nodded. "We will, sir."

Dhatri and Woon knelt and covered the cave entrance. Vasuki-Kai stood imperiously, watching behind them. Bookbinder milled about, feeling useless. Sharp and Archer picked their way up the hillside, sighting down their weapons, steady and silent. When they reached the cave mouth, they braced alongside the entrance, shoulders against the rock. Sharp took a chemlight from his pack, broke and shook it, then threw it inside. They paused, listening. Finally he took out a long mirror and peered into the cave entrance. He returned it to his pack, braced himself, and rolled inside, Archer following.

The darkness swallowed them.

Minutes passed. Bookbinder held his breath. Regret pulsed in his gut and scalp. *Bad call. You have just gotten two more of your people killed.*

He was just about to race up the hill after them when Sharp emerged at the cave's entrance and gave a thumbs-up sign. "It's clear," he called.

Relief swamped Bookbinder with such force that his knees went weak. When he finally mastered himself, he nodded and began to make his way up the hill.

A thump sounded behind them and Vasuki-Kai sent up a hiss that bordered on a roar. Sharp dropped to one knee, pointing his weapon at something behind Bookbinder. Archer followed a moment later. Bookbinder spun.

A man stood behind them. His brown skin was scratched and weathered to the point of old shoe leather, stretched over lean muscle. His hair and beard had grown into short gray dreadlocks. He was dressed in ragged furs, hand-stitched leather. One arm was draped across Dhatri's chest. The other held a short sword across his throat.

His eyes were bright and intelligent. Calm eyes, killer's eyes. Like Sharp's.

Vasuki-Kai had drawn his weapons, hissing murder, but not daring to approach.

"This your boyfriend?" the black man asked the naga. "Put those meat choppers away, or I'll cut his fucking head off."

Sharp and Archer began to advance down the hill. "Drop

your weapon!" Sharp commanded. "Do it right now! Asshole! Do you want to get shot?"

Bookbinder raised his shotgun, remembering to thumb the safety off this time. "Sir!" he said. "Sir, it's okay. I'm Colonel Alan Bookbinder, United States Army. We're the good guys. You don't have to do this."

The man relaxed a bit, but jerked his chin at the naga. "What the hell is that?"

The motion tugged at Bookbinder's mind. He could swear he'd seen this man somewhere before. But where? From his accent, the man was definitely American and likely from New England somewhere.

"That's . . ." Bookbinder said. "That's complicated. What's important is that we're not going to hurt you. That's our friend you've got there. Just let him go, and we can talk like civilized people."

The man hesitated. Bookbinder swept his arm across the rest of his team, motioning for Sharp and Archer to lower their weapons. "This is Sergeant First Class Sharp and Specialist Archer, also army. This is Major Woon, from the air force. The guy you've got there is Subedar Major Dhatri from the Armed Forces of India. This is Vasuki-Kai. Not his boyfriend, precisely, but close enough that he's not going to get over it if you don't let him go right now."

The man hesitated another moment, then slowly lowered the sword. Dhatri scrambled away from him, snatching up his carbine. Vasuki-Kai instantly sheathed his weapons and gathered the subedar major into the coils of his tail, checking him for injuries, a canopy of snake's heads darting their tongues at him, hissing with concern. Bookbinder breathed a sigh of relief. "Thank you."

The man stood and nodded. "Stanley Britton. Colonel, United States Marine Corps, retired."

The familiarity hit home with a bang. Bookbinder gasped. "My god. You're Oscar Britton's father."

Stanley Britton's eyes narrowed. "You know Oscar?"

Bookbinder nodded. "I do. We thought you were dead. How the hell have you survived out here?"

Stanley jerked his chin again, this time at Sharp and Archer. "I was Force Recon in my fighting days. You learn a thing or two about how to keep on keeping on. This place hasn't thrown anything at me that I couldn't handle. Mostly those little monsters out here, but they scare easy." He nodded toward the stakes outside his cave and Bookbinder realized he was talking about goblins.

Bookbinder motioned to Archer, "He's a medic. Mind if he checks you out?"

Stanley shrugged. "Not necessary. I'm fine."

Bookbinder paused, trying to decide whether or not to force the issue. The man had staked the heads of goblins outside his cave. Maybe his injuries weren't physical. Stanley spoke before he could. "I didn't expect to see . . . my own kind out here. How did you get here? I thought I was alone." The relief in his voice helped Bookbinder breathe easier. Whatever trauma this man had suffered, and what it had caused him to do to goblins, he still had attachments to his own kind.

"We've got a . . . presence out here," Bookbinder said.

"If I'd known that, I wouldn't have holed up in this dump." Stanley gestured to the cave.

"It's a good thing you did," Bookbinder said. "We're in the middle of hostile territory, you'd have had one hell of a fight to reach us."

"I can handle it." Stanley's look was frank.

"I bet you could."

"My son is there? At your base?" Stanley asked, his expression hopeful.

"He was," Bookbinder said. "He's gone now."

"But he's okay? What about Desda? Is she with him?" Stanley's voice rose, the words coming faster.

"I'm sorry, Mr. Britton. I don't know who that is. And I can't speak for your son. I don't know where he is or how he is now."

"Desda is my wife. What happened to Oscar?" His concern increased Bookbinder's trust. The man cared about his family, and Bookbinder knew that ache well.

"He . . ." Bookbinder paused as he tried to figure out how to explain it. After a moment, he decided on the truth. "He's a fugitive. We had him, but he escaped. I don't know where he is now. But we really need to get him back. Maybe you can help with that."

Stanley shook his head ruefully. "The last time we saw each other we . . . we had words. It was bad."

He looked up at Bookbinder, his eyes wet. "I just . . . I just want to talk to him."

Bookbinder nodded. "I've got two girls, Mr. Britton. I can't wait to get back to them. Come with us, and we'll try to reunite you. You might be talking to your son through bars, but you can still talk."

Stanley paused. "Back to your base? You're doing a patrol out here?"

"Not exactly. It's an A-to-B run. But we'll be getting back there eventually."

Vasuki-Kai hissed, waving his arms. "His Highness says he will not travel with this animal. This *Saala kutta* attacked his *Bandhav* and this is the same as an attack on his own royal person. He commands you to shoot him." Dhatri translated.

Bookbinder turned and stabbed a finger at the naga. "Tell His Highness that I respectfully decline. This man is a citizen of the United States of America. As far as I know, I am the ranking officer from that country in this entire plane of existence. That makes this man my ward and my responsibility. We will not shoot him. We will protect him. With our lives if necessary."

Dhatri hesitated.

"Tell him!" Bookbinder said.

Dhatri turned and translated haltingly. The naga prince's heads weaved an irritated dance, and he paused, several of the heads locking gazes with Bookbinder. After a tense moment, Vasuki-Kai hissed a single syllable and turned away. Dhatri following.

Bookbinder turned back to Stanley. "I'm afraid I have to insist you come with us, Mr. Britton. For the reasons I just stated."

Stanley seemed even less impressed than Vasuki-Kai. "Can you get back to my wife and son?"

"I can't promise anything, but you have a better chance of finding him with us than just staying here."

Stanley thought for a moment, then nodded. "Okay."

Bookbinder sighed. "Outstanding. We're in something of a hurry. Is there anything you need from your . . . home . . . before we go?"

Stanley nodded. "I'll just be a minute."

Sharp, ever practical, halted his jog up the hillside with a touch on his elbow. "Sir, we're low on supplies. You got any food? We also need water. Nasty stuff'll do. We can clean it."

Stanley nodded. "Hope you like devil-horse jerky. I know of a spring not far from here. Just give me a minute."

He disappeared inside the cave and returned a moment later, a hide bag tied across his chest. He carried several bundles of dried meat that gave off a pungent, smoky odor, and distributed them.

He paused. "This run is dangerous?"

Bookbinder nodded. "It has been so far."

"Then I don't suppose I can prevail on you for a firearm?" He tapped the sword, now slung at his side. "This is kind of old-fashioned."

Vasuki-Kai hissed what Bookbinder assumed was a concerted objection. He thought for a moment, then shook his head. "You're a civilian, sir. I can't just go dispensing you weapons. We'll keep you covered."

Stanley gave him a hard look. "I was a full bird like you. I've got more ops under my belt than—"

Bookbinder cut him off. "Sir, I am not going to stand here and compare dicks with you. This is my team and my mission. You want to get back to your son? Let's get moving."

They locked eyes for a long moment. That might have made him uncomfortable before, but Bookbinder was having none of it now. He held Stanley's gaze until the man looked away. "All right," he said.

"Glad we got that cleared up," Bookbinder said. "Welcome to the outfit. Now let's go find that spring."

CHAPTER XXI
FOB SARPAKAVU

This levy and seawall system was built in partnership between the SOC and the US Army Corps of Engineers in response to Lake Pont-chartrain's rising water levels post-Katrina. Scientists estimate that without it, the City of New Orleans would have been completely submerged years ago. Just one of the ways Terramantic Engineering is working hard to keep America safe! Please check out www .magicinaction.gov to learn more.

—Text from a sign on the Lake Pontchartrain Causeway

Stanley was true to his word. Five kilometers north of the cave, they arrived at a kidney-shaped pool of water, bubbling between a broken tumble of rocks. Stanley led them there effortlessly, walking smooth and silent like Sharp, his eyes alert and his sword drawn. Bookbinder relaxed a bit seeing the man prove trustworthy, but kept a close eye on him. He doubted that any man could have survived out here on his own for as long as Stanley Britton had and not be at least a little crazy. Vasuki-Kai's assessment of Stanley was clear. He always kept between Stanley and Dhatri, never allowing less than three heads to watch him at all times.

Sharp pulled Bookbinder aside once they reached the spring. "Good call on the gun, sir."

"You think he can be trusted?"

The sergeant was pensive. "Retired Marine colonel? Probably, but he's got a crazy eye."

"You've got a crazy eye." Bookbinder smirked. "You ever look in a mirror, Sharp?"

Sharp shrugged. "Not a whole lot of call for mirrors out here, sir."

"How the hell did he survive out here on his own?" *We've lost two, and we're a highly trained and well-equipped outfit, with a naga to boot.* The thought of those two lost men plagued him. He knew that the SOF operators thought of themselves as independent, but this was his team and his mission. Of all the times he'd dreamed of command, he'd never imagined what it would be like to lose the people who worked for him.

Sharp took a quick look at Stanley. "Wiry son of a bitch, sir. Tough. Recon's no joke. He's a fighter."

"So were Anan and Fillion."

"Don't do that to yourself, sir. People die in this line of work. That's just how it is."

Talking about it made Bookbinder feel worse. He changed the subject. "Well, you just keep an eye on our guest there," he said, gesturing to Stanley. "I can hardly deny him a sword, but if he tries anything . . ."

Sharp nodded and tapped his carbine's trigger guard. "Got it, sir."

Stanley was eerily silent as they washed themselves as much as they could stand in the cold air and filled their water bladders. With the boomers gone, they saved their decontamination tablets, trusting in the fresh-flowing spring to be clean. Bookbinder had to admit that he was happy just to drink the stuff fresh from the ground. The boomers completely sterilized the water they touched, leaving it tasting . . . bland. Freshwater had a metallic thrill to it, especially in the enhancing air of the Source.

Stanley kept his eyes on the horizon and his weapon close. Bookbinder stood amazed by his self-possession. *The man has been stuck out here for months, hasn't seen another person in all that time. I would be bubbling over with questions, desperate for the chance to talk to someone. Anyone. But he's more concerned with overwatch. I guess that's what kept him alive.*

Bookbinder judged the setting sun and gave the order to make camp. "We might as well take advantage of the water while we're this close to it."

As Vasuki-Kai took up his fan-headed watch, Stanley finally relaxed, grounding his pack, never keeping his hand far from his sword. He washed carefully, giving little heed to the cold.

He gestured to Sharp's pocket, where the sergeant's knife peeked out above its securing clip. "That sharp?"

Sharp nodded. "You could shave with it."

Stanley smiled. "Precisely what I had in mind."

Sharp tossed it to him, and Stanley set to work. An hour later, as the sun dipped below the horizon, he finally emerged from his crouch, his face and head completely shaved. The wild man was gone. In his place was a handsome older gentleman; distinguished, even regal. Bookbinder could see the Marine colonel he had been.

"That's more like it," Stanley said. "Kind of hard to keep a blade as sharp as it should be out here."

"You look good," Bookbinder said.

"I feel good," Stanley said. Then he paused, frowning.

"Thank you," he said. "I never said that. I never really said that enough to anyone."

Bookbinder nodded. "We're all in this together."

"So, what's been happening in my absence? Walsh still president?"

Bookbinder sat on a low flat rock beside him. "Last time I checked. It's been a while since I phoned home."

"Tell me about it."

Bookbinder did. The wall of Stanley's reticence broke, and he interrogated Bookbinder long into the night about the state of things on the Home Plane, the FOB, any scrap of detail about his family. He told Bookbinder how his son had gated him here, how he'd survived, dug out a home in that cave, resigned himself to a life of solitude, scratching to survive.

"God was teaching me a lesson," Stanley said. "I was a hardass before this all happened. I guess I still am, but I get it now. It thawed my heart. And you know what I'm thinking now?"

Bookbinder looked a question at him.

"I'm thinking God sent you to give me a second chance. I think he's done with this phase of my learning. Now it's time for me to make amends. I'm going to start with Oscar. Then Desda. I'm ready."

"But he gated you out here. The papers were saying it was murder."

Stanley was silent for a moment. "I won't lie. I'm . . . angry.

He put me here, and it's been a tough row to hoe, but there's . . . some things."

Bookbinder was silent. He had enough experience with taciturn types like Sharp now to know that was the best way to encourage them to talk. Eventually, Stanley went on. "He reached for my hand, as I fell through the gate. He tried to grab me and missed. He shouted a warning. I think it was an accident. When I see him, I'll know the right of it. And you're going to make that happen for me." He jerked his chin in Bookbinder's direction.

Bookbinder nodded. "Happy to help."

"So, you going to tell me where we're going? The base is cut off and surrounded by hostiles. We're just running?"

"No," Bookbinder said. "The Indians have a FOB a few days from here. Dhatri says they have a Portamancer of their own. Without your son, it's the only way home for us."

Stanley shook his head. "I don't believe this. To think I was nearby not one, but two human outposts out here, and I never knew."

"No reason you should. You don't exactly have GPS."

"Or even a map." He paused. "We're not heading east, are we?"

Bookbinder thought about it. "Due north, I think. You'd have to ask Sharp. He's the one with the built-in compass."

"East is tough," Stanley said. "I struck out in that direction a few times, but it's not safe."

"That's something coming from you. What's going on out there?"

"Monsters. Big, black, horned things. Teeth like knives. I tangled with one once. It almost got me."

"You killed it?" Bookbinder asked.

"I hurt it. At least I think I did. They bleed smoke. They've started ranging farther and farther since they got a new queen. I was thinking about pulling stakes anyway for that reason. Cave wouldn't be safe much longer."

"Queen?" Bookbinder asked.

"I saw her once when I was ranging. Pretty woman. Looks like a human, but don't you let it fool you. She's a walking corpse. Those things adore her."

Bookbinder frowned. "If there's another person out there . . ."

Stanley's expression hardened. He put a hand on Bookbinder's forearm. "Leave it, Colonel. You've got to trust me on this one. I've seen her. She *looks* like a human. Pretty one, too, but there's nothing human about her. She'd kill you just as soon as look at you. She's got nasty, rotting magic. You tangle with her, you die. I nearly did."

Bookbinder thought for a moment, then nodded. "Okay."

"Good," Stanley said. "North sounds right as rain."

A few days later, FOB Sarpakavu hove into view in the greatest anticlimax of Bookbinder's life. No fanfare, no cresting a ridgeline or fording a river to see their prize suddenly before them. They just trudged along, exhausted and bored, and there it was.

The distinction between the Indian Army's dwellings and the Naga Raja's palace compound was painfully clear. Bookbinder guessed that the palace and the Indian Army encampment around it were easily the same size as FOB Frontier. The palace rose, grand and beautiful, thick white towers arcing gracefully into billowing onion domes topped with brass finials that glinted in the sun. Thick walls, far more businesslike, linked them, sporting rough-looking crenellations and narrow arrow slits. Beautiful scrollwork graced nearly every surface, visible even at a distance. Bookbinder couldn't make out the details of the intricate carvings from so far away, but he guessed they might depict serpents in some way.

The Indian FOB sprawled around the outside of the defensive ring wall, a shantytown by comparison; little more than a collection of cheap military tents huddled against the grander stone. A vehicle park was visible below one tower, Humvees and tanks side by side. Dots scurried to and fro around them. *People,* Bookbinder realized, his heart leaping. *Real, honest-to-God humans.*

Vasuki-Kai crossed his arms and hissed in satisfaction. "His Highness welcomes you to Sarpakavu Raajbhavan, the home of His Lordship Raja Ajathashatru the Fifth, Great King of the World, Uniter of the Spheres." Dhatri translated. "It is by his will that you are brought here."

Bookbinder stood for a long time, trying to soak in the sight. "It's straight out of Kipling."

Dhatri frowned. "Hardly."

"Sorry," Bookbinder said. "I didn't mean anything by that. It's just . . . it's very storybook."

"Wait until you see the rest of it, sir." Dhatri's pride was evident.

Sharp chucked Bookbinder's elbow. "Congratulations, sir."

Bookbinder looked over at him. Woon and Archer stood beside him, beaming.

"What are you all smiling at?"

"You did it, sir," Woon said. "We're here. We made it."

Bookbinder was so absorbed with the sight that the realization hadn't yet dawned on him. Now it did, and pride flushed upward through his throat, making his chest swell. "Yes, I suppose we did."

"Huah, sir," Sharp said.

Bookbinder found himself embarrassed by the praise. *Two dead. Besides, what the hell did I really do? Nothing. Just pointed in a direction and made everyone walk. It's the rest of you who did the work.*

He coughed, nodding. "All right, enough of that crap. We're here. Now let's finish the mission."

Sharp nodded, gesturing toward the palace. Two nagas approached, Indian soldiers trotting along at their sides. They were smaller than Vasuki-Kai, with fewer heads and arms, their scales only two or three colors against the rainbow that covered him. They carried huge bows, taller than a man. Bookbinder guessed it would take more than one set of hands to draw them. The Indian soldiers carried carbines of the same manufacture as Dhatri's.

The naga and their *Bandhavs* prostrated themselves at the sight of Vasuki-Kai, the humans touching their foreheads to the ground and the naga spreading their many heads in a fan across it beside them. Vasuki-Kai acknowledged them with the barest incline of his heads, hissing in greeting. After they rose, the naga hissed back and forth for some time, heads shaking, tongues darting, and hands gesturing at the humans several times. The Indian soldiers clapped Dhatri on the shoulder and spoke with him in Hindi in hushed tones. Their eyes flicked to the Americans several times as they spoke, and Dhatri seemed to be placating them, patting the air with his palms.

We're not supposed to be here, Bookbinder thought.

At last, the naga gestured to the Americans to follow, and the group fell in at the rear of a procession that made its way toward the Indian military-tent encampment, Vasuki-Kai at the head.

After living on MREs for so long, Bookbinder salivated as the smell of fresh-cooking food wafted toward him. Familiar sounds began to reach him; the grumbling of internal-combustion engines, the dull thrumming of generators. Industrial sounds, human sounds. Normality. He had to stop himself from running toward them.

Sharp began to frown as they went. He punched Stanley's shoulder and pointed ahead of them. Bookbinder followed his line of sight to the ground around the human encampment. He blinked. Then blinked again. The ground was writhing.

Snakes. Snakes of such variety they boggled the mind. Long and short, thick and fat, all the colors of the rainbow. Striped, spotted, monocolored. Bookbinder spotted some with horns, some with tiny, vestigial wings. A few had heads at both ends of their long, sinuous bodies. They were draped over every surface. They cavorted on top of the Humvees and slithered around the bases of the tent poles. Bookbinder looked up at the palace ring wall to see them sunning themselves in the arrow slits and sliding atop the crenellations. He stifled a shudder, already guessing what the naga's attitude toward their lesser cousins might be. The Indians were stepping gingerly as they went, careful to move around them.

"Ugh," Woon breathed. "Sir . . ."

"Major," Bookbinder said, his tone low and commanding, "I don't care if fear of snakes is the greatest phobia you've ever had. You will get over it *right now*. Do you understand me?"

Woon swallowed, grimacing. "Yes, sir."

As if on cue, Vasuki-Kai stopped, scooping up a double handful of the creatures, letting them move across his arms. He hissed gently to them, twining his heads against theirs, before setting them down again. Dhatri smiled. "It's good to be home."

Sharp reached down and touched one of the flat rocks that littered the ground at regular intervals. "It's warm, sir," he said, looking up. "Pyromantically heated, I'd guess. Unless they've got some system under the ground."

Bookbinder nodded. "For the snakes. They're cold-blooded."

Sharp nodded, standing. A ring of Indian soldiers and naga had formed around the group. Bookbinder noted that the parapet walk on the ring wall was beginning to fill up with naga though he didn't see any humans there.

The naga and humans prostrated themselves before Vasuki-Kai, who began to speak before they rose. Dhatri translated into Hindi, briefly pausing to salute as an officer joined the circle of onlookers, the dark green epaulets on his khaki uniform showing three gold suns.

At last, the naga and humans bowed together. The officer came forward and saluted Bookbinder. "Sir, I am Captain Ghaisas," he said in English so heavily accented Bookbinder could barely follow him. "I am honoring to having you in our base."

Bookbinder returned the salute. "Many thanks for having us, Captain. I can't begin to tell you how happy we are to be here."

Dhatri turned to Bookbinder. "Sir, His Highness has directed that you be lodged in one of the Raja's guesthouses. This is a great honor. You will be hosted inside the palace walls, where very few humans ever go. You can rest after your long journey."

"I appreciate that," Bookbinder said. "But we're plenty rested, and the FOB doesn't have a lot of time. Please inform His Highness that we need to connect with your Portamancer as soon as possible."

Vasuki-Kai had already begun hissing a response before Bookbinder finished speaking. Dhatri patted the air again. "Sir, please understand that the Raja does things in his own way. For now, you must go to the guesthouse and refresh yourself. I have to make my reports here."

Bookbinder opened his mouth to respond, then thought better of it. Dhatri had been clear. He was in foreign territory that he wasn't even supposed to know existed. Better not to push it. "Please thank His Highness. We're honored to stay wherever he is willing to house us."

Vasuki-Kai nodded, and the procession moved on, careful to avoid the scattering of snakes at their feet. As they moved through the encampment, Bookbinder marveled at its sparseness.

There were no sandbags, no barricade walls, no permanent structures. The soldiers looked cheerful enough, the encampment had the air of a street fair, with men cooking food on open grills, some in their undershirts playing cricket on a stretch of open field. Unlike the American FOB, there were no women at all. All stopped and stared as the Americans moved past. Bookbinder quickly abandoned any hope that, Portamancer or no, the Indians could come to FOB Frontier's aid. They were far too few, and Bookbinder counted only a handful of helicopters.

They approached a giant set of arched wooden doors, banded with scrolled iron. The iron and the rich, dark surface of the wood were decorated with intricate patterns of snakes and naga cavorting together. Bookbinder spied what he thought might be battle scenes and a couple of images of naga embracing humans, clutching them protectively to their chests.

The doors creaked open, and they moved into an enormous paved courtyard crowded with naga. A few of them were as large and colorful as Vasuki-Kai, but the majority were the smaller, plainer variety. A very few Indian officers dotted the throng, high-ranking to judge by the gold piping on their dress uniforms and the richness of their epaulets. Towers soared all around them, as thick at their base as apartment buildings, forcing Bookbinder to crane his neck. The whiteness of the stone was nearly blinding, and the magical heat rising from it made him sweat under his gear despite the encroaching winter.

Vasuki-Kai turned and motioned. A dozen smaller naga formed a tight column around the Americans and herded them along the inside of the ring wall. Vasuki-Kai stood and watched, and Dhatri saluted Bookbinder as they were separated. Bookbinder felt an anxious pang at being separated from the only friends he had in this strange place but let himself be herded along with what remained of his team. The naga marched them along for a full kilometer before the paved ground gave way to packed earth and frostbitten grass, rising to a white stone pavilion that sat at the base of one of the enormous towers. Its sloped roof was supported by eight carved columns, their capitals carved in the likeness of clustered snake's heads, fanned out to look in all directions. The pavilion was open on all sides, and Bookbinder could make out several bed-sized white stone slabs within, carved with broad grooves. He spied a white stone pool just outside the pavilion, maybe six feet across, with a brass fountain in the middle, spouting clear, sparkling water.

The naga motioned them inside, then arranged themselves to form a ring around the pavilion, backs to the humans, most of their heads looking inward. They froze in that position, eerily silent. The pavilion floor was heated, the grooved slabs even hotter. Here, as everywhere, snakes basked in abundance. The place was uncomfortably hard, but at least they wouldn't be cold, despite the lack of walls. Bookbinder looked up at the backs of the silent, immobile naga. "Well, I guess we're not going anywhere. Best get comfortable."

They grounded their packs and weapons, took off their helmets and body armor gratefully, then laid out their bedrolls and sleeping bags to try to provide some padding against the hard stone, careful to avoid the snakes who lounged about them. When Bookbinder made his way out to the fountain to wash himself and drink, one of the naga guards silently detached itself from the ring and joined him.

He glanced up at it. "You speak English, by any chance?"

It ignored him. He took a tentative step past the fountain in the direction of the tower. The naga hissed a warning, one of its heads jerking firmly in the direction of the pavilion. "All right, all right," Bookbinder said. "I've got it."

When they were all cleaned and had drunk their fill, they lay on their bedrolls, waiting. Before long, Bookbinder fell asleep despite the hard surface of the stone beneath him and the nearness of the many snakes.

Woon sprawled against one of the stone slabs, snoring with her mouth open. An enormous black snake had crawled into her lap and lay half-draped across her pack beside her. Bookbinder shuddered to think what Woon would do if she awoke to find it there. He rose to his knees and slid toward her, reaching for the animal.

Dozens of the naga guards' heads followed his movements, tongues rapidly flickering through the air.

Bookbinder sighed and backed off. Maybe they wouldn't mind if he handled one of the snakes. Maybe they would. Best not to risk it. Woon was an air force officer. She'd have to find a way to deal with it.

They lay, resting and waiting, until darkness began to fall.

Archer and Sharp rested at the other end of the pavilion, keeping their own counsel. Woon was thankfully snake-free when she finally awoke and joined Stanley and Bookbinder. "Guessing we're going to be here a while, huh, sir?"

"Guess so," he said.

"Anybody got a deck of cards?"

Nobody did.

Shortly afterward, two Indians approached, accompanied by a naga guard. They brought two large woven baskets full of food. The first appeared to be a rifleman, his uniform marked with a single chevron, but the second was an officer, wearing epaulets marked with two golden suns. The naga parted to let them pass, and they set the baskets on the pavilion's stone floor. Bookbinder stood and returned the officer's salute, eyeing the baskets hungrily. They were filled with piles of flat, fresh-baked bread, dishes full of creamed vegetables and thick sauces, skewers of savory meat. His mouth began to water from the smell.

The officer said. "I am hoping you will enjoy this food. You are well?"

"We're all fine, thanks, and I'm sure we will." He spoke quickly as the officer turned to go, hurrying. "We've been sitting here all day. We really need to get moving. We need to speak to . . ." *The Naga Raja? Wasn't he a king?* ". . . um, whoever is in charge. Your commander. We have a crisis back at our base. That's why we came here." He tried to keep his tone neutral, patient. It proved very difficult.

The officer froze. "I am asking you to please be patient. We are . . . having talks. Please enjoy the food." He motioned to his man, and they hurried away, their naga escorts keeping up easily.

Two hours later, as full darkness began to cloak the pavilion, Bookbinder found himself pacing the perimeter. He'd made two more attempts to leave the immediate area, both rebuffed by the naga guards that surrounded them. He heard sounds of human activity from all around the palace compound, and even shouts, laughter, and barked orders from the Indian human encampment on the other side of the ring wall. Once, he heard the throaty rhythmic thumping of helicopter rotors.

This was getting ridiculous. He turned to one of the naga guards. "We have got to get moving! My people are in trouble.

They need our help. We can't just sit here while you negotiate! We need help, now!"

The only indicator that it heard was a slight shifting of the few heads that regarded him. Sharp touched his elbow. "Sir, don't make yourself crazy. These guys are going to move at their own pace. I ran with the Yemenis for a while, and it was like this. No sense in pushing it. It won't help, and you'll just piss them off."

Bookbinder swallowed his anger with some difficulty. *Sharp lost two men on your watch. He's never said a word about it to you. Show him a little fucking patience.*

"All right," Bookbinder said, biting down on the words. "But, damn it! Every second counts here! We wait too long and the post gets overrun and then what the fuck did we come here for in the first place?" *What did your men die for?* Bookbinder tamped down on his magic with a will and steadied his shaking hands.

Sharp only looked at him calmly. "I get it, sir. But this isn't something we can do anything about right now. You just have to chill."

Bookbinder sighed. "You're right. So how the hell did you deal with the Yemenis?"

Sharp shrugged. "We waited. We waited until they were good and ready."

But two days later, the Naga Raja was still neither good nor ready. Apart from the regular deliveries of food, the Americans remained confined to the pavilion and the short strip of ground around it that led to the fountain on one end and a latrine pit on the other, behind an intricately carved wooden screen.

They were easily the longest two days of Bookbinder's life. The Americans did their best to occupy themselves. Sharp led them in rounds of push-ups and sit-ups, under the amused eyes of the naga. They chatted about home and played word games. Each time food was delivered, Bookbinder demanded that the officer send word to his commander that they had to get moving. After the second time, the officer stopped coming, and two troopers, neither speaking a word of English, only stared blankly at Bookbinder's demands.

As night fell after the second day, Bookbinder rounded up his team. "We can't sit like this. We have got to get out of here."

He whispered, looking over his shoulder at the Naga. Even if they could hear them, could they understand?

Sharp was silent. Stanley nodded. "We can't do that, sir," Woon said. "If we just wait a little . . ."

"We don't have time! What if they want us to wait a week? Two weeks? A month? The FOB could have fallen by then! We're already well past the window I told Crucible we would take. He's probably given up on us already!"

"Sir." It was Sharp.

"What?"

"Sir, could I have a word?" Sharp's voice was hard. He jerked his head in the direction of the fountain.

Bookbinder met the eyes of the rest of his team, saw the concern there. He felt his throat, slightly raw. Had he been yelling?

"Come on, sir." Sharp stood.

They walked over to the fountain. Light from the Source's huge moon had begun to cast a soft glow over the playing waters, the trickle of which masked their conversation from those still seated in the pavilion.

"What's up, Sergeant?" Bookbinder asked, trying to sound as authoritative as possible.

Sharp wasn't buying it. "Sir, I know you're taking the guys we lost hard. You have to remember that they signed up for this. They knew what was coming. That's just how it is."

Bookbinder looked at him. "What are you going on about? We've got a FOB to save! That's why we came here!"

Sharp put his hand on Bookbinder's shoulder. "Sir, it's okay. It's not your fault. They knew what they were doing. We made it. We're here. We don't want to screw that up now. Not after we've come so far."

Bookbinder opened his mouth to refute him and found he had nothing to say.

Sharp's voice was soft. "I'm proud to follow you, sir. But you have to keep in mind that you're in charge here. If you try to arrange some kind of jailbreak because you're feeling bad about the guys getting zapped, well . . . that's going to cause trouble isn't it? For all of us. The FOB will keep a few days, sir. We just need to sit tight and keep it together is all."

Bookbinder was silent. His throat clenched with humiliation and grief.

Sharp touched his shoulder again. "Those guys didn't die in vain, sir. They really didn't. We just need to keep it together. Do you think you can do that?"

Bookbinder found his voice. "Yes."

Footsteps sounded on the courtyard beyond. Bookbinder and Sharp turned to see Dhatri approaching. At his side was a tall, regal-looking older man. His khaki uniform was immaculately pressed and covered with ribbons. Red facings adorned his lapels. His black beret bore a gold wreath around a sun. His epaulets were a gaudy design of three gold suns surmounted by an equal number of lions. His immaculately trimmed moustache twitched disdain. Vasuki-Kai stood behind them, nodding greeting as the Naga guards prostrated themselves.

Dhatri saluted and gestured to the man beside him. "May I present Brigadier Hazarika, who commands our presence here at FOB Sarpakavu."

Bookbinder did the mental rank comparison and saluted smartly. "Sir, a pleasure to meet you."

Brigadier Hazarika returned Bookbinder's salute but said nothing. Vasuki-Kai however, hissed something from behind him.

Dhatri translated dutifully. "His Lordship Raja Ajathashatru the Fifth, Great King of the World, Uniter of the Spheres, summons you to appear before him."

Bookbinder and Sharp exchanged glances. The wait was over. They were to see the Naga Raja after all.

CHAPTER XXII
AUDIENCE

The strength of British magic lies in is diversity. Modern militaries emphasize uniformity out of necessity, and they're right to . . . in a nonarcane world. The Great Reawakening has made that kind of thinking obsolete. The Welsh "Bog Style" Terramancy complements our "Branded" Highland Battalion. Mesh that with the "Court Sorcery" coming out of London, and you have a range of abilities we bring to bear to face a diverse range of threats. If we'd streamlined all that into a single, conforming style? We'd have lost far more than we would have gained. It's a united kingdom, to be sure, but it's the parts we're the sum of that win the fight in the end.

—Thegn Albert Harrow, Blackpool Warband, Red Ravens

Bookbinder asked Stanley Britton to stay behind with Archer and Sharp. The Naga had given every indication of being rank-conscious, and this was an official embassy, so he thought it best to bring only senior officers. He silently thanked his luck that Woon was a major.

They proceeded through the courtyard beyond the pavilion, passing around the thickness of the tower and into the main plaza. Bookbinder caught his breath at the opulence. A long reflecting pool, broken by several fountains, spanned the plaza, which was at least a hundred feet long. The white stone expanse was ringed by domed buildings, also of white stone, their surfaces expertly carved in interlocking images of serpents, humans, men with the heads and wings of birds. Bookbinder spotted at least one agni danav, lying on its back, a naga triumphantly astride it, thrusting a sword through its chest. The

vanity of the royal naga was underscored by the scattering of
giant, man-sized gold-framed mirrors that hung on the inside of
the plaza walls, lining the entire courtyard all the way from the
ring wall's entrance to the main gates of each building.

Vasuki-Kai led the way, the humans behind him, a double
line of naga guards falling in on either side. Clusters of naga,
all of Vasuki-Kai's greater size and coloration, stood at the
entrance to what Bookbinder assumed was the palace.

The building dwarfed all the rest, a massive central dome
ringed by eight smaller towers, too narrow and delicate to be
anything other than decorative. A brass finial at the top of the
dome depicted a coiled, multiheaded snake, basking in a burning sun. The walls of the structure were pierced with such skill
that they had become stone latticeworks, dappling all with the
patterned firelight that flowed from inside. The huge iron gates
were open, revealing a massive promenade that stretched out
into the distance, lit on either side by giant, black, iron braziers,
burning scented oils. The same jeweled insects that Bookbinder
had seen over the river they'd crossed earlier cavorted above the
promenade, drawn to it by bowls filled with a thick, sweet-
smelling liquid that stood on white stone pedestals interspersed
among the braziers.

The ground was, of course, carpeted with snakes. Bookbinder
caught his breath at the beauty of it all but didn't forget to chuck
Woon's elbow. "Don't step on 'em, for the love of God."

She rolled her eyes as they advanced into the promenade.
After a few steps, a magnificent dais hove into view. A white
stone fan spread behind it, carved in the likeness of a naga
reclining. A grooved slab, much like the ones in the pavilion,
stood before the stone fan, flanked by naga guards of princely
rank judging by their size and coloration. They bore no weapons, but Britton could feel strong magical currents off them even
from far away.

In the center of it all, reclining on the grooved slab, was the
creature that Bookbinder guessed had to be the Naga Raja,
Ajathashatru the Fifth.

The Great King was a monster. He lacked even the nods to
humanity that the other naga showed. He was all serpent; gigantic, his coiled length as thick around as a tree. His scales, each
the size of a dinner plate, blazed in a rainbow of colors so

dazzling that Bookbinder had to squint to look at him. His coils stacked, length upon tree-trunk length, raising his neck at least twenty feet in the air to where it blossomed into a forest of snake's heads more than double what Bookbinder had seen on any other naga. Each one was the size of large man's head, each wearing a silver crown that dripped with glittering jewels.

At their approach, the Naga Raja reared to his full height, the heads stretching out in a fan that spread at least eight feet at its ends, and hissed a greeting that echoed the length of the promenade. Vasuki-Kai, Brigadier Hazarika, everyone in the room went down on their bellies. After an instant's hesitation, Bookbinder tugged on Woon's sleeve, and they imitated them, knocking their foreheads on the floor. Bookbinder's gut rebelled at the gesture. He was an American, his forefathers had fought a revolution to end customs just like this. But there was no America in the Source. There had been no revolution here. New world. New rules.

When at last they rose, Ajathashatru hissed again in an echoing bass that rattled Bookbinder's teeth. Brigadier Hazarika translated in English nearly as good as Dhatri's. "His Royal Majesty welcomes you to his Raajya and says that his loyal *amatyan* Abhijit Vasuki-Kai has spoken highly of you and your people. He says you have been kind to his wards and children." At this the king inclined a few of his heads toward Dhatri and Hazarika. "His Royal Majesty welcomes this and is pleased to note that you are learning civilization. It was ever his wish that his *amatyan*'s tenure among you should teach you this. It pleases him to see it is so."

Out of the corner of his eye, Bookbinder saw Woon swallow and guessed the Naga Raja's tone rankled her as much as him. *Easy. This isn't a democracy.*

"Please inform His Royal Majesty that we are very grateful for his hospitality and assistance. We are very comfortable in our quarters and have been well fed. Thank him for his generosity. This can only help improve relations between the United States, the Republic of India, and His Majesty's great Raajya. I will ensure that my government knows of the king's kindness when I finally establish contact with them."

Hazarika translated, Ajathashatru's heads nodding in time with the words. "His Majesty's *amatyan* informs him that you lost *sipahis* on the journey here. His Majesty notes it is your custom to mourn even your lowest and so he has assigned one hundred mourners on their behalf. They are even now interceding with Chitragupta to ensure your men are well treated by Yamaraj in the next life."

Bookbinder swallowed, glad that Sharp and Archer weren't here for this. "Thank His Royal Majesty for me. It is a great honor."

"His Royal Majesty's *amatyan* informs him that you have a special and rare magic. He says that you can steal the magic of others and make it fast into nonliving things. His Majesty asks if this is true."

Bookbinder paused, his stomach doing somersaults. *You have nothing to bargain with here. You are completely at their mercy. Here, at last, is something they want from you.* Better to keep his cards close to the vest for now until he was sure they were going to help him.

He took a deep breath before answering. "Inform His Majesty that it is true, but it doesn't work all the time. I was lucky on the road here. Much of the time, I cannot make it work. I think my magic is . . . broken somehow."

Dhatri looked over his shoulder, frowning at Bookbinder, his expression saying, *You never told us this* . . . He whispered rapidly to Hazarika, who nodded, looking over at Bookbinder. Woon was stone-faced. Bookbinder thanked her inwardly yet again.

There was a short burst of conversation between Vasuki-Kai, Ajathashatru, Hazarika, and Dhatri, interspersed hissing and Hindi. After a moment, Hazarika translated again. "His Royal Majesty is quite curious to see you demonstrate this ability. Two of his sorcerers attend him here. He commands you to steal their magic and bind it to this brazier."

As he spoke, two lesser naga approached the dais, carrying another one of the large iron braziers, this one unlit. They set it down with a thud and stepped back as the naga to Ajathashatru's side slithered forward. It reached forward with four of its arms and Bookbinder felt its flow intensify, Binding to the air molecules between its outstretched hands. Wind picked up throughout the promenade, making the flames in the braziers flicker and sending the crystalline insects scattering. After a moment, a crackling ball of lightning, several feet across, blazed before the naga's chest. All eyes looked expectantly at Bookbinder.

He bowed and stepped forward, shunting back his magical flow as it surged instinctively toward the naga Aeromancer's spell casting. He stretched his hands forth and gently let his current intersect with the naga's. The creature's eyes widened as the ball of lightning before it began to shrink. Bookbinder extended a hand and pointed to the brazier, grunting and straining as dramatically as he could, willing himself to sweat. He dragged on the naga's current, but only slightly, not fully allowing himself to capture the flow before he halfheartedly slapped a tiny portion of it at the brazier. The black iron surface began to sizzle slightly, tiny tendrils of electricity playing across its surface.

Ajathashatru hissed in excitement, and all in the chamber pressed forward to look. Bookbinder grunted more, reaching hard for the brazier. Internally, he began to roll the magic back, shunting the tide away.

After a moment, he let out a soft cry and dropped his arms. The brazier ceased to sizzle. The naga's lightning ball returned to full size. Bookbinder shook his head and put on an expression of disgust. "I beg His Royal Majesty's forgiveness. It isn't working right now."

Hazarika translated, and Ajathashatru hissed back urgently. "His Royal Majesty commands you to make it work."

Bookbinder prostrated himself. "Please beg His Majesty's mercy and forgiveness. It works sometimes. Sometimes it does not. Perhaps it is the presence of his might that has frightened my powers away."

Vasuki-Kai hissed a long conversation with Ajathashatru, gesturing frequently to Bookbinder. Hazarika joined the conversation, and they talked for a long time before pausing. At last, Hazarika said, "His Royal Majesty speculates that perhaps this is like the fear-sickness that sometimes plagues his lesser children"—Ajathashatru gestured with his heads toward the snakes all around them—"when they will not eat or pass their waste. Or maybe this is like the fear-sickness in humans, when they cannot mate with their women."

Bookbinder caught Woon smirking out of the corner of his eye and felt himself flush. He stood. "I'm sure His Majesty is right."

"His Majesty says you must rest and become comfortable in

your surroundings. He asks if you have enough heat. Are you fed well? Are you wanting to mate with a woman?"

Bookbinder shook his head. "Thank His Majesty for his generosity. I am perhaps concerned only for the safety of my people. If His Majesty would help us to assist them, then I could perhaps defeat this fear-sickness and demonstrate my power to his satisfaction."

Hazarika stared at him, horrified. He did not translate. Instead, he said, "Colonel, you do not bargain with the Great King."

Ajathashatru hissed angrily and Hazarika turned and spoke quickly in Hindi, bowing deeply.

The Naga Raja straightened at the brigadier's words. Everyone in the room stiffened. There was a long pause before Ajathashatru spoke again. "His Royal Majesty understands that you are only learning to be civilized. Therefore, he will forgive your rudeness. He says this is not a boon-begging audience, but an introduction. His Royal Majesty does not hear entreaties for another two days. He will consider your request on the proper day."

Bookbinder bit down hard. Two days! They'd already wasted two damned days. *Relax. Remember what Sharp said. If you want help, you've got to dance to their tune. Two more days or never.*

Bookbinder only bowed, not trusting himself to speak.

"His Royal Majesty commands you to return to your quarters and await his next summons. He commands you to shed your fear-sickness and be prepared to demonstrate your abilities when next you are called before him."

Again, Bookbinder bowed and managed to respond without anger in his voice. "Thank His Royal Majesty for speaking with me."

Hazarika nodded, and said. "Now you will back out of the audience. At no time are you to turn your back on the Great King."

All prostrated once again to a slight nod from Ajathashatru's many heads.

Bookbinder and Woon followed the rest of the procession, backing away, eyes cast down, until the giant monster that held them captive was out of sight.

Sharp and Archer took the news with mere nods. Stanley shook his head impatiently but said nothing. Bookbinder sighed as they settled in for the night, ready to get some rest before another two days of long waiting.

Woon caught up to him when he was washing at the fountain. "That was all bullshit about your magic, wasn't it, sir?"

Bookbinder shrugged. "So what if it was?"

"If you've got a plan, I'd like to know what it is."

Bookbinder shook his head. "No plan, really. It's just the one thing we have that they want. Figured it would be smarter to hang on to it for a while."

"What do you plan to do with it?" Woon asked. "Brigadier Hazarika was pretty clear that you can't negotiate with this . . . guy . . . thing. Whatever."

Bookbinder smiled. "I'm still working on that part. I'm running mostly on instinct, Major. This is all new to me, in case you haven't noticed. I don't exactly have my Ph.D. in negotiating with giant snakes."

She snorted. "We have that in common, sir."

The sun was scarcely up the next morning before Captain Ghaisas arrived with two Naga guards and a trooper of his own. He was empty-handed, which surprised Bookbinder because humans only ever approached them here to bring food.

Ghaisas saluted. "Good morning, sir."

Bookbinder returned the salute. "Good morning, Captain. Nice to see you."

"It is nice to see you. I am thinking you are very unhappy sitting here with nothing to do. I am inviting you to play games with my men. His Majesty has given permission for the playing."

Bookbinder stood, working kinks out of his shoulders from sleeping on the hard stone floor. He felt a snake drop from his knee, where it had been curled up to sleep. He had become so used to them now that he barely noticed. He looked over at the rest of his team, most already awake, stiff and annoyed from enforced idleness and sleeping on stone. He turned back to the captain. "That would be delightful."

Ghaisas chatted amiably as they headed over to the Indian

encampment. "We are a combined force here, sir. All of our best come. We have Assam, Madras, Gurkhas. I am from Fourth Rajputs. Subedar Major Dhatri is Sikh Regiment."

They passed through the curtain wall out to the tent city that comprised the human presence. The smells of cooking and sounds of conversation were rain in Bookbinder's desert after being cooped up in that pavilion for so long. "This is it?" He gestured to the camp around him. "Are there more of you here?"

Ghaisas shook his head. "His Royal Majesty only permits a small number of peoples to be living here. Most of them are officers inside the palace."

"You like it?" Bookbinder asked, unsure of what else to say.

Ghaisas grinned until his moustache tickled his cheeks. "It is the biggest honor to be coming here, sir. We are living with our gods."

They passed beyond the line of tents to a broad field covered in semifrozen grass that was miraculously free of snakes. A cricket pitch had been laid out, complete with wickets. Bats, balls, helmets, and pads lay haphazardly along the side. A group of young Indian soldiers mulled around the stumps at one end. They looked up, smiling, as the Americans approached.

One of the troopers handed Ghaisas a basket of flat bread, which he passed to Bookbinder. "Only a little eating. You are running a lot today! Has anyone played the game cricket before?"

Bookbinder shook his head and noted that the Americans around him were following suit. "I did once," Stanlcy said. "On a liaison tour with the Brits. But that was ages ago. It's a little like baseball . . . and a little like golf."

Ghaisas nodded. "You are right. We are dividing you up on two teams, and you will learn fast. This is an easy game to play."

Sharp and Archer shook their heads. "We'd like to sit this out, sir, if it's okay with you. We're happy just to be out of that gazebo."

"It's not okay with me, Sergeant. You'll play and you'll do your best and we're all going to have a good time and get along with our friends here, okay?"

"Okay." Sharp shrugged, as unflappable as ever.

"No using magic," Bookbinder joked to Ghaisas as they

headed over to the knot of Indian soldiers to make their introductions.

Ghaisas smiled back. "No worrying about that. Humans are not allowed to be bringing magic to this place. His Majesty makes special permission for you and Major Woon. It is a great honor."

Cricket was precisely as Stanley had described it, a lively game that felt part baseball, part soccer, and part golf. Near as Bookbinder could tell, it consisted of whacking a ball with a short flat bat and then running back and forth between a couple of sticks while the pitcher tried to get him declared "dismissed" through a variety of confusing ways, most consisting of knocking down the sticks they were running between. It was tough to follow, but the Indians seemed to be playing honestly, and the mere act of being around people and stretching their legs to run in the bright sunshine was an absolute blessing. Bookbinder found himself smiling and wasn't surprised to see Sharp, Archer, and even Stanley doing the same despite their original refusal to play.

The Indians were affable and playful, poking fun at one another when a swing at the ball was missed or the sticks were accidentally knocked over during a run. There was Nishok, a Nepali lad from the Gurkhas who was missing three of his teeth. It didn't stop him from grinning incessantly. He was the fastest runner Bookbinder could remember seeing and in the habit of disputing referee calls with Ghaisas, who served as the game's umpire, shouting "Howzat!" at the top of his lungs every time he felt a player should be declared out. There was Jivan, a *Naik* cavalryman from the Kashmir Rifles, who could throw the ball with such accuracy that he often hit the sticks before a batter could finish the run, keeping him from scoring even once. Dhatri turned out to be the best bowler, what Bookbinder thought of as a pitcher, in the entire camp.

They ran and sweated and laughed, and Bookbinder felt better than he had in a long time despite the maddening wait for the Great King's pleasure. He looked up about halfway through the game to see many naga clustering around the parapets of the ring wall, watching them play. Much of the Indian encampment seemed to have turned out as well, standing alongside the oval pitch, shouting encouragement in broken English as the Americans fumbled their way through the bats and runs. Sharp and Archer, gifted natural athletes, took to it quickly, and what Stanley, Bookbinder, and Woon lacked in athleticism, they made up for in the charity of the opposing team, who worked hard to let the Americans off easy when they were up at bat.

After a couple of hours, they broke for a snack, sitting around the stumps and making halting conversation in their limited common language. Bookbinder was trying to comprehend some joke Nishok had told in his broken English when he heard a throaty rumble of vehicles. A small row of trucks had gathered on the opposite side of the pitch in a clearing just beyond the camp. Indian soldiers massed around it, waiting for something. Bookbinder stared for a moment, and was about to turn his attention back to Nishok when the air before them shimmered.

A giant gate rolled open before them, as large as the one he'd passed through when he'd first come to the Source.

A convoy of military trucks rolled through, and the Indian soldiers swarmed them, rushing to move stacks of heavy wooden crates into their own vehicles.

Resupply by Portamantic gate. Bookbinder snapped his eyes up to the ring wall. After a moment's scanning, they alighted on one of the naga princes, leaning from one of the wall's turrets, arms outstretched. His current was wickedly strong. Even from this great distance, Bookbinder felt the faintest hint of it thrumming in the air.

Their Portamancer. Bookbinder tried not to stare and failed. Here was the answer to their problems. Right beside him and not helping him for reasons he couldn't understand.

Bookbinder bit back on his anger. Ghaisas followed his gaze and noted his expression. "Perhaps Colonel Bookbinder is feeling tired from too much playing," he ventured. "Maybe now is the time to go back to the guesthouse for resting. Maybe with rest you can finish the fear-sickness and give His Royal Majesty the requested demonstration."

The Naga Raja summoned them again the next day, right on schedule. They proceeded into his presence, Hazarika and Vasuki-Kai in the lead, just as before. Ajathashatru reclined on his dais, just as before. The only thing to distinguish this visit from the last was the presence of a single naga sorcerer by his side. Bookbinder still had trouble telling any two naga apart, but this looked to him to be the Portamancer he'd seen during the cricket game.

Once they had performed their prostrations, Ajathashatru addressed them. "His Royal Majesty notes that you are enjoying playing games with his children. This pleases him. Cricket is a silly game, but it is a mark of civilization, and taking to it can only improve the lot of your people."

Bookbinder bowed. "His Majesty was kind to permit it. Captain Ghaisas has been very gracious and patient in teaching us."

Ajathashatru's many heads nodded. "His Majesty says that you have been a polite guest. He will hear your entreaty now if you wish to beg a boon of him."

Bookbinder glanced at the Portamancer. The formality of the request making perplexed him. Surely Vasuki-Kai had informed his king why they had come here. Why bother with the asking? He shrugged inwardly. This was a different race, a different culture. He couldn't begin to understand how their minds worked. Best to play along in the hopes they were getting somewhere. The Portamancer couldn't help but be a good sign.

"Please inform His Majesty that my government's presence in this plane is cut off from resupply and aid. We are under siege by hostile goblin tribes and cannot hold out for very long. If we are not rescued, many thousands will die. I ask that His Majesty use his Portamancer to help us to return to my home to obtain relief for my men before they are lost."

Ajathashatru hissed to one of the naga guards, who bowed, slithered away, and returned with a bundle of arrows. A princely naga joined it, a strong current emanating from it. The tenor of the tide came clear to Bookbinder, soft, cold, fluid. A Hydromancer.

"His Majesty asks if, now that you are rested and accustomed to life among us, you can work your magic as a demonstration."

Bookbinder sighed inwardly. It seemed that while he could not bargain, the Great King most certainly could. The naga Hydromancer stretched its hands forward, Binding its magic into a shimmering ball of ice that hovered before it.

"His Majesty asks that you magic the tips of these arrows, as you did the bullets of your *sipahi* when you fought the agni danav on your journey here."

There was no playing games now. If he wanted to use the king's gate, he was going to have to put something on the table. He stepped forward and did his grunting drama as before, but this time, he worked his magic properly, siphoning off the naga's current in full to its hissing surprise, then channeling it into the arrowheads, one by one, until they crackled on the stone floor of the promenade, blue with cold, sparking frost.

One of the naga guards slithered forward at a gesture from the king, retrieved one of the magic arrows, and nocked it to a man-sized bow. At a nod from Ajathashatru, it fired it into one of the stone pedestals that fed the clouds of glass insects. The arrow slammed into the base of it, the frost spreading outward, the stone crackling from the cold. After a moment, the pedestal shivered, then shattered, frozen pieces scattering across the promenade, sending the snakes sliding away.

Ajathashatru hissed in frank admiration, then paused, assuming his usual regal mode. "His Majesty says your magic is very impressive. He asks how long these arrows will stay ensorcelled."

Bookbinder shook his head honestly. "I regret I do not know. I believe they expend their magic as they are used."

"His Majesty is pleased with your demonstration. He grants your boon and will direct his *amatyan* to return you home to your people soon. Unfortunately, the time is not auspicious for the working of this particular magic. The great rain that indicates the end of the *Vassa* is late this year. Until these rains come, the magic you request cannot be worked."

Bookbinder seethed. Fucking liar. He had just seen the Portamancer working his magic right in front of him yesterday. He chose one of Ajathashatru's heads and met its eyes. The head stared back, daring him to challenge the patent falsehood. Bookbinder swallowed his pride and bowed. "Of course, I will be patient and await His Majesty's pleasure."

Ajathashatru nodded. "His Majesty commands you to do so. He will summon you again when he next desires an audience. Go now, and know that His Royal Majesty is pleased with you."

Bookbinder backed out of the audience again, eyes down, blood boiling with fury, digging deep for scraps of patience.

When next the Indians brought them out for cricket, Bookbinder noted soldiers busily cleaning up the tents and doing their best to put their gear in order. Regimental standards were being raised. A golden Maltese cross surrounding a horn beneath three lions fluttered above one tent pole; an elephant paraded across a round shield before two crossed swords on another. The number of dress uniforms had spiked sharply.

"What's up with that?" Bookbinder asked Ghaisas, indicating the fluttering standards, the sudden interest in order and cleanliness.

Ghaisas grinned. "Very soon it is Army Day in my country. We celebrate a very famous general. He was our first once India became a free democracy. There will be celebrations here and also at home."

"Outstanding. Do we get to celebrate with you?"

Ghaisas thought about it for a moment. "Maybe we are having special 'grudge' cricket match?"

Bookbinder nodded. No doubt they'd find a way to use that as an excuse to further delay them. He knew the cricket games were an attempt to distract them.

The next day, two naga guards escorted the same naga Hydromancer and deposited a larger bundle of arrows beside the fountain, hissing and nodding at Bookbinder until he transferred the creature's magic into them. He looked up once the bundle was fully magicked, gingerly lifted by the guards, careful not to touch the blue tips, and carted away. "Tell His Royal Majesty that I sincerely hope those rains come soon," Bookbinder said. But if the naga understood him, they gave no sign.

This became a daily ritual. Bookbinder would magick bundles of arrows in the morning, as well as the occasional sword or magazine of ammunition. In the afternoon, Captain Ghaisas would collect them for cricket. The captain was tight-lipped about the coming rains, and his men all studiously avoided the topic, Dhatri included. After a while, Bookbinder stopped bringing it up.

Each day, the Portamancer would come to the turret to open

the gate for the Indian soldiers to transfer equipment or personnel. Bookbinder would look at his lap, knowing he was expected to ignore this flagrant dishonesty.

When, after another week, Hazarika and Vasuki-Kai came to summon him before the Naga Raja again, hope stirred in his breast. Perhaps he'd finally passed whatever test of patience they'd laid before him. Maybe this was it.

But his heart sank when he saw that the promenade before Ajathashatru had at last been cleared of snakes. Instead, there were heaps of ordinance. Arrows, swords, bullets, even larger artillery shells and rockets. They stretched all around Bookbinder, forcing him to turn his head to take it all in.

"His Royal Majesty is exceedingly pleased with your magic," Hazarika translated. "The frost you have put into his arms persists, and has given him a great tool to strike at the heart of his enemies. He is most pleased with you and has decided to make an exception. There is no need to wait for the *Vassa* this year. His Majesty will employ his magic to aid you."

Bookbinder shuddered as he waited for the "but" that was surely coming. It did.

"But," Hazarika added, "His Majesty asks that you first complete this task for him." He swept his arm across all the ordnance spread around him. "You must first magick these instruments of war for the glory of His Majesty's army."

Bookbinder nodded and bowed. All anger was gone. His blood was as cool as his mind was clear.

Because now he knew. He had seen the vast expanse of the Agni Danav Raajya. He knew that a full-scale offensive against them would take months, that it would require magicked ammunition far beyond even the piles that lay all around him now.

He knew the truth: Now that Ajathashatru knew what he could do, the Great King would never, ever let him go.

CHAPTER XXIII
OFF THE PITCH

The notion of "Probe" or prohibited magics is completely arbitrary. It's much like passing judgment on homosexuality, or euthanasia. The physical world isn't interested in human moral judgments. It simply ticks along as it always has. In the so-called "pariah" states in Africa and the Caribbean, where Necromancy is embraced and openly practiced, the idea of death and the sanctity of burial are different. The Mexican "Dios de los Muertos Exception," and the fact that the United States recognizes it, underscores this flagrant hypocrisy. There are so-called "Probe Selfers" rotting in prison, or even dead, for the crime of practicing magic that would have been perfectly legal if they'd been lucky enough to be born in Nigeria, or the Southern Sudan, or Haiti.

—Loretta Kiwan, Vice President
Council on Latent-American Rights
Appearing on WorldSpan Networks *Counterpoint*

Bookbinder returned to the pavilion, stretched, and tapped Sharp on the shoulder. "A word." He motioned toward the fountain. Sharp nodded and followed. The naga guards, now confident that Bookbinder and his team would keep to the pavilion and its environs, no longer followed them to the place where the loud pattering of falling water obscured hushed conversation.

Bookbinder was fairly certain that the naga guards couldn't understand a word of what they said, but he still made a great show of scrubbing down, and was sure to pitch his voice low when he said to Sharp, "We're leaving."

Sharp looked up, surprised. "Sir . . ."

Bookbinder plunged his hands into the water, scrubbing them hard and splashing loudly. "You're in receive mode now, Sergeant. I am not asking for your opinion. I am telling you what our course of action is."

Sharp paused only briefly. "Roger that, sir. What are your orders?"

Bookbinder nodded. "The first thing is that the only people who know are you and I. That doesn't change. I don't want Woon or Stanley accidentally letting the cat out of the bag."

"Got it. What's the plan? It's a long walk back to the FOB."

"We're not walking back to the FOB. Listen, when this happens, it's going to be a big surprise. I'm telling you because I know I can count on you not to hesitate. If anyone holds back when this kicks off, you grab them by the short hairs and make them move."

"Make them move where?"

"You'll see."

Sharp nodded. "All right, sir. When does this pop off?"

"Tomorrow's their big celebration, right? Their national Army Day or something?"

Sharp thought about it for a moment and nodded again. "All right, they'll be distracted and busy. We'll be out on the pitch for our grudge match.

"That's when we get out of here."

Bookbinder barely slept that night. He was up at dawn, pacing the pavilion, waiting for his escort to arrive. He watched the tower's base, willing his eyes to see through it. At some point, Indian officers would round that tower to fetch him away. Would it be Captain Ghaisas, coming to fetch him for another round of cricket? Or would it be Brigadier Hazarika and another day of ensorcelling Ajathashatru's weaponry? Panic and elation warred in his gut.

At long last, two khaki uniforms appeared around the tower's base, naga guards in tow. Bookbinder froze, staring hard as the men hove into view. One of them wore epaulets and Bookbinder strained to make them out. At long last he did.

Three gold suns. Ghaisas. Bookbinder swallowed hard and nodded to Sharp. The sergeant nodded back and said nothing.

Ghaisas saluted, grinning. "Today is a very special cricket match, sir."

Bookbinder cocked an eyebrow. "Why's that?" But his stomach was doing somersaults. He hadn't forgotten about the promised grudge match.

"Today is Army Day that I told you about. So we are having our grudge match, and we are not taking it easy on you, Colonel! Very tough cricket match." He smiled fiercely.

Bookbinder laughed. "Well, in honor of your holiday, I suppose we'll try to lose with as much grace as possible."

They headed through the plaza toward the main gate in the ring wall. Bookbinder motioned to Sharp to keep close by. The sergeant matched his pace, his face blank.

The Indian encampment was festive. Pennants flapped from staves shoved into the muddy lanes that intersected between the Indian tents, proudly displaying the regimental arms of the various units making up the Indian presence on the FOB. The red Indian Army flag, white swords crossed below white lions, was everywhere. Soldiers chatted happily around grill fires. He saw more than one dress uniform, starched jackets, red silk turbans, white feathers. They looked ridiculously out of place among the mud and tents.

Ghaisas was true to his word. The Indians did not take it easy this time. They put all the Americans on one team, then proceeded to crush that team, despite Dhatri and Jivan's valiant efforts to save them. For the first time, the crowd of Indians cheered loudly as the team hosting the Americans was defeated, and Bookbinder smiled along with them, seeing it for what it was, national pride. Only Stanley Britton seemed irritated by losing, throwing himself into the game with a ferocity that did not match his skill. Bookbinder played worse and worse as his impatience grew. His eyes kept returning to the turret on the ring wall closest to the pitch. He played on, waiting. The naga didn't appear. His heart sank. The Portamancer had been opening gates for resupply on a daily basis since he'd arrived. Maybe the holiday had delayed the daily occurrence?

He turned back to the game just as Jivan scooped up the ball and threw it hard at the stumps, knocking them down and saving their team from a more miserable trouncing than they'd have suffered otherwise. With that last dismissal, the teams came to the center of the pitch, clapping and shaking hands as they switched sides.

Bookbinder heard the rumble of trucks. He turned. The Portamancer had appeared on the balcony, hands spread lightly over the parapet. Bookbinder took an instinctive step toward it, then stopped himself. He wasn't going to be able to get closer to the point of making a difference. He dabbed at his eye and waved to Ghaisas as he stepped off the pitch, as close to the turret as he dared, sitting this round out. Another Indian soldier raced in to play for him. Bookbinder sized up the side of one of the Indian trucks parked closest to the field, eyeing its large, enclosed cargo bed.

The trucks pulled to a stop, freshly washed, with the Indian Army flag fluttering brightly from their antennae. The Portamancer spread its arms wide and Drew its magic to open the gate. Bookbinder strained toward it, summoning his own current. The naga had to be Binding the magic to the air just before the Indian convoy at this very moment. But he could feel nothing.

Maybe the distance was too far? Maybe he was having an off day? It didn't matter. He looked at the truck bed, so close and yet so useless, and swallowed his disappointment.

And then he felt it. A flicker, a tiny tendril of the naga Portamancer's magic, deep and sonorous, transporting.

Now or never, all in. Bookbinder yanked his own flow, surging it through him with everything he had, sending it to latch on to that tiny flicker of the Portamancer's current. For a moment it slipped, and he worried that he'd missed the opportunity. The gate slid open before the trucks, huge and shimmering.

And then Bookbinder's magic caught. He hauled hard on the naga's flow, feeling the Portamancer spin in the turret, many pairs of eyes searching for the thief siphoning off its magic.

He felt his own body suffuse with the double magical load, puffed up and strained, fit to burst. He turned and bound hard to the truck bed. The metal side vanished. In its place was the shimmering static of a gate. Beyond it, he could see asphalt and rows of trucks. The Home Plane, in India probably, but home nonetheless.

"Sharp! Go!" he shouted, breaking into a run. "Everybody through there right now! Gogogo!"

Sharp and Archer motioned to Stanley and all three broke into a run. Woon hesitated for a brief moment, then followed, all pelting as hard as they could for the shimmering gate that now flickered in the side of the truck. The Indians stood stunned, trying to understand what was happening.

But only for a moment. Shouts erupted from all around them as their hosts moved to intercept.

Bookbinder hoped a moment was enough. Ghaisas threw himself in Sharp's path, but the sergeant brought his elbow up across the captain's face without breaking stride, sending him sprawling in the dust.

The Indians lounging in the truck had leapt backward as the truck's bed became a gate, but they now raced forward in front of it, trying to cut off the Americans' escape. Woon reached forward without slowing and the ground bucked, sending the men flying, leaving the truck rock steady.

Stanley was the first to jump through, the gate's light washing over his back as he thudded out onto the asphalt surface on the other side. Sharp and Archer took up positions to either side, crouching, ready to fight. Woon was slower, nicely hurdling an Indian solider who dove at her and crunching down hard on the back of his hand before reaching the gate and passing through it. Bookbinder felt a hand grab his elbow, and spun to see Dhatri's face frowning up at him, anger and betrayal scrawled across it. He yanked on Bookbinder's arm, checking his run. His eyes were wide, the expression reading, *How could you do this to us?*

Bookbinder spun and brought his knee up into the subedar major's crotch. Shaking his arm free. "I am not going to let my people die," he snarled, as the man sank to his knees. "Not for anyone!"

And then he turned and raced through the gate, Archer and Sharp turning and following close behind. At long last, shots rang out behind them, rounds churning the ground and thudding into the truck's frame. Bookbinder skidded to a halt on the asphalt surface of what looked like a military parade ground, ringed with low buildings. He rolled his magic back, the gate sliding shut as his tide dissipated. Only then did he look up and make a quick check of his team. They stood around him, winded and puffing, but unharmed. The sense of the Home Plane washed over him, disappointing in its muted quality. Every-thing was . . . less here, the glow of the sunlight, the smells of engine oil and human sweat, the sound of Woon gasping for air beside him.

A long line of trucks stood before him, piled high with cargo, Indian soldiers standing in shock to either side. A banner strung over the plaza showed the Indian Army flag, with writing beneath it in Sanskrit, Chinese, and English. INDIA SAHIR WEL-COMES SHANGHAI COOPERATIVE ORGANIZATION PARTNERS TO ARMY DAY!

A large stand of bleachers had been set up alongside the plaza, presumably to watch the gate open. It was crowded with Indian officers, but Bookbinder noted a few others in the press; Chinese sorcerers in long, traditional robes, officers from another Asian country in dark, tiger-striped camouflage. He spotted a redheaded man with the Russian flag stitched to his shoulder. All gaped openmouthed at Bookbinder and his team.

For a moment, everyone stood, frozen. Most of the men were in dress uniforms and unarmed, but a few armed soldiers ringed the plaza. They raised their weapons tentatively, then lowered them, unsure of what to do.

Bookbinder sucked in a breath and mustered all the com-mand he could. "We are Americans!" he shouted. "We demand to be taken to the office of our defense attaché or the nearest US embassy immediately!"

He picked out the closest Indian officer, judging by his dark green epaulets. "Do any of you speak English?" Bookbinder shouted again as he approached. "We are Americans, and . . ."

"I speak English," the officer answered him. "And now you are being detained."

The paralysis broke, and the Indians surged forward, taking hold of Bookbinder and his team, binding their hands behind them.

CHAPTER XXIV
HOMEWARD BOUND

Hurricane season used to be our big mobilization time, but good Hydromancy and Aeromancy pretty much put paid to that. Add in the legalization of marijuana, and we were nearly a service without a mission. Then the Bosporus Incident blew up, and the navy had a ton of egg on its face. They didn't have the authority to operate against what turned out to be US citizens. But we do. Globally, there are seven major maritime choke points that threaten US trade on the high seas. Guess who keeps 'em open now? I'll give you a hint. It ain't the navy.

—Chief Warrant Officer 4 Janice Heligg, Skipper
United States Coast Guard Cutter *Hammerhead*

Detention by the Indians wasn't all that different from being guests of the Naga Raja. Bookbinder and his team were ushered into one of the low, aluminum-sided buildings that ringed the plaza. The inside was featureless save for a stack of gray folding chairs and a single long folding table. Cinder-block walls had been painted a sick shade of yellow. Bookbinder cracked a smile. The thought that the military was the military, even here on the other side of the world, amused him.

They were released from their bonds, and two guards were posted in the room's single entrance, not that they would try to escape anyway. Where would they go? They were in the middle of what Bookbinder guessed was the nerve center of the Indian military's magic-using arm. Food and water was brought by a couple of troopers, all of whom Bookbinder guessed had been carefully chosen for their inability to speak English.

And then the waiting began.

"They're going to put us right back through that gate," Stanley groused.

"I don't think so," Bookbinder said. "If they were going to do that, I figure they'd have done it already. Every second they delay, it's going to be more of a problem."

He looked around the room, meeting the eyes of Woon, Sharp, and Archer. "I had to do it," he found himself saying. "This wasn't about impatience. Ajathashatru would never have let us go. That shell game would have gone on forever."

Sharp didn't look convinced, but he nodded. Woon cracked a smile. "That was balls to the wall, sir. I can't believe you did that."

Bookbinder discovered he was smiling in spite of himself. For all he knew, he'd just created an international incident as well as an interplanar one. He kept telling himself that time was on their side, but that didn't stop him from expecting the guards to haul them out of this room and toss them back through a gate at any moment. "Honestly? I can't believe I did it either."

"You stole the naga Portamancer's magic, Bound it into that truck," Woon said.

Bookbinder nodded. "I wish I could control where it went. I guess this is where the naga was opening the gate. Would have been a lot easier if he'd been opening it on Washington."

After a few hours, an Indian man in a suit entered the room. He was tall and good-looking, his hair military-short and his face clean-shaven. He carried a pen, notebook, and handheld digital recorder. He smiled at them. "Colonel Bookbinder, I presume," he said in perfect English. "You gave us all quite a scare."

Bookbinder was expecting this. He stood. "That's nice. Neither myself nor any member of my team has anything to say to you."

The man frowned, managing to look surprised and wronged at the same time. "There's no need for that, sir. I'm not here to interrogate you."

"Are you a duly authorized agent of the United States government?" Bookbinder asked.

The man smiled and spread his arms.

"Then we're not talking to you." He turned and faced his

team. "As your commanding officer I am ordering you on pain of an article fifteen at a minimum not to speak to any foreign national. Not a single word until I say otherwise. You will only speak to the US consul or defense attaché. Everyone clear on that?"

"Yes, sir," they replied in unison, even Stanley.

He turned back to the Indian, who was already speaking. "Sir, this isn't necessary. As I said, this isn't an interrogation. I just have a few basic questions so that I can . . ."

Bookbinder stabbed a finger at his chest. "Not. One. Word. If you're going to use torture, you better get started. But keep in mind that we're going to resist with everything we have. US consul or defense attaché." He took a step closer and did his best impression of Colonel Taylor. "We're done here."

The Indian's face became equally serious and angry. Under the diplomatic smile was the expression of a man clearly not used to being disobeyed. "Very well," he said, and left.

Bookbinder turned back to his team. They met his eyes with varying degrees of uncertainty, but at least they had the respect not to say anything. Once he'd called the anger, it was difficult to dismiss, and he paced the room for a full hour, before his head had cooled enough for him to realize the butterflies in his stomach were competing with hunger, exhaustion, and an almost overwhelming urge to pee.

Well, Julie, bunny, at least I'm back on the same plane as you. That's a start, right?

The idea gave him comfort through the hours that followed. He stared at his wedding band, toying with it as he lost track of how long they waited. Twenty-four hours? Maybe twice that long? He lost count of how many times the guards were rotated. There were no more visits. No one brought food or water, no one checked on them. They simply sat, slumped in their chairs, not speaking. A part of Bookbinder yelled at him to search the room, to try to find another avenue for escape. But he was an empty cup. He had risen as far as he could to the task at hand. He had led them this far. It was either enough, or it wasn't. He was done.

He found himself slumped over one of the folding chairs, his sore ass reporting that he had fallen asleep in it, when the door finally opened again. He squinted, shading his eyes against the bright daylight streaming in from outside, silhouetting another man in a suit.

Bookbinder stirred, working the kinks out of his lower back. "I thought I told you, we're not going to . . ."

"Colonel Bookbinder, sir?" the man said. He had sandy blond hair and a slight Midwestern accent. An American flag was pinned neatly to his lapel. "I'm Paul Krieger from the US embassy. I'm here to take custody of you."

Bookbinder only stared, suddenly noticing that the guards were gone. Woon let out a short bark of a laugh. Sharp and Archer stood and dusted themselves off, all business, Stanley close behind.

"I don't believe . . ." Bookbinder finally managed.

Krieger grinned. "You tumbled through that gate in front of visiting dignitaries from half a dozen countries, all of whom have relationships with us. The naga might be nasty in the Source, but the US Navy is nasty right off the coast. It wasn't exactly a hard sell. There's a chopper waiting for us outside. Let's go."

Bookbinder pressed his face up against the tiny window of the Greyhound airplane as the catapult whipped it forward. The thrust briefly pressed Bookbinder back into his seat, but a moment later he was back at the window, watching the deck of the carrier *Gerald R. Ford* disappear behind them. He glanced around at the rest of his team. Only Stanley was awake, his eyes locked on the C-2A's closed rear hatch. Sharp, Archer, and Woon were fast asleep.

Bookbinder couldn't blame them. He'd barely slept since the same aircraft whisked them off the Indian base to the waiting carrier. Thus far, they'd been more closely guarded by their own countrymen than by the Indians. A doctor silently examined them, asking no questions and telling them nothing. Six MPs and a Suppressor stood by, keeping them confined to the carrier's bridge until the plane was ready to launch again. The team huddled together, feeling alien back on their Home Plane and closer to one another. Bookbinder thought briefly of asking to contact his family, but decided against it. Sooner or later, they would be questioned, and that would be the time for answers and requests. Yelling at enlisted MPs wouldn't do him any good. Besides, he promised himself that no matter how it twisted in his gut, his family would wait. They were safe. His FOB wasn't. First things first.

Bookbinder eventually dozed himself, waking only when the Greyhound touched down on a smooth and well-maintained flight line abutted by rows of waving palm trees. The plane finally came to a shuddering stop before a sign depicting a blue shield broken by a waving gold chevron. UBON ROYAL THAI AIR FORCE BASE WELCOMES THE WOLF PACK! it read. *Thailand,* Bookbinder thought. *How can someplace so exotic seem so mundane to me now?* But after the intensity of every sensation in the Source, he figured the Vegas Strip would be an anti-climax.

The Greyhound's rear hatch descended with a whir, stirring the rest of his team awake as MPs and Suppressors trooped aboard, led by two men in sunglasses and dark suits totally inappropriate to the near-eighty-degree heat. Bookbinder stood and shook himself as the suits silently motioned him and his team off the aircraft and into a closed white van. They rode in silence for just a few minutes before being dropped off in front of a plain white aluminum building at the line's edge. It was completely surrounded by troops, and Bookbinder noted at least one armored Humvee before he was ushered inside.

He nearly laughed out loud.

Though it was cleaner, and the furniture in better repair, the building's interior almost exactly matched the Indian structure they'd just left. Same crappy folding chairs and tables. Same featureless walls. Same temporary structure.

A tall army major in his class A uniform met him. His short blond hair was cut exactly to regulation, his blue eyes frosty. His jawline was as pronounced as his uniform creases. He looked every inch the textbook soldier. THORSSON, his nameplate read. Bookbinder could feel a solid Aeromantic current emanating from him, disciplined, like everything else about the man.

"Colonel Bookbinder, welcome to Ubon and welcome home."

Bookbinder nodded. "Thanks. Forgive me if I don't stand on formality just now, I'm about on my last legs."

Major Thorsson smiled. "You and me both, sir. I was on a plane from DC the moment we got word you were on our side of a gate. I was so anxious to get here that I actually dropped myself and flew the rest of the way on my own. C-130s are slow."

"You're an Aeromancer," Bookbinder said, though he already knew.

"They used to call me Harlequin," the man said, extending his hand. "Now I go by Major Jan Thorsson, Special Advisor to the Reawakening Commission. I'm here to take care of you, and also to find out just what the heck is going on."

Bookbinder slumped in one of the folding chairs, completely drained. He heard similar sounds around him that told him his team was following suit.

"You need a doctor?" Thorsson asked.

Bookbinder waved. "We're fine, just tired."

"Okay." Thorsson approached Stanley. "It's good to see you alive, sir. I captured your son after he tried to kill you. I'm sorry that he escaped—"

"Do you know where he is?" Stanley cut him off. "Can you get me to him?"

Thorsson looked at him in silence, shocked by the urgency in his voice. He turned to Bookbinder. "Sir, I think it's best if we speak alone."

"Absolutely not," Bookbinder said. "There's nothing I know that this man doesn't. He's part of my team, and I'm not talking to anyone without him. You want to debrief us, you debrief all of us."

Thorsson hesitated. "This man is not . . ."

"You're wasting time, Major," Bookbinder said.

Thorsson shook his head. "So, give me the bottom line, sir. Why are we in the middle of a political meltdown with India? And what happened to FOB Frontier?"

"The FOB's cut off . . ." Bookbinder began.

"We know that," Thorsson replied. "Britton killed our one Portamancer before he flew the coop. We need to know what happened to the FOB."

Stanley looked at his lap.

"What the hell do you think happened to it?" Bookbinder said. "It's cut off, surrounded, running low on supplies. The goblins get bolder every day. I left my XO in charge of the defenses. He told me he could hold for a month, and we're already way past that. Things are dialed back a bit due to the winter, but he assured me that the fighting will pick up with the spring thaw. The Sahir liaison informed us they have a FOB appended to this kingdom of snake creatures called . . ."

"Naga," Thorsson finished for him. "I'm aware of FOB Sarpakavu, sir."

"Did you know they had a Portamancer?" Bookbinder asked. "Did you contact the Indians and have them send a team out to get us? Why the hell did I have to come to you?"

Thorsson was silent for a moment before gesturing to five even stacks of paper on the folding table behind him, one for each of them. "Sir, you will of course understand the necessity for complete individual debriefs of you and each member of your team. I'm afraid my security people are insisting on polygraph tests, and there will be these additional nondisclosure req—"

"Nondisclosure! What the hell is wrong with you?" Bookbinder exploded, leaping to his feet. "There are people dying in a FOB that's cut off from home. We should be mobilizing a team to get them out, and instead we're spinning our wheels worrying about bad press. There has to be a way to work this out. You need to call the Indian ambassador. If they've got a Portamancer, then we've . . ."

"You've dealt with the naga before, sir. Getting them to assist is . . . something of a challenge. They have a differing perspective on the value of human life than we do."

Bookbinder thought of the wasted idle hours in the opulent stone pavilion and nodded.

"There has to be a way," he said. "Some other military with gate capabilities? Another Selfer? Even if the naga are tough, there's got to be a way to work it out. There's got to be, damn it."

The door opened and a group of men in suits entered carrying briefcases. "We've got the debriefing rooms prepped, Major," one of them said, not bothering to remove his sunglasses.

Bookbinder turned to protest but Sharp stopped him with a wave of his hand. "Archer and I'll go, sir. We've got nothing to hide. We came with you to accomplish a mission, and it's been done. You're in command, sir, you decide what's the best course from here on out."

Woon stood. "I'll go, too, sir. If that's all right with you."

Bookbinder gaped at them. "Are you sure?"

Sharp met Woon and Archer's eyes before turning back to him. "We're sure, sir."

"I'm not going anywhere," Stanley said through gritted teeth as Woon, Archer, and Sharp left with their debriefers. "And I'm not telling you shit until you tell me what's going on with my wife and son."

Stanley's debriefer started forward, reaching into his jacket. Thorsson stopped him with a wave. "Give us a few more minutes, please," he said. The debriefers paused, looking askance, before leaving.

"This is bullshit," Stanley said. "You've got a base full of your own about to get fried, and you're so full of shit that you squeak going into a turn when I ask you about my son. He's my family. My blood. Now you have got to tell me the truth. I've got a wife, too, damn it."

"Desda," Thorsson said. "She's fine."

"Jesus!" Stanley said. "What about Oscar? My clearance was still active when I retired. I have a goddamn need to know!"

"We're doing what we can," Thorsson said, looking at his feet, his face flushed.

"Something tells me that's not entirely true," Bookbinder said evenly. "There's a division's worth of people on that FOB, Major."

"This comes from the president, sir."

Bookbinder amazed himself with what he said next. "I don't give a rat's ass. Do you know how many people are in a division?"

Thorsson was silent for a long time.

"The naga," Bookbinder finally said. "We've got to get back in touch with them. Get me that consul who got us off the . . ."

"Sir, please." Thorsson looked at Stanley. "If I have to, I can have you forcibly removed."

Stanley opened his mouth, the words "do it" forming on his lips. Bookbinder waved him back. "Just step outside, sir," he said. "Give me a minute with the major here."

Stanley swore and left. Bookbinder spun on Thorsson. "Now, just what the hell is—"

Thorsson cut him off. "The naga aren't the only ones with a Portamancer."

"What the hell are you talking about?"

"I'm talking about Oscar Britton," Thorsson said. "We've got him."

"Take me to him," Bookbinder said. "Right now."

Thorsson shook his head. "He'll never help us."

Bookbinder paused, his mind trembling with exhaustion, with panic, with missing his family. All he wanted to do was throw up his hands, sleep, eat, let someone else deal with this.

But instead he stood and stabbed his finger at Thorsson's chest.

"He has to," Bookbinder said. "He fucking has to."

CHAPTER XXV
TALKING POINTS

The issue isn't fear of upsetting the established social order, it's fear of upsetting the genetic one. What if Selfers aren't just the latest brand of insurgent malcontents? What if they're the next rung on the evolutionary ladder? I doubt Neanderthals were big fans of the first Homo sapiens *either.*

—"Render," Houston Street Selfers
Recorded "Message for SOC Sorcerers" distributed
on the Internet and the streets of New York City

Once the debriefs were completed, Thorsson had Bookbinder and his team bundled onto a plane back to the States.

He watched the plane take off and kept watching as it dwindled to a speck, before returning to the temporary offices the Royal Thai Air Force had been kind enough to set up along the flight line for his use.

He entered, dismissed the guards, and sat, cradling his head in his hands. If what Bookbinder had told him was true, then Colonel Taylor was dead and Crucible in command of a division-sized outpost on the verge of being overrun. Hell, thanks to the nagas' delaying tactics, it might have been overrun already. The computer on the desk before him had at least three hundred unread email messages, most of them pertaining to what Ambassador Buchar and the State Department were already calling "The Incident."

He ignored them, swallowing hard. Buchar could handle it.

When Britton had escaped him, Thorsson had watched him fire his pistol through the gate, watched the bullet tear through the army's only other Portamancer. *I don't think you're coming for anybody,* Britton had said. *Not anymore.*

Horror had curdled in Harlequin's gut.

Because he knew from that moment, FOB Frontier was cut off.

A tiny proportion of the population came up Latent. Count out those who went Selfer, and the SOC was a very small force, indeed. Most commissioned Sorcerers knew one another, and the personnel at FOB Frontier were no exception. Taylor might have been a petulant bully, but he had also been a mentor and a friend.

Crucible even more so. They'd played golf together in Arlington before he'd shipped out to command SAOLCC. Thorsson had lent him a listening ear as he prepared to break the news that he was "going away for a while" to his wife. "What's good for a career is bad for a marriage," Crucible had said. "That's the army."

Thorsson, single, had taken the advice to heart. He tapped the gold pen in his breast pocket. Crucible had had it delivered as a promotion gift when he'd made captain. Crucible had been a major himself then, leading the fifth district's "Recovery Teams," ensuring no Selfer ever threatened the District of Columbia.

Thorsson had few friends; Crucible was one.

Every day since Britton had killed Billy and gated Thorsson onto the White House lawn, Harlequin had shouted to anyone in the SOC who would listen about the danger FOB Frontier was in. Could they capture another Portamancer? Maybe a foreign partner had one who could help?

The answer always came back the same. Wait. Be patient. The FOB was a powerful force, they could hold. A way would be found eventually.

When Oscar Britton was recaptured, Thorsson had fully expected that answer to change, for a relief expedition to be mounted.

But the answer stayed the same, the weeks dragged on, and Thorsson's horror mounted.

Thorsson logged into the computer and double-clicked on the icon the technician had set up for him before he'd taken the computer from Washington. It was labeled, simply, DIRECT CONNECTION.

The face that appeared on the screen was craggy, serious. "Gatanas."

Thorsson's involvement in the incident with Oscar Britton had seen him appointed to the position of Special Advisor to the Reawakening Commission. Apart from spending much of his time on television interviews, it made him one of the most trusted men in SOC. The position had its privileges.

General Gatanas, the SOC Commandant, had hounded Thorsson daily since Britton's escape. While his recapture had brought Thorsson back into the general's good graces, the man still didn't look thrilled to see him.

"It's done, sir," Thorsson said. "The full breakdown is in the report I emailed. Bookbinder—"

Gatanas cut him off. "Rescued Britton's father, I know, I read the report. I'm giving orders for them to be detained until we can get to the bottom of their involvement."

"They're telling the truth, sir," Thorsson said. "We have to evacuate the FOB. Taylor's dead, sir. Crucible is running the post now."

Gatanas's eyes narrowed. "That's not your call. Do I need to remind you of your title? 'Special Advisor.' That means you advise. You don't order."

"I understand that, sir. I am *advising* you to bring Crucible and his people home."

"And how the hell do you propose we do that, Harlequin? Your ward, Oscar Britton, shot our Portamancer between the eyes on his way out the door."

"We use him. Oscar Britton. We have to."

Gatanas was silent.

"Sir, we . . ."

"That's enough. I've been on the horn with Senator Whalen and the Joint Chiefs since Bookbinder pulled his little stunt with the Indians. They've got questions for you. Pack up whatever you're doing at Ubon and get your ass back to the Pentagon."

"Sir, Crucible's a friend. We have to . . ."

"I am just about done being told what I have to do, Major,"

Gatanas said. "Get on a plane, or fly yourself, I don't care. But I had better see you back in the Pentagon, or it's your ass."

"How soon, sir?"

"Now, Major. Right fucking now."

Thorsson knew something was wrong as soon as he got out of his car. The Pentagon's expansive north parking lot was packed with black SUVs and cordoned off around the edges with orange traffic cones topped with yellow police tape. The usual crowds of morning commuters, civilian and military, were absent. He glanced up at the bridge leading past the athletic club and over the highway and counted at least two snipers walking slowly back and forth. A helicopter circled conspicuously overhead.

This was a lot of security, even for Senator Whalen. Had there been a death threat? He took a deep breath and quickened his pace across the parking lot.

He fumed as he went, thinking of all the time he'd wasted flying here from Thailand. And for what? A face-to-face meeting that could just as easily have been held over the Internet? They were wasting time. With every second that ticked by, FOB Frontier was at greater and greater risk. To hear Bookbinder tell it, the attacks were coming pretty much nightly now. Who knew how many men and women were dying with each step Thorsson took across the parking lot?

What if one of them was Crucible? Was his friend even now commanding the perimeter defenses, assuring his people that help was on the way?

The main entrance was completely blocked off. Harlequin could make out a small squadron of Pentagon police hunkered down behind bulletproof barriers, geared for war. He tried to slip into the crowd heading for the alternate entrance, being herded along by impatient Pentagon police officers, similarly equipped. As he stepped into the stream of commuters, one of the officers tapped his elbow, glancing down at a photograph on his cell phone. "Major Thorsson?"

"That's me."

"This way, sir." He led Thorsson out of line and over to the main entrance he'd originally avoided. The police there waved him through without checking his ID.

Inside the long foyer, he was led east, past the escalators that would have put him on the path to his office. After a few feet, four hard-looking Secret Service agents took over from the police and resumed their escort. Thorsson smirked at the direction they were taking. "We're going to the gift shop?" The Secret Service agents were stone-faced, silent.

They stopped outside the fire doors that led to shopping concourse, shut tight. Thorsson had never seen that before. The area, normally the busiest in the building, had been cleared.

"Go ahead, sir," one of the agents said, motioning him through the doors.

Thorsson straightened his uniform one last time and went through.

The shops were shuttered, steel gates drawn down over their doors and windows. The lights were dimmed, but Thorsson thought he could make out figures in the distant gloom, men standing on overwatch, weapons ready.

A man stood immediately before him, back turned, in a windbreaker, jeans, and docksiders. Thorsson recognized the forced casualness of his stance from hours of television, but the man's voice confirmed it.

"Major Thorsson. Thank you for coming."

Thorsson swallowed. "Sir, I was expecting to see Senator Whalen."

President Walsh turned, giving him a grim look. "The senator is attending to some urgent business for me. I'm taking a personal interest in this matter. It's a hell of a thing, Major, wouldn't you say?"

"I would, Mr. President."

Walsh gestured with a sheaf of papers. "I've looked over your report. Thorough. Precise. I wish I could get my staff to write like this."

Praise from the commander in chief was never a bad thing, but there was something in Walsh's sugarcoated tone that put Thorsson on edge. "Thank you, sir. I've lost a lot of hours over poor communications. I try to secure that wherever I can."

Walsh smiled. "That's good. That's good. It's quite a

kerfuffle he's stirred up with the Indians. Ambassador Buchar has got his hands full trying to get that put to bed. Not to mention that we've got the Russians, Singaporeans, and Chinese all demanding answers. It's a hell of a headache."

"He did what he had to, sir. The naga are . . . tough to figure out."

Walsh's eyes narrowed. Apparently that wasn't what he wanted to hear.

"So, you agree with Colonel Bookbinder's assessment?"

He's being clear on what he wants to hear. Too bad. Thorsson was an officer. He owed it to his superiors to be honest with them, whatever the cost.

"I believe him, Mr. President. I was at FOB Frontier. The war season is gearing up now as winter fades, and they're going to be seriously hard-pressed come spring. If there's any chance that Britton would be willing to help us, we have to try."

Walsh's face narrowed until it looked positively pinched. "This is Oscar Britton we're talking about, Major. This is the man who nearly killed you. The man who nearly wiped out that FOB you're now talking about using him to save."

"He's the man who saved my life," Thorsson said. "He returned our dead to us, laid them respectfully in Arlington Cemetery, sir. I've thought a lot about Oscar Britton since the last time I faced him. He's a loose cannon. He marches to the beat of his own drum. He's dangerous, no question. But he was a good officer. He put his men first. He took care of them. That's not affectation, that's character. Oscar Britton cares about soldiers. If we ask him, I believe he'll help."

"That's one hell of a risk to be taking, Major. Moving a division's worth of military members, support personnel, and equipment through a gate operated by a convict currently being tried for treason?"

Thorsson held Walsh's eyes. "Respectfully, sir, that's better than letting those same military members and support personnel die."

"We don't know that they will die," Walsh answered immediately, looking irritated. "And I'm not sure that you're right about Britton. Regardless, we can't put the option before him; it's way too risky. We've got less than a year before the election, and I don't think the public is ready to handle FOB Frontier, Shadow Coven, and everything else we've got going on there."

"Sir"—Thorsson gritted his teeth—"the staff understand the OPSEC requirements of being posted to FOB Frontier, they know better than to talk. They know the consequences."

"Sure, in ones or twos," Walsh answered. "But a mass evacuation? Treated at a single medical facility? Without proper time to debrief them all? And with Oscar Britton as the principal logistical element? Leaks are hard enough to contain normally. This would be a disaster. We're already reeling from the press coverage from when he gated you onto the White House lawn. We can risk an op after the election. The FOB will have to hold until then."

Thorsson choked on his rising anger. *This is the President of the United States. Be careful.* "Sir, respectfully—"

"Spare me that, Major. We're both public servants here. Speak plainly."

"Mr. President, Colonel Bookbinder assures me they're not going to last eight more days, let alone eight more months."

Walsh took a step toward him, his posture giving the lie to his talk about being a public servant. "And I can assure you that this administration is the only one equipped to handle magic in this society. Would you prefer a Fareed administration? His so-called 'real magic' legislation?"

I wouldn't have. Until now.

Thorsson didn't bother answering. This whole conversation had been an excuse for Walsh to monologue. At least Fareed wouldn't be willing to sell out a division's worth of men and women just to win an election. Thorsson carefully kept his face neutral.

Walsh's eyes narrowed. "I can trust you on this, Major? Can't I?" *He's doubting my loyalty,* Harlequin thought. *Worse, he's worried I'll blow the lid on this, or do something crazy.*

Because he knows he's wrong.

Walsh put his hand on Thorsson's elbow, his voice going soft and smooth. "Sometimes being in charge requires you to make hard choices, and sometimes those choices cost lives. If you hesitate to make those calls, you can lose more lives than you save."

"Sir, you asked me to speak plainly. We're talking about a division here."

"I know precisely what we're talking about, Major. We'll lose a lot more than a division if we don't keep a lid on what the Reawakening has unleashed on the world. You're not seeing the forest for the trees. I'm going to have to be able to rely on you here. Can I do that?"

Thorsson inclined his head. This man wanted obedience. "Of course, sir." Inside, he seethed.

"Good." Walsh didn't look like he trusted him at all. "Tell me about the refugees. I've got two SF operators and an air force Terramancer, is that right? My staff tells me they're cooperative, signed their nondisclosure agreements, and passed polygraphs. They're confident they can be trusted. What's your take on them?"

Thorsson's tongue felt thick in his mouth, his stomach sick with anger. He had sworn to obey this man who was effectively condemning an entire division to death. What did the rule book say about this? *You know what it says. It says you do what you're told.*

"I'd concur, sir. They're company people."

"Good." Walsh nodded. "What about this administrative colonel, the one who took command when Taylor was killed? I hear that Britton's father is here as well. Can you deal with them? We can't have them stirring up the media. The last thing we need are any father-son reunion sob stories. You've got them on lockdown at Quantico still? That was quick thinking."

"Leave them to me," Thorsson heard himself saying, his voice coming as if from far away. "I can handle them."

Walsh nodded. "You do what you feel is necessary. I would prefer to have them cooperative and released back to their families if you can make that happen."

The rest of the order was left silent, hanging in the air. *And now you want me to commit murder?*

"Leave it to me, sir," was all he said.

"I intend to. You'll have a full report ready for Senator Whalen by the weekend?"

"Absolutely."

Walsh touched Thorsson's elbow again. "I appreciate being able to rely on you, Major. It's important for me to have a presence in the ranks that I can trust. The Joint Chiefs are political animals. I need a real soldier I can reach out to, to get things done, especially in the SOC. Gatanas is far too much of a public figure to be getting his hands dirty. But I served twenty years in the army, and I know that dirty hands are precisely what war requires. That's rough sometimes, but this nation doesn't stay safe because men like us shied away from roughness."

"Roughness." That's what he calls condemning people to die. Thorsson felt filthy. "Of course, sir."

"I'll be keeping an eye on you, Major. I see bright things in your future."

"Thank you, sir."

"Dismissed."

Thorsson executed a perfect about-face and pushed his way back through the fire doors, falling into step with his Secret Service escort. He was completely numb, transiting the Pentagon's foyer and the parking lot in a fog, barely remembering the trip. *The rule book says I should obey my commander in chief. But it also says something about illegal orders.*

And a lot of soldiering wasn't found in any manual. No chapter laid out how to be valorous, or honorable. No text ever told him that on the battlefield, saving lives was every bit as important as taking them.

But he'd learned it just the same.

Thorsson stared for a long moment at his car, then put his keys in his pocket and radioed his intention to fly to the tower at Reagan National Airport. The SOC controller there approved him instantly, filing the flight plan on his behalf, and he was airborne in a matter of minutes, wrapping himself in an envelope of heated air as a buffer against the cold. His dress uniform fluttered in the wind, wrinkling, catching bugs, likely ruined.

As he blasted over the Potomac Mills Mall, he noticed a plain blue air force helicopter dispatched to escort him, keeping pace to his left. The pilot shot him a thumbs-up and he waved back, managing to force a smile. They hung in formation over the gridlocked traffic on Interstate 95 until Quantico's training range came into view, dotted with FBI recruits, probably doing push-ups, far below. The helo peeled off as Harlequin descended to land before a low, gray concrete building ringed with plain chain-link fencing topped with razor wire. The sign at the front read, MARINE CORPS BRIG, QUANTICO. SECBN QUANTICO— CRIMINAL INVESTIGATIVE DIVISION—PROVOST MARSHAL.

The guards on duty saluted and waved Thorsson in without

checking his ID again, for the second time in his military career. *Having friends in high places helps,* Thorsson thought as he made his way to the elevator and waited through the long descent to the holding facility. A Suppressor stood just outside the thick, windowless steel door at the far end of the passage. The Marine sergeant outside the door glanced up from his laptop and frowned. "You look like hell, sir."

"Long day," Thorsson answered. "How are our guests?"

The sergeant smiled and punched a button on his desk. There was a puff of air as the lock disengaged, and the door eased open a crack. "Compliant," he said.

"I'm going to have to move them in a few minutes," Thorsson said. "That's coming from the president." He turned to the Suppressor. "You can let him go, Lieutenant."

The Suppressor nodded, and Thorsson felt his current shift as he pushed through the door, closing it behind him. Bookbinder was stepping off his bunk, shaking his head in surprise at the sudden return of his magical current. Stanley Britton stepped out from the corner to Thorsson's left, fists clenched. Thorsson turned to him, amused. "Were you planning to jump me? You wouldn't have gotten very far."

"I still would have had the pleasure of punching you in the face." Stanley smiled. "Tell me you've got good news."

Thorsson shook his head.

"What did Whalen say?" Bookbinder asked.

"Not Whalen," Thorsson replied. "The president himself. We're on our own."

"You mean that FOB is on its own," Bookbinder snarled.

Thorsson took a deep breath, let it out, then glanced up at Bookbinder. "You ready to commit high treason, sir?"

Bookbinder paused, looked at Stanley, looked back. "Absolutely."

"Good," Thorsson answered. "I didn't join the army so Walsh could get reelected while a whole division goes up in smoke. Let's go get Oscar Britton."

CHAPTER XXVI
JAILBREAK

*If you can heal with a touch, that's an easy call. You have to do it.
But what if you can kill just as easily? Aren't there times when you
have to do that, too?*

—Howard Dienst, Director of Compliance
National Counterterrorism Center
Fifth Annual Conference on Magic and Military Ethics
Geneva, Switzerland

They stepped out past the thick door and into the hallway, Bookbinder and Stanley nodding at the guards, who nodded back as
Thorsson went up to the sergeant's desk. "Call over to Charlie
Block and let 'em know we're coming? President wants a
tête-à-tête with Prisoner One and these two. I'll be mediating."

The sergeant nodded, picking up a phone. "You want me to
send someone to take notes?"

Thorsson produced a pad from the breast pocket of his bug-
spattered, wrinkled uniform jacket. "I've got it, thanks. I want
the surveillance booth empty. No recordings. This is on my pad
and in my head only. Got it?"

"Aye, sir," the sergeant said, dialing numbers into the phone.
He looked at Thorsson, a little starstruck. It still made Thorsson
uncomfortable after all this time. "My wife wanted me to tell
you that she's seen you on TV, sir. She didn't believe it when I
said I was working with you."

Thorsson ignored the fact that the sergeant shouldn't be telling anyone that he was working with him and smiled. "That's
great. Give her my best."

The Suppressor moved to fall in with them, but Thorsson waved him back. "I've got it," he said, interdicting Bookbinder's flow.

"You sure, sir?"

"This man is a colonel in the United States Army, Lieutenant. He's not charged with anything. He's being held here for his own safety and to facilitate the debriefing process."

The Suppressor blanched and nodded to Bookbinder. "Of course, sir. Sorry about that, sir."

Bookbinder nodded back. "No problem, Lieutenant. We all just do our jobs."

"This way, sir." Thorsson gestured to Bookbinder, who stepped in and led the way down the hallway. When they reached the elevator, Bookbinder turned to him. "Where the hell are we going?"

Thorsson smiled. "Around the corner, actually. Do me a favor and stay in front. People tend to give you less crap when they see a full bird leading the way."

Bookbinder smiled back. "Don't I know it."

Stanley fumed. "You mean my son was just a few feet away from me all this time?"

Thorsson shrugged. "You're going to see him in about five minutes, Mr. Britton. Just hang with me. If we make it through this, you can kick my ass later."

"Are we going to make it through this?" Bookbinder asked.

Thorsson followed them into the elevator and punched the button for the brig's main floor. "Highly doubtful, sir. But I'm not going to be able to live with myself if we don't at least try. If you'd rather opt out, I'll take you back to your cell."

"I'm already dead if you believe the newspapers," Stanley said. "Makes no difference to me."

Bookbinder was silent so long that Thorsson expected him to turn around and head back. "No, you're right," he said at last. "I want to see my family again, but so does every man and woman on that FOB. We swore to give our lives if we had to, right?"

"That we did, sir," Thorsson said.

"I just really hope we don't have to," Bookbinder said, as the elevator chimed, and they stepped out into the lobby.

"Feeling's mutual, sir," Thorsson said.

Charlie Block turned out to be on the brig's opposite side, a plain concrete lobby furnished only with a guard desk manned by four tough-looking Marines and guarded by a locked door that opened easily to Thorsson's badge and thumbprint.

"Major Thorsson," the desk sergeant said, punching a button that chimed the elevator, sliding the doors open. "Prisoner One is prepped for you."

"Thanks," Thorsson said. "Keep that recording booth clear. That one comes all the way from the top."

"Booth clear, aye, sir," the sergeant said to his back as the elevator doors slid shut behind them. A similar long and featureless hallway greeted them at the far end, with an identical desk occupied by two identical guards and a Suppressor. The door was already unlocked and cracked open behind them.

"Here we go," Thorsson whispered. "Hope you guys are ready."

"Not sure you can be ready for something like this," Bookbinder said, as Thorsson nodded to the guards, and they pushed through the door. Oscar Britton sat on his bunk. He looked exactly as Thorsson remembered him, tall, well built, shaved head shining under the dull fluorescent lights. He quirked a smile at them as they walked through the door, straightening his orange prison jumpsuit as he stood to greet them. "Well, well," he said. "The dreaded Harlequin comes to visit me." He didn't so much as glance at his father. "To what do I owe the honor?"

"Oscar," Stanley said, but Britton didn't look at him, and Bookbinder cut him off, saying, "We don't have much time, we're here to get you out. We need your help."

Britton snorted. "For what?"

"The FOB . . ." Thorsson began.

"The FOB is cut off," Britton said, shaking his head. "I saw to that personally."

"That doesn't sound like the Oscar Britton I know," Thorsson said. "We've got a chance to save them, and you're the only one who can get them out of there."

"Fuck them and fuck you," Britton said. "Maybe you should have thought about how much you needed my help before you threw me in this place."

Thorsson took a step back. "Jesus, Oscar. Is this what all that time on the run did to you? A lot of people, a lot of soldiers are going to die unless you help us."

"Did I stutter?" Britton asked. "Fuck. Them. And. Fuck. You!"

Bookbinder jumped backward as if he'd been bitten by something. "Major, he's not a Portamancer."

Thorsson turned to Bookbinder. "Wait, how can you tell . . ." He reached out for Britton's flow, and felt it strong and steady. He spun back to face him. "You're not Suppressed."

"And you're not very bright, you fucking traitor," Britton said, reaching forward. His hand blurred, melting. A long bone spike shot out, Britton's arm thinning as it reached across the room. Harlequin dove out of the way, and the spike caught Stanley Britton, piercing his upper chest, pushing through his shoulder and pinning him to the wall.

His face melted, the black man's skin blurring and re-forming, the torso slimming down, until the orange jumpsuit adorned a man with corpse gray skin, slick black hair plastered to his forehead. "Fucking amateurs," he said.

Thorsson knew only one contractor on the SOC payroll whose Physiomancy was so talented that he could impersonate another person.

The Sculptor. President Walsh must have suspected that he might try to break Britton out. This was his insurance policy.

Thorsson Drew hard and Bound lightning to his fists, only to feel a Suppressor's current flow through the wall to roll his own magic back. He cursed, ripping his pistol from inside his jacket and firing twice into the Physiomancer's torso, which oozed sideways as the bullets opened ragged holes in the flesh. The Sculptor grimaced in pain as another arm sprouted from its wounded side to grab Thorsson's throat. "Give it up," the Physiomancer hissed. "I've got orders to take you alive, but I can make it hurt as bad as I want to."

Stanley screamed weakly, beating uselessly against the bone spike that kept him pinned to the wall. Bookbinder gestured from the corner of Thorsson's eye, pointing one hand toward the door and the other at the Physiomancer. Thorsson gasped as he felt his own tide flood back into him. The Sculptor snarled as his own form coalesced, retreating back into itself. The extra fist released Thorsson's neck. The bone spike retreated, dropping Stanley Britton to the floor. His torso re-formed, the actual meat of him only grazed by Thorsson's two shots. He launched himself forward, reaching for Thorsson, screaming to the guards outside.

"I've got him!" Bookbinder howled, tackling the Physiomancer sideways, driving him into the wall, just as the door flew open and the Suppressor came stumbling into the room, pistol drawn. Thorsson whirled, slamming the butt of his own weapon into the man's face, feeling an eye squelch under the gun's impact. The Suppressor began to howl, and Thorsson kicked him squarely in his chest, driving him back into the guards who now crowded the hallway outside, as he Drew his magic hard and stepped out after them. He could hear Bookbinder and the Physiomancer grappling behind him, cursing and punching, but he couldn't deal with that now.

He stepped out into the hallway in time to see eight Marine guards coming at a run, leveling their rifles. The Suppressor knelt before them, hands clasped to his crushed eye, calling on them to shoot.

Men following orders, Thorsson thought. *Just as I've always done.*

He closed his eyes and Bound his magic to the air, agitating the molecules until they blazed, the hallway filling with sizzling lightning. Gunshots rang out and he waited for bullets to tear through him. He heard the crack of chipped masonry as they collided with the walls around him, felt the stirring of the air as they passed him. At last, the hallway fell silent and the stink of cooked meat and ozone reached him. He kept his eyes closed until he turned back into the cell. He opened them to see that the Sculptor, his magic restored by the Suppressor's death, had sprouted eight additional limbs, crushing Bookbinder to him.

A bolt of lightning leapt from Thorsson's hand, engulfing the Physiomancer's head. The Sculptor went rigid, his head smoking, until the extra limbs went limp, and Bookbinder staggered backward, breathing hard.

"Jesus hopping Christ, what . . ." Bookbinder said, staring at the thing's corpse, still now, the head burning brightly.

"No time," Thorsson said. "Get Stanley and come on."

Bookbinder nodded and yanked Stanley up to support him

over his shoulder. The older man screamed as he came upright, blood pouring from the wound. "He's going to bleed out. I'm not sure if it perforated his lung."

"Nothing we can do now," Thorsson said, stepping into the hallway. "Follow me . . . and . . . don't look if you can avoid it."

The hallway was a charnel house. Thorsson picked his way over the cooked bodies of the Marines, still smoking from the lightning storm's aftermath. *Servicemen. Just following regs.*

Walsh's words echoed in his mind. *Sometimes being in charge requires you to make hard choices, and sometimes those choices cost lives. If you hesitate to make those calls, you can lose more lives than you save.* FOB Frontier was an entire division.

He heard Bookbinder catch his breath as he came out into the hallway, and they made their way farther down the corridor, past a stenciled sign on the wall reading PRISONERS 2 AND 3. The second cell was unguarded, but the third had a Suppressor crouched in front of it, back flat against the door. "Don't, sir," the young man begged Thorsson. "If you let him go . . ."

"You can Suppress him or you can Suppress me," Thorsson said without breaking stride. "The difference is that I'll give you five minutes to get topside and start running. Make the call, Lieutenant."

The Suppressor didn't hesitate, bolting past Thorsson, picking his way past the bodies and jumping into the elevator.

"I figure we've got about two minutes," Thorsson said as he turned back to the door. "Now, I've just got to figure out a way to get this open and . . ."

A blazing rectangle of shimmering light sliced through the door's right edge, sliding up and around until it had neatly carved it off its hinges. The block of metal stood for a moment before slowly drifting forward to slam on the floor with a boom that echoed down the length of the hallway.

"Well," Thorsson said, "that solves that problem."

Oscar Britton stood in the doorway in the same orange jumpsuit. His eyes drifted immediately over Thorsson's shoulder to his father, pale and sweating, suspended between Bookbinder and his own hand on the corridor wall. "Dad?" Britton whispered. "Dad!"

He raced to the man's side.

"Oscar . . ." Stanley said. "Did you . . ." he began, then his speech faltered, and he slumped, caught by his son before he could hit the floor.

"What's going on?" Britton looked over his father's shoulder. "We've got to get him to a doctor!"

"We've got about a minute before the whole US military comes pouring out of that elevator, Oscar," Thorsson said. "You need to get us out of here now, or we're all dead. I can explain everything once we're safe."

Britton hesitated, staring.

The elevator chimed down the hallway's length.

"Thirty seconds, Oscar," Thorsson said. "I'm not Suppressing you. If you want to run, I won't stop you. But there're a lot of soldiers who will die if you don't help."

Britton nodded, and a gate slid open behind Bookbinder. The colonel spun and gasped.

"Go!" Thorsson said, pushing the man through, then gesturing to Britton to follow along with his father.

The elevator chimed again, the doors sliding open. Thorsson saw men with guns begin to pour into the hallway as he stepped through the gate himself, gesturing to Britton to shut it behind them.

They stumbled into a clearing at the center of what looked like the set from a Renaissance faire. The clearing was dotted with earthen huts and surrounded by hand-built structures, rammed earth for the most part, with thatched roofs. Packed-dirt paths intersected them, dotted with herb gardens. A low wooden palisade wall was visible in the distance. A pool of clear water snaked its way across one side of the clearing, and a large central fire pit dominated the middle.

All around them, goblins were stopping in stunned amazement, leaping backward from the gate suddenly standing in their midst. A few leveled spears, the majority simply stood, openmouthed. A few of them took off running, shouting and waving their arms.

Britton closed the gate and opened it again, this time on the bowl of rose moss in the Vermont forest where he'd hidden before. "Be ready to move," he said. "I'm not sure what kind of welcome we can expect."

The goblins began to chatter at him, clustering forward. Thorsson saw one white-painted sorcerer among them, felt the eddying of magical currents farther out, but none moved to Suppress them. The faces around them were open.

"Oscar," Thorsson said. "What the hell did you take us here for? We don't have time to—"

Britton cut him off with a wave of his hand. He gently laid his father on the ground. "He needs help, and he needs it now. I'm not doing a damn thing for you until he gets it."

A moment later, a large cluster of goblins arrived and began pushing their way to the front of the throng of the creatures that was gathering around them. Several warriors mounted on wolves led them, waving scavenged carbines or spears to clear the onlookers out of the way. Behind them, Thorsson could see the white-painted heads of a group of their sorcerers. In the midst of them was a solitary figure, his dotted scalp marking him as their *Hepta-Bak*, their prince and leader.

Thorsson Drew his magic and took a step back, letting lightning sizzle along his clenched fists.

Bookbinder marked the move. "Should we be worried here?"

"We'll know in about three seconds," Britton said, moving closer to the gate. "Just be ready to move through there if . . ." And then his face melted into a smile.

The crowd parted, revealing the goblin contractor that Thorsson knew used to drink with Shadow Coven in the cash. The tiny creature looked positively regal now, wearing a fur-trimmed cloak and carrying a short spear. His head and face were covered with patterns of swirling white dots.

"Marty!" Britton shouted. "Man, it's good to see you."

The goblin smiled and came forward. "Uskar," he said. "I think you die."

"So did I," came a woman's voice. The Physiomancer Therese Del Aqua stood at the goblin's side. Her hair had been combed into haphazard braids adorned with leather thongs that suspended feathers and beads. She wore a leather dress in goblin fashion. Beside her came that damned Swift, the head of the No-No Crew. He saw the last remnant of Shadow Coven, Simon Truelove. One side of the Necromancer's body was painted white, and he was robed in leather sewn with bronze discs like an indig.

Therese started forward, arms outstretched. "We thought you were dead, Oscar. We thought we were trapped here, and you were dead."

Britton permitted her the briefest embrace. He spoke quickly, pushing through a throat choked with emotion. "I thought I'd never see you again, either." He pushed away from her with an effort. "But I need your help. This is my dad. He's hurt bad, please."

Therese leaned over Stanley. Thorsson could feel her magic Drawing hard, Binding into the wounds. Truelove came along beside her, grabbing Britton's hand and pumping it, grinning like a fool, speaking so quickly that Thorsson could barely follow him. "I can't believe you're alive! Marty took us in. There was some trouble at first, but he handled it. We thought we were stuck here forever." He paused. "Where's Sarah? What happened to her?"

Britton sighed. "I'm sorry, Simon. She stayed. It was her call, and she made it."

She's detained, being questioned. Even I couldn't get to see her, Thorsson thought. *They didn't trust her, either.*

Swift smiled at the sight of Britton. Then his eyes swept over Harlequin, and he snarled, "What the fuck are you doing here?" Thorsson remembered their last encounter and Suppressed his flow, drawing his pistol and sighting down it at the Aeromancer's scarred forehead. "Don't," he said. "There's no fucking time."

The goblins raced to Swift's side, leveling spears and shouting at Thorsson.

"Everyone settle down!" Bookbinder called out. "I'm Colonel Alan Bookbinder, commander of FOB Frontier. We need your help."

Stanley was sitting up, patting Therese's hand, thanking her in a brittle voice.

"It's okay," Britton said. "I don't know what the hell is going on here, but these men just broke me out of prison. How the hell did you find my father? Dad, I thought . . . I thought you were dead."

"Later," Bookbinder said. "The FOB is completely cut off. We're late to get help to them as it is. All those people are going to die when it's overrun. There's only one way to get them out of there, and I'm afraid you're it. We can deal with everything once they're safe, but we need to do something now. Like, right now."

Britton cursed, turning in a tight circle, hands on his hips.

"Come on, Oscar!" Stanley called to him, also standing.

"Oh, you're one to fucking talk," Britton yelled back at him, tears in his eyes. "After everything, you show up at my cell door needing help? And now you want me to work for the army again?"

"We've got some talking to do," Stanley said, "but there's no time for it now. For now you need to know that the reason we never got along is that I taught you too damned well. You knew how to make the right call even when I forgot.

"Well, you know what the right call is here. You have to help them, Oscar. No son of mine would turn his back on so many people in need, no matter what they'd done to him. The army may have turned you out, but you're still an officer in your bones. The Brittons have been officers for five generations. That never changes no matter what the army says."

Oscar Britton swallowed and looked away. "No time, Oscar," Harlequin said. "We need to go right now. Take us to the FOB."

Britton hesitated. Stanley put his hands on his hips. "Damn it, Oscar! I didn't just spend I don't know how long clawing a life out of this fucking wilderness to come back here and watch you walk out on your countrymen! Now you cowboy up and do the right thing!"

Britton looked from his father to Thorsson and shook his head. "Looks like Dudley Do-Right went rogue. How does it feel to be a fugitive from your government, Harlequin?"

"I'm doing the right thing," Thorsson answered, "so I'd say it feels just fine. I'm guessing you felt the same way when you got out of the FOB."

Britton nodded. "I did."

"Well, we'll talk about that. But for now, we need to get to that FOB."

"We're not finished!" Swift shouted, stepping around the earthen wall. "We've got business!"

"No, you don't," Britton shouted at him. "Right now, the only business is saving that base."

He turned toward Swift again but was intercepted by Therese, who dragged him into another embrace, clutching him tightly. "Oh, God, Oscar. I thought you were dead. I thought you were dead, and I wasn't going to get a chance to . . ."

Britton allowed himself to bury his face in her hair for a moment. "It's okay," he said. "It's okay. We'll . . . we'll . . ."

An obvious cough from Bookbinder brought him back to himself. He stepped away from her with a will. "Later," he said. *It's always later.*

"Can you convince some of these indig to help?" Bookbinder asked.

"Let's see what we're up against first," Britton said, opening a gate. "We'll have to head back to the Home Plane first. These things only work between worlds."

"Fuck you." Swift took a tentative step forward, then checked himself as Thorsson raised his pistol again. "We're not helping you."

"I am," Therese said.

"Thank you," Bookbinder breathed.

Britton shook his head. "I've dragged you around enough. I thought I'd lost you all back there in New York. I'm not gating you into a potential war zone without a look-see first. Stay here. I'll be back when I know what the story is."

"I'll talk to Marty," Therese said. "I'll tell them to be ready if you need us."

"Will they help?" Bookbinder asked.

Therese nodded. "It's their religion. They have a commandment to keep you safe. They're already skirmishing with the *Prendehad* Defender clans on a daily basis."

Bookbinder looked incredulous.

"She's right," Truelove said. "I've been learning about their religion. They don't get many Necromancers out here, so . . ."

Britton silenced him with a wave. "You can tell me after. For now, let's go. Everybody stays here. Dad, you too."

Stanley Britton laughed over the chorus of protests. "The hell I will. I've been fighting to get back to you for months. I'm not letting you out of my sight until we put paid to this mess and go find your mother."

Britton shook his head. "No, Dad. Christ, I thought I'd killed you once. I'm not going through that again. I promise you, we'll be back. Just sit tight. Can you just listen to me this once?"

Stanley made to argue, but Thorsson waved him down. "No time, damn it!"

Swift's eyes never left Harlequin, but he stayed put as Britton rolled open another gate, stepped through, and looked around. "Okay," he said. "It's clear. Follow me through, and we'll gate to the FOB from there."

"Be ready," Bookbinder cautioned them. "We have no idea what we're walking into."

CHAPTER XXVII
RELIEF

*Sir, our presence in the Source is absolutely vital to continued com-
bat overmatch capabilities in the arcane domain. Every day the
special projects activity at FOB Frontier is in operation, we make
leaps forward. We are discovering entirely new schools of magic.
We are learning how to adapt the flora and fauna of that plane to
augment systems in every arena, from medical to offense to logistics. The FOB's existence is a boost to our military capabilities far
beyond any technological breakthrough in history. It is critical to
this nation's continued security to expand the base, and ensure our
adversaries do not gain a similar foothold.*

—Lieutenant General Alexander Gatanas
Commandant, Supernatural Operations Corps
Briefing to the Senate Appropriations Committee (Special Session)

The FOB's main plaza was unrecognizable. The MWR and
DFAC tents were gone, the entire space given over to a vast Terramantic garden. Rows of fat fruits and vegetables trotted out in
all directions, basking in magically warmed air. Bookbinder
counted at least five cisterns bubbling freshwater in just the first
sweep of his eyes across the ground before him.

Gunfire rattled faintly in the distance, followed by the
crackle-boom of magical lightning. Bookbinder didn't hear any
air traffic, which was unusual when the enemy was on them.
They must be running seriously low on fuel. Or aircraft. A few
soldiers gaped as they stepped through the gate, first raising
weapons, then lowering them at the sight of Bookbinder.

"Sir!" said an air force tech sergeant, trotting toward them.

Bookbinder's gut twisted at the man's appearance. He was unshaven, sunken-eyed, and filthy. "We thought that . . ."

Bookbinder stopped him with a wave. "I'm fine. We're bringing help. What's the SITREP?"

"We're in a bad way, sir. Pretty much out of ammo and medical supplies. We ran out of food ages ago." He gestured at the gardens around them. "We just regrew this last night. They burn it up pretty much every time they come. It's touch-and-go, sir."

"Sounds pretty quiet."

"They're just getting warmed up, sir. It'll pick up as the day wears on."

"Casualties?"

The tech sergeant shook his head. "I couldn't say for sure, sir, but it's a lot. Maybe 20 percent. They make it past the perimeter most nights now."

Bookbinder tried not to let his horror show on his face. He kept his voice even. "Where's Crucible?"

"Should be in his office, sir. He usually doesn't head out to the perimeter until after chow."

"All right, as you were. Don't spread the word about us, please. I want everyone's head in the fight until we can execute a plan. But we will get you out of here, you understand me?"

"Yes, sir."

Bookbinder gestured to Britton, his father, and Harlequin, and they made their way toward the camp commandant's office. "That kid won't keep his mouth shut," Bookbinder groused. "Everyone is going to know we're here by the time we get to Crucible. But at least the FOB's still here."

Britton looked around. "I never thought I'd see this place again."

"We're only here long enough to get everyone out safe," Bookbinder said. "Then you'll never have to look at it again."

Crucible was rushing out the door toward them before they'd turned onto the muddy, potholed track that led to his office. Someone must have radioed ahead as Bookbinder predicted. Carmela was at his side, her office clothing replaced by boots, cargo pants, and military parka.

"Holy shit, sir." Crucible choked on his words. "God*damn* but it is good to see you. We all thought you were dead." He slammed to attention and saluted.

Bookbinder, uncovered and out of uniform, returned it anyway, then embraced him. "We're here to get you out. You recognize this guy?" He gestured behind him.

Crucible's smile faltered. "Oscar Britton. I guess it's good to see you, too."

Britton nodded. "No love lost, sir. Let's get everyone to safety, and we can hash out differences later."

Crucible turned to Harlequin. "Jan," he said, grinning. "There are no words."

Harlequin smiled back. "Later, Rick. I'm glad you're okay."

"I can have Britton open a gate in the main plaza," Bookbinder said. "How soon can you give the order to pull back?"

Crucible swore. "I could give it now, but I might as well order them to lay down their arms and give themselves up. We've lost too many. The goblins come twenty-four/seven at this point. We abandon our positions now, they'll cut us to pieces as we fall back."

"Some tech sergeant told me you're at 20 percent casualties," Bookbinder said.

Crucible hung his head. "That's about right. Though, I haven't gotten last night's count in yet."

"Jesus, Rick. I'm sorry," Bookbinder said.

"Doesn't matter," Crucible said. "If we're going to fall back, we need breathing room."

"You need the enemy repulsed," Thorsson said.

"That's right." Crucible nodded. "For at least an hour. That would do it. But it'd just be people. Everything else would stay here. Gear, documents, you name it."

"Repulse them at 20 percent casualties?" Thorsson said. "Jesus, you'd need an army."

Crucible cursed. "I don't suppose you guys have one of those in your pocket?"

Bookbinder thought for a moment, then turned to Carmela. "Can you grab me one of my spare uniforms out of my office? Is it even still in there?" Carmela answered by racing back into the building.

Bookbinder turned to Britton. "You ever been to Colorado Springs?"

Britton frowned. "You mean the Air Force Academy?"

"Close enough."

"Once. Joint service familiarization. Why?"

"Can you get us back there?" Bookbinder asked.

Britton shrugged and rolled open a gate. Bookbinder glimpsed the inside of an empty auditorium through the shimmering surface. Carmela returned and tossed him a bundle of digital camouflage, then handed him a pair of boots. He thanked her and turned to the gate.

"Let's go," he said, stepping through.

"Where the hell are you going?" Crucible called after him.

"To get you an army," Bookbinder said. "Hold tight. We'll be back soon."

Bookbinder directed Britton to gate-hop himself and Thorsson a few miles outside of town with a brief pause to change clothing. Looking the colonel again, he directed Britton to jump back to the FOB's plaza, then to a point on the horizon that Bookbinder identified. After fifteen minutes of it, a tall fence came into view, surrounding a sprawling compound of the prefab plastic-sided buildings they'd all come to associate with deployed military forces. Next to the Stars and Stripes, an eagle fluttered before a map of North America. A sign affixed to the gatehouse read US NORTHERN COMMAND—QUICK REACTION FORCE POST 6. THE IMMOVABLE OBJECT!

Bookbinder began to stride purposefully forward, mustering every inch of the command presence he had. "What the hell are we doing?" Thorsson asked, as they walked.

"I am being a high-and-mighty colonel," Bookbinder replied. "You are being the guy in the class A uniform that everyone knows from TV. Now straighten your crap up and get out in front."

Thorsson did his best to brush out the creases and wipe off the worst of the debris as they approached the gate.

The two privates on duty snapped to attention, saluting crisply.

Bookbinder flashed his ID. "Colonel Alan Bookbinder, Commandant, Forward Operating Base Frontier."

The privates exchanged glances, frowning. "Excuse me, sir? But I . . ."

"Never mind that." He gestured at Thorsson. "This is Major Jan Thorsson, Special Advisor to the Reawakening Committee."

One of the privates nodded. "Seen you on TV, sir."

"Hopefully I didn't embarrass myself." Thorsson grinned.

"Not at all, sir."

Bookbinder continued the good cop, bad-cop routine. "Who's in charge here?" he growled.

"That's Lieutenant Colonel Blake, sir."

"Great. Give him a ring and have him meet me in front of the squadron bay. The QRF is getting scrambled."

"Scrambled!?" The private stammered. "Sir, we didn't get a cable, or a call or . . ."

"Damn it, I don't have time for this!" Bookbinder shouted, taking a step forward. "*I'm* your fucking cable, son. Now open this goddamn gate!"

"Sir, I'm not supposed to do that. I don't even know who this guy is." He gestured at Britton.

Bookbinder took another step forward, letting his saliva mist the private's face. "Son, you are addressing a field-grade officer in the United States Army."

"Flag officer, actually," Thorsson added. "Colonel Bookbinder just got picked up for his first star."

The privates exchanged another look and scrambled to open the gate.

Bookbinder, Thorsson, and Britton strode through and headed for the hangar-sized building in the middle of the compound.

"Flag officer?" Bookbinder muttered to Thorsson. "That was a bit much."

"Got us through, didn't it?" Thorsson smiled.

"You're one to talk," Britton added, looking at Bookbinder. "Beating up on privates? As a full bird? Not cool."

Bookbinder shrugged. "Got us through, didn't it?"

"What the hell is this place?" Britton asked.

"USNORTHCOM's QRF. It's a ready unit for homeland defense. They should have at least a company ready to scramble inside of fifteen minutes. It's not much, but it might do the job," Bookbinder said.

"How the hell did you even know about this?" Britton asked.

Bookbinder shrugged. "I wasn't always the dashing leader of men you see before you now. I used to be AMC's J1. I authorized this unit's budget line for the last five years."

A heavyset lieutenant colonel raced toward them, puffing at the exertion, straightening his patrol cap. "Just what in the hell is going on here!?" he shouted as he reached them, irritatedly returning Thorsson's salute.

"I'm scrambling the QRF," Bookbinder said, showing his ID. "By order of the President of the United States."

Lieutenant Colonel Blake saluted, red-faced, and sputtered. "I don't have any official comms on this! I need time to . . ."

Bookbinder crossed his hands behind his back and raised his chin. "I'm sorry, Colonel. I was under the impression that this was USNORTHCOM's Quick Reaction Force, ready to jump on fifteen minutes' notice when needed for homeland-defense matters. Was I mistaken in that?"

"No, sir, but . . ."

"Outstanding. The homeland is under attack. Scramble the ready company. We're jumping right now."

Blake turned to Thorsson, his eyes narrowing. "You're that major on TV. The . . ."

"Special Advisor to the Reawakening Commission, yes. That's me," Thorsson said.

Blake turned back to Bookbinder. "I've received no higher authorization, and no word that the homeland is under attack. I don't know what the hell you're talking about."

"I'm talking about a United States military base under siege at this very moment and in danger of being overrun. Last time I checked, any American embassy or military outpost is sovereign soil. Your QRF is needed, and we're standing here jaw-jacking."

"Where?" Blake's jowls quivered as he looked from Thorsson to Bookbinder and back.

"Show him the SASS perimeter," Bookbinder said. Britton opened a gate. Through the flickering curtain of light, Bookbinder could see tumbled blocks of masonry, the broken chunks of gabions and blast barricades taken down by magical fire. Dark shapes swarmed in the burning grass beyond. Bookbinder could see a Marine fire team crouching behind an earthen wall, exchanging fire with something beyond it. A SOC Aeromancer streaked overhead, tossing down a grenade from one hand, blazing lightning from the other. Another group of soldiers ran past, then froze, staring at the open gate.

"That"—Bookbinder seethed—"is what's left of an entire fucking division, Colonel. We are getting them out of there right now, and you are going to scramble your QRF to provide the rear guard."

"I . . . I can't just . . ." Blake stammered.

Bookbinder seized the man by his lapels and dragged him so close that he was practically kissing him. "What you can't just do is let a division's worth of men and women die because you're worried about the bureaucracy. I am your goddamn authorization. You have the goddamn right hand of the Reawakening Commission standing next to you. These people are out of time, Colonel. I know you thought this assignment meant sitting around with your feet up for a few years, but that just changed. This is what you joined the army for. Now get off your ass and *Save. Lives.*"

He gave Blake a shake with each of the last two words, then released him. The plump man stood there, bug-eyed, so red he bordered on purple, frozen.

"Colonel Blake," Thorsson added. "There are Americans dying there. You can choose to save them, or you can choose to worry about your career."

Blake blinked, rooted to the spot, his eyes still fixed on the gate.

"Go!" Bookbinder finally shouted at him, breaking Blake's paralysis and sending him racing back to the hangar-sized building behind him.

Bookbinder slumped. "That's it."

"I don't think it'll work," Thorsson said.

Bookbinder shook his head. "If it doesn't, I'm all out of ideas." He turned to Britton, "Get ready to open another gate and get us the hell out of here. What about your indig buddies back there? Would they help?"

Britton frowned. "I . . . I think so. It's their religion to help us, and I've seen them fight for us before . . ."

"But?" Bookbinder asked.

"But it's been a little while since I talked to them." He shook his head. "They'll help. I'm sure."

"You don't look sure," Thorsson mused.

Bookbinder pursed his lips and stood, hands on his hips, too tired to muster anything approaching a look of authority, and waited for Blake's MPs to come and arrest them.

They waited a full five minutes, during which time Bookbinder's stomach did cartwheels so badly he put a hand on his abdomen.

The squad bay's huge metal doors began to inch slowly upward. "Here we go," Bookbinder said. "We did our best, guys." He set his stance and waited for the MPs.

Instead, soldiers began to pour out of the blackness beyond, strapping on helmets, tightening carbine slings, hopping aboard rolling Strykers. They looked grim-faced and determined.

They looked ready for war.

CHAPTER XXVIII
REAR GUARD

Samantha. My Sam. They are coming every day now, pushing farther each time. It's time to come to grips with the fact that Bookbinder didn't make it. There is no cavalry coming. I have done all I can here. We are dug in and fighting like lions, but there's a limit to what people can do. I am ashamed to be admitting defeat here, but comforted somewhat in knowing this letter will never reach you. We are stranded in another world, completely cut off. What comforts me more is knowing that, for ten wonderful years, I lived with and loved you. I had that privilege, that honor. We raised a child together. We knew one another as few people ever do. Many dream of such a thing and never get to experience it. Oh, Sam. I have been so lucky. I am so incredibly fortunate to have loved you.

—"Death Letter" allegedly from Lieutenant
Colonel "Crucible" Allen to his wife
Found in the ruins of Forward Operating Base
Frontier after its destruction

Bookbinder was the first through the gate and the first wounded. A javelin arced out of the seething mass of goblins and clipped his side, digging a furrow below his arm that sent him spinning and dropping behind cover.

The soldiers around them sent up a hoarse cheer as the first Stryker rolled through, followed by running guardsmen who paused, blinking in wonder at the rocs streaking overhead, at the horde of the enemy beyond.

Thorsson was with them, stripping off his uniform jacket and leaping skyward, angry clouds boiling around him. "I know it's strange!" he called down. "That's the enemy! Suppressing fire! I want this line held!"

Bookbinder shrugged off a navy corpsman who rushed to his aid. "I'm fine! Where the hell is Crucible?"

Crucible turned out to be leading from the front as well. Bookbinder found him taking cover in an earthen pillbox, one of many the FOB's Terramancers had raised along the hard-pressed perimeter. He squinted through the slits in the hard-packed surface, Binding his magic in the midst of the goblin throng, raising pillars of fire that sent the creatures shrieking. Their own Hydromancers set up impromptu aid stations, mist clouds that roved among the horde, drenching the burn victims and occasionally launching a stream of ice shards toward the defenders.

"You're a sight for sore eyes," Crucible said, glancing briefly at Bookbinder before turning his attention back to the fight.

"There's a company of fresh troops securing this area right now," Bookbinder said. "Is this the only flash point?"

"It is right now, but it's early."

"Good, get your people organized and start pulling them back. Once I have the full QRF in position, I'll have Britton gate them out from the main plaza. If you have anything you've been holding in reserve, fuel, ordnance, now's the time to expend it. This is the only chance we get. Unleash hell."

"Got it, sir." Crucible raced out of the pillbox, shouting into his radio. Bookbinder followed him, watching as the exhausted defenders began to pull back, their positions taken over by the fresh guardsmen of the QRF. The Strykers rolled through the wreckage, tanks full of gas, machine guns thundering into the massed enemy. Horns sounded among the goblins, to what end Bookbinder couldn't tell. He heard the grind of rotors over-head and grinned as the QRF's Kiowas raced aloft, guns and rockets firing, the rocs and wyverns of the goblin forces shriek-ing in surprise.

One of Britton's shimmering gates arced horizontally through the goblins' front rank, a dazzling cleaver, cutting them to pieces. Bookbinder pumped his fist as one of the giants went down howling, cut off at midthigh, crushing his smaller com-rades beneath him. Sheets of lightning cut ragged rents in the attacking army, Thorsson's work and that of the other Aeromancers energized by his sudden appearance.

Bookbinder raced along the impromptu barricade line set up by the Strykers. "Britton! Britton!" He found the man standing on the back of a Stryker, working his magic.

"Get to the main plaza!" Bookbinder shouted to him. "Start running everyone out of here! Once we fall back, this place is going to be overrun."

Britton nodded and jumped off the Stryker. "Where are we going?"

"I don't fucking know!" Bookbinder shouted at him. "Some place safe! A hospital! Get everyone to a hospital!"

Britton smiled. "I've got just the place." And then he was gone, racing toward the FOB's heart.

Bookbinder found Blake sheltering behind an armored Humvee, its Mark 19 pumping a thundering stream of bullet-shaped grenades into the enemy line. The horns were sounding again, high-pitched and plaintive. Bookbinder saw banners wave, space opening up between the combatant lines, a no-man's-land strewn with goblin corpses.

"Okay!" Bookbinder shouted at him. "You've bought us a little time! I need you to hold this position until you've fully cycled the relief! Once you're confident that we're all out, you can start falling back to the plaza."

Blake nodded, raising his radio. Bookbinder stopped him with a hand on his wrist. "Make sure you *wait* until we're fully out, then fall back immediately to the plaza! It's the only way out of here, and this base is going to be totally overrun once we abandon these defenses."

"Where are you going?" Blake shouted back at him.

"I'm staying here," Bookbinder answered. *At least until I'm sure everyone is ready to go.*

With that he was up, racing among the FOB's original force, shouting at them to head for the plaza, settling the QRF guardsmen into their old positions, shoving them into the pillboxes, exhorting them on.

The gap between the two groups widened. Bookbinder threw himself behind a Stryker and peeked around its giant tire, then back along the perimeter line. The uniforms around him were all fresh and clean-looking, QRF guardsmen. He leaned back and shouted to Blake. "It's clear! Start falling back to the plaza!"

Bookbinder heard a thud behind him and spun to face Thorsson, filthy, bleeding, and grinning like a wolf. "Looking pretty bad for the enemy."

"Outstanding. Help me get everyone the hell out of here. Britton is gating us out from the central plaza."

Thorsson gave a thumbs-up and leapt skyward again.

The QRF guardsmen began to move backward in good order, following the original defenders toward the plaza, moving and covering as they'd been trained. Bookbinder retrieved a fallen carbine and moved with them, firing in three-round bursts. The weapon bucked and it was impossible to hit anything, but he figured the stream of bullets would make the goblins keep their heads down, and that was something.

The goblins sensed the change in the defenders' posture and surged forward. Squadrons of rocs clouded the skies over them as the air cover fell back to circle over the plaza. The good order of the guardsmen began to flag as they sensed the enemy's surge in momentum. Within moments, the first of them had turned his back on the enemy, running pell-mell for the plaza. Bookbinder shouted to no avail. The stream became a river and the guardsmen abandoned all pretense at order, running for escape.

Bookbinder cursed and ran with them. Men fell around him, javelins quivering in their backs. A column of fire jetted through their ranks, sending men howling to roll in the mud. Elbows jostled Bookbinder's ribs, and he nearly went down as a goblin Terramancer raised a doglike thing with spiked teeth made of glittering rock, sending it lurching into the column. He dodged around it, pushing along the muddy track, screaming at the men to move faster. He glanced skyward, grateful for the circling air cover, the only thing keeping this rout from becoming a massacre. Horror rose in his gut.

Even with this relief force, the enemy was not sufficiently repulsed. The goblins were hot on their heels, leaving them the choice of standing and fighting until their ammunition ran out or running for the gate and being cut to pieces, backs to their enemy.

One army wasn't enough.

An arrow whistled by Bookbinder's ear, and he heard the

horns sound again, answered by a howl of victory from the goblins as they began to pour past the now-abandoned perimeter, hot on the retreating soldiers' trail. Thorsson landed beside him, his eyes wide with worry.

"What?" Bookbinder shouted to him. "I don't need bad news right now!"

"Britton's gone."

Bookbinder cursed as they crested a rise in the track, giving him a clear view of the plaza before them. The gardens had been churned to mud by the FOB's original defenders. They'd arrived first, and now clustered together in confusion, looking for a gate home that was nowhere to be found. A cry went up from them and they began firing. Bookbinder winced for a moment until he realized they were shooting in another direction.

Then he froze. Goblins came pouring into the plaza from the east, cutting off the retreating defenders from the ones clustered in the plaza before them, blocking their escape. The guardsmen let out of cry of despair and stopped, slamming into one another.

Crucible had been wrong. The goblins had hit the perimeter from another direction and punched through.

Worse, Britton was gone, and with him, their way out. For the second time, the defenders of FOB Frontier were cut off.

Bookbinder turned to Thorsson. "Get us some fucking cover!" Without waiting for the major, he turned to the nearest guardsman and yanked on his body armor's back strap, hauling him around to face the pursing goblins. "Pour it on!" he shouted, racing among the other guardsmen, trying to organize them into something approaching a firing line.

It was a stupid way to fight, more befitting Napoleon's troops than a modern force, but there was no cover and no retreat. The narrow track was hemmed in on either side by housing units ringed with sandbags. Ahead of them, the other goblin force was hotly engaged with the FOB's original defenders in the plaza's center, buying them some time from the rear for now. Either those goblins would overwhelm that unit and pin them against their pursuers, or the original defenders' bullets would cut through them and start slicing into the QRF guardsmen's backs.

Either way. They were finished.

He felt his wedding band sliding along his finger, pressed against the gun's grip. *Julie, the girls. You won't see them again.* The sadness was followed by a spike of hot pride. *You led from the front. You stayed with your people, and you are putting down your life for theirs. You're a soldier. No one can ever gainsay that now.*

With that thought, he scrambled with the guardsmen clustering behind the fleeing Strykers. He was done shouting. He'd imposed what order he could, led as best he knew how. From here on out, there was only fighting. The thought brought him a measure of peace as he tapped a soldier on the shoulder, received a full magazine, swapped out, and started firing.

An explosion blossomed to his left, a shock wave swatting him aside like a hot hand. One of the QRF's Blackhawks had crashed into the housing pod on that side of the track, its rotors covered in thick ice. Chunks of the cabin spun away, blazing shrapnel slicing through the QRF's ranks. A guardsman spun toward Bookbinder, his arm sliced off, his face slick pale, mouth working silently before he dropped. Bookbinder forced himself to turn away, pouring fire back the way they had come until the barrel of his carbine smoked. He couldn't see anything through the smoke and spraying earth of the track, but with the enemy packed so thickly behind them, it was impossible to miss.

A shriek sounded, high and piercing, trilling above the din of gunfire and shouting voices. Both sides paused in the silence that followed, craning necks behind the goblin horde. The shriek sounded again, and the goblins began to part, admitting a small troop of giants, shambling their way up the muddy trail. They surrounded three creatures that oozed liquid blackness, gliding over the surface of the ground, shadows from a nightmare. Every soldier who'd seen news clips of the Apache insurgency had glimpsed them before, had heard the rumors of their existence in the midst of the reservation's violent ferment, but none had thought to see them here.

The Apache called them their "Mountain Gods." Everyone else called them monsters. What the hell were they doing here?

The Mountain Gods shrieked again, stuttering forward on the trail, one moment in the midst of the goblin army, the next shifting a hundred feet closer, flickering in and out of vision. Their long, thin limbs absorbed the morning light, the uniform sable of pooled india ink. Their fingers tapered to kitchen-knife claws, equally as long as their teeth, and just as sharp. The white cut of their mouths was the only feature in their narrow, horned, black heads.

"Holy shit," said a guardsman, opening fire. The bullets arced across the intervening distance and vanished in their black mass as if they'd been swallowed. The Mountain Gods cried out once more, flickered, and were suddenly in the midst of them.

What little order remained shattered in an instant. The scream that went up from Blake's force rivaled the shrieking of the monsters among them as they swept about with their long claws, shattering bones and tossing the guardsmen in the air like uniformed rag dolls. Bookbinder shouted for them to hold, but it was useless; as soon as the first few shots passed harmlessly into the Mountain Gods' liquid black skins, the soldiers threw down their weapons and fled in the opposite direction.

Straight into the goblins now battling the FOB's original defenders, who began to turn their spears on the panicked, unarmed soldiers charging into their midst. Bookbinder shouted at them, reached out to grab at the grab-handle on a fleeing soldier's body armor, and missed as the woman ran screaming onto the point of a goblin spear. She doubled over, the plate of her body armor turning the point aside, and Bookbinder got to her in three steps, reaching over her shoulder to punch the goblin in the face as she dropped to the ground. The goblin staggered back, shook off the blow, angry eyes turning to slits as it raised its spear.

Then abruptly widening in terror. The goblin dropped the spear and backed away quickly, until it vanished in the melee behind it. Bookbinder turned just as the Mountain God's dagger claws swept down toward him.

He got his carbine up in time, jarring his shoulders from the impact of the creature's arm. The monster gripped the carbine, wrenching it back, dragging Bookbinder with it. Crouched so close, he could feel the chilly air that emanated from its skin. His hands went numb as the metal in the gun conducted the cold to his fingers, making his arms leaden, difficult to keep up. His hands felt thick, clumsy. He fell back in the mud as the Mountain God wrenched the weapon from his hands and threw it away. Its head flickered forward, dagger teeth glinting wetly.

Then it cried out, wreathed in lightning, as Harlequin swooped over its shoulder, ribbons of electricity arcing from his fingers, engulfing the creature's head and shoulders. Black mist wafted from the wounds, so cold that Bookbinder's teeth chattered despite being several feet away from the outpouring. The creature flailed, covering its head, snarling up at Harlequin, who somersaulted in the air and rocketed upward, dodging the feeble swipe it directed at him. He steadied himself for another blaze of the magic, then jerked aside as a roc dove at him, nearly catching him in its jaws. A white-painted goblin Aeromancer followed behind the giant bird, unleashing a torrent of lightning that Harlequin dove low to avoid. The goblin Aeromancer streaked past him and banked sharply, coming back for another pass.

Bookbinder scrambled in the mud as the Mountain God shook off its wounds and turned back to him, still bleeding that freezing black mist. He dragged himself forward, wincing as a fleeing guardsman stepped on his hand, scrambled to get to his knees. He jerked upright, planting his fists in the dirt to push himself to his feet, feeling his knuckles brush against a wooden cylinder.

The goblin's spear.

He gripped the haft and spun, holding it at waist level, pointing it at the Mountain God. The creature paused, arms spread. The black smoke cascaded from its head and shoulders, rising above its curling horns, Bookbinder gritted his teeth to stop himself from shaking. Over the creature's shoulder, Harlequin did battle with the roc, kicking it in the beak and using the momentum to carry him over backward as he channeled a burst of lightning that ignited the bird's features and sent it flapping backward. The giant bird kept coming, keeping his attention as the goblin Aeromancer finished its turn and came at Harlequin from behind, extending its hand for another burst of lightning.

Bookbinder forced himself to take a step forward, could swear he sensed a look of incredulous surprise in the featureless black space above the giant mouth. Then he extended a hand, Drawing hard for the goblin Aeromancer's magic, Binding it into the spear tip with everything he had.

The goblin Aeromancer screamed and plummeted to the earth, its magic suddenly gone. The Mountain God howled in time as the spearhead blazed into a dazzling cone of crackling blue lightning.

Bookbinder screamed and thrust the point toward the Mountain God's chest. The creature batted it away with one long hand, then flinched as the crackle of electricity singed its claws, unleashing more of the freezing smoke. Bookbinder spun with the spear's momentum, swinging it over his head, bringing the added length down so that the crackling tip cut across the monster's face. It screamed, flickered backward into one of the giants, knocking it to one side. The Mountain God grunted, falling on its back, scrambling flickering arms to get to its feet.

Bookbinder was determined not to give it the chance.

With a yell, he leapt, reversing the spear, coming down to land one foot on the creature's stomach, the cold penetrating his boots and making his knee ache and go numb in a matter of moments. The Mountain God screamed, and Bookbinder screamed back, bringing the point down, straight through the monster's chest, pinning it into the mud and leaping aside as the black smoke fountained into the air, numbing his shoulders as he rolled away.

The Mountain God's death throes drew the attention of the other two, who flickered backward in shock at the sight of their own being felled by a human. The giants stood their ground, dumbly staring at the thing dying at their feet. A moment later, Harlequin seized the momentum, blazing lightning down on another of the Mountain Gods, so that they shrieked, fading backward into the goblin lines.

Bookbinder pointed to the spear, still blazing with electricity in the sinking cavity of the Mountain God's chest. "They . . . duh . . . die!" He managed through chattering teeth. The fleeing guardsmen were mostly engaged with the goblins around them, but a few turned their heads, took in the sight, hefted their guns.

Harlequin blazed in the sky like a flickering star. Tongues of lightning lashed the two remaining creatures, who faded backward once more, until they were gone from sight. He swooped closer to Bookbinder, who knelt in the mud, recovering a carbine with trembling hands, only just beginning to regain some of their feeling. "You okay?"

"Fuh . . . fuh . . . fucking . . . cold," Bookbinder managed.

Then he knelt and opened up with the weapon, emptying the magazine into the stunned goblin horde, still trying to reconstitute around the fleeing Mountain Gods. He couldn't feel his fingers, his own flesh chilled corpse rubber. But pulling a trigger didn't exactly take fine motor skills. A few of the other guardsmen lent their fire to his, spinning goblins in circles before they collapsed in the earth.

Harlequin streaked overhead, making sure the Mountain Gods kept running, while Bookbinder and some of the guardsmen took cover behind a Stryker, pouring on fire. At last, the goblins gathered their wits and came on with a cry. He looked around him. A few of the QRF had found their courage and stood beside him, firing with the cold discipline he expected of professional soldiers. But they were so few. Nothing to be done about it now. Standing and fighting took courage, but it didn't take a lot of thought. Bookbinder was happy to put his brain on hold and concentrate instead on the slowly returning feeling in his finger, pulling the trigger over and over.

As he paused to swap out magazines again, he heard the din of gunfire give way before screams and clashing metal as the first of the goblins slammed into the QRF's ranks and the brutal hand-to-hand combat commenced. A goblin launched itself over the Stryker's turret, gutting the gunner with a short, curving sword before plunging down the other side. Bookbinder upended his carbine and took a baseball swing as it passed him, smacking its skull into the Stryker's side and knocking it off its feet. He jumped onto the Stryker's turret, clubbing with his carbine and calling to the men behind him. "Come on!"

And then he raced down the other side, the QRF soldiers alongside him, batting aside a spear and kicking its wielder in the face. Bookbinder jumped onto the goblin's body and laid about him, eyes half-closed, the tight press of men and goblins barely leaving him room to swing, the heat of bodies like a furnace, the stink of sweat and blood thick in his nostrils.

For a moment, Bookbinder forgot where and who he was. There was only the steady rhythm of the carbine, rising and falling, the pumping exertion of his shoulders, the buzz of the fighting around him, coming to his ears as if from a long way off. He was dead. Every second he breathed, the pain lancing through his thigh as something cut him, was a stolen moment, borrowed from the reaper, filling his heart with joy.

Oh, Julie, he thought. *When I see you in heaven, I am going to have such stories to tell you.*

Up, down, the carbine went. Somewhere in the thick of things, the plastic butt stock had broken off, the heavy upper receiver was rimed with dripping blood, fragments of bone, and gray slop that was probably brain.

A snarling face appeared before him, and he headbutted it, sending the goblin reeling back a pace before it shouted something and dove forward, slashing at him with a knife and sinking its teeth into his shoulder. He didn't scream. The pain was a gift, another sensation, another moment of life. Instead, he thrust his fingers into the goblin's eye sockets, businesslike, and yanked its head back before kicking it in the gut and clubbing it into bloody silence.

The ground shook, and Bookbinder looked up. Before him stood one of the giants, a steel pauldron belted across its scarred chest. It hefted an uprooted tree studded with iron nails the size of railroad spikes and roared at him, crushing a guardsman beneath one massive, hobnailed boot. Bookbinder craned his head, felt for a current. No one nearby was using magic. The broken carbine looked pathetic in his hands, now red and aching as the cold left them.

What the hell, Bookbinder thought. *Might as well go out with a bang.* He howled right back and charged, his stubby, broken carbine pathetic in his hands.

The giant lifted its club, then screamed, gurgling and falling back. Bookbinder swiped at its knee and missed as the creature retreated. He looked up in surprise. A spear quivered in the giant's throat.

A goblin spear.

He looked behind him. A cheer had gone up, horns were blowing. Banners waved, a gnarled tree on a square of blue. They flapped in the freezing wind, snapping back and forth before a flickering gate, its shimmering light dancing over the backs of hundreds of goblin warriors. A squadron of them, mounted on huge snarling wolves, leapt over the Stryker, plunging into the enemy, laying about with short, wicked swords, screaming a battle cry. Behind them, scores of their comrades followed, spears waving.

Bookbinder let the press of friendly goblins surge around him, seeing his exhausted, dumbfounded expression mirrored in the guardsmen's faces. They stood, slack-jawed, fatigue and wonder immobilizing them as the newly arriving goblins pushed their pursuers back.

"Sir!" It was Britton. "Let's go! Get your men out of here!"

His voice broke Bookbinder's paralysis, and he raced to stand on top of the Stryker. The Healer, Therese, rushed past him, disappearing among the retreating guardsmen, putting her magic to use.

With the last of the allied goblins through the gate, Britton snapped it shut. He nodded to Bookbinder and opened it again.

Bookbinder looked into the glowing curtain and smiled. Beyond it, he could see an access gate, tall fencing guarded by soldiers, now shouting and pointing at the portal that had suddenly appeared across the road from them. Bookbinder's smile grew as he recognized that road. It was Georgia Avenue, now crowded with traffic as the cars screeched to a halt, their drivers gawking at the gate in their midst.

Bookbinder recognized the road and the gate. More importantly, he recognized the collection of buildings behind it.

The Walter Reed National Military Medical Center.

"Go!" he shouted to his men. "Everybody through! Right now! Carry the wounded! Ditch your gear! Gogogo!"

Around them, the allied goblins and their enemies fought, slowly creating a ring of open ground, free of fighting. The remaining original defenders and the guardsmen of the QRF poured into the void, throwing down their guns, their helmets, anything that might slow them down. Bookbinder plunged among them, dragging wounded men to their feet, slinging them over their comrades' shoulders. His cold, burned flesh screamed at him, but he ignored it. The pain was thematic now, a dull undercurrent, omnipresent and easily ignored. He tripped over an airman howling in the dirt, clutching his shattered knee. Bookbinder dragged him screaming to his feet, pushed him into the side of the Stryker, and with the help of a Marine, bodily threw him into the portal. He turned back to the throng of guardsmen, seized another man by his carbine sling, and yanked him through the gate. The man went stumbling onto the grassy curb along Georgia Avenue, blinking and staring, milling in the growing crowd of his comrades. Bookbinder took a step through the gate and shouted to the dumbstruck gate guards, "A little help here! We've got wounded coming through!"

He took a quick look around. Traffic had come to a complete halt, and police lights flashed as cruisers pulled onto the shoulder, their drivers shouting into the radios for instructions. A huge crowd of pedestrians was growing all along the center's perimeter as civilians exited their cars or hospital workers left their offices to see what the commotion was about. Bookbinder was pleased to see a few of them have the presence of mind to go pelting back into the buildings behind the fence, presumably for medical supplies.

He heard a shout and felt a sharp pain in his shoulder. He whirled, seizing the wrist of a goblin, yanking it to the ground and crunching his boot down on its neck. There was a sharp snap, and the gnarled creature twitched to stillness in the middle of Georgia Avenue, blood leaking from its nostrils and mouth. The crowd of civilians surged away at the sight, pointing in horror. *The president's going to have a tough time explaining that,* Bookbinder thought. He swiped futilely at his own back before one of the guardsmen put a hand on his shoulder. "Hold still, sir. This is going to hurt." It did. Bookbinder cursed and doubled over as the guardsman yanked something from the wound, then pressed something into it.

He reached around Bookbinder's front and presented him with a short, bloody knife. "Here you go, sir. Souvenir."

"Thanks." Bookbinder's vision swam momentarily, and he steadied himself with a deep breath.

"I stuffed my helmet liner in the hole, sir. You won't bleed out, but it's dirty as hell. You need a medic."

Bookbinder looked down and saw a sergeant's chevrons on the man's body armor. "Later. Do me a favor and make sure everybody here"—he gestured at the now-huge crowd of servicemen and -women retreating through the gate—"gets into there." He pointed at the sprawling hospital complex, which was even now disgorging teams of personnel in blue medical scrubs, rushing gurneys onto the now-still tarmac of Georgia Avenue.

"Got it, sir."

Bookbinder nodded and jumped back through the gate. The plaza was oddly silent. The goblins who had made it into the plaza were fleeing between the FOB's buildings, pursued by squadrons of the allied goblins' wolfriders. The goblins that had pursued Bookbinder and his guardsmen had been pushed down the track a quarter kilometer, but the fighting still raged there. Bookbinder's stomach roiled at the sight of ranks of goblin and human corpses, marching shoulder to shoulder, silently bulling the attackers back. He could feel the magic driving them eddying from Britton's Necromancer friend, painted half-white and dressed like a goblin, standing atop the Stryker, arms stretched forward. He recognized him, Rictus from Shadow Coven. Brimstone reached his nostrils and his eyes swept the FOB to see most of it in flames.

Bookbinder felt a hand on his wound. He started to turn, then stopped as a delicious warmth flooded through him. The pain vanished. He could feel the trickle of blood stop, the severed tissues mending together. He felt the helmet liner dust past the back of his leg and settle to the ground. He turned to see Therese.

"Thank you, ma'am," he said.

She smiled.

Thorsson landed beside him. "Everyone's out, sir. Britton's indig buddies here bought us needed time. Even with your QRF, they'd have cut us up trying to go through that gate."

Bookbinder met Britton's eyes. "Thanks."

Britton grunted. "I saw your rear guard coming apart as you fell back. Figured you wouldn't be able to safely withdraw without more support. You didn't think I'd leave you, did you?" He cocked an eyebrow.

Bookbinder kept his face neutral, pursing his lips.

Britton smiled. "We better decide what's next. I'm giving them another five minutes to get a solid buffer, then I'm going to roll the Mattab On Sorrah out."

They stood in silence at that. *Next,* Bookbinder thought. *What the hell do we do next?*

"This is the second time you've thrown this in Walsh's face," Thorsson said, smiling, glancing through the gate at the chaos erupting outside the hospital complex. The first TV news camera crews were arriving in white vans, giant antennae waving from the tops. "I think he's going to have a hard time getting around it."

Britton grunted again. "Well, he should have accepted my offer when he had the chance." They paused uncomfortably.

"I'm going back," Thorsson finally said.

Britton looked up at him. "You know what they'll do to you."

The Aeromancer shrugged. "No, I don't. And anyway, it doesn't matter. I signed up to serve, and I'm not done serving yet. I'll deal with Walsh and his people inside the system."

"I was the same as you, Harlequin," Britton said. "That system ran me into the dirt."

Thorsson met his eyes. "That system works when you work it, Oscar. I believe that."

"I'm going with you," Bookbinder said. "We'll face whatever's coming together, Major."

"You two are out of your damned minds," Britton said.

"Maybe," Bookbinder said, "but my place is with my family . . . and with my troops." It felt strange to say it, but it was true. He commanded these men and women in battle. He was responsible for them. His people, his family. Maybe the terms were redundant. "Whatever's going to happen to me, it's going to happen to me alongside my own."

Thorsson nodded. "Well, let's secure this Hallmark card moment," he said. "I can't believe I'm doing this, but"—he extended a hand to Britton—"you're a good man and a fine officer, Oscar Britton. I wish the circumstances of our . . . uh . . . interaction had been different. The president's never going to say it, so I will. On behalf of a grateful nation, thank you."

Britton shook his hand, then took a step back, saluting. "Thank you, sir. It's my honor."

Thorsson returned the salute, looking uncomfortable, then smiled. "Thanks to all of you," he said to the other SASS refugees who stood watching the exchange. Then he stepped through the gate and into the chaos of service members, hospital workers, camera crews, civilian bystanders, and police who mobbed Georgia Avenue beyond.

Bookbinder turned back to Therese. She smiled at him, dazzling. He rolled his shoulder experimentally. "Good as new, ma'am. Much obliged."

"Good luck," she said.

"If you, or any of the other . . . uh . . . SASS escapees want to try your luck in the court of public opinion," Bookbinder said, "you can join me. I don't know how much pull I have now, but you'll have my support."

"I'm staying," Therese said, grasping Oscar Britton's hand.

Britton squeezed her hand back, silent, choking back tears.

"I'm staying with you, too," Stanley said. "We've got some ground to cover. Once we're done, we need to go find your mother."

Britton turned from Therese, faced his father. "You're giving orders now?"

Stanley bit his lip. "We need to do this, Oscar."

Britton grimaced and didn't answer.

"Well," Bookbinder said, cutting through the tension, "I guess this is good-bye for now. Thank you all." He reached forward to shake Britton's hand, but the man's gaze was still locked on his father, and he didn't see it.

"Good luck, sir," Britton said absently. "Once things calm down, I'll look in on you."

"I'll be fine," Bookbinder said, not at all sure that he would be fine.

But Colonel Alan Bookbinder certainly felt fine as he turned and stepped through the gate into the crowd of men and women beyond. He breathed deeply, sucking in the muted smells of the Home Plane, thrilling to the buzzing sound of the military personnel around him. The hardest-bitten, most dedicated band of professionals he'd ever had the privilege to lead. Bookbinder reached down to his wedding band, turning it on his finger, rubbing the scratched gold surface. Just a few miles away, Julie might be watching the breaking news on TV, the kids around her, eyes wide. Maybe she'd see Bookbinder and come rushing to the scene. That would be great.

But for now, he had company enough in the throng of uniforms around him. His family, his people.

His home.

GLOSSARY OF MILITARY TERMS, ACRONYMS, AND SLANG

This novel deals largely with the United States military. As anyone familiar with the military knows, it has a vocabulary of acronyms, slang, and equipment references large enough to constitute its own language. Some readers may be familiar with it. For those who are not, I provide the following glossary, expanded from the original that appeared in *Shadow Ops: Control Point*. Many of these terms are fictional. Many are not.

A-10 WARTHOG—A heavily armed fixed-wing, ground-attack aircraft.

ANG—Air National Guard.

AOR—Area of Responsibility.

APACHE—An attack helicopter, also known as a helicopter gunship.

APB—All Points Bulletin. A broadcast alerting law-enforcement personnel to be on the lookout for a particular individual.

APC—Armored Personnel Carrier.

ARTICLE 15—The article in the US Code of Military Justice that provides for administrative/nonjudicial punishment of troops.

ATTD—Asset Tracking/Termination Device. A beacon/bomb that can be placed inside a person to track their movements and, if necessary, to kill them.

AWOL—Absent Without Leave.

BINDING—The act of utilizing Drawn magic in the making of a spell.

BINGO-FUEL—A term indicating that an aircraft has insufficient fuel reserves to accomplish its mission.

BLACKHAWK—A utility/transport helicopter.

BMER—Bound Magical Energy Repository. Also known as a "boomer," a BMER is any object, inanimate or otherwise, into which magic is bound. BMERs normally dispense the effects of the magic bound into them.

BREVET—A field promotion, granted as an honor before retirement or under extreme circumstances when required senior personnel have been killed in action.

BUTTER-BAR—A second lieutenant in land- or air-based service, or an ensign in maritime service. The lowest-commissioned officer rank in the United States military.

CAC—Common Access Card. A government identification card used across all five branches of the US military.

CARBINE—A shortened, lighter version of the traditional assault rifle used by infantry. It is better suited for tight spaces common in urban operations.

CHINOOK—A large, double-rotor transport/cargo helicopter. Larger than a Blackhawk.

CO—Commanding Officer.

COMMS—Communications.

COMMS-DARK—A situation in which communications are either forbidden or impossible.

CORPSMAN—A medic in the US Navy.

COVEN—Replaces a squad for organizational purposes when magic-using soldiers are concerned. A conventional squad contains four to ten soldiers led by a staff sergeant. A Coven contains four to five SOC Sorcerers, led by a captain. Training Covens are led by a warrant officer.

CSH—Combat Support Hospital. Pronounced "cash." A field hospital, successor to the MASH units of TV fame.

DANGER CLOSE—Indirect Fire impacting within two hundred meters of the intended target.

DFAC—Dining Facility.

DRAWING—The act of summoning raw magic in preparation for Binding it into a spell.

DRUID—Selfer slang for a Terramancer.

ELEMENTALIST—A person practicing the prohibited school of Sentient Elemental Conjuration. This is the act of imbuing Elementals with self-awareness. This is different from automatons—Elementals with no thought, who are entirely dependent on the sorcerer for command and control.

FIELD GRADE—Senior military officers who have not yet attained the rank of general or admiral.

FOB—Forward Operating Base.

FORCE RECON—The US Marine Corps special operations component. While primarily focused on deep reconnaissance, it has direct action platoons. These platoons form the basis for the US Marine Corps Special Operations Command or MARSOC.

FULL BIRD—A full colonel in the land and air services, or captain in the maritime services (O-6). The term refers to the silver eagles worn as a symbol of the rank, and distinguishes from a lieutenant colonel (or "light colonel" O-5), who is designated by a silver oak leaf.

GIMAC—Gate-Integrated Modern Army Combatives—MAC integrated with Portamancy. Also known as "gate-fu." See MAC definition below.

GO DYNAMIC—Command given to assault a target without regard to stealth.

GO NOVA—When a magic user is overwhelmed by the current of their own magical power. This results in a painful death similar to burning. A person who has "gone nova" is sometimes referred to as a "magic sink."

HEALER—A Physiomancer. They are sometimes also referred to as "Manglers" or "Renders" in deference to their ability to damage flesh as well as repair it. Offensive Physiomancy is prohibited under the Geneva Convention's magical amendment. Offensive use of Physiomancy is also known as "Rending."

HELO—Helicopter.

HOOCH—Living quarters. Can also be used as a verb. "You'll hooch here."

HOT—Under fire. Usually refers to an arrival under fire. A "hot LZ" would be landing an aircraft under fire. Also refers to a state of military readiness where personnel are prepared for immediate action.

INDIG—Indigenous.

INDIRECT FIRE—Sometimes shortened to simply "Indirect." An attack, either magical or conventional, aimed without relying on direct line of sight to the target. This usually refers to artillery, rocket, or mortar fire, but also Pyromantic flame strikes and Aeromantic lightning attacks.

JAG—Judge Advocate General. The legal branch of any of the United States armed services.

KIA—Killed in Action.

KIOWA—A light reconnaissance helicopter.

KLICK—A kilometer or kilometers per hour.

LATENT—Any individual who possesses magical ability, detected or otherwise.

LATENT GRENADE—An auto-suppressed or "Stifled" Latency. A person who possesses magical ability, is not a Rump Latent, but for reasons unknown, will not Manifest their powers.

LITTLE BIRD—A small helicopter usually used to insert/extract commandos.

LOGS—Logistics.

LSA—Logistical Staging Area.

LZ—Landing Zone.

MAC—Modern Army Combatives. A martial art unique to the United States Army, based on Brazilian Jiujitsu.

MANIFEST—The act of realizing one's Latency and displaying magical ability. Latent people Manifest at various times in their lives—some at birth, some on their deathbed, and at all times in between. Nobody knows why it occurs when it does.

MARK 19—A crew-served, fully automatic grenade launcher.

MINIGUN—A crew-served multibarrel machine gun with a high rate of fire, employing Gatling-style rotating barrels and an external power source.

MP—Military Police.

MRE—Meal Ready to Eat. A self-contained field ration for use where food facilities are not available.

MWR—Morale, Welfare, and Recreation center.

NCO—Noncommissioned Officer.

NIH—National Institutes of Health. Among many other services, NIH runs a Monitoring/Suppression program for those Latents who refuse to join the military but don't want to become Selfers. Participants are monitored continuously and have virtually no privacy. Most are treated as social pariahs.

NODS—Night Observation Devices.

NONCOMM—A Noncommissioned Officer; sergeants in the air and land services and petty officers in the maritime services.

NON RATE—Enlisted personnel in maritime services below the rank of E-4 (E-3s are sometimes rated). A non rate achieves a "rating" when he/she has graduated from "A-School" and can demonstrate certifiable skill in a particular field. At that point, the non rate usually becomes a petty officer.

NORMALS—Selfer slang for those who are not Latent. The term is respectful. The term "human" is sometimes substituted in derogatory fashion.

NOVICE—SOC Sorcerers still in training, before they graduate SAOLCC.

OC—Officers' Club.

ON MY SIX—Directly behind the speaker.

OPSEC—Operations Security.

OUTSIDE THE WIRE—Area beyond the secure perimeter of a military facility.

PFC—Private First Class. A junior enlisted rank. E-3 in the United States Army and E-2 in the United States Marine Corps.

POAC—Pentagon Officers Athletic Club.

PROBES—Short for "Prohibited." Those Latents who Manifest in a school of prohibited magic such as Negramancy, Portamancy, Necromancy, or Sentient Elemental Conjuration.

PX—Post Exchange. A store selling a variety of goods located on a military facility.

QRF—Quick Reaction Force.

R&R—Rest and Relaxation.

READING—Slang for the military practice of using Rump Latents to "read" the currents of other Latent individuals in an effort to discover their magic-using status.

RENDING—Offensive use of Physiomantic magic. See Healer definition above.

ROE—Rules of Engagement. The conditions under which members of the military and law-enforcement communities are permitted to employ deadly force.

RTO—Radio Telephone Operator. A military member who specializes in the use and maintenance of radio equipment.

RUMP LATENCY—A person who Manifests magical ability that is too slight to be of any real use. Such a person can only use magic to a very slight degree but can feel the magical tide in another person. Rump Latents are not commissioned as full SOC officers but make up a small percentage of the enlisted and warrant-officer support in the corps.

SAOLCC—Sorcerer's Apprentice/Officer Leadership Combined Course. Basic training for SOC Sorcerers. This rigorous training regimen teaches Latent soldiers the basics of magic use/control while simultaneously preparing them for their duties as officers in the US Army.

SAW—Squad Automatic Weapon. A light machine gun, capable of being carried and used as a rifle but heavier and with a greater magazine capacity. It is frequently equipped with a bipod enabling it to be used in a fixed position as a crew-served, belt-fed support weapon.

SCHOOL—A particular kind of magic, usually associated with a mutable element (earth, air, fire, water, flesh, etc.). Latent individuals only Manifest in one school.

SEABEE—Colloquial pronunciation of "CB"—construction battalions of the United States Navy.

SELFERS—Latent individuals who elect to flee authority and use their magical abilities unsupervised. Selfers are usually tracked down and killed.

SF—Special Forces.

SINCGARS—Single Channel Ground and Airborne Radio System. A networked radio system that handles secure voice and data communications.

SITREP—Situation Report.

SOC—Supernatural Operations Corps. Not to be confused with Special Operations Command (or SOCOM, under whose auspices the Supernatural Operations Corps falls). The SOC is the corps of the US Army responsible for all magical use. The SOC is a joint corps, which means it handles magic use for all US armed services to include the Air Force, Navy, and Coast Guard (though the Army is the executive agent). The Marine Corps does not participate in the SOC and runs its own Suppression Lances.

SORCERER—A SOC magical operator—an officer of the SOC who employs magic as his primary military specialty.

STANDOFF ARMOR—A type of vehicle armor designed to protect against attacks by rocket-propelled grenades (RPGs).

STRYKER—An armored combat land vehicle.

SUPPRESSION—The act of using one's own magical current to block that of another. This is typically a one-to-one ratio. The strength of a Suppressor's Latency must exceed that of the individual he is seeking to Suppress.

SUPPRESSION LANCE—A US Marine Corps unit that employs a Suppressing officer to block the magical abilities of the riflemen in the unit.

TAR BABY—SOC Slang for elemental automatons. See Elementalist definition above.

TOC—Tactical Operations Center.

UCMJ—Uniform Code of Military Justice.

USTRANSCOM—United States Transportation Command. is one of ten unified commands of the United States Department of Defense. The mission of USTRANSCOM is to provide air, land, and sea transportation for the Department of Defense, both in time of peace and time of war.

WHISPERING—Terramantic magic used to control the actions of animals. This is prohibited by the US Code. SOC Terramancers are not permitted to Whisper.

WIA—Wounded in Action.

WITCH—Selfer slang for a Negramancer. Male Negramancers are sometimes called Warlocks.

XO—Executive Officer.